# WITHIN

## A NOVEL
## BY
## EVAN MILLER

Evan Miller
WITHIN

Copyright © 2018, Evan Miller

ALL RIGHS RESERVED

# DEDICATION

For my closest friends and my family...without you, I would not be the man I am today and this book would not have been possible. I love you all.

For Dan and Ziggy's incredible support, feedback, and critique to make this book happen.

For Jamie and all the work she put into helping me edit and polish the book into its creation. Ich liebe dich!

For Steve.

# CONTENTS

| | |
|---|---|
| CHAPTER 1 | 1 |
| CHAPTER 2 | 14 |
| CHAPTER 3 | 28 |
| CHAPTER 4 | 46 |
| CHAPTER 5 | 58 |
| CHAPTER 6 | 63 |
| CHAPTER 7 | 73 |
| CHAPTER 8 | 87 |
| CHAPTER 9 | 98 |
| CHAPTER 10 | 110 |
| CHAPTER 11 | 121 |
| CHAPTER 12 | 132 |
| CHAPTER 13 | 139 |
| CHAPTER 14 | 155 |
| CHAPTER 15 | 170 |
| CHAPTER 16 | 181 |
| CHAPTER 17 | 203 |
| CHAPTER 18 | 213 |

CHAPTER 19      220

CHAPTER 20      231

CHAPTER 21      247

CHAPTER 22      260

CHAPTER 23      270

CHAPTER 24      286

CHAPTER 25      296

CHAPTER 26      303

CHAPTER 27      316

CHAPTER 28      326

CHAPTER 29      335

CHAPTER 30      352

CHAPTER 31      373

CHAPTER 32      377

ABOUT      383

DESIGN CREDIT      384

# 1

"Tonight on *Live With Caine*: Psychic, Myles Dunn—the man in a shocking video that preceded the grizzly death of a college student—recounts his experience of that horrific and bizarre night in Platteville, Wisconsin."

Tonight was the show's monthly episode, which the usual bright and lively atmosphere was lowered to a calm, somber tone; the lights focused only on the two chairs center-stage.

As the camera dollies started moving, the audience remained silent as the host, David Caine, emerged from the curtain; he walked straight toward the chairs and situated himself under the spotlight. Even with his chiseled jawline, the forty-year old hid his age well behind a smooth-skinned baby-face. His stylized hair glistened under the lights and he wore his atypical grey business suit well.

As the center-camera finally stopped its forward momentum, the corner of Caine's mouth pulled back in a subtle grin as he acknowledged the viewers…

"Good evening everyone and thank you for joining us on this special two-hour segment." He said with a calm strength, "For those who don't know, once every month we try to have a calmer, more serious show. As much as we enjoy entertaining you on a fun level, we also like to sit down with our guests and get their perspectives on…things that aren't necessarily so fun—things in life that require a serious ear. Now sometimes we have such a show that's suitable for everyone but tonight's episode may actually be a little disturbing for some viewers. That said, we're going to take a quick break so any children, or faint-of-heart viewers, can leave the room. We'll be right back." Caine sat in his chair as the network cut to the commercial lineup.

The empty chair faded into darkness, leaving Caine in isolation. After a moment, the evening's guest strolled through the shadows and sat down.

"…*and we're back in 5, 4, 3…*" motioning the final two numbers with his fingers, the stage director pointed at Caine, cuing him back to life.

"Welcome back everyone. Tonight, we'll be speaking with a psychic—a psychic who co-starred in the viral Internet video that, even after two years, still has everyone talking and…just a little frightened. I say, 'co-star' because…well, take look…"

For all the television viewers at home, the screen faded to black and a new picture popped on screen—the shaky video footage from a cell phone camera…

The camera looked all around, recording images of lounge chairs, tables with text books, papers and pencils, a couple *Foosball* tables and a wall-mounted television—no one in sight. The camera then turned in the operator's hand until the lens faced him, revealing a scrawny young man; behind him were all the room's occupying students crammed in front of the large window. The operator shifted himself back behind the camera, approached the crowd and started shoving through until he reached the window; all the camera saw was the operator's reflection off the glass. As everyone yelled at him to move, he ducked down and rested the phone on the window sill; the camera's auto-focus activated, catching the movement of whatever was outside. The camera turned to the left; a young man between his late twenties and early thirties, with long hair pinned under a black, backward baseball cap, stared intently out the window with wide eyes—a non-verbal expression that matched all of the "*oh my god's*", "*holy shit's*", and "*Is this real's*". Scanning downward, the camera revealed the man to be wielding a handgun.

In a nauseating whip, the camera returned to the window at the crowd's unified gasps and shouts. Outside, the lights of the nearby race-track illuminated the area and a shirtless young man was lying on the ground, struggling. His body looked strange—distorted. His chest was arched up, almost hyper-extended. The arch released, slamming his back onto the ground, then arched again— *slam* on the ground—*arch, slam, arch, slam*. Both arms were mismatched in size; his right hand looked swollen with stubby fingers and the left hand gradually increased size; he was growing.

With convulsing limbs, he slowly reached down and tore off the rest of his split jeans as they cut into his skin; off to the side, his empty shoes had burst open. The boy's naked, steaming body wasn't naked; it was layered in rapid-growing hair. His mouth gaped wide open as he gasped for breath; his head jerked upward and his face shook as it expanded out.

"Oh my God...oh my God! Look at his face!" A student shouted.

The boy's growing mouth opened wider and the shining light shimmered a glimpse of his new teeth; they were a crooked mess. As the body appeared to stop growing, everyone fell silent.

Completely covered in hair and almost doubled in size—no longer human—the boy's new body laid back down, finally coming to rest. After a few motionless moments and failed attempts to stand, it finally rose to all fours, staggering; it stopped to stretch—waking up.

Everyone stared as it lay motionless. The camera looked back at the armed man, then back at the students.

"Is he dead?" "What the fuck?"… "He's moving!" The camera whipped back to the window. The hairy-covered limbs pushed upward and collapsed. The camera rose up with its standing operator and turned around, capturing everyone's awe.

Shouts and screams erupted as everyone quickly stepped backward, tripping over each other. When the camera turned, the jogging animal—closed in and smashed its head against the window; the glass only shook from the weakened attack.

The four-legged assailant fell to the ground and wobbled as it stood back up. Its head swayed side to side, glaring at the human-buffet; its mouth opened in lazy snarls. Regaining composure, the animal swung its paw at the window and its claws clicked against the glass; it slowly crept along the wall, sniffing to the end of the window. It turned and continued sniffing back to the other side, then stopped at the gunman, curling its lips with a low growl; it crouched down defensively and trembled, ready to pounce—to kill.

With a snorting growl, its head and body turned, and it froze. Staring for a moment, it finally jogged off away from the building, toward the trees.

The camera operator backed up, never taking the camera off the window...until the gunman approached.

"I'm Myles." he said as the camera focused on his face. "I was invited to do a seminar at the campus; I carry a gun, with a permit, just for protection. I'm not here to hurt anybody."

The camera started to shake, "I-I, uh...I didn't actually ask that, did I?" the operator questioned hesitantly.

"No, you didn't; I heard your thoughts and, quite frankly, I didn't ask for enough money." Myles replied...

Reaching the end of the video clip, the image paused on Myles' face then dissolved back to the show.

David Caine stared straight into the camera and his eyebrows raised as he took a deep breath, "Many of you are probably skeptical of what you just saw but consider this: according to reports, the same night this video was recorded, a student was violently killed on the campus; it was reported as an animal attack. Approximately one month later, three more people were killed in the same fashion—presumably by the same animal." Caine explained with a pause. "Well, without further delay...ladies and gentlemen, please welcome, Myles Dunn."

Dressed further down from Caine, Myles wore crisp, dark blue jeans, a green button-down shirt that was un-tucked and black pair of *Cotrell Oxfords*; wearing no hat, his hair was short now and he focused calmly on Caine with a polite grin.

"Welcome to the show, Myles." Caine greeted as they shook hands.

"Thank you." Myles said, leaning back.

"So...where to start? Um...so you're a psychic?" Caine asked.

"Mm-hmm."

"And that thing where you approached that student holding the camera...care to elaborate?"

Myles looked down and smiled. He rubbed his chin, inhaled deeply, then looked back at Caine, "I, uh—" he began, "First, please understand that *if* I mention any names—other than what you've heard in the news—they'll be fake; I don't want to cause issues for anyone."

"Oh absolutely." Caine said in an assuring tone.

"Alright. Well, uh—with that student...I read his mind." Myles finally answered, at a loss of any subtlety.

Caine stared at him in a temporary paralysis, "...Really? I mean...yeah that makes sense but...huh. How does that work?"

"Well I don't know how it works—like scientific explanations—but for me, in that instance, I felt his energy focused on me; like...if he was one of these *T.V.* spotlights, his energy would've been the light shining on me. Sometimes when I get in someone's energy path, that allows my telepathy to...go to work without physical contact, I guess? So, through his mind, I saw him look at me and my gun and...yeah; then I heard his thoughts."

"Physical contact?"

"Yeah, um...I typically have to touch someone for it to work but, occasionally, it'll work without. When it's activated, things will just hit me if I don't keep it in check."

"So...can you read my mind right now?" Caine continued eagerly.

"No. I have it under lock tonight." Myles answered.

7

Caine nodded, leaning back in his chair, "So you just turn it off and on?"

"Sort of." Myles said, "It's not an easy 'flip of the switch'. I mean, I've strengthened my control since then so now it takes much less focus. When *that* happened, it took a lot of time, patience and strength—a lot of focus to keep it at bay and even *more* suppress it. It just happened to be on at that moment."

"Why would you want to put your ability to rest?"

Myles looked away and grinned; *If they knew what you've been through, the suicide rate would go up to genocide-percent; they might even kill you out of pity. Good thing they'd never comprehend.* "At the time, my abilities became really overwhelming, David." He answered.

"Abili*ties*? You have more than one?" Caine continued, wide-eyed. Myles nodded and Caine just shook his head, "What other abilities do you have?"

*They always need an explanation. Why couldn't we all just go back to when we had an imagination and just believed anything was possible?* "I'm a...um...a Telepath—mind-reading; I have Auric Sight—seeing auras; I'm an Empath—feel what others are feeling; a Medium—see and...*sort of* communicate with the dead; and a Clairsentient—sense good and evil." Myles listed, hesitantly.

Caine nodded in approval as he looked back at the audience for a moment. "That's really impressive, Myles." Then he looked back at his guest whose gaze never broke. "Well, I've got to be honest with you...our producers indicated you declined to perform a demonstration on the show tonight—that you'd rather just stay on the topic of these events, and I respect that; but, personally, I'd really love to see what you do; I think everyone would."...*here it comes...* "I don't mean to disrespect your wishes, and we don't have the allotted time tonight, but is there any way, you'd be willing to set up something with us to demonstrate in the future?"

Almost everyone in the audience leaned forward together like a wave of water—like *they* were psychically linked. Myles' stomach fluttered as everyone waited patiently for his answer.

"Normally, Myles," Caine continued, "I wouldn't ask again after someone says no but I've read testimonies surrounding all of this and they all indicate that you're the real deal and that just rouses the curiosity of...everyone, really. There's been so many frauds out there and if you really are on the level, I think that just gives tonight's story the credibility it *really* deserves."

Myles looked back down at his feet and paused. "...I can do that." he said with a nod.

Fighting a big, excited smile, Caine cleared his throat, "Alright then, before we really dive into this story, how long have you been able to do these things? I mean, is it something you're born with? Something you develop?"

"To my knowledge, anyone and everyone *has* the abilities, but not everyone develops them. It's, uh—it's like any talent. Some people pick it up real easily and learn real quick; others have to work really hard to develop it; in which case, some people never even touch it.

If they do, it's at a real young age but it just vanishes over time."

"So, you're saying I could do some of this stuff?"

"It takes a *long* time," Myles answered with a shoulder shrug that bordered uncertainty and uncaring, "but from what I've read...sure; anyone has the potential to develop the skills."

"How long did it take you?" Caine continued.

"Overall, they've been with me for about twenty-four years or so. It took me about five years to discover all the abilities that came naturally to me; anything else I would've had to work hard to develop and I didn't care that much; for what was in my arsenal, though, I became obsessed. In the following nine years—until I was twenty-one, actually—I just ate up everything I could about the paranormal and honing my abilities. It all became so engraved, it became second nature."

Neglecting the audience now, Caine's eyes bulged wide open, "Uh...you say, until you were twenty-one...what does that mean, exactly?" Caine's voice was no longer that of a professional talk show host, but that of an innocent fan with a free pass to every secret of the world's greatest magicians.

Myles forced the same polite grin, "Let's just say, I dug too deep; and...the things I saw—the things I felt—yeah...I wanted no part of it any more. Unfortunately, I carved those abilities so deep into my being that I couldn't let them go; I couldn't forget them. So eventually, I began teaching myself how to turn everything off. In another eight years, I managed pretty well. Elements still slipped through the cracks—still do—but now I've developed a strong hold on them."

"I see." Caine replied, "So do you use your abilities on a regular basis then?"

"I didn't for those second-eight years but then this situation came along and I pulled them back out. Now, knowing better, I'm trying to use them more responsibly and constructively." Myles said.

Caine nodded, "Well, on a little tangent, can I ask what you do? You have a job?"

"I do. I have my own lawn care business."

"Interesting," Caine replied, "What pulled you to lawn-care as a living, initially? I mean, it's such a far stretch from what you were doing with your life before."

"At the time, it was keeping me isolated from others; I didn't have to work as hard to subdue my abilities and if one accidentally crept up, it was never as...*potent* as when they were completely alert. Most of the time, I just came across ghosts—which have always scared the hell out of me; they still do, actually."

"Ghosts scare you?" Caine confirmed.

"Yup—yeah. They just, uh...they just stop...and stare at me. There's just something that's always been really eerie about that." *The dark, cold energy of a spirit with unfinished business; their sad, miserable eyes desperately searching for some closure; or sometimes even glaring at the fatal wound that brought them to that state. Something eerie...take your pick.*

Caine's eyes squinted while his brain quickly processed Myles' response, "So, if you knew that seeing

11

ghosts was in your range, and that they scared you, what compelled you to obsess over all your abilities? I think that would just turn me off completely."

Myles thought for a moment then leaned forward, "Well, I'll touch on this more later but when I was seven, I visited my grandmother in the hospital and had my first experience; strangely enough, it was actually related to the events I'm here to talk about tonight. Anyway, um...at that age, I guess the discovery of my abilities just pulled at my curiosity in, like, a superhero complex or something."

Caine chuckled and shook his head. "Wow. Okay, so...you've tried to subdue your abilities; you make them sound more like a curse, really. You took a career that kept you isolated from people. You're afraid of ghosts...just how did you get involved with this tragedy in Wisconsin?"

Myles cringed, recalling the winter before his time in Platteville—shuddering as the snowstorm flashed across his mind; his stomach imploded as he recalled hitting that bank of ice. The crunching metal on his snapped truck axel and plow mechanisms were as vivid as the day they happened...and the ghost of that mangled red-headed child flashed a haunting gaze... "I pretty much *had* no choice. I wrecked my plow-truck that winter and I needed the money. So, when I received the offer, I took it; even then, I was hesitant." Myles said, shrugging his shoulders.

"Ah; that *would* be a good incentive to face your fears." Caine added, clearing his throat, "So...the student in this video—the one everyone was watching— "

"Chris...let's call him Chris." Myles insisted.

"Okay...Chris..." Caine continued, "You're basically saying that Chris...was, in fact...a—a, uh..." he grinned with a subtle embarrassment as he tried to force the word, "...you're claiming—as a fact—that he's a—"

"Yeah..." Myles rescued with a nod, "I'm saying, *that's* what he was."

"...was?"

Myles closed his eyes and nodded, "Yeah. Another topic I'll touch on, if there's time."

Caine chuckled and adjusted in his seat, "Thank you; I was finding it more difficult to say than I thought it would be." He then stared at Myles for a clueless moment, "Um, I'm sorry, Myles...this is probably the strangest interview I've ever done. While some part of my mind is teetering on the line of caution and skepticism, I still completely, and without question, believe what you're saying. I don't know if it's in your demeanor, your vocal delivery, or if you're toying with my mind..." he added and the audience responded with quiet laughter, "...regardless, I—*we*, have got to hear about you and this event before we run out of time..."

Caine looked over at the camera where the stage director was signaling for another break, "We've got another hour and forty-five minutes left of the show; you think you can tell the whole story in that time?"

"I'll do my best." Myles answered.

"Fantastic. Alright, we're gonna take a break and when we come back...Myles Dunn tells all."

*Cut to commercial...*

# 2

CRAWFORD PARK—RACINE, WI (three years earlier)—The breeze offset Myles' sweating to just a mild soak as opposed to a drowning. Even in the day's chilled heat, his white t-shirt was drenched down to just above his belly button; the long, wet strands of hair would stick to his face if they weren't pinned by his black baseball cap—just another day in the office.

Slicing the final patch of the seventeen-acre park field, Myles lifted the blade and drove it back to his *super-cab, eight-foot box* pickup truck, where an empty trailer waited to reunite with its loyal, grass-covered passenger. Closing in at a perpendicular angle, he turned just a pinch away from the trailer then quickly cranked the steering wheel, catching the wheels perfectly on the trailer's ramp tracks and onto the bed.

Finishing up the same routine as for the last seven years, Myles secured the mower, hopped off the trailer to put up the ramp tracks and secured the rear gate. He walked around to the passenger side of the truck, opened the front door and grabbed a fresh t-shirt from a plastic bag, setting it on the seat. Still standing outside the vehicle, he removed his hat and grabbed his sweat-soaked shirt with his fingertips, cringing with disgust as he peeled it off his body and lifted it upward.

He stopped and let the shirt fall; he shivered as the instant cold slapped against his warm skin. He stared straight ahead toward the driver side door as the hairs on his body stood up. Dropping his hands, he balled his fists as his pulse grew faster. He clenched his jaw and squeezed his eyes shut before releasing one fist—slowly reaching back on the door.

*...don't be there; don't be there; don't be there.* Myles backed out of the way as he pulled the door shut but held it open just a few inches. He hesitantly forced his eyes down at the door's glossy black finish; in the reflection, an elderly woman in a green t-shirt stood behind Myles staring right at him and from the waist down, her legs were gone—a floating torso.

Myles slammed the door shut with a loud grunt—a controlled-convulsion as his brain shocked his entire nervous system; his entire body clenched just before the point of cramping. As the door echoed against its metal frame, the woman disappeared from the reflection; Myles slowly turned...nothing; the woman was gone.

He closed his eyes and took a deep breath, then slowly released each of his muscles. He placed his arm against the top of the door frame and rested his head on it, dispersing his weight to the truck while his trembling legs calmed themselves. "...*god dammit.*" he whispered with a heavy sigh.

Another nerve-blast shot down his spine as his phone started ringing. He pushed himself away from the truck and dipped his head in defeat as he fished the phone from his pocket—struggling as the cloth-lining gripped to his sweaty hand. The phone read:

*"INCOMING CALL: Billy Church"*

Myles' clammy thumb dragged roughly across the glass screen, answering the call.

"Hello?"

"Myles! How's it going kiddo?" Billy asked.

"Not too bad, Billy. You?" Myles replied as he looked back behind him—ghost-lady hadn't returned.

"I'm good. I wanted to shoot something your way. You have a minute?"

"Uh..." Myles began, examining around the entire truck and the whole vicinity, still finding himself alone, "...yeah, what's up?"

<><><>

PLATTEVILLE, WI—A small town three hours across the state and home to *the University of Wisconsin-Platteville*—where numerous students completed finals and moved out of their dorms during the past week. It

16

was a clean and well-kept campus with wide sidewalks and continually maintained lawns. Though nothing more than scenic farmland existed beyond the town limits, a serene garden of trees grew throughout the whole town, and its old buildings—such as the university's *Ullrich Hall*—were rich displays of the town's history.

After finally finishing her last final, Shanna Madsen strolled out the doors of *Ullrich*. She slung a practically empty backpack over her shoulder and her flip-flops dragged on the concrete, slapping against her feet. A calm look glossed over her face; her eyes looked almost lazy and a slight smirk pulled at the corners of her mouth. The cool breeze seeped through the fibers of her form-fit t-shirt and sweats, playing with the strands of her bob-cut hair. Of the few remaining people she passed—even some she didn't know—she smiled and wished them a good summer.

When Shanna was thirty yards from her car, Amanda Blythe spotted her and sprinted toward her; her long, tightly-braided hair almost whipped her in the face as she ran; when she stopped next to Shanna, she almost fell over from her over-stuffed backpack—filled beyond capacity. Her entire stick-body could have snapped in half from the weight and she looked sickly standing next to Shanna's shapely figure.

"Hey Shanna." Amanda said with a big smile.

Shanna's brain signaled her eyes to roll backward, but she fought the urge and forced a pleasant smile instead. "Hey what's up?"

More difficult than fighting her eye-roll, Shanna struggled to hide her gag reflex as Amanda's cloud of cheap perfume failed to cover her body odor—a nauseating combination of sweat and rotten onions. Crusty stains covered her denim shorts and a faint, yellow tint circled the neck of her white t-shirt; Shanna turned her head to cover her cringing face; *if she would just wear socks with her shoes and took a shower...ever...maybe...no—wouldn't help.* Even Shanna's hopeful nature questioned how lost Amanda's cause was.

Shanna never questioned lacking a mean bone in her body—not anymore. Every time she encountered an odd individual, such as Amanda, she perfectly remembered the rotting in her stomach of how she and her friends treated their fourth-grade classmate, Samantha James; they called her "Blue Pop" on account of her blue skin caused by the hole in her heart. The day they dumped frozen blueberries on her lunch tray and pretended to shiver at the touch of her cold skin forced a river of tears down her cheeks. When she looked up, she locked eyes with Shanna, whom immediately stopped laughing. Behind the tears, Samantha's eyes were bright red and her surrounding skin brightened to a normal flesh-tone. Shanna cringed at the sudden hollow feeling in her chest and became nauseated; that night, she bawled her eyes out in daddy's arms. Per his suggestion, she apologized to Samantha the next day and she smiled; against her blue lips, her teeth were the purest white. Barely one week later, Samantha's heart gave out and she was gone. When Shanna's friends cracked another joke, she snapped at them, pointing out all their faults and silencing the whole table section; she swore to never make fun of anyone again—a pure promise that evolved to an imperfect *"those that didn't deserve it, or couldn't stand up for themselves."* However, it wasn't until Amanda came around that she finally questioned the inability to be mean and punched it into warp speed.

"You want to hear something really funny?" Amanda said with a forced laugh.

"Sure."

"There was this guy in my class for our last exam and he was really nervous—like so nervous his armpits were sweating; everyone could smell it and it was *so* gross; I couldn't believe someone could smell that bad..." Amanda began and Shanna smiled at the irony, still breathing sparingly at Amanda's stench, "...he's one of those weird guys that doesn't really talk to anyone so, makes sense..." she continued with another forced laugh; Shanna's eyes widened in disbelief; he's *weird? So oblivious—stop. She doesn't realize. She* should *but she doesn't. Are you about to tell her? No, it'll crush her little heart. Just suck it up; you most likely won't see her till next year.*

Every time Amanda babbled to Shanna about whatever her mind conjured, Shanna thought about the time they met—putting it on replay and thinking about how it would've been different, had she just been able to disregard even one, single human being. After she threw the dodge-ball at Amanda during their mandatory—and seemingly unnecessary—physical education class, she just needed to apologize and let it be. Instead, she didn't just apologize for demolishing Amanda's nose and releasing a river of blood down her gym shirt, she took pity on the social outcast. Constantly seeing her alone with struggling people-skills, Shanna was compelled to sit with the fragile little girl; she made sure she was okay and went along with a friendly conversation.

For Amanda, it was a sign—that in a world where no one seemed to care, this one person actually did. She had to keep this wonderful person in her life for as long as possible; Amanda would be the most loyal friend—always there to talk to and lend a helping hand. She found the best friend she would ever have and proved her loyalty to Shanna today—once again—bombarding her like a lost puppy, reunited with its owner.

Five minutes after reaching her car, completely prepared to leave, Shanna finally stopped Amanda's rambling; she dug *deep* to prompt their summer-farewell.

In an attempted joking-tone that Shanna saw right through, Amanda made certain that they kept in touch. With that forced smile—which was becoming harder to hold on to—Shanna assured she would try her best. After a tight hug, during which Shanna held her breath, and a pleasant, "I'll miss you." from Amanda, Shanna climbed into her car, instinctively waving to Amanda as she pulled away—yet another mistake that turned Amanda's stomach with a warm excitement. When Amanda disappeared from the rear-view mirror, Shanna shook her head; *You have gotta stop thinking so negatively about her…but she's* so annoying!

After Shanna disappeared from the lot, Amanda went back her own way. Heading toward her car, that excitement from Shanna's wave—from hugging her—trickled all the way down, fluttering her stomach until she was dizzy. When she finally sat in her car, she took a deep breath and shook her body, snapping out of her trance "You're okay." She pulled out her phone and opened it, navigating to one of her numerous social media applications; she opened the LGBT page she follows and swiped the phone screen. A smile grew on her face as she read some of the posts and comments—witty celebrations of the school year's end and best summer wishes. Amanda's thumbs started tapping as she entered her own post...

"Have a great summer everyone. Mine's off to a shaky start for reasons I would rather not get into, but this summer will be great! And there's always next year! Love you all!"

She waited fifteen minutes for the app's algorithm to work her post into the feed, refreshing her page every thirty seconds; a pinch of adrenaline shot through her when she saw new comments:

"Have a great summer!"

"Hope you have a wonderful summer! Be safe!"

"Everything ok? We're here for you! Next year baby!"

"Aww! Summer is here...keep that chin up!"

Finding her only sense of belonging through her phone, even just a small measure, Amanda sighed with a little smirk; she put the phone away and started her car, ready to head home.

<><><>

*Brothers on 2nd* was still alive with college students, despite so many summer departures. Being the celebratory last day of school and still only 4:32 PM, the only ones that *would* be there drinking were students and alcoholics; for some, unfortunately, those terms intertwined.

Shanna sat at a tall table with her friends Molly Hanson and Korbin Voss. While both girls maintained a conversation that Korbin would occasionally add to, they kept an inconspicuous eye on the boy in their trio. After finishing his double-bacon cheeseburger and fries, he washed it all down with the last of his beer, belched and excused himself with: "I gotta pee."

"Thanks for sharing." Shanna replied sarcastically.

"I'm here for ya." Korbin added as he rushed toward the back of the bar in his typical frantic pace.

Neither Molly nor Shanna could ever understand how Korbin could eat so much, so fast and *not* be morbidly obese. When he was out of sight, Molly picked up her glass and asked, "Time?" just before finishing her beer. Shanna pulled out her phone, which had a timer running on the screen; she stopped it at 00:08:14.

"...dammit." Shanna said, shaking her head with a smile. Molly looked at the screen, laughed and clapped her hands.

"*I know him better than you do. And you owe me a beer.*" She said in a sing-song voice and her long hair swung back and forth as she swung her head side to side; Shanna pursed her lips as she started to blush. "Don't worry, I'll get it." Molly added, getting up from the table.

Though slightly smaller-framed than Shanna, Molly's curves were equal to her friend's and they both enjoyed the swooning of their male counterparts. At the very least, in small-town Platteville this year, they discovered their ability to work the bar and con guys into free drinks.

Last summer, however, they tried their luck at a bar in downtown Milwaukee where Shanna's boyfriend, Jake, sneaked them in. Being with Jake, Shanna drank free anyway, but Molly had to test her seductive powers—a test she barely passed. The much larger building and crowd size made her cower at the bar by her friends and she obtained only two free shots. Eventually, both Molly and Shanna admitted it was too much for their *skills*.

One thing Molly pulled out of that night, was that her assumptions about Shanna and Jake's dwindling relationship were proving to be true. They barely spoke and only sat side by side—a foot apart—texting on their phones. Sucked into his own phone, Jake paid no attention as Shanna continued to show her conversation with Korbin to Molly; as always, it was just friendly banter and random anecdotes but it was clear that it was the phone Shanna smiled at and not her boyfriend. Molly never scolded her about it, though; Shanna was stuck with an oblivious boyfriend, in a seemingly dead-end relationship and all she was doing was living life. Molly liked Korbin and grew more and more anxious for them to actually start dating. Unfortunately, as Shanna was still loyally involved with someone *else*, Molly would have to keep waiting; this afternoon was just another friendly hangout and she returned to the table with a fresh pint of beer, smiling as she put the glass to her lips.

"...you failed." She said, taking a sip.

"Whatever." Shanna replied with a snide glare.

"What are we arguing about?" Korbin asked as he returned to the table. Molly set her glass down and sat back in her chair.

"We bet a drink at how fast you'd finish your burger." She said and Shanna smiled.

"And?" Korbin asked, leaning forward and resting his elbow on the table. He stared straight at Shanna and playfully raised one eyebrow, waiting for her answer— which he would hassle her about regardless.

"I lost." Shanna admitted as she looked down at her glass and Korbin pushed himself upright.

"What the hell?! What was my time?" he demanded and Shanna sat back in her chair, laughing; she turned her phone toward him and his eyebrows raised with surprise, "...damn."

"Yeah, I said it would take over eight minutes. She said *under* eight." Molly bragged and Korbin slowly, and deliberately glared over at Shanna with wide eyes.

"...*you bet against me*?!" he began in a low, hoarse voice and Shanna's face grew redder as she kept laughing. He leaned in closer, "...*how dare you*?"

"Oh, *that's* scary, ya puss." Shanna replied through her laughter and Korbin's eyes remained locked on her. "You're so cute when you get defensive." she added just before tousling her hand through his short, messy hair.

"...bitch." he said quietly as he sat back in his chair, pouting.

Shanna put her glass to her mouth, "...dick." and she smiled as she took a drink; Korbin nodded with a childlike grin...

Half an hour later the trio finally walked out of the bar. With all their promises to stay in touch and suggestions of possible get-togethers, Korbin leaned down a bit and wrapped his arms around Molly's torso as she wrapped her arms around his neck. He gripped her tightly and she grunted as he lifted her off the ground; laughter choked out of her constricted lungs. The moment he set her down, she tousled her hand through his hair and he rolled his eyes as he turned toward Shanna.

Both smiling, they closed the distance between them, staring into each other's eyes. Face to face—inches apart—Korbin began closing his eyelids; they lowered slowly until they were shut and he opened them again after half a second. With a confused grin, Shanna's pulse jumped in speed and her stomach fluttered; she shook her head and wrapped her arms around his neck, squeezing firmly. When he wrapped his arms around her waist, a sense of impenetrable security melted Shanna inside; the urge to hold him tightly was the only thing keeping her muscles from falling limp into his embrace. Waiting patiently, Molly pulled out her cell phone and started playing with it, continually glancing over and smiling at her friends.

Shanna shifted her face next to Korbin's head, "I'll miss you." she said quietly—her breath grazing the inside of his ear. He smiled with a deep breath as his eyes started rolling back into his head—her voice sending a warm rush through his body, massaging his nerves.

"I'll miss you too." he replied. After a few more moments, he gently rubbed her back and as they pulled apart, Molly had her phone pointed at them for a photo.

"Smile!" she said anxiously and Shanna instantly wrapped her arms around Korbin's waist; he placed his arm around her shoulder and squeezed as they both put big, obnoxious smiles on their faces. Molly snapped the photo and when she pulled it back on screen, she scoffed, "Oh, *that's* special." She showed Korbin and Shanna who both laughed, "...okay, one more, *good* one..." They posed again with sincere smiles and Molly snapped the photo.

Content with the new image, Korbin nodded, "Sweet. Alright, I gotta get outta here;" he began, "but I'll see you guys soon, okay?"

Shanna reached over for another hug and they pulled apart after only a few seconds this time. Maintaining eye contact, Korbin backed away in the direction of his car, turning his head occasionally to avoid an accident.

Shanna shook her head with a confused grin, "Why the hell you gotta park so far away?"

"You know I love a good stroll...so step off!" Korbin answered, returning the smile. As soon as distance smudged the clarity of Shanna's face, he turned and walked his normal power-walk the rest of the way.

When he reached his car, he stopped and looked back; *go tell her how you feel.* He shut his eyes and shook his head. *Who are you to break up a relationship? She makes it sound so disappointing with him but...dammit. Who are you to even suggest it?* Finally, he opened his eyes and slipped his key into the door lock. *Fuck that guy.*

# 3

Billy's offer to Myles beginning the following school year was simple: come speak to an audience of psychology students about being a psychic and remain on campus the rest of the week for paid, one-hour student interviews or readings. Billy was given a budget of $1,550 to offer Myles, plus whatever he made off the one-hour sessions—$1,200 for speaking on Monday, $50 per day the rest of the week and $25 per session. Myles declined with no hesitation. Billy pleaded, stopping just short of actual begging, and Myles' sympathy for his friend draped over his shoulders. Still, he declined; *You put those abilities to rest for a reason. Yes, Billy's a friend, but you cannot afford to awaken that shit again; it will fuck you up.*

Even as a well-respected psychology professor, Billy struggled convincing the school's event board of his idea's validity in the first place. After weeks of hounding, he managed to get that rate bumped up to $2,500 and the wheels in Myles' head began to turn; *At least consider it; Billy's always been there for you. Besides, he's not paying you out of pocket. Okay, money...after wrecking your truck last winter, you definitely could use the money; but...do this favor and you still only come out even for taking time off. Ugh, but then you have to tap into the shit you put to rest; is it worth the risk? If you do this, they're going to have to bump up that pay.*

Billy's heart nearly exploded when Myles gave his asking price. Still, he took it back to the board. Now, the only way to convince them to even consider such a request would cost Myles an interview and demonstration.

A few days prior to the interview, Myles made sure to ask Billy about ghost stories around Platteville then, using notes from all of Billy's info, he also did his own internet search for stories. Some matched up and some didn't but what he was adamant about were potential hauntings on the actual school campus. Finding nothing on his target, he stopped searching and abandoned everything related. In order to be prepared for this interview, he would need rest and if he scared himself by doing all this reading and searching, he'd have to add insomnia to his list of obstacles...

<><><>

The interview was at 2:00PM; Myles woke up at 5:00AM and immediately opened the garage door with the remote in the kitchen; *Waste no time. After you open*

29

*yourself up again, those energies are going to kick your ass. Sprint from the back door right to the car.*

He sat in his living room recliner with his eyes closed and took three deep breaths; *you can do this.* A light pressure pulsed in his mind as it began tapping into his abilities—like someone terrified of water, repeatedly sticking their hand down and yanking it back before actually touching the liquid surface. On each attempt, his mind pulled back, obeying its instinctive defenses; with no progress, Myles opened his eyes again. He shook his head, rubbed his hands together and sat forward in the chair. Resting his elbows on his knees, he closed his eyes again; *reach...pull back; reach...pull back; ...* nothing.

"Goddammit." he said, opening his eyes and slamming his back into the chair. He shook his head again and grunted; now gripping the arms of the chair he planted his feet firmly on the ground and slowly leaned forward, "...come on!" *Reach...pull back; reach...pull back; reach...pull back...*

An hour and half passed; his forehead glistened with a thin coat of sweat; his muscles ached from his neck, throughout his arms and down to his lower back; his constant grip on the chair's fabric chafed his fingers raw, just before the point of blisters...*Reeeaaach...*

His mind finally snagged; his hand touched the water. Myles felt just an ounce of the same sensations he felt at his peak, years ago. Reaching further, a calm pressure began to grow from the stem of his brain; *Go; deeper...deeper; dig...dig...dig...dig...dig...*

30

That pressure finally consumed his entire mind—his hand was submerged now. A wave of heat shot through his body; like a limb that had been slept on for years, his nerves tingled as his heightened consciousness woke. He smirked as the tickling sensation slowly dissolved.

Vanishing faster than the tickle, his grin and sudden euphoria disappeared when he remembered what lay ahead—the things he knew he would encounter and the internal heat wave was crushed by a freezing chill...

10:58AM—Prepared to finally leave the sanctuary of his house, which had, literally, been exorcised and blessed to ward off anything paranormal—and has worked quite well in his five-year residence—Myles whipped out his phone and prepared a text message to Billy:

"On my way. Be at the school in about three hours."

Slipping the phone into his blue jeans pocket, he circled around a one-foot radius—last minute check. He patted down his hooded sweatshirt and pants pockets then nodded his head; *good to go.* He looked over at the back door, and stared at it for a moment before actually taking a step; after a slow stroll, he reached the door and at half a foot away—reaching distance to the knob, he stopped...*energy.*

Myles had not felt that much energy in years; besides its spiritual cleansing, there was nothing extraordinary about the house to make it "psychic-proof"; but with that cleansing, his abilities in a dormant state and his overall will to avoid the paranormal, nothing ever managed to get in. Outside that door, however, those universal energies radiated through the wood and glass to the terrified flesh and blood conductor shielded behind it.

He closed his eyes and took a deep breath as he reached for the doorknob. He twisted the unusually-cold piece of metal and pulled the door open half an inch. He locked the knob and whipped the door open, slipped out and slammed it shut behind him; needing to reach the safety of his car fast, he skipped the two-second task of locking the deadbolt. He sprinted toward the big garage door that was still open from six hours earlier; fortunately, living on a secluded, dead-end road made it safe to have a huge door open and unmonitored for so long.

Slightly crouched at the car door with the appropriate key ready, he held it in front of the lock entry and the tip hit the side—strike one. Myles pulled back for a second attempt, hitting the key-tip on the bottom of the entry— strike two; *...stupid fab.* Normally the car would've been unlocked without a key, already started and he'd be buckled in but he was still waiting on his replacement fab for the keyless-entry and remote starter; *...come on.*

On the next attempt, the key hit right in the center, pushed the tiny metal plate inward and turned fluidly. He fell into the car seat, slamming the door shut behind him. Leaning back in his Voodoo Blue Scion XB—his civilian vehicle—he started to notice a multitude of colors in front of his eyes; *Ghosts already?! Oh, come on; let's get out of the garage first, at least!* When he felt dizzy and his heart pumped faster, he coughed out the carbon dioxide burning his lungs; he'd forgotten to let it out when he inhaled the oxygen at the back door; *Okay, not a ghost...just suffocation.*

Myles shook his head, getting rid of the colors and dizziness; he slipped the key in the ignition and twisted. The car started perfectly and he flipped the gears to reverse, backing out of the garage; the moment he cleared the door's path, he reached for his visor and pushed the automatic door button, closing it. Making a quick, careless check for neighbor pedestrians—*clear*—he backed out into the road. He put the car in drive and gave too much gas for the sensitive pedals. As the tires screeched, Myles smiled with a subtle nod; *good start.* Obeying the stop sign at the end of the block, he hit the brakes at the intersection with the main road; he checked both directions for oncoming traffic.

The vibrating cell-phone against his leg blasted his nerves, head to toe. He grabbed the phone from his pocket; he tapped the screen to see a text message notification from Billy and he unlocked the phone. The screen opened right to a box that read:

*"BILLY CHURCH: 'Not at the school. Out for summer, remember? :) Meet at City Park off Main Street.'"*

*...son-of-a-bitch.* In all the research Myles did, he found the park was one of the places said to be haunted; *...perfect.* Now he was about to encounter another old woman in the park, if the stories were accurate. Finally, Myles put the phone back in his pocket, grabbed the wheel and pulled out onto the road...*the hell is with old women haunting the parks?*

<><><>

Exactly three hours later, Myles arrived at the park to find it littered with people; *What the hell?!* Myles' directions took him to *N. Bonson Street*, where he would have to circle around the park to find a parking space right by the park's gazebo—the meeting spot—and there were only two. As he turned onto *Market Street*, he came upon the park's far parking lot where only one car was surrounded by eighteen empty spaces. *Park the car with ease and enter from the far side?* He still had not seen anything resembling an old woman in a nightgown; still adjusting to all the energies he was perceiving, he couldn't pinpoint the energy of any specific entity. *Risk running into something? ...hell no. Take the short route.*

He passed all the empty spots and turned onto the unnamed road between the park and some buildings where additional spaces lined the park's side—all taken. *Whatever; going to the front;* unfortunately, as he made his way up *Bonson* and took his moment to debate parking on the opposite end, two cars turning off *Mineral Street* already made their way down the unnamed road and claimed the two spaces. As Myles turned the corner and slowed down to find his targets now occupied, he stopped the car and sighed; *...great.*

For the next ten minutes, he searched all possible parking areas within a fifty-yard radius; everything was either taken or reserved. Finally, he returned to the rear parking lot and pulled into a space; he didn't even bother to straighten his car as the front left corner hung over the

34

white painted line; *bullshit "small town"; this park is busy as hell.* The park was populated with numerous parents, children, and elderly people. After a moment, he stepped out of the car and, with a slight wave of mental pressure, his empathy finally activated.

Myles rolled his eyes and shook his head as he stepped to the edge of the park. As if crossing the street, he looked left, then right and stopped as his eyes locked. Standing off by a tree, an old woman in a nightgown with deep set eyes stared at him. He just clenched his jaw and turned his head forward as the first sweat drips leaked from his pores.

There was a variety of emotions in the air that he couldn't pick out, but they were good overall. The gazebo on the other side of the park was unmistakable and four people sat, waiting. Three sat together while one sat across from them, looking back over his shoulder at Myles— Billy. Already roasting in his jeans and hooded sweatshirt under the cooking sun, Myles placed his hands in its pockets, pinned his arms close to his body and started walking with his legs close together; *Touch nothing.* The collected body heat cued more sweat flow.

Walking at a brisk pace, he kept his eyes forward as he swayed his body out of the way of running children; he was amazed that no one else seemed to pay him any attention. Only looking through his peripheral vision, the old woman reappeared after every time he passed her; switching from the left side of the park to the right, re-emerging from behind objects and even out in the open, her eyes remained locked on the one mortal that knew her existence. As he came closer to the gazebo, she continued to close her distance and Myles' pulse sped up; the hairs on his neck stood taller and taller and he clenched his jaw tighter. Fortunately, the only visible sweat on his sweatshirt were the drips from his forehead; it was a fantastic mask for the stains that already soaked the chest and back of his t-shirt underneath.

He was five paces away from the cement floor of the gazebo when he passed the woman again and when he finally reached charming structure, she reappeared right next to it—right next to *him*. With a loud grunt he bolted to right passed Billy and the school's event board representatives to the gazebo's opposite side. Myles turned to see, not only the woman right outside, but Billy and the three board reps staring at him with confusion.

"...excuse me one sec." Billy said as he walked over to Myles. The lanky 6'2" fifty-five-year old approached his friend with caution, casually scratching the back of his bald head. Myles breathed deep and Billy gently bumped Myles' shoulder with his fist.

"Doin' alright, Kiddo?" he asked.

"...yeah," Myles answered with a nod; he looked up at Billy with a polite grin, "I just saw something." he added in a lighthearted tone; the attempt to play it off as "nothing" wasn't even close to convincing—even to Myles.

"Ghost?" Billy asked. In a subtle motion, Myles tilted his head to the side, looking behind his friend and the old woman remained right at the gazebo's edge.

"...yes."

Billy nodded and, careful not to touch him, gestured Myles off the barricade, guiding him toward the rest of the group—one man in his late forties with a receding hairline that should be shaved off already; an older, elegant looking woman who hid her age *very* well; her pale green t-shirt and blue capris suited her; and finally a young woman—similar age as Myles—with long shiny hair tied in a ponytail and sunglasses atop her head. She had a beautifully smooth, pale face with deep penetrating eyes; yet their blue color appeared off and unnatural—*contacts.*

From Myles' perspective, the striking beauty had a nice slender body that was well maintained and partially covered by a blue tank-top and white shorts. There was a half-sleeve floral tattoo on her right arm from the shoulder to the bicep, and a rose with three-dimensional, stone-like filigree and a skull down on her left leg from ankle to shin. Each piece had incredibly vibrant contrast to her skin tone. She almost completely distracted Myles from the lingering entity, to which, everyone else was oblivious. His stomach dropped when the glare of her enormous engagement ring scorched his retina; *Engaged...dammit.*

"Everyone, I'd like you to meet my friend and former student, Myles Dunn." Billy introduced and as the balding man extended his hand, Myles leaned away; the man glared at the seemingly rude guest with insult.

"Sorry," Myles began, "...it's uh...kind of a shady habit. I try not to make skin contact unless I'm prepared or I know someone really well." he added and the man sat back on the bench with an estranged nod.

"That explains the sweatshirt on a day like this." The older woman stated with a polite smile.

"Yeah, are you sure you don't want to take that off?" asked the beauty. Myles nodded with a forced grin and she nodded in response.

"So what spooked ya?" the balding man blurted out. Myles' scoff was poorly hidden by an attempted chuckle as he used his sweatshirt sleeve to wipe his forehead and push his hair back. Suddenly he paused; four different energies hit him simultaneously—emotions—and each one emanated from a different member of the little party.

Excluding Billy from his quick analysis, Myles gripped the sensation and honed in on the energies but suddenly stopped as a fifth energy hit him from further away, outside the gazebo—from the elderly ghost. He stopped, squeezed his eyes shut and clenched every muscle in his body; *no...no, no, no...do* not *feel her emotions, no matter what. Go away; you feel nothing; there's nothing...nothing...nothing.* In what even he would wonder about later on, he somehow subdued the ghost's emotions and slowly returned his attention to the event board; *these three are the only people in the world. There's no one else...nothing.*

At worst, they were all skeptical but with no malicious intent; the balding man just appeared to have a pessimistic, condescending attitude that any normal person could see and it was scratching Myles' nerves. That man actually held the most skepticism; not even an experienced magician could convince him and he had no expectation to give out anything more than the initial offer. He actually seemed anxious for Myles to fail. The older woman's skepticism was accompanied with a guilty hope, as if she just didn't want Myles to be humiliated. The beauty, on the other hand, had just a hint of skepticism, like anyone would, but she was hopeful— hoping to be amazed and prepared to authorize quite a bit to have a true psychic speaking at the school.

"Actually, I'd...rather not discuss it." Myles answered, recalling the man's question. He bit his lip and the balding man stared at him with a look of contempt.

"Well tell us about yourself, Myles." the older woman suggested, quickly changing the subject. Both Billy and Myles sat down on the bench across from the trio; Myles looked down, rubbing his hands together.

"Umm...well, I have a little lawn care business in Racine—where I also live; and um...well that's it really. I work and go home."

"Simple man, huh?" the beauty asked.

"Mm-hmm," Myles replied with a smile and his stomach fluttered a bit when she smiled back at him; failing to hide his curious eyes, his blood temperature rose as he scanned up and down her body; *Take it easy. Not going to happen with that ring on her finger.*

"And you're a psychic?" the balding man asked impatiently.

Myles looked over at him with a straight face, "...yes,"; *that* is *why we're here, isn't it?*

"Intriguing," the balding man stated in an equally flat, condescending, tone; he dropped his folded leg to the ground as he sat forward, "Well from what Bill's told us, you sound very talented. However, the consideration of a higher rate than what we've *already* raised it to, is a little concerning. After all...this idea not being a necessary aspect of the curriculum, $2500 is really generous, considering your lack of experience; you haven't even told us your actual asking price yet. What I wonder is...why should we even continue discussing this?"

Myles' gaze never broke as the balding man made his case; it wasn't until he sat upright that Myles broke the line of sight and made smiling eye contact with the other two members.

"Well, if you don't mind, I'd like to demonstrate my capabilities for you. I'd also like to thank you for not telling me your names as it pertains to my demonstration." he said with a quiet confidence as he stood up. The older woman and the beauty both rested their backs against the bench with eager smiles; the balding man remained forward with a straight face.

Myles took a knee in front of the older woman, wiping his clammy hands on his jeans just before extending out his arm. "Um...your hand, please; I apologize for the sweat."

She leaned forward and held out her hand, placing it in Myles' palm. His fingers gently wrapped around her bony appendage—rolling over the tendon of her ring finger. Placing his other hand on top—sandwiching hers—he took a deep breath and closed his eyes as he dipped his head down.

After a few seconds, the woman glanced over at the beauty and shrugged her shoulders; the beauty smiled. The balding man glanced over to see Billy wearing an anxious grin and when Billy looked back, the balding man sighed and looked back at Myles, who never moved. Another couple of seconds passed and Myles' head slowly turned at the slightest angle; his barely-open mouth began moving—mouthing silent words.

"...*what's he saying?*" the balding man whispered to the beauty.

She leaned forward, focusing on the psychic's mouth and shrugged her shoulders, "...*looks like gibberish.*" she answered and Billy sat back on the bench with a confident smile, waiting patiently for everyone's reaction.

Myles inhaled sharply and held it for a moment before letting out a jagged, tearful sigh; he swallowed the lump in his throat as he let out a quiet whimper; *there it is...empathy is definitely awake now—such sadness.* He calmly released the woman's hand and sat back onto his heel.

"Are you alright?" the woman asked.

Myles nodded, holding back tears, "It's nice to meet you, Bernice." He said with a forced smile and the beauty's eyes widened while the balding man kept a straight face; Myles cleared his throat, "Um...there was one predominant thing I saw and I'm not sure if I should bring it up. I know it's hard for you; that's why I'm...kind

41

of on the verge of crying. I can—uh...I can feel emotions too."

Bernice's throat tightened as she glared at Myles with concern—almost scowling, "...tell me." she insisted. Myles quickly glanced at everyone else, then leaned further forward, close to her ear.

"...*Damon and Annabelle...*" he whispered, and Bernice's eyes widened, almost abandoning her eye-sockets; the tendons in her neck quickly emerged as she sucked her throat inward, "...*I am so, very sorry for the loss of your daughter, Annabelle and your husband, Damon. I'm confid—I know it does them great honor to know that...although you still think about them every day, you've overcome your addictions and moved on with your life.*" He placed his hand on top of hers and squeezed gently as he pulled away. Tiny spasms erupted in Bernice's chest as she fought the inevitable crying; she leaned back into the bench, covering her mouth with her hand. As the tears started rolling, she lifted her sunglasses and wiped them away.

Myles stepped over to the balding man and knelt in front of him, holding out his hand. The man stared at him for a moment, then reached out. In the same fashion, Myles grasped the man's hand and repeated the previous routine.

In seconds, Myles turned his head away. His eyebrows cringed and he immediately released the hand; he shuddered as he sat back on his feet, then shook his head as he opened his eyes, scowling at the man.

"What's up, Jerry?" he began in a condescending tone.

"...Alright...two for two on the name guesses. How come mine didn't take as long?" Jerry asked.

"Because yours is a current thing—right on the surface," Myles answered as he leaned toward Jerry's ear, "...*anyone can see that you're not only skeptical, but you're kind of an asshole. What I saw, in particular, was the cartoon porn you look up on the computer in your office at school; with a username like, "LayMeAmy", you should probably get that addiction checked out. And teaching your dog to, uh..."kiss the kitty", as you call it...is really sick. You're the first person to make me feel like a dirty old pervert.*"

Like plugging in a Christmas light, Jerry's face and head instantly turned bright red and he remained frozen as Myles moved over to the beauty; Billy watched Jerry with concern.

The beauty's hand was already extended out when Myles knelt in front of her, waiting for its turn to be viewed. He smiled hesitantly as he grabbed it. While Bernice and Jerry remained in their temporary catatonic states, Billy was the only witness left; his anxious and confident grins were gone as he glanced back and forth at the two adults, stunned like children. "Myles, uh...maybe you should—"

The beauty quickly held up her hand, cutting Billy off and he simply nodded. A few moments later—more than Jerry but less than Bernice—Myles sucked a breath of air in through his clenched teeth then slowly let out a low grumble—wincing. He finally opened his eyes and released her hand; he looked up at her and smiled. In the subtlest gesture, he rubbed his head just over his eye, alleviating some pressure as he leaned forward...

*"Hello, Jessica. Well don't be too embarrassed about your bird and baseball phobia; getting smacked like that with such a mix would be traumatizing to lots of people; if it makes you feel better, I'm deathly afraid of ghosts,"* he said, now in a lighter tone and a tiny chuckle escaped Jessica's lungs, *"I know how the ball to your eye drastically changed your eye-color and scared a few kids back then, but I can assure you, that accident made your eyes truly unique and I don't think anyone will be scared anymore. You should try going without the contacts 'cause your eyes are very pretty."*

Myles pulled back to see a wide-eyed, jaw-dropped smile on Jessica's face and he laughed as he propped himself back up on the bench. Jessica shook her head and glanced at both Bernice and Jerry, both of whom snapped out of their trances and were waiting on the bench; they still continued composing themselves as Bernice let out a couple more sniffles, and Jerry wiped the sweat off his forehead.

"Wow..." Jessica began, "...what would it take to get you to present at Platteville, Myles?"

Myles glanced over at Billy, who just shrugged his shoulders, taking himself out of the matter. Myles then turned back with a straight face and in a calm, confident tone, he dropped *his* price-bomb.

Flying on an adrenaline high the rest of the day, with the urge to frantically jump up and down and go sprinting on the campus track, Jessica was excited for Myles to spend a week at Platteville. When they voted on his request for a $13,500 paycheck, she immediately said yes, wasting no time weighing pros and cons.

At home that night, she went straight to the bathroom, turned on the light and looked herself in the mirror, staring only at her eyes—her masking contact lenses. She gently ran her hand along the skin around her left eye; *Oh, what the hell?*

She grabbed the plastic contact lens case on the sink and opened it; she removed her contacts, placing them in their liquid-filled home. She now she stared at her real eyes—a pale, almost non-existent blue with a few random spots of rust color—splotches of blood that always remained since the day of her accident.

When the bird slammed into Jessica's face, its frantic flapping was more shocking than painful but the line drive to her head that immediately followed severely damaged her skull and eyes. After a full, functioning recovery, the side effects even baffled the doctors. Only a little blood seeped into her irises and the vibrant blue lightened to a pale, crystal blue. Now, after hiding them since childhood, her stomach turned with excitement at the thought of showing them off...

Back at home, the strain Myles felt when holding back his empathy stirred his stomach with anxiety. While his other abilities were the foundation of his downfall nine years earlier, that empathy was the key. Just seeing the combined memories and experiencing the horrific events those ghosts went through wasn't enough; feeling all their emotions and physical torture was the vehicle to a psychological hell and it actually grew the ability beyond Myles' control. Burying it took more mental strength than he ever had to conjure before.

For the next several weeks, he would lose valuable work-sleep as he made certain his abilities were under his complete control—that his empathy would stay buried in the darkness of his entire being.

# 4

The top three buttons of Shanna's shirt and her tie were already undone when she walked in the door of her family's two-story ranch house that evening; she slipped her shoes off, sliding them to the wall with various other pairs. She stopped and stuck her nose in the air, inhaling deeply; *Mom's chili.*

"Hey." Shanna called out in a tone that dragged as much as her feet after a twelve-hour restaurant shift. The sound of a knife slicing into a cutting board echoed from the kitchen as did a woman's responding voice; "Hey." Despite her exhaustion, that spicy, beef-filled aroma pulled Shanna right to the source.

Shanna's mother, Vikki finished cutting through what was once a large tomato and poured the sliced chunks into a steaming pot. Shanna lifted her nose as she passed the stove and inhaled a savoring breath. She then walked right to the fridge; not even searching around, she reached right in the side of the door and pulled out a chilled bottle of coffee. She inhaled again as she opened the beverage.

"You got some mail." Vikki said, never breaking pace of that night's dinner preparation.

After a swig of the coffee, Shanna returned to the living room; next to the door, opposite the shoe pile was a small, decorative table snug against the wall with a short stack of envelopes. Shanna sifted through it, finding an offer from *Victoria's Secret* and a postcard from New York. She flipped it over and glossed over the tiny, unrecognizable chicken-scratch that read:

*Roses are red, violets are purple (not blue); I have cool hair; these poems are stupid; you're gorgeous and I miss you.*

*Bet you never expected this old school, handwritten mess, huh? Haha I'm havin' a great time rollin' with my dad across country. Hope your summer's good. I can't wait to get back and see you.*

*Korbin*

Shanna's face turned red and she smiled; her cheeks forced her eyes almost completely shut. With an anxious giggle, she gently bit her bottom lip but quickly released at the sound of an empty plastic dish dropping in the sink. She looked back toward the kitchen, then down at the postcard; *Mom'll know what to do.*

Vikki was stirring the pot when Shanna returned; she pulled the spoon out and cautiously shoveled off a small portion of the chili with her teeth. She sucked in an extra breeze of cool air and thought for a moment as she chewed. She grabbed the salt shaker and sprinkled a bit into her household-famous concoction.

Shanna walked up next to her mother, put her face over the pot and inhaled again. "Mmmm—can I have a taste?"

"Mm-hmm." Vikki sounded as she pulled another spoonful. Shanna grabbed the spoon and blew onto the steaming meat while Vikki turned to the sink. In a perfect mix of savory and sweet, the chili's flavor blessed Shanna's taste buds and her eyes rolled toward the back of her head.

"Taste alright?" Vikki asked.

"Amazing." Shanna replied, placing the spoon back in the pot; she wiped the corner of her mouth with her fingers then walked around to the bar-counter and propped up on one of the tall chairs. "Care to impart some advice?"

"Sure. What's up?" Vikki answered.

Shanna curled her toes around a metal crossbar on the chair legs and leaned forward, resting her elbows on the counter top. "Okay, umm...You know how I said Jake and I have been getting really distant?" She asked and Vikki nodded. "Well I've been feeling like that more and more—to the point of where I don't even wanna try anymore. Like, I still love him but...it's like we've drifted so far apart that I'm not *in* love with him anymore."

"That's pretty serious, hun; you two've been together a long time...does it bother you?"

"Not in the normal sense. Actually, I'm not mad about us drifting apart. The thing that's bugging me is that no matter when I bring it up, he plays off like everything's fine and *I* continue playing the waiting game. Here I'm holding myself in place when I could be moving on."

Vikki shut off the faucet and dried her hands before walking over to the counter. She stood directly across from her daughter and looked her in the eyes, "Sounds like you may have to give him an ultimatum. Figure out what's going on or be done, 'cause he shouldn't be stringing you along like that."

"Right; but I mean...I don't really *wanna* give him an ultimatum." Shanna hesitantly admitted, staring at her hands.

"No?"

Shanna shook her head before looking up at her mother, "...no. It's like, I just wanna move forward."

"Sounds like you've already made up your mind sweetie." Vikki added as she rested her chin on her hand.

"I haven't yet. This is where I start getting confused...my friend Korbin and I have gotten real close and, honestly, I adore him. If I wasn't with anyone, he's who I'd pick to be with. He, basically, makes me feel the way Jake used to make me feel. So now I dunno if I'm doing what I'm supposed to be doing, or feeling what I'm supposed to be feeling. I'm stuck on whether or not I should wait to resolve this with Jake—because of how much we've invested in our relationship; or is it time to let go and pursue something that feels like it's working? Would pursuing a path with Korbin be 'moving on' or would it be 'giving up' and throwing away the history between me and Jake?"

Vikki smiled as she reached over and squeezed Shanna's hand, then turned and walked back to the stove. "Hun, first, you're thinking way too much—too much worrying..." she assured as she stirred the chili; she pulled out the spoon and took another sample. With an approving nod, she set the spoon down, turned off the oven and placed the pot on the back burner. "...in my opinion, you and Jake are definitely in different places now; it's not like how it used to be. Since nothing's being done, I think you should see other people—pursue things with Korbin. Who knows? Maybe that's what you and Jake need." She walked around the kitchen, putting away her cooking arsenal, "Hun, these are still times to test the waters but while you're seeing what works for you, I still believe everything happens for a reason; if you and Jake are meant to be together, it'll happen but if not, life'll go on." She returned to the counter across from Shanna, "Of course, I can't make the decision for you but, honestly, you know what's best for you; you know what feels right so just go with your gut and instinct. Either way, I support you."

Vikki's smile managed to pull a small grin from her stressed daughter, "Thanks, mom."...

Upstairs in her bedroom, Shanna started unbuttoning her shirt when her phone chimed with a new text message from Molly: "*Forgot to send this to you...*" and attached to the message were the two photos Molly snapped outside the bar, just before Korbin left.

Shanna giggled and her face turned red. Withdrawing her long hug with Korbin from her memory bank, her nerves tickled goose bumps onto her skin. When her phone's energy saver dimmed the screen, she quickly tapped it awake and saved the photo to the phone's memory.

Sitting at the edge of her bed, she tapped open the photo album and configured the recent photo's location—sending it from the "*camera roll*" to the album, "*my budz*". She opened the album and examined the photo once more before scrolling backward.

The majority of the photos captured Shanna, Molly and Korbin. Some showed other people with them and a few others were just Shanna and Molly. After a few more scrolls, she stopped and her eyes squinted with confusion. She quickly scrolled back to the photo of her and Korbin by themselves; *The only ones with just you and Korbin.* Shanna shook her head as her lips mouthed the word: "*wow.*" Then with a smile, she sent a copy of the photo to a freshly-created album: "*Korbin*".

Swooning at the photo again, her eyes began to wander when she was hit with a notion: *where's Jake?* Shanna went back to the "*my budz*" album and started scrolling through; she scrolled too long and too far back for her liking before she found a photo with her and Jake—one that Molly took the night at the Milwaukee bar; though Jake's arm was around Shanna's shoulders, they sat next to each other looking bored. She scrolled twice as far back before she saw any enthusiasm displayed in their photos. With her smile gone, she shook her head and pressed the phone's "*Home*" button.

Shanna opened the ongoing conversation with Molly and started tapping her thumbs on the screen...

"I made a decision."...*message sent*

<><><>

Molly made an interesting—if not good—point about Shanna's timing. Perhaps she could have waited for Jake to get settled back in from his trip before she officially broke up with him; of course, Molly couldn't deny Jake's lack of concern whenever Shanna tried to bring up their problems. Shanna always considered others before herself and this rarely-occurring concept of selfishness was euphoric. Her mother said to go with her instinct and all it said was: "*Korbin*"

Shanna parked her car along the curb outside Jake's parents' house; even the idea of parking in their driveway rattled her nerves; *You're barely a couple anymore; you're a stranger.* After six years, being a stranger couldn't be further from the truth but that seed was planted deep into her mind, regardless.

The butterflies in her stomach started partying immediately at home, before she even got in the car and it quickly escalated into a full-fledged rave as she drove. When she stepped out of the car, they turned into giant bats tearing away at her insides; *Oh Jesus, don't puke.* She took a deep breath and pressed on her stomach, fighting the nausea as she walked to the front door; *They're gonna hate you;* he's *gonna hate you.* Each step on the already ten-year journey to the door continued to piss off the bats so she switched her normal, yet, currently jarring pace to a slight tip-toe—another ten years.

Finally reaching the door, she rang the bell instead of just walking in; *Shit...they're gonna know something's off now...whatever, you're not here to hide anything.*

Jake's mother answered the door with a confused smile. "Why did you ring the bell?" she asked. Brushing it off as *"just not feeling well"*, Jake's mother invited her in. No, Shanna wasn't there to hide anything, but she had no intention of doing this directly in front of them. *Why the hell are you getting sick? Wasn't it obvious that this was coming? Yeah...yeah, of course it's obvious; just chill out.* Learning of Jake's whereabouts in his room, she continued further into the house, down the hall and her nausea was about to reach a new level of discomfort.

When Jake suddenly popped into the hallway, a shock blasted down her spine and throughout her nerves, paralyzing the sickness in her belly. *Oh, thank you!*

"Hey." Jake said in a flat tone as he walked over and kissed his girlfriend, leaning down from a towering six-foot height; he didn't even reach out to her and while she'd grown used to that, she definitely missed the embrace of his strong, muscular arms—when they still had emotion. Though still soft to the touch, his lips felt tight against Shanna's; *...nothing.* Noticing a slight tremble in her body, he asked if she was alright and, thankfully, she was able to say, "Yeah, you just scared me."

He went back to his room and traded his shorts for a pair of sweats, covering his toned legs; the fitted *Iowa State Hockey* t-shirt he put on over his wife-beater couldn't hide his large pecs and flawless v-shaped back— nor did he want it to. His freshly-trimmed, crew-cut hair was perfect but he needed a complete deforesting from his chiseled jaw, down to his thick neck.

After stopping at the front door for a clean white pair of running shoes, Jake walked outside; instead of holding the door open until Shanna was completely outside, he held it for only an extra second while she was still in the house, then let it go for her to catch as she crossed the threshold; *Uh...I'm not* "one of the guys" *dick.* While the door didn't slam on her, just the lack of chivalry—lack of consideration—was affirming and her nerves began to settle; *Yeah, this is the right decision.*

They walked down the road of the fifteen-year old subdivision and only made uncomfortable small talk about their summer thus far. Another moment of silence passed and Shanna's stomach started waking up; *God, just do it. Just say it,* "We're done."*—not like that. Let him down easy. Do it...grow a pair, dammit. Do it! DO—*

"Okay," Jake chimed in, "I know things have gotten weird between us." With another nerve-shock, Shanna's stomach went back to sleep. "I know that...like...it's like we just go through the motions at this point and we've gotten pretty stale, right?"

"Right." Shanna replied as a new anxiety fluttered in her stomach; she searched her mind for the logic behind it, finding nothing; *he's trying to fix it. Please don't do this now.* As torn as she was before, she was practically shredded now. Jake was *finally* showing that neglected consideration she was missing; *Aww—wait, how could he let that happen in the first place? Korbin wouldn't do—maybe Jake's just been losing himself at school; he pushes himself so hard. No, he's telling you right now, he's known about this; he brushed it off every time you tried to bring it up.* She started to sweat during Jake's prolonged explanation—full of stray babbling details—and her shredded emotions were scattering all over the neighborhood as they walked; *He misses you; he knows now what he's been missing. This might be a sign—he still hasn't actually apologized; he* should *apologize but he's never been good about feelings. No, this has gone on way too long; you've waited and waited until you finally started moving on. It's time for* your *happiness; it's time for* you. *Be strong.*

"So yeah. I'm sorry we got to this point." Jake finished.

*...and the apology. Was it really both of us? He knew we were in trouble the whole time and would never discuss it. Okay, not a completely accurate apology, but still an apology—NO! Be strong goddammit!* "Well, I really appreciate that, Jake—all of it; but...I gotta be honest..." she began, feeling sick again; a deep breath subdued the urge to vomit, "...we've been on this road for a long time now. You even knew about it; but whenever I tried to bring it up, you played it off like nothing was wrong."

Jake waited for the historically proven moment where Shanna would give in—something in the hopeful words of, *"how do we know...",* or *"what are we gonna do..."*—

something that would open his opportunity to convince—

"I waited for you, Jake. I waited and waited and waited but nothing was changing and...life kept going on and I moved forward with it."

Jake glanced at her with confusion and he stopped his pace. He turned and glared sternly in her eyes, "What's *that* mean?" he asked condescendingly.

Now *he has emotion? Be strong; Be strong, be strong. Say it. Just...say...it.* "I think we need to see other people."

Jake's eyes widened, "...you serious?"

"Mm-hmm." Shanna nodded hesitantly and pressed her hand into her stomach. *...be strong. It's about what you want now; be strong.* Jake stepped back and shook his head as he looked up—an empty, celestial search for an explanation that he *actually* found. He looked back down at Shanna right as the notion hit him, "You said you moved forward...are you already seeing someone else?"

*Really? Did he just actually ask that? After six faithful years, he's got balls to question your loyalty?!* The party in Shanna's stomach finally died as a policing offense took over, putting up her guard. "No, and I'm really offended you just asked that."

"You gave me reason to!"

"No I didn't! But to answer your question, no; I haven't gotten involved with anyone else. I *have* gotten very close to a friend of mine at school..." *why did you mention* "friend"? "...and, yes, I'm gonna give things a try with him."

57

Jake rolled his eyes, flinging his hand in the air as he walked a quick circle, "Wow, Shanna; you really must not give a shit—rubbin' it in my face like that."

*...really?* "No, I *do* care and that's why I'm telling you; I figured you should know. Besides, *you* asked." *Suck on that, asshole. No, he's not an asshole but he's really acting like one.*

"Who is it? It's probably that little faggot friend that's always posting on your page."

*Okay...asshole. Never talk shit about my friends ever again.* The slur sliced her nerves and her muscles clenched as she resisted the urge to attack, "First, you know I hate that word and when people talk shit about others. Second, whoever it is, is none of your damn business. After all this time, I thought you deserved to know what was going on with me. Now I'm not even sure I want to know *you*."

"Whatever. This is bullshit. Yeah, I'm a little late with it, but I just tried to start making things better and you're dumping me like it's nothing—like you don't care."

*I'm sorry,* who *has the vagina?* "I told you I care! You're taking everything out of proportion and twisting it around. Who knows? Maybe this won't work out and we'll eventually get back together; if it's meant to happen it'll happen. Either way, I want you in my life, even if we're not together; but this ball started rolling and I went with it. I couldn't wait anymore and I decided before you finally decided to do something about it—about the problem you already knew about."

Staring at the ground, Jake smiled and shook his head, turning back toward the house. "...whatever," he began.

He turned back toward his ex, walking backward, "You go ahead and have fun with that little prick. I give a shit." He took a few more steps, then again, turned his back on her, picking up a storming pace back to the house.

Shanna clenched her muscles, taking frantic steps in numerous directions around her spot. *How the hell could he be that immature?* She stopped and crossed her arms against her chest as tears filled her eyes. She tightened her muscles further, fighting a heavy crying session and walked back to her car.

# 5

In an upscale neighborhood of Madison, Wisconsin, stood a large, two-story house with a big, well-maintained front yard and an in-ground swimming pool in an even bigger backyard; adjacent to, and four feet above, the pool was a Philippine Mahogany deck equipped with built in seats, a fire-pit and a hot tub. The spacious garage reserved spaces for three vehicles worth, easily, over $100,000 together

Inside the four-thousand square foot house were four full bedrooms *and* bathrooms, a large living room with a sixty-inch full HD television—with surround sound—an enormous kitchen and a basement sectioned off as a laundry room, a small gym and a game room with a bar.

As Dr. David Blythe an accomplished brain surgeon and Mrs. Emily Blythe a legal secretary for a successful firm, they found great joy in spoiling themselves; while not snide or condescending to anyone, they loved showing off at frequent parties and gatherings with friends. As social as they were—with all that they had and the advantages they've provided—they've never been able to grasp the mindset of their daughter, Amanda—why she never did well with making friends or why she was so *odd* as they considered.

On yet another, beautiful summer afternoon, Amanda sat in her room watching *Grease 2* on a break from drawing; she hadn't even changed from her t-shirt and pajama pants. The movie always made her smile and gave her goose bumps when *Maxwell Caulfield* thwarted the rival gang and revealed his identity to *Michelle Pfeiffer*. Typically, after the movie—sometimes during—Amanda would pull out a jacket from her bedroom closet and start prancing around as a *Pink Lady*.

Numerous art pieces were scattered over her walls, leaving no room for pictures or posters of any kind. Sitting on an elaborate drafting board were numerous art tools and a recent sketch—a self-portrait of Amanda crying as she held a rotting heart.

People that encountered Amanda always commented on and questioned her antics; they questioned her entire being from her decisions to her actions and her speech. Family and her parents' friends made sure to do so behind her back for fear of her reaction. Their apprehensions were well earned whenever she lost her "*cool*". While she could handle things not going her way, Amanda had moments that triggered angry outbursts that always led to over-dramatic crying. No one could ever calculate a pattern; the moment had to be just right.

As with Shanna, Amanda's irrelevant and compulsive speaking struck the nerves of everyone. What really made people chuckle in disbelief, was her tendency to talk as actors did in movies—even using direct quotes, as if she couldn't find her own words to express her thoughts. Even Amanda's parents questioned her cognitive development. After some testing during her high school years, her brain was diagnosed as completely healthy with no abnormalities. However, she did receive a diagnosis for a personality and social anxiety disorder. After some ineffective therapy—constantly denying any problems— she stopped going when she turned eighteen.

The only person she ever admitted anything to was herself. All of her problems and concerns were merely expressed through her art and her social outlet came from movies—the only exposure to the world she really allowed herself; her hopes to, someday, connect with someone grew tremendously when Shanna first gave her the time of day and continued to care afterward.

Shanna was the first, and only person Amanda was willing to open up to. Despite the general acceptance of today's standards, being a socially-handicapped lesbian proved a constant struggle for her. Specifically, she believed she'd never find anyone to love her romantically—that she'd never find her "one". That changed when Shanna came into her life. Amanda never really learned to read people and while Shanna never even *hinted* an interest in women, Amanda was convinced there had to be something. She couldn't explain any other reason for Shanna showing so much compassion and while she may have to find and trigger her true nature, Amanda believed with all her heart and soul that Shanna was meant for her.

When the movie finished, Amanda shut off the player and television. She walked to the small desk next to her bed, waking up her laptop; she opened her email and refreshed the "Inbox" to find no new mail. Her heart sank a bit, having to continue waiting for Shanna's response to her last message. In that whole summer, she emailed Shanna every week but only received one reply that, apart from basic summer inquiries, stated Amanda's exact assumption: she'd just been really busy. Being the best friend she could be, Amanda replied immediately, telling of her summer and how she completely and totally understood her being busy; she would always understand.

After the disappointing email-check, Amanda closed her laptop and walked back to her drafting table. She placed her portrait on a floor pile next to the table's leg, then reached to the other side and grabbed a purple pocket folder. Despite its solid durability, she handled it with extreme caution and gently placed it on the table. She opened it and pulled out a small stack of folded printer paper; printed on the first one was a photo of her and Shanna that she was fortunate enough to get in their sophomore year. She set the picture down, then scattered the rest on the left of the table—all printed pictures of Shanna, thanks to social media. Finally, she pulled out the remaining contents of the folder—a piece of sketch paper with a full body drawing of Shanna in nothing but a large, partially held up t-shirt, revealing her stomach just below her breasts. Amanda marveled at her ability to use numerous references to interpret her subject into an art piece. Staring at the drawing, she gently ran her fingers across the paper's surface. She then closed her eyes and kissed her fingers, pressing them against the drawing.

"*You're the most beautiful woman in my life.*" she whispered.

# 6

Saturday night of Labor Day Weekend—twelve hours before his seminar—Myles settled himself into the couch of Billy's living room. When Myles made his case about potential hauntings in the local motels, his former professor graciously invited him to stay at his home; with his wife out of town on business, there would definitely be more room in the small house.

With continuously wandering eyes, Myles rose from the couch and strolled around the edges of the living room, glancing over all of Billy's visible decor and possessions. From the big screen television to his contemporary furniture setup, Myles shook his head as a sense of surprise brewed in his mind.

This was Billy's second house, which he and his wife bought after he landed the teaching job at *UW-Platteville*. The walls mostly held photos of Billy with his wife and kids and two paintings, which Myles could never place the work or recognize the signatures. Billy's office was just as surprising—a plain brown desk, matched by an even plainer brown bookshelf. A much smaller television sat in the corner, next to a stereo from the mid-90's and the walls were decorated with various music posters and sports memorabilia—*The Doors, Lynard Skynard, Van Halen, Milwaukee Brewers, Wisconsin Badgers, Green Bay Packers, Marquette Golden Eagles and Milwaukee Bucks.* The neon *Miller Beer* light was the affirming seal that Billy was an ordinary, but true, Wisconsinite. Myles grinned with a quiet chuckle. Discounting the smaller size, the house was a spot-on replica to the first that was just outside Milwaukee.

Despite Billy's ability to talk to students in an easy and comprehensive manner—and the fact that they called him "*Billy*"—Myles' initial impression was that his psychology professor would have the typical house full of books—more than his office actually held—with no television or indications of a sports fan. He saw Billy's furniture comprised of dark wood, elegantly carved in acanthus scroll-work; dimly-lit lamps with fancy shades; an antique radio—or record player—playing classical music; he even pictured the big, throne-like chair by the fancy lamp, with a small table to the side holding an intricate sculpture that held Billy's smoking pipe. Myles never even suspected him to be married or have kids but when the troubled dropout was first invited to Billy's old house, those assumptions faded almost completely away. As they lingered in his mind by a mere thread, he grew accustomed to the notion that the professor he held in such high regard was so...*regular.*

Continuing around the room, Myles glanced at the table next to the recliner; he reached and picked up the book that held a bookmark half way through; Billy was reading *Pet Sematary* by Stephen King; he shuddered and set the book back down; *No thanks...*

When they first met at the *University of Wisconsin-Milwaukee*, they were both turned in completely different directions—Billy at only ninety-degrees and Myles at a complete one hundred eighty-degrees. Obsessed about his abilities by that time, Myles was completely confident and optimistic about his chosen path in psychology; being up to date on numerous societal topics, he was incredibly outspoken and always ready to weigh in on conversations. He had no hope of hiding the overall joy and life-enthusiasm displayed on his face.

Billy, however, maintained the same personality that he held now, but his mind wasn't nearly as opened—specifically with the paranormal. With unwavering skepticism, Billy believed in science and facts and when he began his unit on psychic abilities, the battles commenced.

Despite his excitement, Myles maintained a solid cover of his abilities in attempts to not frighten anyone. During the entire unit on psychics, he and Billy would constantly counter each other's points with theories, if not facts. They bantered back and forth but the atmosphere never became hostile; it actually provided entertainment for the other students.

Catering to the excitement throughout the unit's duration, Myles approached Billy after class on the last day to reconcile; laughing it off, they both assured no intended disrespect. Before they parted ways, Myles convinced his professor to allow a quick mind-reading. Rolling his eyes and shaking his head with a smile, Billy extended his hand and Myles held it firmly as he closed his eyes; after a moment's focus, he began citing everything Billy's mind conjured up—random numbers, skeptical thoughts of lucky guesses, involuntary embarrassing thoughts, shuffling music—one right after the other.

When Myles opened his eyes, Billy was staring right at him with his mouth wide open; he slowly pulled his hand back when Myles released his grip, fidgeting with excitement. Billy questioned the anxiousness and when his student explained his additional abilities, he began laughing uncontrollably, laying the first blocks to their friendship.

The following year, Myles' class was assigned a pseudo thesis project; intending to turn it into a book one day, he approached it as the beginning of his dissertation. Of course, Billy approved the subject matter; after three years of endless approval, the answer was obvious—almost inevitable—and Myles just waited on the formalities. While he researched some external sources, the plan he drew out consisted heavily of self-studies, documented with journal entries, audio and visual samples and witness testimonies. This was going to be his mark on the world.

An element he declared as part of his thesis was to challenge himself and the notion gave him an adrenaline high. One way was to see if he could discover something about a person or place that had been hidden from public records. Another was to see if he could see into the mind or consciousness of an entity. Being in Milwaukee, the *Oxford Apartments* was an obvious first choice; *la casa de Jeffrey Dahmer.*

Having been demolished in 1992, *Jeffrey Dahmer's* home was now a vacant lot in the neighborhood of Walker's Point on Milwaukee's south side—gang territory. As much as his pride ached to admit the cliché, Myles' peak point of ghostly encounters was at night, just as was the criminal activity; there was no convincing him not to request a police escort. With all available officers out in the field that night, Myles would have to meet them at the lot.

At 10:00PM, he pulled up along the curb in front of the site—no cops yet. Before he could put the car in park, entities of people faded into view, one by one. While they all stood fifty yards away on the spot where the building once stood, they each turned toward Myles and glared at him. An assuring grin grew on his face but the chill down his spine forced him to look away, where his eyes locked on the group at the end of the block, standing under the street light.

Five guys dressed in combinations of dark baseball caps, dark hooded sweatshirts, and baggy pants glared right at Myles; his spine blasted him as they started walking in his direction; *Shit! Where are those cops?!*

69

Each group member swaggered with each step, continually turning around or leaning over, whispering to one another and Myles' gaze unlocked, looking back over at the lot—at the "*people*" he actually came to see; he shuddered, then looked back toward the group that was already half-way down the block, closing in on him; *Jesus Christ, please stop and turn around; stop...and turn around. If you're not going to stop, just keep walking passed. Please, though, turn around; turn around, turn around, turn around...*

Closer now, the group spread apart as three of them walked into the street and the other two remained on the sidewalk; none of them ever removed their eyes from their target. Myles looked down and clenched his fists; *c'mon, cops...c'mon. Get here* please. The five swaggered closer and closer—ten feet. Myles clenched tighter until his entire body ached and he squeezed his eyes shut. When the diffused light shining through his eyelids suddenly darkened—*right outside! They're right outside the fucking window! They're going to rob you and kill you! Oh God, oh God, oh GOD!*

The chirping of a police siren sounded from around the corner behind Myles; still looking down, he opened his eyes and his body relaxed as the blue and red lights bounced off their surroundings. From his peripheral vision, he saw the bodies that surrounded his car quickly step away and he instantly lifted his head; the five were already heading back the way they came and Myles took a deep breath as he leaned his head back against his seat...*knock, knock!*

An officer banged his knuckles against the window and he jumped off the seat; shaking his head with embarrassment, he rolled down the thin glass shield that one of the five would have surely broken. A second officer stood on the sidewalk, opposite his partner.

"Mr. Dunn?" The officer asked and after Myles nodded, the officer invited him out of the car—lecturing him about the neighborhood's dangers at night; *No shit. You asked for an escort and had to settle for a meet up.* After an explanation of his research and assurance of no malicious intent, they allowed him onto the restricted property.

When Myles turned, the *Dahmer* victims were all still staring at him; with the cops' skeptical eyes burning a hole in his back, he paused a moment. He looked back toward the two officers, nodded his head then looked back to the vacant lot and grinned; *...of course they feel skeptical; well they'd piss themselves dry if they saw what you're seeing right now.* With a deep breath, Myles stepped off the sidewalk and onto the gravel.

His steps were slow at first but he sped up until he reached the perimeter's edge and stopped—the exact location of one of the building's outer walls. There was an invisible barrier that Myles could only feel—a wall of energy. He raised his hand and placed his palm in front of it, stopping when his gut suddenly twisted into fleshed-origami; *Turn around now—no...no, this isn't anything out of the ordinary. It's just a manifestation of all the victims' emotions—unfinished business; okay, you've never experienced it as a wall before—so what...you're strong; your abilities are incredibly strong. You just have to be brave and deal with the ghosts staring into you. Suck it up.*

Myles inched his hand forward against the invisible wall and it pushed right through; startled, the cold, tingling sensation against his skin forced a tiny convulsion and he immediately pulled his hand back; *...turn around—stop. Get it over with.* He shook it off and exhaled with a low grunt. He clenched his body, closed his eyes and stepped forward, passing completely through the wall.

If the silence of the ghosts wasn't deafening enough, each step on the gravel was like a sidewalk-eating jackhammer next to Myles' ears; after one more stone-grinding step, he stopped. It was freezing standing on that lot; the cold tingling gave life to the goose bumps on his skin, like they were crawling; he shivered from the inside out but he didn't open his eyes; *You're here; you know they're here and they know* you're *here. This is the ground level of your life's work; just open your eyes and do what you need to do...do it...do it, open them...now!*

Myles opened his eyes and inhaled deeply, holding his breath; *...breathe.* He slowly exhaled as he looked around at twelve young men who were all in-tact; *oh yeah; he didn't cut them up till after they were dead.* At most, a couple of them appeared to have swollen bulges from hits to the head.

"Um...hi; I'm—uh...I'm Myles." he introduced, clearing his throat and there was no response; *Still won't talk to you; they just stare. Fuck it—no point in small talk;* Myles looked around again and in a group of twelve, dead, terrified and begrudging spirits—ignoring his instinct to just leave—his gut pointed him to one teenage boy and walked toward him—each step grinding his eardrum. The ghost was a statue that never moved as the psychic neared him.

Myles stopped directly in front of the boy, face to face; he fought the urge to close his eyes and turn away; *Ugh, you pussy. You were born with a gift; use it!* His chest trembled, immediately followed by his arms and legs from what he was about to do; *Oh God.* He lifted his hand, slowly pushing it toward the ghost and suddenly stopped; he frantically looked over both shoulders as the other eleven spirits walked toward Myles. They drew closer with faster paces...faster...*faster.* Their eyes and mouths were wide open—terrified. As the paranormal gang closed in, Myles turned back toward the boy and jumped at the ghost's gaping eyes and mouth. Myles pulled his arms close to his body, ready to curl into a ball when all twelve of them reached out and placed their hands into and through Myles' body...

Myles' consciousness suddenly fused to the perspective of a *Dahmer* victim, trapped in apartment *213*. He was drugged just like them. His vision was blurry and his body was weak—barely able to move it—but he was coherent. The pain and fear of every victim coursed through Myles' mind as his attempts to fight off the attacker failed. The infamous murderer straddled Myles, pinning him to the couch as he performed every heinous act he put his victims through—a personal demonstration. Myles cringed at the physical sensations while *Dahmer* raped him and he fell into despair as shame took over his mind twelve-fold. His blood boiled when those hands wrapped around his neck and squeezed; even the sensation of blood flow in his body ceased and he was even colder than when he passed through the invisible wall. Suddenly, his head began to vibrate as the drill dug into his skull; when the hydrochloric acid started to eat his brain, he finally screamed.

Making light jokes at Myles, the two officers stared at him; were it not for the gentle body-sways as his muscles lost stability, Myles would've been completely catatonic with his arms curled into his chest. Immediately after his loud, echoing scream, he fell to the gravel convulsing; the officers sprinted to his aid. Myles' seizure rolled his eyes into the back of his head and his nose started to bleed...

When Myles was discharged, he no longer had control of his abilities; he could not turn them off. He was receiving everyone's thoughts and absorbing all their emotions regardless if he touched them or not. After a nervous breakdown at school—afraid of everyone and anything with a spirit or living consciousness—he dropped out and began the task of regaining control of his abilities; immediately after, he would push them as far down into his being as he could and never touch them again.

Seven years passed before he was comfortable again and though he'd been living in peace for the previous two years, he was never the same—seven years to suppress his abilities and only minutes to bring back to life. Yet, as hard as he tried to fool himself and as terrified as he was, a small part of Myles' spirit was gratified at the notion of reuniting with his *gifts*—like being separated from a sibling. Money or not, that small part of him always wanted to conjure them again but it needed a reason; *Thank you, Billy.*

# 7

Shanna fell into a depression that only lasted two days when she broke up with Jake; it even started getting better the very next morning when Korbin greeted her with a text: "*WAKE UP! B-)*".

She lingered on the memory of her times with Jake and how hurt he must have been but it was a slippery grip on a bar being pulled by Korbin. By the third day, thoughts of Jake were completely gone as she fantasized possible outcomes of revealing her feelings to Korbin; *How are you supposed to tell him? What's gonna happen with—shut up. It's gonna be fine. You saw how he looked at you before summer. It's gonna be good.*

Though moving in a week early, Shanna's routine of the new school year played out the same as the last three years; she registered, moved in and said goodbye to Mom and Dad. The only difference, this year, was her living quarters. Being a senior now, she had the option to live off campus in a sorority house or an apartment and she jumped at the opportunity. Going half and half with both their parents, Shanna and Molly rented a furnished unit in *Washington Place Apartments*, on *Washington Street*.

Shanna told Korbin where she and Molly were staying but he never showed. She watched for a revealing text every day, saying something obnoxious such as: *"Let me in! It's 85(degrees) and cold as hell!"* but instead, her gut hollowed out when her phone screen was blank or filled with someone else's message; the last message he sent came on Tuesday and consisted of only basic chit-chat; three days went by and on Friday, a new message finally appeared. Korbin was still out of state; *What the hell?! School's gonna start. How can he still be traveling?!*

The final Saturday before classes began—Shanna left to rent out her textbooks for the semester while Molly slept in—having already rented hers. Arriving early, she breezed through the line and was out in under ten minutes. When she walked out of the tiny textbook-specific library, she almost completely stopped in her tracks as the student line wrapped all the way up the stairs. Waving excitedly to a couple friends as she passed by, she giggled when she saw the line extending out the doors and around the corner; *Only ten minutes for that mess...good job early-girl.*

Heading down the sidewalk, Shanna looked over at a couple benches and immediately recognized the seated position of the girl drawing away on a sketchpad; were it not for those two factors of sitting and drawing, she would never have guessed the girl dressed in black—now with short hair—was Amanda. Even those bird legs that supported her little torso didn't connect the dots.

*Just go say hi before she hunts you down; don't engage, just say you gotta go.* With a contemptible sigh, Shanna changed course toward her number-one fan.

What...*is she wearing?* Amanda traded her *Chuck Taylors* for some shin-high, spike-tipped, platform boots; her "girl-next-door" t-shirt and shorts were now a black tank-top and leather skirt. As Shanna got closer, she noticed Amanda's fingernails and eyes were covered in heavy black; a spiked bracelet wrapped around her wrist and her middle-finger bore a piece of metal finger armor; *You're no expert, but didn't those finger things go outta style? Hey...to each their own; at least she's not dressed like you— stop. Stop judging the poor girl.* As Shanna's hair already grew down to her shoulders in the past three months, she excused the, seemingly fresh, bob-haircut Amanda was now wearing.

"Hey there." She said from ten feet away and her neck clenched.

Amanda quickly jerked her head up, instantly locking her eyes with Shanna's and she smiled; her brain released "warm and fuzzy" endorphins, proving a powerful ally to the adrenaline shot when Shanna broke her focus; "Hi Shanna!"

"How was the rest of your summer?" Shanna asked, keeping a safe distance from whatever potential fumes Amanda might radiate.

"It was good. I drew a lot and saw some friends." Amanda lied.

"Awesome. I see your new look; why the change?"

Amanda looked over her body from the large bottoms of her boots, up to her chest and started to blush; she looked back at Shanna with an embarrassed grin and giggled, "Guess I'm just trying to express myself."

"How's that?"

"Umm...goth? Well, actually..." Amanda looked around elaborately; no one was near them, "...can I tell you something?" she asked, leaning forward.

Shanna held back the laughter trying to escape; *Feels like fourth grade all over again—big dramatic secret—oh Jesus, just suck it up; she's strange—of course—but apparently, she has no clue. You're not about to tell her so just play along; she'll learn one day...hopefully.* She nodded and sat on the bench.

Still holding her sketchbook in her lap, she turned slightly toward Shanna and leaned closer, "So, with all the drawing I did this summer, I realized a lot of it was dark; and, no...of course I didn't realize it till I was done with, maybe thirty pieces. You know me, when I get into drawings I can't stop and I have no idea what I'm actually drawing. It's like this powerful force that just comes out of me..."

*Oh, spare me of all the crap you just said—ugh, stop! What is* wrong *with you? Let her do her thing;*

"Well I realized, there's something inside me—something dark that's trying to get out. So, I thought, maybe if I do my part and make myself look dark, then it'll finally find peace and leave."

"...Interesting." *Wha—darkness?*

Then Amanda dropped an assuring bomb that one of her life-goals right now was to impress Shanna, "You don't like it?"

"Hey, if you like it, that's cool." Shanna answered. *Well now we know you're doing this to, somehow, impress—fail, by the way—and it really doesn't help—ugh! Stop being such a bitch! She can't help it!*

What Amanda would never admit was that being an outcast already, dressing in a "gothic" style felt perfect. She'd seen numerous movies with outcasts of all cliques; specifically, most of the misfit-artist characters were portrayed as "goth" or "dark". Not seeing herself as a "nerd" and uncertain how to express herself—with subtlety—as a lesbian, "gothic artist" gave her that feeling of certainty.

"Guess—" Shanna jumped at the voice behind her ear. She smiled when she saw Korbin staring at her, one inch away from her face; he laughed as he stood upright.

She stood, rushed over to Korbin and punched his arm, "Ah! You ass! Don't do that!" Flinching from Shanna's attack, Korbin stepped away from the assault. Shanna took a giant step forward, wrapping her arms around him and he returned the hug. They squeezed each other firmly and he lifted Shanna off the ground; she clung to him. "I missed you." she said.

"I missed you too." Korbin replied, setting her down.

Shanna released her grip and took half a step back, "What happened this last week? Did you just get back?"

"Nah, I got back, like, two weeks ago; I wanted to surprise you."

Shanna scoffed and smacked him once more.

An overwhelming sense of shame and defeat shot to Amanda's stomach, practically carving out an ulcer and she began packing her things.

"Oh, I'm sorry..." Shanna said, "Korbin, this is Amanda. Amanda—Korbin."

"What's up?" Korbin greeted with a nod.

"Hi." Amanda answered in a flat tone, never looking up.

Korbin's eyes were pulled to Amanda's sketchpad, "Oooh; can I see what you're drawing?" he asked and Amanda stopped moving; she let out a big, obvious sigh and picked up the book, turning the paper toward them, "Oh, damn," he said. He stared in awe at an abstract composition of organic material fused with, what appeared to be metal. "I love those spikes. What is that? Like an alien type thing?"

Amanda nodded, "It's called Biomech."

"Wow, Amanda; that's awesome—like, *really* awesome." Shanna added, completely stunned by the drawing. A single butterfly fluttered in Amanda's stomach after seeing Shanna's reaction and it was immediately squashed when she remembered Korbin standing right next to her.

"Thanks." Amanda said, slipping the sketchpad into her bag, "I actually have to get going."

"Alrighty," Shanna said in a much lighter tone, "Good luck with your first week; I'll see ya 'round."

"Bye." Amanda answered with a wave as she turned in the opposite direction.

Shanna turned back to Korbin and smiled, "So you gonna come see the apartment?" Korbin grinned, tilted his head and slowly *blinked* his eyes at Shanna and she shook her head with a giggle.

"'Bout damn time." She said.

Following the sidewalk around the bend, Amanda stopped and turned at the corner of a building, scowling at Korbin as he continued teasing Shanna; *Don't be mad; never be mad at Shanna. She's just confused by what society tells her; she doesn't know. You just have to show her how to follow her heart—that you'll be better to her—and for her—than any man could hope...to hell with him...*

In the late afternoon, Shanna played around on her laptop while Molly scrolled her finger up and down her phone screen. Each of their *zones* created an oblivious shield of silence until the loud apartment buzzer sounded—jolting the girls out of their seats. Shanna gripped her laptop tight, avoiding the same fate of Molly's dropped phone; she picked it up and examined it.

"All good." Molly said, examining for damage.

Shanna laughed and walked to the buzzer, pushing the "talk" button, "Hello?"

"Hey...it's Jake." said a voice through the intercom and Shanna's eyes widened; she looked at Molly whose facial expression perfectly mirrored Shanna's. In clueless gestures, Shanna shrugged her shoulders and Molly shook her head; "...can I come up?" Jake added. Shanna sighed, then shook her head as she pushed the "front door" button.

Molly sat forward on the couch, holding her hands open, waiting to receive an explanation that she wouldn't get. "Did you know he was coming?"

"No!" Shanna said as she sat down; she reached over and closed her laptop, "I mean, I gave him the address at the end of summer, if he wanted to visit but I thought he was gonna call and make a plan."

"But you're trying to go further with Korbin."

"I know. Jake apologized, like, two weeks ago and asked if it would be alright if he tried to come visit sometime. I don't wanna completely drop him from my life so I said, 'ok'."

Molly nodded in acceptance, "But Korbin's coming over, right?"

"Yeah..." Shanna began as she stood up; she glanced at the clock, "...soon." The butterflies in her stomach started another party—only a small social gathering at the moment.

"Oh, man—wonder what Korbin will do." Molly added.

"I'm worried about what *Jake's* gonna do." Shanna said just before the door knocked. She gritted her teeth and threw her clenched fists in the air before letting in

Jake. Not even looking through the peephole, she opened the door and was greeted with a large bouquet of roses; *Oh great.*

Standing behind the flowers, Jake took a deep breath, "...hi."

"Hey." Shanna said with a forced smile and stepped out of the way, allowing Jake inside. When he reached the living room, he waved, "Hey Molly."

She waved back, "Hi!" She held a stronger "poker-face" as her smile appeared more natural.

Jake turned back to Shanna and handed her the bouquet, "...for you; if you...didn't notice."

"Thank you." she said, grabbing the flowers and still forcing a smile as she searched around, "...I don't think we have a vase." She walked into the kitchen and checked through the cabinets, finding nothing.

"It's all good ba—" Jake suddenly stopped as Shanna's habitual pet-name, "*babe*" started to creep out his mouth. He looked; she was still checking the cabinets.

Kneeling down to the bottom cabinets, Shanna shook her head and clenched her jaw again as the butterflies livened up; *This isn't happening; this is* not *happening.*

Jake glanced around the front section of the apartment, examining the living room and kitchen, "...nice place guys."

"Right?" Molly added, still playing on her phone. Finally, Shanna stood up and gently set the flowers on the counter.

"Yeah, we need to pick up a vase yet." she said from the kitchen through the wall's opening.

"That's cool." Jake assured.

After only a few seconds—that felt like elongated minutes—of silence, Jake asked to use the bathroom and Molly pointed it out right away. As soon as he shut the door, Shanna buried her face in her hands and pulled her hair back.

"...*awkward*." Molly whispered and Shanna nodded, "Look, we both know what he's gonna ask so I'm gonna go to my room. Just be strong; I'm right in there if you need me."

Shanna nodded and Molly left her in privacy. One second after, the toilet flushed and Jake returned, looking around.

"Molly go hiding?" he asked, pointing down the hall; Shanna smiled and nodded as her face turned red; *Don't get sick this time; Molly's right here.* Jake walked over to the little breakfast bar, separating the kitchen and living room; he leaned on the counter across from his ex-girlfriend. They glared at each other for a moment.

"I really wish you would've called; ya know, planned beforehand." Shanna said.

Jake closed his eyes and nodded with embarrassment, "I know; I'm sorry. I just...wanted to surprise you."

"I appreciate the gesture." *It won't amount to anything. Had this been planned, it'd be great to talk but, today...say your piece and leave...please.*

"Look, um...can you please reconsider? Can we give this another chance? I'm so, sorry for everything, Shanna and I hate being without you," *Hmm...points for being honest with his feelings for a change;* "and talkin' like this is

85

*really* hard for me so I better be gettin' some mad props." he confirmed with a chuckle; Shanna let out just a subtle cough of a laugh—barely able to force any more enthusiasm. "I'm ready to be the man you need me to be, babe; I really am. Whatever you need me to be, I can be it."

*Oh, God. Why did he have to get so negligent in the first place? Wish Korbin was here—just him and you. Gaaahhh! Why did you have to meet Korbin and...fall for him? Holy shit...you fell for Korbin...*

"So? You think we can salvage what we have? Rebuild?"

Developing her response, Shanna's mind circled around Korbin instead of a possible patch-job with Jake. After a few seconds, she finally forced the consideration of her and Jake getting back together and there was nothing. No excited-adrenaline shot through her veins; no oozing dread churned her stomach. Even the butterflies stopped dancing. *Well yeah, the answer's obvious; but now you gotta deal with his reaction when you let him down.*

"Jake, I really do appreciate the gesture; I appreciate the apology but, I'm sorry...I'm sticking to my decision."

Jake sighed as he stared at Shanna for a moment; then he quickly looked away and pushed himself up, off the counter, "I don't get this, Shanna. You wanna throw away everything of ours for some new crush that you *only* developed because we were having problems?"

*Ooooooooookay; here we go again,* "I'm adapting, Jake. I'm living my life as it moves forward; like I said this

86

summer, I tried to bring up our issues but you continued to play it off."

"Okay, I'm not perfect. Why do I have to get shit on for it?" Jake insisted.

"Jake...this isn't a good time right now. You're getting upset again and I can't talk straight with you like this. I'm happy to discuss everything another time, but—"

The door buzzer sounded and Shanna closed her eyes, shaking her head, "...*oh please, not now.*" she whispered. Jake glared at the door, then back at Shanna as she walked over to the intercom and pushed the button, "Hello?"

"Hiii!" Korbin said in a drunk voice. Shanna sighed and rested her head against the wall; she pushed the button again,

"Gimme a couple minutes?" she asked.

"Mmkay." Korbin answered.

Shanna returned to the living room, standing in front of Jake with nothing to separate them and the butterflies started again.

Jake stared at Shanna—his eyes full of contempt, "That's him isn't it?"

"...yes," Shanna answered with a defeated sigh, "and I'd really appreciate it if you left before I let him in."

"What the hell for?! I was here first. Let him try somethin'...see what happens."

*Be strong...be strong,* "I'm not worried about him; I'm worried about *your* reaction."

"What's that supposed to mean?" Jake demanded, taking a step back.

"It means you always overreact and I don't want you hurting anyone. So please, just leave!" Shanna shouted as she pulled the door open; Jake stood awestruck for a moment, then slowly walked to the door. Before stepping over the threshold, he looked at Shanna; he turned his head back and as he stepped through the door, "...fuck you."

Shanna's eyes widened as her boiling blood burned those nervous butterflies to ashes. She stormed out the door after Jake who was already half way down the hall; she sprinted to him, grabbed hold of his shirt and pulled him to a stop as she whipped around in front of him. "Who do you think you are?! Who the *hell* do you think you are?! Don't you ever talk to me like that! I gave you six years! Six years I was loyal to you! I gave you all my love! I stuck it out when you were playing '*Oh, everything's fine*'! I've been your girlfriend and your best friend since high school! I've never done *anything* to deserve this guilt-trip shit!"

Molly rushed out to the hall and put her arms around Shanna, pulling her apart from Jake. "Okay, okay..." she said and Shanna started to cry.

Down the hall and around the corner, the elevator doors opened and Korbin stepped off, thanking the woman next to him for letting him inside. He turned the corner and stopped; when he noticed Shanna standing in front of the big athlete with a troubled, red face, he started jogging. Passing Jake, he stopped right in front of Shanna, "What's wrong?" the concern in his eyes was a complete one-eighty from his typically, lighthearted smile.

Shanna's jaw dropped when her eyes locked on Korbin and she turned her head in disbelief. Korbin turned and locked eyes with Jake.

"Got a problem?" Jake asked. Korbin looked back at Shanna, then back to Jake.

"I think you better leave, man." Korbin answered, taking a step toward Shanna. Jake pulled him to a stop, turned him around, and slammed his fist into Korbin's face.

"Fuckin' bitch." Jake said as Korbin fell to the floor. Holding his right eye and wincing with pain, Molly knelt down to Korbin's aid. A neighboring door opened down the hall and a man in his fifties popped his head out.

After checking Korbin, Shanna ran over and pushed Jake; she knocked him back a step, then he braced himself as she continued pushing. "I told you to leave! I told you I didn't want you to do this! Get outta here! Get out now!" Shanna yelled in a voice muffled by her cries.

Jake's left shoulder was tugged hard and when he turned, his face met with *Korbin's* fist. Distracted by Shanna, Jake failed to notice Korbin standing back up and flanking his left side; the resulting *"hammer fist"* knocked Jake down, leaving him with a gushing, broken nose.

The neighbor finally ran out into the hall and as he reached to shove Korbin back, Korbin held up his hands, backing away. "I'm done; I'm done." he said.

Regaining composure, Jake shoved the neighbor's hands away and stood up; as he walked down the hall, he swayed into the walls, still dazed from the punch.

After explaining how such an incident wouldn't happen again, the neighbor agreed not to call the police and went back to his apartment, as did Shanna—escorted by Molly and Korbin—and she hid in her room the rest of the night.

# 8

9:00AM—It wasn't the alarm that teased Korbin's nerves; he woke on the correct side of the bed. Not hearing at all from Shanna after leaving last night gave his brain the extra kick—next to the headache he already felt. Enraged at being assaulted, proud of his retaliation, worried about Shanna's new impression of him—Korbin's suddenly-frantic mind was a complete turnaround from the issues that usually just rolled off his shoulder and it greeted him again when he regained consciousness.

Walking on the path from the dorms to the lecture hall, he replayed the incident in his head and concluded nothing else could have been done. Like a conflict between countries, he made his civilized stance, defending a friend; inevitably, when diplomacy failed and he was attacked, the only logical response was physical force—make the enemy see he wouldn't stand down but raise the bar and make him pay. A broken nose from a significantly smaller foe was perfect.

While some of his pride swelled at the little victory, most of it quivered at the uncertainty of Shanna's opinion; *...their relationship was already dwindling and he just pissed her off even more—before you got there* and *after he punched you—so now what's she think of him? God...she was* really *pissed...but she didn't seem any better after you hit him back. Well how the hell were you* supposed *to respond?! Fuck it; you defended yourself. Just text her when you get to the hall— moment of truth.*

Though not reaching the full one hundred eighty-six seat capacity, numerous students filled the rows of the *Thomas B. Lundeen Lecture Hall*, waiting to see if the psychic presenter today was the real deal.

Sitting in the middle row, toward the right, Korbin's thumbs rapidly tapped the screen of his phone. The top of the conversation box read: "Shanna Madsen" and, having been sitting for nearly half an hour—contemplating his words—the message itself stretched from the top of the virtual keyboard to the very top row of screen pixels:

*"Okay I had this on my mind since last night and I gotta get it out...I know yesterday was a shitty day for u. I'm sorry u and ur bf reached that kinda level. I'm not sure if ur mad at me for what I did. If u are I guess I can understand but I need u to understand that I don't go looking for fights but I'll be damned if I'm gonna lay down after some asshole sucker punches me. Sorry but yeah I think ur bf is an asshole for how he treated you yesterday and for punching me. If that*

*offends you I apologize again but thats my impression. If I came between u two and I'm causing problems I'll step back and leave you alone if you ask. I hope that's not the case cause that would be really sad but if it is I'll respect it. Okay gonna wrap this up. I hope u feel better today. TTYL."*

After pressing *"Send"*, the message delivery confirmed and Korbin stuffed the phone back in his pocket. He looked around the hall a bit more—still not a capacity-crowd. When he glanced down toward the front row on the left side, he spotted Amanda scribbling some more in her sketchbook. His eyebrows jumped at the uncertainty of what to take from the girl; *Shanna never talked about her before and she seemed a little shady...whatever.*

Suddenly the hall broke into applause as Billy took the stage. Korbin quickly checked his phone and the time read: 10:01AM; *...could'a sworn it was 9:30...okay then.* He started to put the phone back in his pocket when it suddenly vibrated; the speed at which he pulled it almost threw it from his hand. The screen showed a preview of Shanna's reply to his lengthy message; he slid his finger on the screen before the phone's sensors could catch up and react and the device lagged. Korbin's patience dwindled as the screen remained a blank white and as he was about to push the *"Home"* button to refresh, the message appeared:

*"I'm not mad at you. I understand why you did what you did. Honestly, Jake got what he deserved. I will always care about him but he really deserved it. I didn't get a chance to tell you but I broke up with him this summer. It had nothing to do with you. Things between him and I just weren't getting any better and I finally had enough. Besides,*

*no one can tell me who I can and can't be friends with. He never had any reason to suspect dishonorable intentions from you or unloyal ones from me. If he had legit reason, that would be a different story but since it's not we won't worry about it :) You don't have to step back. Actually, I prefer you stay right here with me. You wanna meet up today?"*

Korbin's pulse jumped five speeds and he couldn't fight the smile on his face. The hairs on his body stood as his brain served a round of endorphins to his nerves and he began a reply:

*"Absolutely! B) I'll text you when I'm done."* He held onto his phone after sending his reply this time. Not a minute later, Shanna replied:

*":) later!"* Finally, he placed it back in his pocket and turned his attention to the stage.

Myles stood behind an exit-door as Billy introduced him in the hall. Early that morning, Myles woke his abilities yet again; having already triggered them during the summer, the process wasn't *nearly* as difficult or jarring this time. Each ability—but one—woke to their top potential and he was able to hone on energies at will. The one he left dormant—the one he managed to put in a vice-grip restraint—was his empathy. Swelled with an unexpected pride and holding his head high, he prepared for the day and accompanied Billy to the campus.

Despite his extra-sensory preparations, Myles felt another strange sensation when he arrived at the lecture hall. Stranger than the overall, abnormal feel he couldn't place, was its familiarity digging deep in his mind—a tiny itch that he just could not reach—and it consumed his focus. Waiting outside the lecture hall's side exit as Billy made his introduction, Myles kept digging and digging into his memory—scratching every spot but the one that actually itched; *...focus now; you've got to focus. You're about to present—Goddamn! What the hell is that?! What the—*

"*It's with great pleasure that I introduce Mr. Myles Dunn!*" Billy's voice muffled through the door; applause followed and Myles quickly entered, hesitantly walking toward the small wood podium, where he only waited a few moments as the applause gradually died down.

His eyes scanned up and down the seats in the hall and his auric sight revealed numerous colors surrounding each student. Even Jessica, from the school's event board, was in attendance; noticing she left her contacts out, displaying her true eyes, Myles fought a smile, avoiding her embarrassment. When the excitement of the applause subsided, the familiar sensation tickled at his brain again but stronger now; it was actually somewhere *in* the lecture hall. Myles scanned the crowd again, following the direction from which the sensation radiated. His eyes moved up and down the rows—right to left—until he finally pinpointed the source. In the effort to avoid an awkward staring contest, Myles' eyes scanned right passed Korbin while his peripheral vision remained locked on target; You're *the culprit. Where have I seen you before? Somethi—they're all staring at you; they're waiting.*

"Hi," Myles finally said, addressing the audience, "Um...excuse me. I was just...getting my bearings." he continued, clearing his throat, "Um..." he bit the inside of his lip then used his hand to scoop his hair backward, out of his face for a few seconds, "...well, like uh...Professor Church said, I'm Myles; and...I'm a psychic."...

Following his story, his experiences as a psychic— skipping the details of why he abandoned his abilities— and a slew of questions, the inevitable requests for proof and demonstration ensued and he grinned at the sudden surge of excitement.

An attendance checklist was used to confirm everyone signed a non-disclosure agreement. Assuring that none of this was staged, he asked everyone in attendance who had met him previously to raise their hands; the only acknowledging two were Billy and Jessica. He then invited everyone to take a moment and, honestly, discuss with each other—friends and fellow students—whether or not they ever met with him; no one confirmed. When he asked again who'd met him, no one raised their hands. After he insisted the unlikelihood of a great student conspiracy, he noted the fact that any and all of their student records were private and, because he was considered part of the "public" he had no access to them. His empathy was in a dormant state but the students' obvious skepticism was plastered right on their faces.

"Okay..." he began, "...here's what I propose: my demonstration will include everyone in the audience, except Billy and Miss Jessica, over there. It'll be entirely based on your decisions and this is what I'll need: I need two of you to escort me out the exit door, as far as you like—within reason, of course. Once we're outside, you both will *carefully* examine the bandanna in this brand new, unopened package..." Myles pulled the package from his back pocket and waved it around at the audience; *ugh...just call me David Copperfield. You sold out for money and you're eating it right up; you're just a dancing monkey—stop; it's not a gimmick. You're helping Billy,* "...you will then tie it around my eyes, blinding me. While this is all happening outside, everyone in here—except Billy and Jessica—gather two representatives of your choice; come up with something to put on paper—drawing, phrase, numbers...whatever—make sure what each representative puts on the paper is as different from the other as you can make it. When you're ready, one of you come out to get us; my two escorts will bring me back in, right in front of this podium, facing you all. One at a time, each representative will come stand *behind* the podium, facing the back wall. Actually, they can sit behind the podium to help block the paper from me; I'll just need to be able to reach their hand. Now notice all around me—besides being blindfolded and blocked by a solid wood podium—there's no mirrors or anything; any additional piece of glass in this room are in a location that would fail to help me. So, that said...who wants to escort me out?"

A male and female student approached the front of the audience; as the girl reached Myles first, he handed her the wrapped bandanna. "Before we head outside, check in my ears and make sure there's no earpieces in there." The boy and girl looked inside Myles' ears finding nothing; they turned to the audience and shook their heads. They proceeded to walk the presenter out the side-exit door from which he entered, heading down the hall and through a door leading outside the building.

When the crowd of students gathered, they quietly deliberated on who would represent and what they should write down. The first choice came down to a detailed, hand-written fitness schedule—including previous weights, sets and reps—offered by a muscular young man in the audience; to throw the psychic off, Amanda was designated to present it. In a hearty, group laugh, the second sample was a list of names from some girls in the audience; next to each name was a date and a description; Korbin blushed when the group volunteered him to represent.

Outside, with Myles standing an additional ten feet from his two escorts, the girl opened the package and thoroughly examined the bandanna; everything appeared normal and intact with no holes or tears. After the boy examined it and reached the same conclusion, he walked behind Myles as he rolled the bandana, placed it over his eyes and tied a knot in the back. Myles cocked his head a bit, "Go ahead and tie that tighter; you can make it uncomfortable."

The boy untied the knot then retied it, pulling as hard as he could until the knot was a thick chunk of cloth; Myles winced, despite his approval for discomfort. A minute later, a student emerged from the door and invited Myles back in. He carefully placed his hands on his escorts' shoulders, avoiding their skin, and they slowly guided him back to the lecture hall.

When he reached the front of the podium, Amanda was already seated behind it—tucked in the small storage nook with the fitness schedule in her lap. Myles asked for her hand and she adjusted herself, reaching around the side. Grabbing the podium and reaching back, Myles crouched down a bit; as soon as he touched Amanda's hand, he stopped, "...can I get a chair? This is a little more awkward than I figured." Obliging to his request, a student grabbed a chair, quickly examined it and delivered it up front. Myles carefully sat down, facing the front at just the slightest angle, "Whoever's behind the podium, don't say anything and make sure you focus on your sample." Finally, he grabbed Amanda's hand once more and took a deep breath.

While the tiny hand was a clear indication of either a girl or a severely weak boy, images of Amanda's spiked boots and black clothing appeared in Myles' mind; tightening his focus, the image of the fitness schedule appeared; there was a name at the top, a few scribbles of spelling errors and number adjustments and a few stain droplets on the side margin. Myles finally tilted his head up at the audience, "Well, Ben; this is an impressive fitness routine. I know I can't lift *nearly* what you're putting up. Actually, it looks like you bench about twice what I weigh—three times for squatting, if my math's correct..." The muscular student, Ben, sat frozen with his eyes locked on Myles, "...and don't feel too bad about all the scribbles and spelling mistakes; hatch marks and heavy scribbles took up most of my notebooks in college. Let's just hope you have a backup, in case your sweat drips onto the writing."

Like "Big Ben", the remaining students stared at Myles, awestruck. He let go of Amanda's hand and she stood up, heading back to her seat; her face was red with a big smile.

"Next?" Myles said, rubbing his head with a quiet grunt, then paused when Korbin—the source of the mysteriously familiar sensation—stood up; *...you. Good—sift through his memory quick to see how you know him.* Myles rubbed his head once more and adjusted his position in the chair.

Korbin stood up with the paper in his hand and was quickly stopped by a neighboring student that quickly whispered in his ear. He nodded with a smile and walked toward the front. When he sat down behind the podium, he gently laid the paper upside-down on the carpet and reached his hand back.

The sensation grew stronger as Korbin approached and now it grazed Myles' spine. When he sat down, Myles turned his head toward the podium, "Ready?" he asked and Korbin reached back. When Myles grabbed Korbin's hand, the foggy image of the paper and the thought of a big, random number appeared; Myles skipped right passed those and pushed his way back through Korbin's memory.

Moments passed before the psychic stated anything he saw at the present moment and Korbin, still blocked by the podium, cocked his eyebrows with confusion and looked back, "see anyth—"

"Shh!" Myles interrupted, "...sorry. Talk throws off my focus." he added and Korbin sighed.

With a heavy throbbing in his head, Myles managed to project his consciousness back to Korbin's childhood and suddenly, it came to a stop; there was nothing else but a wall of fog—a dense cloud that never moved; *What the hell? Nothing? You didn't even get passed age five and it stopped? In that whole time-line, you both never met. Who the hell is this kid?!...Oh shit! Get back to your demo!* Myles' consciousness flew back to the front of Korbin's memory, in his present state of mind, and examined both the paper and the large number.

"The number you're thinking is \$4,845,295,461.12; can you pick up the paper?" With a large grin that represented each student's astonishment, Korbin obliged and turned over the paper; he stared at the list, "Thank you." Myles continued, "As for this list...well, I could read off all the names, dates and symptom-descriptions, but I'm not sure you ladies want me to reveal such information about your periods."

One single clap triggered an avalanche of applause and Myles slipped the bandanna off his head; he rubbed his eyes, blinking them tightly as he refocused them. With completely blurred sight, Myles looked over and nodded as Korbin headed back to his seat; passing Amanda along the way, he peripherally noticed a snide glare from her—as if he'd violated her honor. He simply grinned with confusion and continued on. As the hall burst into applause and whistles, Myles stood up and—like any great showman—acknowledged the audience's praise with a simple wave and a small bow.

# 9

Monday morning, Myles actually woke with pure optimism. Immediately after his presentation the day before, almost every student in that hall signed up for a one-hour time slot with him. When they tallied the slots, they counted one hundred twenty-two requests—an extra $3,050—and after giving his seminar without any complications or loss of control, excitement rose up right next to his swelled pride...

10:00AM—Myles' third appointment that day arrived exactly half an hour early. All her buckles, zippers and spikes jingled a dull, flat tone as she nervously shook her legs up and down. Leaning forward in a chair outside Myles' temporary office—her palms braced firmly against the plastic seat—she continually stared at the door. At the first sound of the doorknob, Amanda practically jumped out of the chair and started walking; she stopped abruptly and slowed her pace until the appointment before her—walking with a big smile—passed, then she sped back up until she reached threshold.

Inside the small classroom, Myles stood by a window, snacking on crackers and sausage off the platter ordered by the event board. When he looked over at the door and noticed Amanda, he held up his index finger, cuing her to wait; he took a few gulps from a can of soda, "...sorry 'bout that;" he said politely as he motioned her to enter, "take a seat."

The room setup remained the same as every other day; rows of seats with attached desks faced the front of the room where a small table sat; a chair for a class instructor sat on the opposite side, facing the students' seats. Today, however, an extra chair sat at the table, opposite the instructor's and after closing the door, Amanda sat in it, making herself comfortable.

Myles walked back to the table and sat down. Amidst all of his excitement, he failed to realize that she was the first tester with the fitness schedule from the seminar; not even her spiked boots triggered his memory and he looked at her with fresh eyes, "Hello," he began, "...interview or reading?"

"Reading." Amanda said hesitantly.

Myles adjusted his position in the chair, rubbed his hands together for a few seconds then placed one on the table, palm-up, "I just need to hold your hand and for you to think your name."

Amanda placed her hand in Myles' palm and he grasped it, placing his other hand on top, "Okay, Amanda...just clear your mind the best you can. What would you like me to look into?"

Amanda smiled and looked down at her hand, "There's a girl that I want to know if she wants me and if she has the same feelings. I truly believe she does, but...I'd like some evidence."

*Evidence? Let's hope she realizes this isn't that cut and dry; you're not even reading the other girl so how the hell are you going to determine that? Body language?* Myles nodded, "I shall do my best. Just remember, though...I'm not a psychologist; anything I see is just observation and opinion—no guarantees." He closed his eyes, taking a deep breath.

After a couple seconds, Shanna's face immediately came into his view as he immersed his consciousness in Amanda's perspective—staring through her eyes. Shanna was surrounded by trees but all color was stripped from her face and the surrounding environment; *Black and white? This one must be color-blind.* Looking right at him—at Amanda—Shanna was smiling and gently biting her lip. Teasing with her eyes, she continually looked away, then looked back. When Myles looked down, Amanda's hands reached for Shanna's; their fingers fiddled around each other's for a moment before their hands completely locked together. When he looked back up, Shanna's face moved in close until she was partially out of sight; she was kissing Amanda.

Myles pushed himself to another memory where Shanna was laughing and joking with Amanda; they shoved each other back and forth then after Shanna lightly slapped Amanda's arm, Amanda leaned forward and kissed Shanna. In another memory, Amanda was staring at a large drawing pad, working on a portrait of Shanna; she was completely nude, on a bed. Amanda looked passed the drawing pad where Shanna was lying on a bed; ... *Titanic in real life.*

Myles quickly moved his mind to the next memory where Shanna was laying on her back. Amanda slid her body downward until her eyes met Shanna's stomach; Shanna lifted her t-shirt and began sliding her hands into her panties—

Myles immediately released Amanda's hand, breaking their connection and returning him to the classroom. With wide eyes, he let out a nervous chuckle.

"Is everything okay?" Amanda asked.

Myles nodded, turning away slightly, "Yeah, just uh...give me a quick second." *Well* obviously *something's not right. How could Amanda not know that girl's feelings? Clearly the mystery girl's into her. Is she* that *insecure? She didn't seem like it in her head but right now, she's got* no *confidence. It's too perfect to not know—wait..."in her head"..."too perfect"...black and white...those weren't memories; they were damn fantasies!* Myles turned back to her, "Amanda, are you really looking for the honest answer, or are you just hoping to hear what you want to hear?"

106

Frozen, Amanda stared at Myles without blinking and her face turned red.

"...because I saw the girl that, I think, you're referring to and I tried to find memories with her but...all I could see were fantasies."

"...no," she started quietly, "I want the truth."

Myles nodded and leaned back, folding his hands in his lap, "Well, having never really experienced this kind of thing before, I have two theories: you're either hiding behind the fantasy and unwilling to show me the truth—even at an unconscious level—or your fantasies are so ingrained, that you can't get passed them. Now, because I don't know you, I can't say one way or another. All I know is, if I can't see beyond what I saw, I can't give you any real feedback."

As Amanda slumped back in her chair, she dipped her head and after a moment, she sniffled. Myles' eyes widened and he sat forward, looking around frantically; *oh shit; someone crying from the visions you get is one thing. Someone crying out of embarrassment is something else. Wrong tears! Wrong tears! Stop please!* He looked over at the food table where an unopened box of tissues sat; his first two appointments didn't cry so there it stayed. He quickly ran over, opened it and returned with a few tissues in hand. Amanda grabbed them and, instead of wiping her face, started twirling them in her fingers. Myles looked at her with confusion that quickly turned to disgust when she wiped her nose with her sleeve.

"Hey, it's alright; it's not your fault," he began, leaning forward, "...we can't control our unconscious mind. That much I *do* know."

Amanda nodded, finally using the tissues as intended.

"...maybe this is fate's way of saying you're strong enough to handle this on your own. You know?" *...no; this girl's probably got some issues.*

Amanda nodded again then finally looked up; the skin around her eyes was bright red and her eyeballs were drowning in tears, "...wha—what should I do?" she asked.

Myles raised his eyebrows and tilted his head as he tried to forge a solution, "Well, honestly, I could try again, but I think we'd just get the same thing. The visions I saw were really strong; they felt like actual memories. So even if they're just your fantasies, they're locked in there real tight."

"What should I do about Shanna?"

"Umm..." he began, biting the inside of his lip, "Well, I don't have anything to go on, really—just on my own life experiences. While nothing I say guarantees anything...I can only say, go with your gut. The things we regret most in life are the risks we didn't take, right?"

"Right." Amanda replied with a nod as she looked down again. Wiping her nose with her sleeve once more, she looked back up with a forced grin, "Okay, I'll go tell her how I feel."

"Good for you. If you're certain she has feelings, then everything should be fine."

Amanda reached out and grabbed Myles' hand and he fought the instinct to cringe; *uh...what are you doing?* She placed his hand against her wet cheek and his eyes widened. "Thank you; from the bottom of my heart, thank you Myles. You're an amazing man with a beautiful soul." she said.

"Thank you." he answered; *Give me my hand back! It's touching fluids from your body! You wiped your nose on your sleeve when I gave you tissues! Nasty!*

Still holding his hand, Amanda nodded, then turned her face and kissed it. When she finally set it back on the table, she squeezed it firmly before releasing her grip. She stood from the table, heading toward the door and Myles just stared at his hand, letting it lay covered in salty tears and mucus.

Amanda opened the door and before walking out, she turned back, looking Myles dead in the eye, "I won't forget what you've done for me."

Myles simply forced a smile, nodded and she walked out. When the door closed behind her, he stood up and rushed over to the food table. He grabbed the can of soda, held it over the garbage can and dumped it on his hand; the soda's acid revealed the invisible stains with extra bubbles and he left for the men's room.

After wiping himself clean, then washing in the nearest bathroom, he came back to the room and sat down with forty-eight minutes to kill; *Be glad the school and all these students signed accountability waivers. It's only fair after signing theirs,* essentially *saying they couldn't be held accountable for student snot.*

Immediately after arriving back at her dorm, Amanda pulled out her phone and started typing a new post to her group. Her stomach already fluttered with excitement, but her apprehension still nauseated her..."Hey everyone. I am getting ready to tell my crush how I feel. I just spoke with a very strong authority who said I should go with my gut. So I'm going to do it. I'm going to tell her how I feel."; she tapped the button to submit.

She swiped her thumb on the screen, refreshing the page every few seconds; her heart skipped a beat when the comment notifications appeared...

"Good for you! Go win that heart!"

"Aw! So happy for you!

"You got this girl. NO FEAR!"

Amanda could not contain her smile and her nausea subsided. She put her phone down, opened her drawing pad, and went right to work with her where she'd bury her face for the next five and a half hours and upon that first pencil stroke...the whole world disappeared.

Shanna returned to the apartment at 7:14PM. She set her bag down and grabbed a chilled coffee from the fridge, then walked to the living room and sat on the couch. She popped open the glass bottle and was consumed with a gratifying euphoria as she took a slow drink of the cold coffee; *Hours of homework...bring it.*

She set the bottle down, grabbed her laptop, and opened it; she pushed the *space* key, waking it from *sleep* mode. The monitor woke, displaying a bright background photo of the Vegas Strip at night; scattered all over the desktop were various files and folders. She clicked on her "Email" application and waited as it booted up. When her mailbox appeared, the loading icon spun and spun; when it finished, a few junk-emails appeared as well as one from Amanda; *...oh boy.* She deleted the junk then paused for a moment, staring at Amanda's message; the headline read: "No Subject". Finally, she hovered her cursor over it and clicked open the message:

*Shanna, there are things I would like to talk to you about, but I am not sure of how to say them. I realize things and I am confident in what my gut tells me but I do not know how to properly express it through words. Perhaps you will know and then we can talk about it. For now, here is the best way I can express what I want to say. Talk to you soon.*

*Amanda*

Shanna sneered at the message then moved her eyes to the top of the email box; directly underneath Amanda's information it read: "1 Attachment". Needing to know what it was, she wasted no time in clicking on the file. It revealed itself in segments as it downloaded and when the completed image displayed, Shanna's jaw dropped and her eyes widened; *What the fuck?!*

111

Molly arrived back an hour later, "Hey." she said and received no response. She peeked her head into the living room and Shanna just sat in the corner of the couch, staring at the Vegas photo on her computer screen. Molly's face scrunched with confusion and she headed down the hall to her room. She dropped her bag on the floor, her extra books on the bed, and walked back to the living room.

She sat on the couch looking at Shanna, whose face was tense with angry eyes and a clenched jaw; she was huddled in the corner with her knees close to her chest and her arms were pinned between them.

"What's wrong?" Molly asked.

"You know that girl, Amanda?" Shanna replied, still staring at the screen.

Molly looked up as she searched through her memory. "That weird girl that worships you?"

"Yup."

"Yeah. What about her?"

"...she's in love with me."

Molly smiled and pulled her feet onto the couch, "Uh, yah...clearly."

"No. I mean *really*. She's in love with me." Shanna repeated.

Molly's smile disappeared, "What do you mean?"

In a slow gesture, Shanna looked over at Molly, "I mean, she...is...in...*love*...with...me! She wants to date me, hold me, kiss me, fuck me...whatever; she wants to do it!"

Molly's eyes widened, "She told you that?"

"More or less..." Shanna answered as she leaned forward and pulled up the email; when the image displayed again, she turned the computer toward Molly whose jaw dropped as far as Shanna's; her eyes were glued on a digital copy of a drawing that showed Shanna and Amanda's embracing in the nude.

"What am I supposed to do?!" Shanna asked in a panicked tone, "I think *she* thinks that I like her that way too! I mean...I never gave any signals like that! I felt sorry for the girl and just tried to be a friend!"

"...damn!" Molly said with a nervous giggle.

"Don't laugh! It's not funny!"

Molly hid her mouth behind her hand and her chest started to convulse as she fought back her laughter. Finally, she released her grip, buried her entire face in both her hands and started laughing; still trying to muffle it, short gulps sounded from her throat.

"It's not funny!" Shanna repeated. Finally, Molly composed herself. She wiped the tears from her eyes and took a few deep breaths.

"I know; I'm sorry," she began, "Okay...just calm down; alright? Just tell her you're not interested that way."

"What if she goes psycho on me?! I mean, look at this shit! This looks exactly like me—all that detail! It's like she's been watching me in the shower!"

"Oh c'mon," Molly pleaded, "we're on the second floor. How is she gonna watch you in the shower?"

"I don't know! I don't know anything and it's scaring the hell outta me!" Shanna yelled.

Molly scooted over and put her arm around Shanna's shoulders, "Okay, so you just tell her you're not interested; if she goes nuts, we can call the cops or, if we have to get malicious, we can hire some butch ex-con from the women's penitentiary to smack her around." She started to laugh and Shanna failed to hide her own laughter by covering her face with her hands. After discussing the plan of approach, Shanna emailed Amanda, asking her to meet her outside the student activity center tomorrow morning.

# 10

In an immediate response to her email Monday night, Amanda wrote an enormous paragraph full of forgiveness-begging apologies and a prolonged explanation as to why they'd need to meet Wednesday morning instead—a reply that Shanna, or anyone else, would've summed up to: *"Would Wednesday work? That'll be better for me."* Regardless, Shanna's anxiety began the moment Amanda's response appeared in her inbox. As when she broke up with Jake, Shanna was nauseous all of Tuesday and her stomach continued to churn when she woke up this morning.

Agreeing to accompany her friend, Molly forced Shanna out of bed with a grin, "No procrastinating!"

Shanna cringed at the comment as she reluctantly dressed herself; a simple addition of a hooded sweatshirt, socks and shoes to her pajama pants and tank-top was all she bothered to put on.

Molly parked the car in the Activity Center parking lot; barely awake, Shanna slumped in her seat with her arms crossed.

"Wake up." Molly said.

"I'm awake." Shanna groaned. She turned her head toward Molly, looking passed her at the open grass by the school's track, "...she's not even here yet." Then she leaned her head back against the seat and allowed her eyes to droop; *Amanda's late? How the hell did that happen?*

Peripherally noticing a building door open, Molly looked up and made a subtle double-take, pulling her head back in surprise as she stared at the girl, overly-dressed in black, peeking her head out. As Amanda looked around—almost frantic—Molly tapped on Shanna's leg, "Uh...is that her?"

Shanna turned her head forward and rose up in her seat. As she laid eyes on Amanda, she scoffed and immediately sunk back into the seat, scooting further down and covering her face with her hood, "...yes." *Why would you think she was late? How dare you?*

"Well? You gonna go?" Molly asked, ready to push Shanna out of the car. Shanna scoffed again and pulled herself back up. She opened the door and dragged herself out. Molly unbuckled her seatbelt and leaned over the middle console, "You want me to come with, then?"

Shanna leaned hear head back in the car, "No. Just, wait here and, like...I dunno...just make sure she doesn't go nuts. I'm gonna pull her over to that grassy area," she indicated, pointing her finger out Molly's window, "...hopefully save her some embarrassment."

Molly looked out the window and nodded, confirming Shanna's directions, "Alright, I'll be here. Just be strong."

"Thanks." Shanna said as she shut the door.

The echo of the slamming metal stopped Amanda before she completely disappeared back into the activity center; she looked out to the parking lot and focused on the hooded girl walking toward her. She started to smile, then stopped herself, holding it back.

Shanna stopped a few feet from the door and forced a little smile and a wave, "Hey."

"...hi." Amanda replied as her pulse increased; she held the door open and Shanna shook her head.

"Actually, let's go over there, by the track. Get a little, um...privacy."

"Oh, um...yeah, okay. Just let me grab my coffee."

Amanda rushed back into the building—practically running—and Shanna took a deep breath and rolled her eyes. Her stomach tightened in attempt to hold the chaos at bay; *It'll be fine. You'll tell her and it'll be done. She can't be* that *oblivious.* Her stomach clenched tighter when Amanda returned with two cups instead of one, "Here, I got you one too." Shanna's smile was now a well-hidden cringe as she took the cup and all she could do was nod.

They said nothing as they walked; Amanda sipped her coffee and Shanna just held her cup, never even popping the plastic tab. At the tip of the track's outer ring, Shanna stopped and turned, looking around; with no one in sight, she looked down at the cup, "Alright, we're good right here." Gripping the Styrofoam container with two hands now, Amanda giggled before taking another sip. After a moment, Shanna forced herself to look into Amanda's eyes, "...okay, um...getting right to the point...I got your email on Monday; I saw the drawing."

"Did you like it?" Amanda asked—her face bright red.

Shanna's entire body clenched; *calm down...let her down easy.* "It's a very good drawing."

"...did you get the meaning behind it? What I was trying to express?"

Shanna nodded, "I think so." Amanda exhaled a deep breath, bending over slightly as she laughed. She nervously gulped the air in her mouth when she stood back up. Shanna glared at her, desperately fighting the urge to slap the scrawny girl upside the head. "Amanda, what do you think is going on between us?"

Amanda froze; she slowly licked her lips but her jaw still hung open when her tongue retreated back into her mouth; blinking her eyes rapidly, she twitched as she came to, "Uh...I, uh...I thought you...got the message behind it." She stammered.

"Well, I want you to tell me, in case I'm wrong."

Frozen again—brain-fried—Amanda's eyes wandered everywhere that Shanna's gaze wasn't.

"...Amanda?" Shanna called to her.

"...um..."

Shanna sighed, "Okay, I see this is kinda hard for you. Look, I'm sure you think there's something...romantic between us and, while I'm flattered," *bullshitting's just gonna make you puke,* "...I'm sorry, but I'm not interested in you like that."

Amanda's eyes stopped moving and she slowly lowered her head; she gripped her cup tighter, indenting it, "but...we have a connection." she finally uttered in a barely-audible tone.

Shanna leaned forward, "What?"

"Nothing." Amanda said, shaking her head.

"Amanda, what did you say? I couldn't hear."

Amanda's lip quivered and the temperature in her eyes grew, pulling the red from her cheeks up to her eye sockets, "...we...we have a connection." she finally said, one octave higher.

Shanna pulled back, "No, Amanda. We're friends," *ACK!* "but that's it. I'm not interested in *any* woman."

Amanda hesitated, "...what if you just haven't realized it yet?" she asked, releasing the tears.

*No; don't get mean. Calm down...she has no clue. You're doin' good; just keep your pace.* "Amanda...I don't know how else to say it, but you need to understand: I will *never* be interested in women. I like *men*; I'm attracted to *men*; I will only date *men*."

Amanda's eyes wandered again, faster now and Shanna stared at her; she looked over toward Molly, then back at Amanda whose head was still down. Amanda's eyes moved faster and faster. She pulled her head up and lunged forward; she tilted her head, closed her eyes, partly opened her mouth and reached for Shanna as she tried to steal a kiss. Back at the car, Molly immediately opened the door and stepped out.

Shanna stiffened her arms and stopped Amanda's attempt cold, "Whoa..." *...holy shit.* "...listen to me, right now. If you try that again, I'm not even gonna be your friend. I already told you—"

Amanda lunged again, harder this time; her hands just reached around Shanna's shoulders and the moment their lips made the slightest contact, Shanna put her hands on Amanda's chest and her coiled arms sprung forward, pushing Amanda to the ground; both cups of coffee spilling over her clothes,

"Fuckin' dyke!" Shanna yelled, following her words with a heavy gasp; *Oh God...did you just say that? You did* not *just say that. Oh God, oh God, oh God...you bitch.* Amanda's chest started convulsing from hiccups as she sobbed uncontrollably and Shanna just stared at her; *You're horrible. You're a horrible person. Just go; put your hood up, get in the car and go home.* Shanna pulled her hood tight over her head and started back toward the car, cursing herself the entire way.

Standing in Myles' temporary office gripping a notepad and pen, the student standing one foot taller than the psychic gave his thanks and walked to the door; he turned his already-slim body sideways, creating extra room for Jessica as she walked in. Myles nodded at her with a smile, "Hi."

"Hey there." she replied, "I'd ask how everything's been going but based on word around campus, it seems to

120

be going fantastic. A lot of students are actually discouraged that this is all limited to just the psychology majors."

Myles chuckled as he placed his hands in his pockets, "Well, good; I'm glad."

Jessica nodded, "Alright, well I don't want to waste too much time...I'm wondering if you'd like to grab some dinner tonight. Billy's already in; I'd just like to get to know more about you; I'm incredibly curious."

Myles thought for a moment, "Yeah; sounds great."

Jessica smiled, "Pizza?"

"Pizza works." Myles answered.

"Great. Um...there's a place on *Main Street—Steve's Pizza Palace*? You wanna meet there?"

Myles nodded, "Sure. Any good?"

Jessica laughed and shrugged her shoulders, "Well *I* like it."

"Then I'll trust your word."

After setting the always suitable time of 7:00PM, Jessica handed Myles a business card with her office phone number for any possible issues, then left him alone to his remaining appointments. As she was walking out, Myles' next appointment walked in the building, heading right to the classroom in a fast pace.

"I'm sorry. I overslept." She said, panting as she entered the room. As she set her backpack down, another set of fast footprints sounded from outside the door; they were heavy with thick soles. When Amanda walked in the door, Myles immediately looked down at her boots; ...*oh shit.* Tracing his eyes back up, they squinted when he focused on her soaked clothes; faint, brown stains covered her neck and part of her face.

She stormed right up to him, "You told me to go with my gut! You told me that! Now she hates me...because of you!"

"Whoa, whoa, whoa! Take it easy." Myles said calmly, holding his hands up in defense. He turned to the startled student, "I'm sorry. Can you give us a moment?" The student nodded and quickly walked out of the room, shutting the door.

Myles looked intently at Amanda—her eyes still fresh with tears, "Okay, calm down, alright? Start from the beginning."

"...she called me a dyke." Amanda said as another crying fit ensued.

"That can't be the beginning."

With a few deep breaths, Amanda composed herself and Myles pulled out the chair; as he took his chair opposite her, she sat down and took a deep breath, "I decided to tell her. I sent her a drawing 'cause I was more comfortable telling her like that. She saw it and asked me to meet this morning. I was so sure it would work out..." she bit her lip as the hiccups started again and Myles handed her the box of tissues; she ignored it, wiping her face with her hand, "...I gave her the coffee; it was even her favorite: caramel latte. I had the same...God, what did I do wrong?"

Myles sat patiently, staring at the sobbing student; *c'mon, c'mon. There's another student waiting...to the point please.*

Amanda sucked in a deep breath of air, "She took me out by the track so we could be alone—she's so sweet—and then she asked me what I thought was happening. Then...like she read my mind, she figured out I had feelings for her but...instead of feeling the same, she said she wasn't interested in women—that she'd never be interested. Then she pushed me to the ground."

"...really?"

Amanda nodded, "Yeah—for no reason...she didn't have to do that..." She dipped her head as she released the sobs again. Covering her face with one hand, the other hand remained on the table and Myles focused on it; despite the glistening snot on her fingers, he reached for it and squeezed.

"I'm sorry to hear that." he said; *alright that sounded odd...*"for no reason"? *Let's check that out.* Honing into Amanda's mind *this* time, Myles could actually see color now. In Amanda's perspective, he pushed through her memory to the point where she and Shanna were standing by the track and he focused on Shanna's face; the muscles around her eyes were clenched, forcing her lids slightly closed and her body was stiff—defensive; *well she's clearly on edge.* Shanna started her interrogation and Amanda looked around, dropping her focus; *can't tell how either of them are feeling—no...do* not *engage your empathy.* Throughout the incident's entire replay, Shanna never displayed any romantic gestures toward this girl—the complete opposite scenario of Amanda's first beautifully dreamed visions; *thank her vulnerability for showing you the truth.* Finally, Myles came to the lunge Amanda made toward Shanna; then, despite her warning, Amanda lunged again and Shanna finally shoved her to the ground—indeed using the derogatory term. Immediately after the word exploded from Shanna's vocabulary, her eyes widened and her jaw dropped with a gasp; she tightly covered her mouth with her hands; *oh she regrets using* that *word*. When Shanna walked away, Amanda stood up and Myles broke the connection.

Amanda was still sobbing when Myles pulled his hand back, "Amanda, I'm sorry but...you provoked the outburst."

"What?"

Myles nodded, "Yeah. I mean, she was wrong to use that term. However, I don't know how you didn't see but she was incredibly disturbed standing in front of you—I'm guessing from the drawing you sent her—and even after she told you how she felt, you didn't accept it and trying to steal a kiss was...not only crossing her personal boundaries, but stepping into harassment territory.

Amanda froze—a deer in the headlights, "...you said to go with my gut."

"Yes but there's a few problems with that now," he began as he leaned back in the chair, "first and foremost, it was made clear that anything I said had no guarantees of anything; I just relayed my findings. Second...I couldn't see the truth of what was going on in your mind; it was blocked by the fantasy you created and it wasn't until you hit this vulnerability that I saw it. I only had your word to go on, which leads to the final issue: I was under the impression that you had awareness of others.

I'm sorry, but, based on what I saw, you not only lacked the awareness with this girl, you wouldn't accept what she told you. I don't know if you were incapable of accepting it or if you just disregarded it—I'm not a psychologist—but, just the same, you didn't accept it."

Still frozen with blank eyes, a few moments passed and Amanda finally stood up from the chair, never breaking her gaze from Myles.

"...I'm sorry." he said and she *slowly* turned, dragging her feet as she walked toward the door. She maintained her zombie-esque stroll down the hall until she disappeared through the building's exit door.

Back in the room, Myles sighed deeply and shook his head; the appointments rightful client hesitantly peeked her head in, "...everything alright."

Myles looked over, smiled and nodded, "Yeah, everything's cool; sorry 'bout that. Um, come on in and make yourself comfortable; I have to go wash my hands quick."

# 11

*Brothers on 2nd* pulsed with life on Wednesday night. The bar-side opposite the dart board and pool table typically reserved the area for tall tables and chairs; tonight, they were moved to two neat, perpendicular lines, creating an "L" shape with an open walking space in the shape's corner. A few patrons remained at their tables while others stood in the open space, focused on the three-member band in the corner. The standing lead singer also played an acoustic guitar and on either side of him were two more guitarists sitting on stools; one played another acoustic and the other, an electric. Moving enthusiastically with the cool rock sound, the crowd's response was a clear approval.

Earlier that day, Shanna told Korbin she could really use his company that evening and after a slight consideration of his homework, he inevitably agreed.

When they arrived at the bar, Shanna ordered a shot of rum and a *Belgian* beer.

Korbin chuckled, ordering an *IPA* for himself, "*That* tense, huh?" he asked and Shanna just scoffed.

Grabbing their drinks, they headed toward one of the tables and situated themselves; gently eyeing Shanna, Korbin took a hesitant breath, "I know you need to vent, but before you start, can I ask you something?"

"Go for it." Shanna said.

"Okay…um, I don't mean any offense to your other friends, but…what's with that Amanda chick? I mean, the day I met her she had this attitude, then I saw her at that seminar and she gave me this really *pissed-off* look. Is she always like that?"

Shanna stared at Korbin with a blank grin, then reached for the shot glass and slammed the liquor down her throat; she immediately followed it by chugging half her beer. She shook her head with a chuckle as she wiped her mouth clean and Korbin's eyes were wide with confusion.

"*Ohhhh* Amanda…" Shanna finally began with a condescending tension, "…Amanda is out there. The poor girl has no social skills—no friends—and, actually, she's an introverted, self-conscious lesbian who hasn't even really found her identity yet. I guess, out of pity, I gave her friendship."

"…well, it could be just me, but you don't sound too happy about it."

Shanna shook her head with a heavy sigh, "It's weird. Like…I tried to give her a chance. I figured if she was able to have one friend, then maybe she'd learn things and grow. Instead, she's just stuck in this...*weird* mentality and she hasn't changed a bit. It's like she relies *completely* on me to make herself feel better but she won't even try to build herself up and step out of this zone. I thought I was a patient person but after these past couple years, I've actually gotten really tired of it. Honestly, she really is *very* annoying. At the same time, I haven't had the heart to tell her the truth because I didn't wanna be the one to break her heart. Plus...I have *no* idea what she's capable of and I'm afraid to think about it."

Korbin nodded after a sip of his beer, "Yeah I can understand the frustration." Shanna nodded then sipped the second half of her beer...until Korbin chimed back in, "So...what was wrong today?"

Shanna rolled her eyes back in her head and immediately opened her throat; her sips turned to large gulps and the brown liquid instantly vanished.

"Jesus...you gonna be alright?" Korbin asked as Shanna placed the empty glass on the table.

"Yeah." she answered, followed by a mild belch.

"You're not drunk yet, are you?"

Shanna grinned and shook her head, "Not yet." Korbin nodded with a look of uncertainty and sipped his beer. Shanna leaned forward, still in control of her body. "Don't worry, I'm not gonna get tanked."

Korbin smiled, "You do what you gotta do. I just don't want you to get sick."

"Psshh! Please. I don't get sick."

128

"Fair enough. Besides, you haven't told your story. I wanna hear the rest of it while you're still coherent, ya lush!"

Shanna's jaw dropped as she smacked Korbin's arm, "Oh now the truth comes out! You don't care about me; you just wanna hear the bullshit, you gossiping—you gossiping dick!"

"Oh, *that's* clever." Korbin responded with a smug grin and Shanna turned her body away, leaning over on the table. After a few moments, she glanced back at him leaning back in the chair, sipping his beer and staring right at her—waiting. She turned her head away once more for a moment, then sat back in her original position, "...you're lucky you're cute."

"Nah that's *skill*."

Shanna scoffed and picked up her empty glass. Remembering the lack of beer, she set it down, pouted her lips, saddened her eyes and leaned closer to her companion, "...could you please get me another beer?"

"Oh, you don't care about me! You just want beer!" Korbin shouted.

"If you get me another beer, I'll tell my story."

"...done." Korbin said and immediately left the table toward the bar.

By the end of re-telling that day's incident, Shanna's second beer had barely been touched—save for a few sips. Her smile had disappeared, as did Korbin's; he reached over and caressed her arm that was resting on the table.

"I just can't believe I said that," she said as her mind continued searching for some justification, finding none, "I don't even know where that came from. I try so hard to be accepting, then all the sudden *bam!*...one person flips my *Bitch-Switch* and I become something I never thought I could be. I mean, yeah, I sometimes wondered if I was able to be mean—*just a bit*—and maybe she'd get the hint, or would start feeling uncomfortable and just go away but...*Gah!* Instead I completely lose it and attack her—physically *and* verbally."

"I suppose," Korbin began, "but keep in mind, she crossed your lines—lines that you spelled out right to her face. I'm not saying calling her that is justifiable, but everyone has their breaking points, right? Well, mostly everyone. You're human and you had a bad moment—

"An *awful* moment..."

"...an *awful* moment, but ask anyone that knows you; losing complete control isn't a common thing for you—let alone throwing out offensive terms. You're not planning on doing it again are you?"

Shanna glanced at him and shook her head.

"There ya go. So...try not to beat yourself up over this; really." Korbin added and Shanna sighed as she lowered her head to the table. The band broke into a slow, somber tune and Korbin slid his hand down Shanna's arm, grabbing her hand.

A new sensation of warmth coursed through her body and she lifted her head; she stared at her hand for a moment, smiled and looked at Korbin. He smiled back at her then pulled her hand toward him, "Come with me." he said.

They both stood from the table and Shanna followed Korbin's lead toward the crowd of people—some of the couples were already embraced, slowly rocking back and forth in little designated circles. Picking a spot, Korbin turned to Shanna and mirroring her, grabbed her right hand with his left; he pulled her closer to him as his right hand gently grasped her lower back. He laughed as she giggled and before placing her hand on his shoulder, she used it to muffle her nervousness.

"I'm sorry. I'm good." she said, then settled her hand in the customary shoulder placement.

As with the other couples, Korbin rocked Shanna back and forth in a small circle in-sync with the song. When she smiled at him, he locked on her eyes and slowly lowered his eyelids—his unique, prolonged *blink*.

Still smiling, Shanna cringed her eyebrows and gently shook her head, "What is that?"

"What?" Korbin asked playfully.

"*That*. That blinking thing you do."

Korbin shook his head—taunting Shanna, "Does it bother you?"

"No. I'm not exactly sure why, but it's sweet. I'm just wondering what it is."

"Well, then no worries; just know that you're the only one that it's ever meant for." he explained.

Shanna rolled her eyes and scoffed then leaned her head forward onto Korbin's shoulder; she wrapped her arms around his neck. He wrapped his arms around her waist and gave her a gentle squeeze, triggering the security that always accompanied his hugs. Feeling the same euphoric warmth, goose bumps rose on Korbin's skin as his pulse grew faster.

Halfway through the song—when the vocals broke for an instrumental segment—Shanna lifted her head and they looked into each other's eyes. Their faces slowly closed the distance and as their lips made contact, they both fell into the kiss—both sets of lips massaging one another as they expressed the mutual passion—and Korbin's knees weakened.

A heatwave and pressure blasted through Korbin's entire body; the shock escalated the euphoric sensation to a nauseating level, triggering a sense of vertigo. It popped Korbin's eyes wide open and he quickly pulled away from Shanna.

Still embracing each other, Shanna's eyes scanned Korbin's face, "What? What happened?" She asked—her voice laced with a slight undertone of panic.

Staggering back a step, Korbin shook his head, blinking his eyes tightly. Finally, he looked back at his worried date and smiled, "I knew kissing you would be awesome but...holy shit, woman."

Shanna laughed and turned her head as her face turned red, "You okay?"

"A little lightheaded; uh…can we go sit for a minute?" Korbin asked and Shanna nodded, keeping him steady with her hands on his sides as they carefully walked back to their table.

<><><>

Mirroring the life of *live music night* at *Brothers on 2nd*, *Steve's Pizza Palace* was bustling with guests dug into their night of dinner and sports.

That very moment, sitting with Billy and Jessica, Myles' thought was interrupted by a sharp sting in his brain stem; Jessica and Billy stared wide-eyed as he grabbed the back of his neck and cocked his head in the opposite direction. His eyes were squeezed tightly shut and his shoulders shrugged up to his ears in a compulsive strain and his clenched fists started to shiver.

"Myles? You okay?" Jessica asked as she reached over and touched his arm; the muscles were steel fibers beneath his flesh.

His mouth opened slightly as he forced an exhaling breath from his lungs and somehow, he extended his index finger and turned it upward; *...one...moment...please.* When his thoughts disappeared, his consciousness was consumed by total darkness until one strand of smoke appeared from below, slowly floating upward; he overlooked the paralyzing sting as the familiarity he felt on Sunday increased in its potency and a weak, faded image of Korbin came into view.

When Korbin and the smoke disappeared, Myles' thoughts took their time returning and his muscles relaxed as the sting faded. He opened his eyes—blinking repeatedly to overcome the sudden blurriness—and when he regained his bearings, Jessica and Billy leaned forward, staring at him with a look of concern.

"...I—uh...I'm sorry." Myles said in a trembling voice.

"You alright?" Billy asked.

Myles' eyes widened and glanced away as he took a deep breath; *"okay"? I suppose so, considering;* "Yeah. I think so."

"What happened?" Billy continued.

He searched throughout his memory, coming up empty. Even recalling the memory he saw in Korbin's mind, the only thing he could see was that wall of fog; *smoke...that kid... what the* hell *is so goddamn familiar about him?* "Honestly, I'm not really sure. Like...this energy just hit me, all the sudden. You know when your ears ring?" he asked and his temporary contractors nodded, "well, that's what it felt like, in the back of my neck—like manifested into some kind of stinging. My whole mind went black for a moment."

Jessica leaned forward and quickly glanced for potential onlookers, "Do you need to leave? Go to the doctor or something?"

"No. I'm good now; it's just...I'm going to have to try to figure it out later." He assured. Jessica nodded and sat back in her chair as Myles sipped his soda, "...what was I saying?"

Jessica smiled, "You were about to tell me something that you were a little nervous to say." Billy smiled, anxiously looking on.

"Oh yeah..." he said, taking a moment to adjust his entire upper torso and smiled; *guess that outburst exhausted your nerves;* "...I wanted to tell you that I'm really glad you took your contacts out. I knew you had beautiful eyes."

Jessica smiled as she started to blush, "Thank you."

Myles smiled then the back of his neck grew warm—blushing when he noticed Billy looking away with a big grin; *Shut it old man;* He glanced over her body again; despite her ridiculously large engagement ring—his stomach still fluttered from attraction.

Gratitude eased his mind, knowing that his nerves were no longer responding defensively. Even when Jessica questioned him about the day's earlier incident with Amanda, he remained confident and steady; *You probably shouldn't be discussing a student's reading—going on psychology rules. No, it's alright; given the instability of the student, someone in authority should know; besides,* you're *not a psychologist.*

"I don't think you'll have to worry." he assured Jessica, "Based on what I saw, I think they're both too stunned to take any action. I think they both just want to forget about it." Myles added; *oh, if only that were true about* Miss Amanda—*the unpredictable time bomb.*

"Were you wrong, though?" Jessica asked.

Myles' eyes looked up and rocked back and forth, contemplating the answer, "...I guess it depends on how you look at it. Was it wrong to tell her *'go with your gut'*? Maybe; but, then again, I didn't know how oblivious she was to reality. I mean, I couldn't even get an accurate reading the first time around; all I saw was a group of fantasies that were dug into her consciousness. It wasn't until she was, like, shaken and vulnerable 'till I could see the truth."

"How'd she take it?" Billy asked.

*Horribly! The girl's insane!* "She was pretty upset and I honestly didn't see what was going on in her head right before she left; but like I said, from what I saw, I think they both just want to forget and move forward."

Eventually, Jessica nodded in acceptance and attempted to push the concern from her mind, "I believe you." she said and Myles smirked hesitantly. "So, now...how's everything going with you so far? I've got my own observations—which look perfectly fine—but what are your thoughts?"

Myles leaned forward, resting his elbows on the table and looked around for a moment—actually giving thought to his own assessment of his current endeavor, "It's actually going really well, I think."

"Yeah? No...complications?" Jessica hesitantly asked as she pointed to her head.

Myles laughed, "Uh, no. I know I put a lot of work into re-honing my abilities over the summer—keep them under control; but still I'm a little surprised."

Jessica leaned back in her chair, "How so?"

"Well...for one thing, it's kind of a comfort zone. Despite old fears and inhibitions—even new ones I developed—I always felt good when I was using my abilities; it just felt right. So being here, doing this...I guess it's familiar and gives me a fulfilling gratification. The really great thing, though, is the control I've been able to maintain. Like how you asked about complications...I've held a really strong grip and, for the most part, nothing unwanted has slipped through the cracks."

"That's really great, Myles." Jessica added.

"That it is." He continued, "As much as I refused to ever tap into my abilities again, a part of me always wanted to and right now, it's proving to be a good decision."

# 12

Shanna saw right through Korbin's claims of "feeling fine". He only had a couple beers then suddenly got dizzy and lightheaded; his sluggish mannerisms and playful attitude grew worse and worse in a combination of a drunken-high. He would occasionally cringe—like in pain—and shudder before shaking it off and returning to a happy Korbin.

Twenty minutes passed before he began to sweat and finally suggested leaving; Shanna reached out in a comforting gesture but when she touched his hot, clammy hand, her eyes widened, "Oh my God, Korbin..." she reached up and touched his forehead, cheeks and neck.

"Tha- feels gooooooooood." he slurred.

"You have a fever! C'mon." she said in a stern tone as she stood from her chair. She grabbed her purse and started toward the bar, stopping next to Korbin's chair,

"Hang on a sec; I gotta go close the tab." Korbin winked at her and she squeezed his hand again; she wiped his sweat from her palm on her pants.

Resting his elbow on the table, Korbin let out a loud sigh as he propped his chin in his hand. Glancing around incoherently, he caught a glance of someone eating a platter of nachos—complete with all the works. Fighting the sudden nausea, he ripped his eyes away, squeezing them shut. Turning his head back toward the bar, he caught Shanna waiting patiently; he scanned his eyes up and down her body, absorbing every inch of her shapely figure and the heated pressure flared once again.

When she finished and started back toward him, Korbin immediately pushed himself off the table; his bearings and rubbery legs failed, dropping him straight to the floor.

The slew of people in the crowd stopped and turned their attention to the seemingly drunk young man. As he propped himself up, Shanna came to his rescue, helping him stand.

"He gonna be alright?" someone asked.

Shanna nodded, "Yeah, he just got sick with somethin'." Ignoring the undertone of skeptic disbelief in the background, *"He's annihilated let him own up to it,"*...Shanna lifted Korbin to his feet, wrapping his arm around her supporting shoulder. Closing his eyes and holding back another bout of nausea, he turned to Shanna, glaring at her with lazy eyes, "We really should go now."

"Don't worry; we're leaving. I need your help though; you gotta walk with me." Shanna insisted then the limp weight suddenly lightened when another man lifted Korbin's other arm over his shoulder.

"I'll help you get to your car." he said

"Oh, thank you *so* much." Shanna replied.

"No problem. He's definitely warm, though. This just happened?"

"Yeah—just like, twenty minutes ago."

The man glanced over Korbin's face for a moment, "I wouldn't blame the alcohol then. He probably caught some bug—you guys eat here tonight?"

"No." Shanna answered, shaking her head. People cleared the way as they drew closer to the door.

"Could be food poisoning from somewhere." he added.

"Maybe...you a doctor?" Shanna asked with a grin.

"Nurse Practitioner." the man replied.

Decreasing their walking time by half, the trio reached the door and left the building, heading to Shanna's car.

In his delusional state, Korbin complimented Shanna all the way back to her apartment; even when he mentioned having sex—in a failed attempt at subtlety— she just smiled and shook her head as she was tickled with excitement; *Why did you have to get sick? I soooooo wanna make love to you.*

The lack of a second assistant to her apartment wracked Shanna's nerves with each of Korbin's stumbles. Despite his significantly smaller size than her ex, that extra hundred-some pounds was more of a workout than she'd had in a while. When they reached the apartment, Molly was on the couch doing homework; Shanna guided Korbin right passed the living room, down the hall to her room and she let him drop onto her bed. With his sluggish help, Shanna pulled him up to the pillows and pulled the blankets back. Her only frustration sat with the difficulty of helping Korbin walk but it immediately faded with each compliment he threw at her. After she took his shoes off, she pulled the blankets up over him but stopped before leaving and felt his forehead again; *...still warm.* She pulled the blankets back off then leaned over, put her hand on the side of Korbin's head and kissed his forehead.

"I think I'm gonna throw up." Korbin confessed. Shanna grabbed his arm, pulled him up from the bed and, using his forward momentum, guided him into the bathroom; not even a second after reaching the toilet, he purged the contents of his stomach. Shanna held his waist as he collapsed to his knees and she gently caressed his back.

Molly rushed to the bathroom with a concerned look and stepped inside. She tapped Shanna's shoulder, *"He gonna be alright?"* she whispered.

Shanna nodded, "I'll be out in a bit; just gonna finish with him." Molly nodded as she left.

"Wait; Molly."

Molly backtracked and peered in the door again, "Yeah?"

"Can you get a glass of ice water and put it on my nightstand?" she asked.

"Mm-hmm." Molly said, heading to the kitchen at a brisk pace.

Shanna continued caressing Korbin's back and after a final heave, he rested his head onto the toilet seat.

"All done, sicko?" Shanna asked with a grin but Korbin didn't respond. Through his labored breathing, he smacked his lips and groaned. Shanna tilted her head and examined his flushed face; *...still alive.* She felt his forehead again, which had actually increased in temperature. Her face straightened from her lighthearted look and she lifted him up, dragging him over the side of tub and holding up his head. "Molly!"

Molly returned to the bathroom, "Glass is on your nightstand."

"Thanks. Could you actually get me another empty one?"

Molly nodded and headed back to the kitchen while Shanna turned on the shower's cold-water faucet. Molly returned with the glass then retreated back to the living room; Shanna filled the glass and carefully poured the water over Korbin's head, covering as much area as possible before having to refill. After a second soak, she set the glass down and gently combed her fingers through his hair, spreading the water.

Korbin's head popped up with a heavy gasp that shocked Shanna's nerves. He frantically jerked back and forth until Shanna grabbed his chest with one hand and placed her other hand on his neck. His head stopped moving when his eyes latched onto her face and she rubbed his neck.

142

"Shhhh...it's okay." She assured. Panting lightly with a nervous swallow, Korbin struggled to keep his eyes on his caregiver.

"I'm sorry." He said.

"It's alright. Here, put your head back down."

Korbin obeyed and leaned back over the tub, allowing Shanna to continue her water treatment. As the adrenaline subsided, the drunken haze returned, forcing more of his affectionate gibberish; this time it wasn't full of compliments, "I'm sorry Shanna. Tonight was supposed to be fun; I'm sorry I ruined your fun. I didn't mean to ruin it."

She smiled as she poured the water, "It's fine, Korbin. I think you just caught something."

"I'm sorry I caught something and ruined your night." He continued. For the next ten minutes, Shanna poured water over his head, breaking to run her fingers through his hair and Korbin continued to apologize and express his gratitude for having such a good *"friend"*—a word Shanna playfully smiled about; *Wait till tomorrow to remind him it's more than that.*

After getting Korbin back into bed, Shanna shut the light off and walked out to the living room. She fell into the couch, bouncing on the cushions and Molly set her homework on the coffee table.

"Man..." Molly began as she looked back toward the bedrooms, "...he got *shit-faced!* I thought *you* were the stressed one that needed a drink."

"He didn't. He got sick—caught, like...a bug or somethin'."

Molly's eyes squinted as she processed the notion, "Seriously?"

Shanna nodded as she looked at the ceiling, "Yup. He only had two beers and was fine—*I* was getting buzzed—then all the sudden he gets dizzy and lightheaded and after a little while he *did* sound drunk...and high."

"Damn." Molly added, "Well...how'd the rest of it go—up to that point?"

"...*goooood.*" Shanna said playfully; she smiled as a red tint filled her cheeks then she sat up, pulled her feet onto the couch and turned toward her friend, "It was the same as always for the first hour or so, then the band started playing this slow song, and he asked me to dance."

Molly's eyes widened and her jaw slightly dropped with a smile; she leaned her side on the back of the couch and folded her hands together. "Your first dance?" She said with an extra excitement.

Shanna giggled, "Mm-hmm." then stared at Molly, saying nothing.

Molly twitched with anticipation, welcoming more information by a wave of her hand, "Then what?!"

Shanna shrugged her shoulders and shook her head but Molly leaned forward; her eyebrows turned upside down as she burned a hole in her friend's eyes. Finally, Shanna broke and started laughing, "...we kissed."

"Yes!" Molly shouted, rapidly clapping her hands and Shanna's hands covered her face as she shook her body back and forth. They rated the rest of the date—

specifically the kiss—and fantasized about possible what-if scenarios well into the wee hours of the night.

# 13

It was already mid-afternoon on Thursday when Korbin finally woke in Shanna's bed; as soon as his brain cleared enough to translate his surroundings, he glanced around the room—cringing his eyebrows with confusion; *What the hell?* When the microwave beeper sounded, Korbin's eyes rolled slowly toward the door.

Standing up too fast, the fluid in his skull turned upside down, flipping his vision and he staggered toward the wall. Pressing his hand against it before falling, he pulled his legs back underneath his torso and held his head as the fluid settled; *...at least it's not a headache.* He gathered himself and carefully stepped toward the door, grazing his hand along the safety-net wall until he reached the living room.

With an open text book and highlighter on the cushion next to her, Molly sat on the couch, watching the television as she ate her freshly-nuked microwave dinner. When Korbin emerged from the hallway, Molly looked up and quickly set her food on the couch's arm; she got up and walked quickly to Korbin, holding out her hands for a potential fall, "Hey dude. You alright?" Korbin rubbed the heel of his palm against his eye and nodded, "...you wanna sit down?" Nodding again, Korbin slowly made his way to the soft, empty seat while Molly walked back to the kitchen.

He sunk into the cushion and leaned his head back; his eyelids were half closed as he looked around. Molly returned with a glass of water and two aspirin tablets; when Korbin grabbed only the glass, she set the medicine on the coffee table in front of him. Chugging the water quickly, he handed the glass back to her, "...could I get another one, please?"

"Mm-hmm." Molly said, grabbing the glass and going back to the kitchen. This time, she returned with two glasses of water, handing one to Korbin and setting the other on the small table.

"Thanks." he said in a whisper; he downed the second glass even faster than the first, "Shanna's at class?" he asked, setting the glass down.

Molly sat back down and picked up the cardboard food tray and nodded as she took bite; she inhaled a deep breath of air, cooling the food in her mouth, "How're you feeling?" she asked after swallowing the chunk of food.

"...tired as hell." he responded, leaning his head back against the couch.

"Yeah I bet."

Korbin grinned, then looked over at Molly. Thinking for a moment, he glanced at the television, then back at Molly, "...okay; so...what happened last night?"

Her eyebrows raised as she looked at him, "You don't remember?" Korbin shook his head and she leaned back into the couch, "Oh you were gone. You were, basically, drunk—slurred speech, staggered walking...puking."

"Damn..." Korbin said, shaking his head, "...I don't remember drinking that much."

"Shanna said you didn't."

Korbin squinted his eyes and glared at Molly, "No?"

"Mm-mm;" she began with a mouth full, "she said you caught a bug or food poisoning—something. You were fine, then all of a sudden you were all kinds'a looped up. I guess the girl's got some powerful lips." Korbin smiled as he started to blush and Molly playfully wriggled her eyebrows up and down, grinning as she chewed her food, "Awwww! You remember *that*, huh?"

"Perfectly." he said with assurance.

"And how was it?"

Korbin took a deep breath and slowly released it from his lungs as a warm chill coursed through his body—from his chest, out his fingertips, "...it was amazing. All I can remember is dancing, kissing and getting the weakest knees I ever had in my life; then it's all a blank until right now."

Molly giggled; fighting the urge to clap with occupied hands, "Well, between you and me...it was the same for her."

"Yeah?" Korbin asked with a smile.

"Uh-huh. She said it was the most amazing kiss she ever had." Korbin let out a little chuckle, then tightened his lips together; the trapped laugh forced small tremors in his chest and, in an instance of contagion, Molly giggled, "I gotta tell ya, Korbin...she cares about you. I mean...she doesn't just *like* you; she really cares about you and I *love* the idea of you two being a couple."

"And I love *her*."

Molly stopped and slowly looked over at Korbin with wide eyes; in an equally slow gesture, he lifted his head forward from the cushion and stared straight ahead with astonishment in his eyes.

"You *love* her?" Molly asked.

"Without a doubt." he insisted and his eyes cringed; *...maybe you do, but why the hell are you spilling the beans?* "I'm not even sure why I'm saying that so freely; you'd think I'd have more tact but right now...it almost feels outta my control."...the warm pressure from last night was slowly building again, "After all this time, she's become the greatest girl I've ever known."

"Know what?" Molly started as she set her food back on the table, "I think I always knew and, quite frankly, I think that's great. You go ahead and say it all you want."

"I love Shanna." Korbin repeated.

The intoxicating heat and pressure exploded through his body—three times what it did last night; before he could even express his sudden repeat of drunkenness, his eyes rolled back into his head and he keeled over on the couch.

Molly stared at him for a moment, "...Korbin?" He didn't move, "...*Kooorbin*?" He remained still on the couch, "...*really* dude?"

Molly set her tray down and reached her hand to Korbin's burning forehead, "Shit. C'mon, we gotta go." She woke him just enough for him to hobble as she carried him to her car and drove him to Southwest Health's urgent care where they injected him with a fever reducer.

When Korbin finally woke an hour later, the doctor informed him he most likely sustained an allergic reaction, as he displayed no other symptoms. With Molly there, they waited to call his father, but Korbin assured them he would let him know when he returned to his dorm. They released him a half-hour and three cups of water later, and the moment Molly left him, he fell to his bed and passed out.

That very instant, across town—as he just finished with a student's reading—Myles paused in his chair. Instead of frozen, locked muscles, a surge of heat instantly rose up his spine from zero to five hundred degrees and a sharp pain stabbed into his right arm—claws. In his mind, his thoughts and vision were replaced by a red smoke cloud—smoke that dripped like liquid vapor—that carried a deep, loud growl; *...oh God...not again...*

The red smoke burst into a flame and released a deafening roar. Myles jumped from the chair and was stopped by the dry erase board as he stepped backward; his jaw dropped as he gripped his arm.

As the fire in his mind faded into darkness, his thoughts and vision returned and the pain in his arm disappeared. He looked around the room, then out into the hall; *...no one.* Myles reached forward and pulled the chair out, falling into it. In a defeated scoff, he buried his face into his hands.

Straining himself through the rest of the day's readings, Myles returned to Billy's just as his host was finishing some work. They watched the *Green Bay Packer's* pregame, a couple sitcom reruns then Billy turned in for the night. Asking about Myles' night, noticing the troubled look on his face, Billy offered him a drink and Myles refused. Strangely, it wasn't until Billy retired to his bedroom that Myles got an urge for—what would be considered, tonight, as—a spiritual soother. Skipping the few options in the cupboard, Myles grabbed the whiskey that Billy initially offered and poured the brown liquid into an intricate scotch glass. The desperate urgency to calm his nerves forced him to slam the first round; his cringing face held his gag reflex at bay.

Sitting at the foot-end of the couch—and his makeshift bed—he held the glass with both hands, taking small and seldom sips; he still cringed after each drop hit his taste buds. All the while, his mind and muscles relaxed, starting to feel like chocolate's first sign of melting—solid but softening and moldable. Unfortunately, a mushy mind couldn't keep him from circling around the vision he saw earlier; it couldn't keep him from replaying the day in the hospital so many years ago...

<><><>

Ava Moore's heart attack brought her to the emergency room of *Saint Mary's Hospital* in Milwaukee. After stabilizing her an hour later, they transferred her to the Intensive Care Unit where her daughter and son-in-law were finally able to visit.

She was transferred the next morning to the general ward on the fifth floor for her recovery where it was quiet and calm. Besides Ava resting down the hall from the reception desk, there were two other patients checked in. While her daughter stayed overnight, falling asleep in a chair, her son-in-law drove home to pick up his seven-year old son, Myles, the next morning; he brought Myles along to visit his *Oma*, who was sleeping when they arrived; ten minutes later, Myles' morning breakfast finally made its call to nature.

When Myles emerged from the bathroom, he dried his freshly clean hands on his pants; he started back down the hall to Ava's room but when a faint, deep rumbling teased his ears, he stopped. He looked around to find only one nurse up and about and the rest were tending to the other tasks of paperwork and supply stocking. Dismissing the sound, he continued walking and after three more steps, the rumbling sounded again.

Turning completely around, Myles' eyes scanned the hallway, examining everything in sight; the nurses hadn't changed as they continued with their tasks; *They can't hear?* He heard the sound again but it was shorter this time; the sound popped in half-way into its duration like a shorted speaker. Myles walked over to the wall next to the bathroom door and leaned back, listening intently. Tuned in, the sound rippled through the air from the beginning again but was rudely interrupted by a loud cough. The sound stopped as Myles' focus was broken by the overweight nurse at the desk; he stuck a finger in each ear, wiggling them around trying to clear them and he heard the sound again. Now, it had a direction—up the hall, toward the reception desk.

When Myles changed course and started toward the desk, it sounded again...then again after a few more steps—louder now and to the left. He moved in the apparent direction, close to the wall and continued forward. With an even louder exertion, Myles was definitely getting closer; ...*in the wall.* Continuing further, a slight pressure traveled through his body when the rumble sounded this time then the source's direction revealed itself. Myles glanced ahead at the next door along the wall and the warm, fuzzy sensation in his neck compelled him toward it.

He was too short to look in the door's window; only the tip of his nose could reach the glass. He took a quick glance around the hall; all the nurses were still occupied and his parents were still in the room with Ava. The rumble sounded again and his eyes jumped right to the doorknob but as he reached for it, he stopped. Completely consumed with curiosity, he hadn't even been touched with the sensation of fear, let alone considered any possible dangers; the idea of getting caught was what held his hand at bay but when he heard the sound again, he grabbed the doorknob and gently turned it.

The clinking of metal mechanisms was deafening and the door itself weighed three tons on his little arms; *It's a bajillion pounds!* With just less than one foot of clearance, Myles snuck into the room; he held the inside handle, stopping the door from closing right at the edge of the frame. He quickly glanced at the patient's bed, then looked around the room identical to Ava's but the rumbling pulled his attention right back to the bed; *There you are. Why can't they hear? It's so loud.* Feeling a stronger pressure, Myles cringed and shook his head, forcing a tolerance and it sounded again.

He hadn't even looked at the patient; his eyes were on their legs at the foot of the bed while he pondered over the sound and sensation he was receiving. Switching that focus, he looked up toward the wall as the bed inclined; lying unconscious, was a young woman with bandaging on her chest and wrist. He looked back at the foot of the bed, spotting her chart and still holding the doorknob, he leaned forward and—tuning out the mysterious, continual sound—started reading…

"JANE DOE; AGE: UNKNOWN; SEX: FEMALE;"

He then skipped to the bottom of the page, disregarding a scrambled slew of foreign words; *huh?* Then his eyes were comfortably drawn to a more common-looking paragraph…

"EXAM SUMMARY": *"Patient was found unconscious behind a bar with a severe laceration to the right wrist and a stab wound to the chest that punctured patient's heart."*

*...bar...right wrist...stab...chest...heart; what are the rest of the words?*

"TREATMENT SUMMARY": *"Emergency blood transfusion was administered followed by surgery to re-attach wrist and seal chest wound."*

Myles' eyebrows raised with confusion as he stood back up and looked back at the patient; he jumped as the rumble sounded in a louder, deeper tone with a ragged consistency and the pressure squeezed his chest, grazing upward. While honing his focus on the sound, a red aura around the woman's body faded into view for a moment but disappeared as the pressure subsided. The sound jolted Myles' nerves when it erupted again, even louder and hoarse now; the red aura reappeared and the pressure focused right to Myles' head—even slower to fade away.

He gripped the back of his head with his free hand, squeezing as he winced with pain until it was gone. After a few moments, the pressure built again, growing faster and faster—a thermometer about to peak. When it finally stopped, the pain disappeared; his mind and body felt completely clear and free.

The rumble blasted at Myles, knocking him to the floor; it finally revealed itself to be a growl and as it crashed through the room, the red aura fully appeared around the woman's body and Myles became deaf to the room's earthly ambiance; everything surrounding the woman was now in an unusual haze and despite the room's new strangeness, he couldn't pull his eyes from the woman.

Now in a faster rhythmic pattern, the growl sounded in calmer segments; ...*breathing?* His eyes widened as they scanned over her body; the red aura maintained a flow of whisking strands, moving over, under, around and even through themselves; ...*smoke?* With the normal smoke strands, the cloud was also dripping—liquid vapor—in *every* direction—up, down, left, right, diagonal; Myles took a slow step forward.

Numb to any and all emotional sensations, he continued forward and the growling grew faster—shallow breaths. Obliviously releasing the doorknob and with his feet spaced wide apart, his face was just over the bed's side edge. The air around the aura was warm and almost suffocating; keeping an open airway, he stopped reaching his face any further. After examining for another moment, he cautiously lifted a hand and reached forward, pushing through the muggy heat. Finally, his fingers penetrated the smoke; his brain actually interpreted the physical sensation of a rough and gritty texture and he slowly stirred his fingers around.

The cloud grabbed his wrist and squeezed; he saw nothing but felt sharp objects stabbing into his skin. His body froze; he saw nothing but darkness and the growl burst into an earth-shaking roar; his adrenaline spiked and he trembled as fear finally took hold.

When the door opened, Myles' hand was released and his normal consciousness returned. Once again, he saw a normal, hazeless room; the red aura was gone and the growling silenced. Finally coming to, he turned to see a nurse calmly staring at him.

"...you lost hun?" Torn between lie and truth, Myles' head bobbled a few directions before he gave her an affirming nod.

Whatever fear he felt being in that room left him as soon as he walked out—as soon as the nurse distracted his focus—but he ran back to Ava's room, calling for her; his mother *shushed* him as she was sleeping. Waiting to for her to wake up, he sat in the chair his mother had next to the bed and fell asleep.

Ava woke half an hour later and smiled at her grandson sleeping in the chair. "Myles?" She quietly called out in a German accent, "Myles...wake up."

After a moment, her grandson fidgeted as he woke. When the disorientation subsided, Myles looked at his grandmother, jumped out of the chair and wrapped his arms around her. She smiled and squeezed him tightly, gently rubbing the back of his head.

"Are you okay?" he asked, pulling away from her.

"Yes, Oma. How are you?"

He stared at her for a moment, then wandered his eyes around the room, searching for an answer, "I'm good." was all he could say as his mind was in a tornado of confusion.

Ava tilted her head and glared at him, "...are you sure?"

Myles looked around again and took a step back as his face turned red. He looked out the door where his mother and father were speaking with a doctor in the hall, then stepped back toward Ava—actually leaning closer, "*I saw something, Oma.*" he whispered.

"I know; but are you alright?" she repeated.

"I think so?" he answered, searching his freshly blank mind for the next words to use; *wait...how did she know?* "How did you know?"

Ava smiled, looked out the door, then turned back to Myles, also leaning closer, "I could feel it; and I could feel you with it."

"But...no one else could."

Ava smiled and caressed Myles' cheek, "No sweetie; they don't have a gift like you and I."

His eyes widened and he looked toward the wall—imagining through it to Jane Doe's room—and with a sudden cringe, he squeezed his eyes shut until he turned his head back to his grandmother, "*...it was so scary, Oma. I wasn't scared until I touched it.*"

Ava's eyebrows raised as she looked away, pondering. She glanced at the door and Myles' parents were still talking to the doctor. She then turned back to him; her smile was gone, "You touched it?" Myles lowered his head in shame.

"...yes." he admitted and Ava drew a quick, deep breath, grabbing her chest as she carefully exhaled, "Are you okay?!" he asked in a panic. Ava nodded and when she was recomposed, she held out her hand.

"Give me your hand, Myles." she said and he obeyed without hesitation. She took it with both hands and held it firmly; her warm skin eased his nerves. Ava then closed her eyes and remained completely still. After a few moments, she inhaled another deep breath when the image of the growling red smoke entered her mind; eventually, she exhaled as she opened her eyes. Still holding his hand, she looked at Myles and smiled; *it didn't latch on to him.* "Myles, I want you to listen to me..." He straightened his back at full attention, "...I realize this is your first time with this gift; you didn't know anything about it when you went into that room so, Oma's not mad." She smiled and caressed his hand, lifting it to her lips and kissing it, "If you choose, someday, you can develop it; but, until that happens, you must *not* attempt to use your gift without me. It's nothing to play with. Oma's been using her gifts for many years and knows exactly what to do with them but you're too young to use it by yourself. So, I need you to make me two promises: first, you must promise to never use your gift without me..." she paused a moment, never breaking eye contact from Myles, "...say it, please."

"I promise, Oma." he said

"Second, when you visit me here in the hospital, you must promise to never go in that room again."

"I promise." he repeated. Ava held her arms open and Myles leaned forward from the chair, wrapping his arms

159

around her; she kissed his head, then he looked up, "What if it gets out? Will it get you?"

"Don't worry about it, sweetheart. Oma can take care of herself."

Five days passed before Myles returned to visit his grandmother. She was sitting in the same position as when he left her and she smiled brightly when he walked in the room. Not a minute after his arrival, Ava asked permission to take Myles for a walking chit-chat around the hall; his mother, father and the doctor hesitantly agreed but laughed when Myles vowed to protect her from the monsters.

Walking hand in hand down the hall, Myles' cheerful demeanor dwindled when he saw the door they stopped at—Jane Doe's door.

"...Oma?"

Ava carefully knelt down to one knee, lifted Myles' hand and kissed it, "Remember when you asked me '*what if it gets out?*'?" Myles nodded with his eyes glued to the door, "...well, it's gone. It won't bother you anymore."

"Really?" Myles asked.

"Really. Come and see." She insisted and her steps were halted as Myles remained in place. She backtracked with a smile and only bent over this time, "Do you trust me?" Myles looked in her eyes and nodded; when she pulled him along, he followed this time.

Ava opened the door and allowed Myles through; the bed was empty and the room looked the same as Ava's.

"Can you try to use your gift?" She asked. Myles glanced at her hesitantly, then looked back at the bed; he squeezed his eyes shut and began to concentrate—nothing. After a few moments, he opened his eyes and wobbled with a dizzy head.

"Careful, Myles." Ava said with a smile.

Myles chuckled and turned back to her, "How did you make it go away?"

Ava looked at the bed and sighed, "Oma gave it a good talking to."

"Yeah; stupid monster." Myles said confidently and Ava guided him back through the door.

As the years went by, Myles occasionally questioned what Oma did with the entity he encountered and she always replied with, *"I'll tell you when you're older."*; she passed away before he reached the designated age.

*"It won't bother you anymore."*—the phrase kept circling his mind as he still held the scotch glass that now had only a dribble of alcohol from his second helping. Even with the booze relaxing his body, he couldn't shake the irritating guilt of questioning his grandmother, *"It's here again, Oma,"* He whispered quietly, *"It's bothering me again. You said it wouldn't bother me again and, now, here it is. I was having a great date—a great week—then it pops up and I'm terrified again. I thought you took care of it."*

Rising from the couch, he slammed the remaining alcohol down his throat and took the glass and bottle back

161

to the kitchen. As soon as he staggered across the threshold back into the living room, he flicked the light switch off, dropped to the couch and passed out.

# 14

Korbin woke Friday morning feeling completely normal, physically. However, the first image that came to mind was Shanna's face; he painted a perfect mental image of every detail from her eyes, to the bridge of her nose and down to her lips. Her hair flowed gracefully with every movement of her head. When she smiled during a teasing moment, her lips remained sealed and she ambiguously glanced around the room. When she was about to tell him a story, she took a short breath and her jaw dropped slightly. In a moment of victory, the right corner of her mouth pulled back as she pursed her lips, followed by a single nod of her head. If he had her at a loss for words, she either, stuck out her tongue and shook her head with a mocking groan or she scrunched her face, wrinkling her nose. The mere memory of her scent was intoxicating and that of her voice reached forward in time, massaging his ears; the memory of her lips penetrated his hazy memory like a wet piece of paper. Warm to the touch, they were soft and they coddled his lips with passion—claiming her territory. While the intricate thought of her soothed Korbin's body, a strange, yet, toxic sensation of missing her ate away at the stem of his brain and it triggered an even stranger loathing of ever being apart.

Ignoring his tiny, sudden ounce of frustration, he prepped himself for the morning as today was his appointment with the psychic presenter—Myles' first appointment of the day.

Having never been a big drinker, even the two glasses of alcohol left Myles a headache that morning. Every movement of his head rocked the fluid in his brain like a hurricane at sea, crashing against his nerves and he continually stopped to re-collect himself; he simply froze, placed his hands over his eyes and took a few deep breaths, allowing the mental rapids to settle. He had taken some aspirin at Billy's and despite being too early to tell if they'd work or not, he looked forward to some strong coffee at the campus as his backup plan—the motivation to actually get up that morning.

Already on his third cup of coffee at 9:45AM, Myles sat in the classroom wearing his hat for the first time that week—front-ways this time—and it sufficed to shield the light from his eyes; *Oh...why couldn't you have been raised as a drinker—had a higher tolerance?*

164

He slowly looked over when Jessica knocked on the open door, "Hey." she said as she walked in.

"...hey." Myles greeted in a low, tranquilized tone.

"How you doing today?"

*Hung over—fuck it; just tell her. If she gives you shit, oh well.* "I've been better."

She sat in the chair opposite Myles and leaned on the table, "Still rattled from the other night?"

"No, something happened *last* night, actually," Myles said, forcing a grin that his facial muscles lacked the strength to hold, "sorry; um...I actually had a drink when I got back to Billy's last night. I don't have a tolerance for the hard stuff so now I'm hung over."

"Wow. Was it *that* bad?" Jessica asked.

"Yeah; I was pretty rattled. I needed something to calm the nerves."

"...you want to talk about it?"

Myles *carefully* shook his head, "I'm not really prepared right now."

"Okay, well I'll be in my office if you need." Jessica said

Myles nodded then she bid him a good day and left the room. Keeping his head still, he moved his eyes to the side—obeying the urge to examine her behind as she left—but he stopped and cringed with pain, sending his eye muscles into a spastic tantrum. Giving in and relaxing his eyes, he finished his coffee then pulled out his phone and squinted as the bright display popped on: 9:53AM; now, obeying his bladder, he carefully stood up and headed to the bathroom.

He was finishing his business at the urinal—actually resting his head on the wall with his eyes closed—when his neck started to burn; the smoky-red aura was nearby and was creeping closer and closer. With his eyes still closed, his curiosity compelled him to turn his head toward the wall, in the direction of the building's entryway; from what would be the parking lot, his *Extra Sensory Perception* translated the sensation into a vision of the entity—surrounded in darkness—actually walking toward the door. He turned his head back to the wall in front of his face and he opened his eyes wide, zipping up his pants.

Myles walked hesitantly toward the bathroom door and stopped when he reached it; he closed his eyes, honing his *E.S.P.* again, and the entity was in the hallway walking toward the classroom; it was a brighter red now and its vapor-consistency flowed even faster. No longer a dripping mist, it acted as normal smoke—coursing upward and dissolving into the atmosphere.

Hidden beneath the bright red smoke, a tiny micron of the lingering familiarity reached out and just grazed his consciousness; when he forced his focus on it, Korbin's face slowly appeared and Myles' eyes exploded open, even wider.

*...maybe ten—twelve steps till he reaches the classroom;* as quickly and silently as he could manage, he reached for the door handle, stepped to the side and pulled the door open a tiny crack. Peering through the opening, his eyes captured Korbin as he casually strolled to the classroom door; he stopped before entering the room and looked

167

around, clearly searching around for the psychic that was supposed to be there. Korbin leaned back and scanned the hallways left to right then after a short pause, continued into the room.

Myles gently closed the door and released the handle as he fell back into the wall; his inhaling breath was long, straining to fill his lungs but once it consumed their capacity, he held it. He had to force it out in choppy exertions. His heart was beating with such force, his chest, wrist and neck arteries visibly bounced. He pushed himself off the wall toward the paper towel dispenser and pulled out some sheets, wiping them all over his sweaty face. Crippled by his symptoms and the memory of his first encounter, Myles reached into his pocket, pulled out his phone and started dialing.

Typing at her desk computer, the phone rang three times before she stopped to answer it. Slowly leaning over as she finished typing her last few thoughts, she finally picked up the receiver, resting it between her head and shoulder, "Event services; this is Jessica."

*Good; she's there;* "Hey, it's Myles."

Jessica's eyebrows cringed as she glanced away from the screen, "Myles? Umm...what's up?" she asked with a grin, "Why didn't you just walk to the office?"

*...stupid—no, stop. Your problem's legit; she'll understand,* "Uh...I'm having a little issue."

"...okay?"

"I need you to go into the classroom and tell the student waiting inside that I got sick and I can't come in today."

Jessica glanced quickly out the door then turned her chair toward the wall, tucking her chin to her chest as she lowered her vocal octave—just short of whispering, "Myles...this doesn't really look good if you have to leave because of a hangover."

"It's not; I swear. I'll explain myself later but I'm having a serious problem right now. Can you help me out?" Myles pleaded.

His sudden tone of fear canceled out Jessica's skepticism, "So then, you'll finish with your remaining appointments today?"

Myles stared straight ahead and said nothing; *You can't; get outta there. Get away from that school. Do whatever you gotta do but get the fuck out of there.* "...no."

"Myles..." Jessica began in a new anxious tone, "...I understand if you're having another...problem. I really do; but you can't abandon the rest of your appointments without repercussions—one student, maybe, but we have a contract."

"That's fine; we can make the necessary adjustments to my pay, give those last students a refund—whatever. I just have to get out of here. Please go tell him; and make sure he leaves. I ju—" he took a deep breath, "I can't be near him."

Jessica nodded, "Alright, I'll take care of it. Will you tell me about it later, though?"

"I don't know, Jessica." Myles answered immediately; *Hell no! Keep your thoughts on anything but that.*

"Well I'll tell you what...you promise to tell me and I'll go make sure whoever's in the room leaves." she conditioned.

Myles scoffed and shook his head, "...alright, I'll tell you about it later. Just please help me out."

"You got it." Jessica said as she hung up the phone. She saved the document on her computer, scaled the window down to her desktop and put the machine to sleep. She grabbed her cell phone as she stood up then left her office in a calm pace.

When she reached the classroom, Korbin was sitting in a chair, playing on his phone. She knocked on the door before entering, "Excuse me," she greeted with a smile, "you're waiting for Myles?"

Korbin nodded, "Yup. Supposed to have an appointment at ten."

"Yeah, he actually just got a hold of us; he's not going to be able to make it in today. He caught some bug yesterday and he's feeling really lousy this morning."

Korbin cringed as he locked his phone and placed it in his pocket, "That sucks; I actually caught something a couple nights ago. It was only a twenty-four-hour thing, but it was *baaaaaad*."

"I guess it's going around." Jessica added, "Well neither of us are exactly sure how he's going to be, or when he'll be better—and today's his last day, so we're not going to be able to fulfill your appointment."

"Really?" Korbin asked.

"Afraid not."

Korbin stood up, placing his hands in his pockets, "Well, not to be inconsiderate but, am I able to get my money back?"

"Absolutely," Jessica answered without hesitation, "we'll get an email out to everyone, letting them know the situation and we'll get right to work on refunds."

"Alrighty." Korbin said with a nod. After a quick check of whether or not he left anything, he headed toward the door and Jessica followed.

She walked him to the exit door, apologizing with false explanations. When Korbin was out of the building and nearing the parking lot, Jessica turned around and Myles was walking toward her; the bathroom door slowly closed behind him. He took his hat off and ran his hands through his hair; she walked forward, meeting him half way.

"Thanks." Myles said in a quiet, groggy tone.

"You're welcome." Jessica answered, "...so what's going on?"

On top of the false email she sent out to the remaining students on Myles' schedule that day, Jessica lied to her colleagues and superior about an "emergency" and was excused—with the encouragement to return if there was time. She met Myles out near the parking lot and he followed her to her car.

Myles reached for the door and stopped, "Wait...where are we going?"

"*City Hall Park.* That should be safe, right?" Jessica answered as she opened her door.

"No."

"Why?"

*Oh yeah...you didn't exactly tell that little secret;* "There's a ghost there and...I'm under enough pressure right now." he said, massaging his temples.

Jessica looked around for a moment, "Where, then?"

"Can you just follow me back to Billy's?"

"Can you drive?" Jessica asked in a stern tone, piercing her gaze through Myles' throbbing head.

"I can manage." he said. Jessica nodded and they both got in her car and she dropped Myles off at his. Despite the painful hangover, he moved quickly, getting into his blue box on wheels; he backed out and they were on their way.

Immediately rushing to the front porch for a spot to sit, Myles leaned his head on the railing and never moved it. When Jessica repeated her question of what was wrong, all he could think was to warn her with: "*It's really,* really *fucked up*". Nonetheless, she encouraged him to proceed; *...just tell her. What've you got to lose?*

Unfortunately, his warning never actually broke through to her; Jessica's face was paralyzed after Myles' last sentence. Despite the few things she'd seen from him and other, unexplainable, things he told her, her mind was expecting something of less caliber—less bizarre—like a trauma one of her friends may have gone through. She had the experience to listen, assess and either advise or just be the shoulder to cry on; perhaps she'd experience a bit of empathy and cry along with a friend but nothing ever jarred her mind the way Myles' story did and her face was a perfect representation. Her eyes were wide—looking full of pain—her jaw hung open, her cheeks were flushed and goose bumps covered her body.

Clearly seeing his pain and discomfort, she'd be the one to break the silence but with a suddenly blank mind, she had to search her vocabulary for a moment and force her words.

"Uh—umm...whoa." *Oh my God! Is that even possible? Can that be real? Of course it's real; look at everything you've seen from him so far. Okay, just calm down; let it sink in. Do you really want it to sink in—stop. Help this poor guy; just...be here for him.* Jessica glared at Myles and a hollow sensation dug into her stomach.

"You okay over there?" Myles asked with his face buried in his hand and she jumped at the sudden question.

"Yeah, I'm fine. I just, uh...just trying to process it." Jessica answered, fighting the nervous shake in her voice; *Okay, whether it's in his head or his soul—Jesus Christ— Stop! Just gather yourself. Okay, first bad experience as a child...growling red smoke...scary but not deterring; second bad experience in college...Dahmer victim...terrifying and made him quit; but...*

"Okay..." she finally began, "...first, I apologize for the silence; you just caught me off guard."

"I said it was bad." he said calmly.

"I know, but that's something that words can't prepare you for and it's a little harder because I believe you, yet, I can't even fathom such things."

"Understood."

Jessica sat up straight and took a deep breath, letting it out in a nervous chuckle. She looked at Myles and scooted closer to him, "Can I hold your hand?"

Myles nodded; *fifty-fifty shot you'll start seeing her mind right now.*

Jessica reached over his wrist and wriggled her fingers between his; she squeezed firmly when their palms touched.

"Myles," she began in a soft voice, "I know you're feeling real crappy and your experience today put you more on edge, but I'd like to ask more. It has nothing to do with business...I'm asking as a friend. Is that alright?"

Myles took a slow, deep breath—his brain fluid still painfully sloshing around at the slightest motions—and, still leaning against the railing, he gently turned his head, making eye contact with Jessica; he simply closed his eyes and uttered the approving sounds: "Mm-hmm".

Jessica placed her other hand on top of his, sandwiching it between her two palms and gave another squeeze, "So, I get why you stopped doing all this to begin with. What I don't exactly get is...the experience in college was traumatizing, while the one as a kid wasn't. You said the thing today was the same from that first experience, right?" Myles nodded, "And you weren't afraid of it then, but you are now; I'm just not getting the connection."

Myles shrugged his shoulders, "I guess...well...when I dealt with it in the hospital—and I like, *touched* it? That *was* scary; but after I went back to my Oma, the fear was gone. When she took me in front of the door again, I was afraid but then I saw it was gone and I wasn't scared anymore. The possibilities of what I could do actually fascinated me. I think at that age, I just didn't understand enough about life to be really terrified. As I got older, I didn't completely forget about it, but I pushed it out of my mind and just forgot to *think* about it—especially since Oma said it wouldn't bother me anymore. I understood way more about life when I was in college and when I went through that...yeah it definitely did something. As for today...I think the mix of everything— all my fears—just limits all of what I can handle. I didn't know what I was feeling when I first got to this school but each time it hit me, it was stronger; when it finally manifested into this, I remembered and that was it. I let my guard down—pushed too hard—and now, I have to stop it all again."

"Well, I mean...you also said you worked really hard on your defenses and that it was going really well. If you didn't think about this, specific thing, obviously you wouldn't prepare for it. Maybe you don't have to stop all your abilities this time; maybe you just gotta take some time and develop some defense against this." Jessica insisted.

"I don't know what this thing is, Jessica." Myles defended. He slowly turned his body, facing her—now leaning his back against the railing, "My Oma died before she could tell me and, for whatever reason, ghosts don't talk to me. On top of that, I can't get passed that phobia I have for them."

"Even for your Oma?" Jessica asked in a surprised tone.

"Even for Oma. I have no idea what would happen if I try to develop a defense against this thing—if it'll tap into any other parts of me, or what—all I know is that it would be bad."

Jessica stared at Myles for a moment, "...but, if it's bad...what about the student? The one that's actually carrying it?"

Myles glanced at her and paused; *...there's nothing you can do; this thing will get inside you and devour your entire being; it'll probably drag you right back to hell with it;* "...I don't know."

"Well, shouldn't you try to help him? I mean, you have these abilities; you can see what others can't."

"Jessica, I don't know how to help him. I don't even know where to begin looking for a solution."

"I can help."

*Stay calm; ignore the burning ends of your nerves. Come up with some excuse; don't tell her you're just too chicken shit;* "I don't know how long it'll take. Besides...looking at him in a normal perspective, he looks fine. I think if this thing was going to do something, it would have done it a long time ago."

"Yeah, but just because he looks fine, doesn't mean he is. We're not even talking about a disease." she insisted.

*No; keep your cool. Keep...your...cool;* "Jessica...please."

Jessica pulled his hand closer, "I promise, I can help." Suddenly, Myles yanked his hand away from her grasp and Jessica jumped.

"Stop!" he shouted in a fierce tone, "Just stop! Leave it alone! You don't know anything about this shit or how it'll hurt you!"

Jessica stared at him. She coiled her arms close her stomach, tightening herself into a defensive pose; *He's just having a rough moment; he didn't mean it. C'mon, he's a good man...but* goddamn...*that hurt. Okay, just, head back to campus—let him do what he's gotta do.* "I'm sorry, Myles. Look, um...I'm gonna let you be and get some rest. I'm gonna head back but, I'll keep you posted on whatever adjustments they make to your contr—"

As Jessica pushed herself off the porch—starting to stand—Myles reached out and gently grabbed her arm, "Don't go. Please...don't go." Jessica paused and closed her eyes for a moment, then she looked down at his hand around her arm; it held firm—keeping her from moving—but loose enough for her to pull away with an ounce of effort. He was sitting up and forward now, and his hat was tipped up as his exhausted eyes stared right at hers, "...I'm sorry."

"It's okay." she said.

"No, it's not. I don't care what condition I'm in right now, you're just trying to help and I shouldn't have snapped—guess I just have some shitty control." Jessica

177

sat back down, loosening up and Myles pulled his hand back, "I'm sorry."

"It's alright. I'm not mad." she said with a little grin, "But...what about that student?"

Myles took a deep breath; *Oh, thank you adrenaline for numbing my head;* "...honestly, I know I *should* try to help; but when the thought of actually trying crossed my mind, I ignored it—for the reasons I mentioned."

Jessica nodded, "I understand, Myles; I really do...but maybe, that's what you're meant to do."

"Jessica, these aren't, like...magical or superpowers. They're not of anything normal, either but..."

She dipped her head in defeat; *Why can't he see? I know he's afraid but he says this kid has something bad in him and he has the ability to do something;* "I know you're scared, Myles; but please, tell me that's the only thing holding you back."

He bit the inside of his mouth and leaned forward again, staring at the ground, "Yeah; I'm terrified." He then looked up into her crystal blue eyes, "...when I get home, I'll start looking into it. I promise."

Jessica simply nodded with a pleased smile.

# 15

Getting back to his daily routine at home wasn't as difficult as it was exhausting. After a heavy debate the Friday night Myles returned to Racine, he decided not to subdue his abilities again but rather maintain whatever control he had over them; *Maybe you'll get stronger.* Unfortunately—even if his theory would prove correct— like physical training for a shredded body, it was going to take time before he developed the necessary endurance and strength. By Saturday, that wear on his mind already manifested into his body's exhaustion.

Unable to let go of the fact that something bad was stirring inside an innocent and oblivious student—unable to forget the promise he made to Jessica—he went out on Sunday afternoon to two discount book stores and a *Barnes & Noble*, buying whatever books on psychics and the occult that seemed legit. When he got back home, he immediately began reading. He switched back and forth between the books and various internet searches, learning nothing new. More often than not, he found himself scoffing, rolling his eyes and even laughing at some of the material he glossed over. Fighting—what felt like—sleep deprivation, he finally passed out around midnight and woke up the next morning feeling even worse; *You maintained a level of control at the school last week. What the hell's the problem? The excitement and adrenaline may have been helping.*

Myles returned to his regular work on Monday, pushing himself through the fatigue. The consistent vibration of the riding lawnmower actually soothed his muscles—hypnotizing them—and the relaxation therapy inevitably lulled his mind toward a dormant state. The muscles in his eyes would release their grip and his eyeballs would start to cross, followed by drooping lids. He opened his eyes just as he was about to drive into a neighbor's fence; he yanked on the steering wheel and slammed the breaks, bumping the fence with the side of the lawnmower.

Even when finishing up on Tuesday and Thursday, he missed the tracks to the trailer on the back of his truck; he had to back it up for a second, slower attempt. Despite the struggle, he never attempted to put his abilities to sleep and continued his research every afternoon and evening after work.

<><><>

Barely able to move on Friday, he shut off his alarm and rolled over, allowing himself some extra, necessary sleep and he skipped the entire day.

<><><>

On Saturday, he searched around for local psychics—within a twenty-mile radius—finding four and only able to get an appointment with one that day.

Arriving at 12:47PM for a 1:00PM appointment, he got out of his car, shut the door and paused as he stared at the house. The blinds were shut on the big front window with black peel-away stickers that read: "Maria Cortenger: Psychic Medium". Under the big headline was a smaller line: "Accurate Spiritual Readings". Myles eyebrows raised as he allowed a small grin on his face; ...accurate *readings? Bullsh—stop. Just keep an open mind. Yeah, yeah, they're mostly full of shit and you can't trust them...but what choice do you have?* With a small shake of his head, he walked toward the front door.

Reaching the sidewalk path, he glanced up under the lip of the roof of the opposite corner and stopped; a small, out of place-hole practically screamed at him and he rolled his eyes; *Is that a camera? Oh, that door better not* magically *open before you knock.* He started walking again and as soon as he reached the door, the metal workings of the door knob turned and the door pulled open; *...oh God.*

181

A small, woman in her fifties, with a small pair of glasses on her head, answered the door with a smile; *...don't say it.*

"Hi there." she greeted with a polite smile, "I've been expecting you."

*...she said it. Of* course *she has; you made an appointment. Just get the hell out of there—no. She may have some use.* "Hello." Myles replied as he stepped in the house. His muscles relaxed some when he noticed that it was just a normal house inside; there weren't any bizarre decorations or strange music playing to force a mystical atmosphere. Maria didn't even talk strange; she simply offered Myles something to drink but he denied.

"Well, what can I do for you?" she asked.

"Actually, I'm not really here for a reading. I just wanted to ask your...*professional* opinion about something." *"Professional"? Wash your mouth out with soap when you get home, young man.*

"Fair enough. Would you like to sit?"

Myles nodded and they sat down on the small sofa beneath the big window. He coughed as he defensively crossed his leg over the other and folded his arms against his chest, "What do you know about entities and possession?"

Maria's eyes widened and she chuckled, "Wow, um...in regards to what?"

"Well, a good friend of mine was *perusing* the internet on psychics and such and she came upon this thing that said something about being possessed by a red, smoky,

182

cloud thing. I actually tried to look into it and I couldn't find anything. Ever hear of anything like that?"

"Hmm..." she sounded out.

Myles fought the laughter shaking his chest; *"Hmm"? Her eyes are already clueless—suppose you can commend her for the effort.*

"Ya know, honestly, I haven't. Now, to be a good psychic, I'm not gonna lie and pretend that I know exactly what you're talking about, cause then that'll get back to me." She said with a big smile.

*Ugh...she just lost her effort points.*

"Now, I've been doing this close to thirty years but I've never heard of anything like that; and actually, entities are my specialty..."

Myles fought both laughter and the urge to smack the woman upside the head as she continued on with her useless self-praise. After a couple minutes, she asked if he intended to make actual contact with the entity, then lectured him on how bad it was. After his convincing assurance, she eventually invited him to the room just beside the small living room.

In the room, there was a small table with a white cloth draped over the top and a single candle on top. Off against the wall was a shelf that housed some books and, what appeared to be some tarot cards and other miscellaneous nick-knacks; *...her little tool shelf.* Despite the begging of his pride, he wasn't about to tell this woman about his own abilities but stopping her in the middle of any remaining nonsense was definitely in the cards.

183

She pulled out a book from the shelf and handed it to Myles, explaining how it might have some answers.

"Now be careful with this, it's very old and only one of a few copies left." she said.

Myles handed it back to her, "No, I couldn't."

"I insist; I can sense you're a good man with pure intentions. I know you're not going to try conjuring anything of these sorts but perhaps you can find what you're looking for."

"Are you sure?"

"Absolutely."

After his most sincere attempt at a meaningful "thank you", Maria guided him to the front door and let him out. He quickly turned and held up the book, "Thanks again; I appreciate it. I promise, I'll take good care of it."

"Don't even worry about it; I have another copy." she said. Suddenly, her calm politeness turned hasty as she simply said, "Bye" and quickly shut the door.

*...one in a few copies left but you have another? That explains the sudden "good-bye"...shot yourself right in the foot, lady.* Myles smiled and shook his head as he walked back to the car.

When he sat down inside, he opened the book and the publishing year read: 1982. He then pulled out his phone, activated the internet and searched for the book's title; the same book had at least thirty copies on *Amazon.com*; *Bullshit, old. It better have something you can use.*

<><><>

184

Korbin and Shanna met for lunch in the campus cafeteria on Monday and she struggled to hide her excitement; the moment they sat down, Korbin dove right into his food and Shanna smiled, shaking her head, "You want me to keep time?"

Korbin looked up and extended his middle finger toward her; she scrunched her face and shook her head; he just chuckled.

"How was the party?" Korbin asked.

"It was fun. Molly got totally sloshed." *And revealed a little secret.*

Korbin smiled, taking another bite, "And how 'bout you?"

"I didn't get too bad. I was a little paranoid about the mess people might make so I tried to stay *somewhat* sober."

"Good thinking." He added.

Shanna nodded then took a drink of her iced tea; *Just tell him. You already know how he feels; it's mutual.* "I wanna tell you something."

"What's up?"

"Um...can you stop for a second?"

Korbin looked up as he was chewing and smiled, setting his fork down. He wiped his face with a napkin, then folded his arms, staring into Shanna's eyes; *...god she's amazing; even for a little request like that; okay, you gotta step back. Dunno what the hell is wrong and why you're so immersed; is this obsession?*

Shanna took a deep breath and set her own fork down. She looked at Korbin and her straight face quickly failed as she turned her head, laughing.

"What?" Korbin asked.

Shanna covered her mouth with her hand and shook her head, "I'm sorry...um...okay...we've known each other a few years; so maybe this isn't as strange as it feels. I know that..." she paused as she lost herself in his eyes; her pulse raced and her stomach fluttered. Her eyes scanned his torso, from his stomach, along his arms, to his hands; the warm euphoria in her chest trickled all the way down to her knees; *...holy shit; stop...get it together;* She leaned forward and her tone lowered to a soft pitch; Korbin leaned forward to meet her in the middle of the table, "...I think I know what it means when you do that blinking thing."

"Yeah?" he asked with a smile.

Shanna nodded, "Mm-hmm; and, uh..." Shanna paused and mimicking Korbin's "Shanna-limited" gesture, she slowly lowered her eye-lids, closed them for a moment, then slowly opened them up with a bright smile.

Korbin stared into her eyes for a moment, "...Molly told you, didn't she?"

Shanna started laughing and turned her head away, "Yeeeaaahh. She was already drunk, pulled me aside and spilled."

"Wonderful." Korbin said in a sarcastic tone as he sat back.

"Well, if you didn't notice, the feeling's mutual."

He took a drink of his soda and started blushing. He looked at Shanna and *blinked*.

"Are you embarrassed?" Shanna continued.

"A little."

"Why?"

He looked around for a moment, then leaned forward again, "The truth?" Shanna nodded, "...I knew I had feelings before we kissed but after...that shit jumped like, ten stories. It's like—God, this is gonna sound lame—it's like I didn't just feel it; I knew it. Like, I knew the depth of my feelings for you, and that yours were the same for me. It's like something was giving me signals inside and I knew, without a doubt."

"Really?"

"Yeah. It was scary at first 'cause...I never had that before. Then, all the sudden, there it was. I didn't know what was pushing me toward you but something was. I know *why* I feel the way I do—you're amazing—but I dunno what was making it so intense. Then I started to freak out about you finding out, then you'd get scared that I was getting too clingy or some shit. So I've just been trying to keep things as normal as possible but, honestly, it's getting really difficult."

Shanna smiled and *blinked* again then Korbin closed the distance between their faces and kissed Shanna's lips. When they parted, their faces remained the same distance, "You're not sick again, are you?"

Korbin laughed, "Uh...shut up?"

"Well..." Shanna began, "...how bout when we're done here, we head back to my apartment?"

"You wanna play video games?"

"Nah...just your joystick."

Korbin sat back in his chair as his cheeks turned red, then he picked up his fork and continued eating, "I'm game." he said with a mouthful of food.

<><><>

Myles reached Wednesday afternoon that week with nothing to show for his research. He threw away the book he received from the psychic the first day he got it and the other books were scattered on the table. Slumped deep into his recliner, he stared at a blank television screen with a scowl on his face.

*Why the hell would there be anything about this in some book or the* totally *reliable internet? Why would there be a single person that could tell you something you don't already know? That would all just make sense. A goddamn week and a half, killing myself for nothing. Fuck it...*

"Oma?" he called out, "Oma...I don't know if you can hear me—no, I'm sure you can and as soon as you show up, you're going to terrify me but, I'm having a problem here. You remember that red smoky entity at the hospital? You said it wouldn't bother me again? Well, it's back. It's stuck with some poor kid in Platteville and as terrified as I am, I'm trying to find a way to help; so far, I got squat. You left me before you could tell me about it and I have no clue where to start—"

Myles jumped back in his chair, almost toppling it over backward when Oma appeared in the middle of the living room. The fear of falling, alongside his ghost-phobia, caused his heart to skip a beat. He was panting heavily as he stared at his straight-faced grandmother; *She died in jeans and a t-shirt? Hair's only down to her shoulders? She must've cut it right before;* "...Oma?" he asked in a quiet, timid voice, "Oma. Please talk to me."

She just stared at him.

Now his blood boiled with anger; the burning sensation started in his stomach, then slowly crept its way up his spine, to his shoulders and filled his head; his nerves practically pulsated with each breath he took until finally, they exploded.

"Ugh! I hate this! I hate having this, Oma! You called it a gift! It's not a gift! It's a curse! It's a fucking cu—" Myles suddenly stopped his tirade and stared at Oma; she still remained motionless as she stared back at him. His eyes slowly scanned around the room as his brain processed the sudden epiphany, "A curse. The kid's cursed. He's cursed!" he shouted and when he looked back at Oma, she was gone.

Fighting his trembling muscles, he got up from the chair and frantically ran around the house, grabbing his coat, wallet and keys. He double checked that the computer and all the other lights in the house were off then pulled out his cell phone and started a text message to Jessica, *"I think I figured it out. I'm heading back to Platteville now. I'll let you know when I get there."* He pressed "send", then walked out the front door and locked it behind him.

# 16

Myles met Jessica just outside her office at 6:52PM and they retreated to her car in the parking lot; she was consumed with uncertainty as the look on Myles' face was nothing short of fear. As always, he was sweating, but he was severely gnawing on the inside of his mouth—even using his teeth as a flesh peeler for his bottom lip. Her seat vibrated as his leg rapidly shook up and down and he kept looking around.

"Is it that bad?" she asked.

"I don't know how bad it is."

"What'd you find out?"

His head paused for a moment, then he glared at her with hesitation, "...I'm not sure but I think it's a curse."

Her eyes widened, "Really?"

"I think so," he answered with a nod, "...like I said, I'm not sure. That whole time, I couldn't find any information related to what I saw. I even went to a local psychic—God, I think they're full of shit—and still came up with nothing."

Jessica sat back in her seat and looked ahead for a moment, then sighed as she turned back, "What are you going to do?"

Myles shook his head and shrugged his shoulders, "I don't know; what *can* I do? I mean, first, I have to find him. After that...I have no clue."

"Can I help?"

"I'd rather you didn't. I appreciate the offer, but I don't want to risk you getting hurt. If it traveled from one person to another like this, I don't want it to get a hold of you, you know?"

She nodded, "I understand."

"Yeah; um...I just wanted to let you know the situation. Uh...just, you know, head home and I'll take care of it."

"You're not worried about others?"

He looked around for a moment and shrugged his shoulders again, "I think, until this point, no one's been in danger 'cause no one messed with it. If I do something tonight...I mean, people are going to be out and about. I can't make them all go hide—unless you put the whole town on some alert but then you get, like, mass panic. Not like most would believe me anyway. Since you know me, I can make that request."

Jessica flashed a half-smile and nodded in acceptance, then engaged Myles in a few more friendly words. Finally, he said his goodbye for the night and stepped out of the car, heading back to his own.

Myles turned his head as Jessica started the car and pulled away; *She's not going back to get the rest of her things? Hope you didn't scare her too much.* When he got back to his car, he sat in the front seat and locked the doors. Leaning his head against the headrest, he closed his eyes and took three deep breaths; *in...out; in...out; in...out.* His psychic grip reached into his consciousness and released the temporary grips on each ability—except for his dreaded empathy; relaxing that hold lifted a big weight from his shoulders but he had to stop himself from basking in the relief.

His senses alerted him immediately of Korbin and his supposed curse and Myles' adrenaline spiked with his pulse. His breaths became shorter and more labored; *Calm down; breathe. Breeeaaaathe.* Following the direction of those triggered senses, he turned his head and through the darkness behind his eyelids, his mind interpreted the bright red smoke in the distance; *Open your eyes.* Forcing the muscles to work, his eyelids lifted in slow hesitation, begging to remain shut. When they opened completely, Myles was staring at the building that held Jessica's office but despite feeling its presence, he couldn't see the red smoke. He closed his eyes again and it reappeared; *...hold onto it.* His mind flexed, struggling to hold onto the vision as he opened his eyes. The lids lifted slowly—bits at a time—and the vision of smoke actually remained in sight; *Just a little further; open. Hold onto it; further ...further ...further.* As his eyes completely opened once again, they stared at the building and actually held onto the extra sensory vision and the corner of Myles' mouth turned up. *Okay, that's a new one. Now, where are they? They can't be in the building, it's too far—have to drive.*

Across campus in her dorm, Amanda's pulse raced; her breathing shifted to an inconsistent rhythm as Shanna's face dug into her consciousness; it was welded to the neurons in her brain dosing her with euphoria. It was immediately crushed by Shanna's obliviousness to Amanda's advances; how do you tell her? How do you make her see the truth? It's there, she just can't see it. Her rage coursed through her spine, throughout her limbs, and she could not contain the vicious attack on her pillows.

After exhausting herself and panting heavily, Amanda grabbed her phone and went right to her sanctus app, thumbs blazing on the screen..."I do not know what to do anymore. I've tried so hard to be strong and positive, but I'm so stuck and I feel so lost. I didn't want to say anything about this cause I'm not a fan of airing my dirty laundry, but I just do not know what to do. My crush has no idea how I feel and no matter what I do, she just won't respond. Like she can't pick up on what I'm telling her. What do I do?"

She held the phone firm in her hands—thumbs hovering over the screen; the "PUBLISH" button was bright and vibrant, yet, threatening. The flesh between both Amanda's brain hemispheres ripped fiber by fiber...publish the post or not. Her desperation outweighed her inhibitions and as soon as she tapped the button to submit, her stomach twisted with regret. She slammed the phone face down on her desk and sat on her bed.

Ten minutes passed before Amanda's focus broke from picturing Shanna's face; one giant step brought her to her desk and she picked up her phone to find 5 new notifications...

"Don't give up hope! Maybe she's playing hard to get?"

"Sounds like you've just been laying down signals. Have you tried actually asking her?"

"I agree, be persistent, but don't pressure too much. Do what you can and let be what will be."

"Just be you and whatever happens happens. If it doesn't work, it's a huge world!"

The encouragement intended through the comments did little to calm Amanda's mind; the constructive criticism and suggestions even scratched her nerves. They could not compare to the dark electricity the fifth comment would come to charge...

"No offense, but there's a couple things I'd like to address here...one, you say you don't like to air your dirty laundry, yet that's pretty much what you do. I mean, yeah we all do it haha, but that's what you do in a support group. Second, maybe she just doesn't feel the same way and is trying to be nice about it? If I could offer a little constructive criticism, based on other posts you've made, you do come off as a little needy and sometimes pessimistic. Maybe she just doesn't feel your vibe, ya know?"

As her heart sank and dissolved in the acid of her stomach, Amanda's nerves scorched with rage and she tapped hard on the screen; the ghostly finger print in the pixels quickly faded as she typed her response..."Please don't be rude. You don't have to insult me," She began typing, now feeling empowered, "I'm just trying to get some advice on how to help someone who is more confused than me and can't see her true feelings. If you can't be helpful or polite, please don't bother commenting." Amanda's eyes burned a hole through her phone as she watched with anticipation, constantly refreshing the screen. A new notification appeared...

"Well I'm sorry but what you call being rude, I call being honest. I only tried to give constructive feedback on a public post you published. Also, how is your crush confused? How do you know what she can or cannot see? "

A previous user suddenly chimed in...
"Hey just leave it be. Quit egging her on."

"I'm not egging her on. Sorry if she can't handle honest opinions."

Amanda gritted her teeth and typed a new reply...
"I know her and who she is. I can see that she's confused about the boy she's with."

The chain of comments paused. She sat refreshing her screen every second for the following seven minutes until a new notification appeared...

"Wait...she has a BOYFRIEND? Are you trying to convert a straight girl?"

Amanda's throat clenched. Her eyes widened and her lungs failed to breathe. She typed again..."I'm done with this conversation..."

"Yeah if you were you would've ended it already. You need to stop right now and leave her be. You're proving one of the stereotypes that makes every straight person hate us. Your crush knows where she stands. No confusion."

"While I won't go to such a harsh perspective, I do agree. You can't do stuff like that hun, that will just drive her further away and won't even want to be your friend."

"Same. Let it go."

Amanda's stomach turned inside out as even her initial supporters started opposing her; ...this can't be. How can they take that jerk's side?

She quickly backed out of the conversation and into its specific settings. The delete function was unresponsive in her frantic attempts and she slammed her fist on her knee. Finally, she focused and slowly tapped the button. A message prompt asked if she truly wanted to delete the post, "Yes!" She said in a harsh whisper as she pushed the confirming button. After a moment's delay, her screen refreshed and the post was gone; she set her phone down then laid down on her bed; they don't know you, they don't know her. You know. You know and only you can show Shanna the way. Your heart and your love is true. She paused a moment then laid back in her bed, covering her face.

Both sifting through text books during a spontaneous homework date, Korbin sat across Shanna at the library table; they continually disrupted their focus to look at one another. When Korbin would look, Shanna's head would be down and vice-versa; sometimes they would catch each other looking, then laugh as they went back to their books.

After a few more glances, Shanna dropped her pen and folded her arms on the table; Korbin's eyes rolled up toward her.

"So, I need to tell you that at this get together tonight, Jake's gonna come by." Shanna said in a hesitant tone.

"I know. You told me." Korbin replied calmly.

"Did I?"

"Mm-hmm. You texted me during your class on Monday."

Shanna glanced back and forth as she traced back her memory, "Oh yeah; that's right." Korbin smiled as his eyes returned to the text book but Shanna continued looking at him, "So you really don't have a problem with it?"

"Nope." he answered quickly.

"You're sure?"

Korbin set his pen down and folded his arms on the table, mirroring his girlfriend, "Okay, honestly...no, I don't have a problem with it. I get he's your friend and if you want him to stay that way, that's cool. My only concern is him hurting you like last time; but if he can be civil, then I'm good. I'm not gonna tell you who you can or can't be friends with."

"Damn right you're not." Shanna replied with a smile.

"Hey, *you're* the one that just asked for my approval."

Frozen for a moment, searching for a comeback, Shanna just crinkled her nose and stuck her tongue out at Korbin.

"Oh yeah...I went there." he added.

"...dick." she said.

"Damn proud."

Shanna fought an inevitable smile, "...dick."


Only five minutes after his meeting with Jessica, Myles tracked Korbin down to the campus library and parked his car in the lot. Upon his arrival, Shanna walked right out the door, leaving to get ready for the night's gathering; Myles dismissed her as just another student—oblivious to her connection with his target. Unable to discern her face, his brain never even registered her as the girl Amanda was crushing on. His focus remained locked on the bright red smoke that appeared to him from inside the building. The uncomfortable heat of its presence nearly burned his insides and scratched away at his mind. For thirty minutes, he sat patiently—straining from both the mystical discomfort and holding onto the auric image both mentally and physically.

7:31PM—It…Korbin…started to move; the smoke made some mysterious gestures, then started moving closer to the exit; *It's about time.* When Korbin walked out the door, Myles paused until the student walked around the corner of the building, out of sight. Myles opened the car door but stopped as he was getting out. He looked under the dashboard on the passenger side, pondering; *Just grab it; be prepared.* He reached over and pushed down on the grip of a handgun; the spring-lock of the mounted holster disengaged and he removed a *Glock* 9mm. Myles released the magazine from the grip and examined it; *…fully loaded.*

After examining the magazine, he double-checked the empty gun barrel, then locked the magazine back in place. He leaned forward and slipped the gun in the holster on his waistband behind him; draping his shirt over the weapon, he stepped out of the car and followed his senses.

Korbin had not gotten very far when Myles caught up to him. He was following the path around the buildings that led to the dorms. Myles' loud, jogging footsteps compelled Korbin to turn and they made instant eye contact.

Before he even started running, Myles released the grip of his auric vision and all he saw was an unsuspecting student taking a harmless stroll. Yet, the red smoke's presence still dug away at him and he painfully pushed himself into a light run. When Korbin turned toward him, the hot scratching's intensity suddenly grew and stopped Myles in his tracks; he gasped as he swallowed the lump in his throat; *Oh God...oh God get me through this; please.*

"Hi." was all that Myles could say.

"What's up?" Korbin replied, leaning away.

"I'm Myles."

Korbin raised his eyebrows with a little smirk, "Hey...man." Korbin's eyes glanced over as his mind went to work, "Wait...you're the psychic that came in, right?"

Myles nodded, "Yeah, that's me."

"How you feelin'?" Korbin asked.

"Excuse me?"

"How you feelin'? I had an appointment with you that Friday and they said you got sick. You feelin' better?"

Myles' eyes rolled up and scanned around, "Oh, yeah. I'm better; thanks."

"Yeah, I caught something earlier that week; it sucked, man."

"What did you catch?" Myles asked.

"I dunno," Korbin began, "it was, like, this twenty-four-hour bug or something but I was all dizzy and throwing up; it's like I was drunk."

Myles glanced away for a moment, "When did that happen?"

Korbin stared at Myles, then scanned his eyes around, trying to remember, "Uh...the Wednesday night of that week?"

Myles' eyes widened as he recalled feeling the curse's awakening that same night; *Definitely wasn't a twenty-four-hour bug,* "Well hopefully that's all gone now."

"Right?" Korbin said with a smile, "So...what'cha doin' back?"

*How the hell are you going to answer that without sounding like a complete—stop. It doesn't matter; help him,* "Well, I know a lot of people were really anxious to—"

"Sorry; um, can we walk and talk?" Korbin interrupted and Myles nodded as they continued onward, "Sorry; go ahead."

"No problem," Myles assured, "I know a lot of people were really anxious to get a reading from me and I wanted to honor that." Myles lied through his teeth; *...keep rolling with it.*

Korbin shook his head, "Nah, don't worry about it dude. Besides, I spent that refunded $25 already."

"Well I wouldn't charge you; it's the principle."

"Really, I'm good, man." Korbin repeated and Myles nodded, leaving them in silence as they walked. Their footsteps grew louder and the silence became deafening;

the hot scratching teamed with Myles' anxiety, driving him to a breaking point.

"Okay, okay...I'm not really hear to honor a reading." Myles confessed.

Korbin looked at him with confusion, "No?"

"No. I need to ask you something—*you* specifically."

"...okay." Korbin said in a skeptical tone.

Myles' heart rate jumped yet another speed, pounding against his ribcage; *what the hell are you going to ask him?* "Have you ever had any strange experiences growing up?"

"Like what?"

"I don't know. Anything that just didn't seem '*normal*'?"

Korbin stared at the ground, thinking for a moment, then shook his head, "Not that I can think of."

"Any strange things with your parents?" Myles continued.

"...nope."

*Well what the hell? This thing has been dormant this long? Or did it just take hold in the last few weeks? He's giving you nothing to go on.*

"Okay, more specific...do you know *anything* about the paranormal?"

Korbin thought for another moment and again, shook his head, "Probably nothing compared to you. I just seen movies, ya know?"

Myles shook his head; *It's not his fault; he has no clue what's going on. Okay, neither do you, but you can't get mad at the kid. Fuck it, you may as well just put it out there.* He stopped Korbin's pace right in front of the student activity center; a large crowd of students were inside, playing *Foosball* and sitting at tables.

"Okay...no more beating around the bush..." Myles stated with a new sincerity; Korbin grabbed his backpack straps and relaxed his stance as Myles prepared his explanation, "...Since I got to this school, I've felt this presence; I didn't know what it was at first but then it suddenly blew up and...it's not good. It's actually really bad. I had an experience with it once before—a long time ago—and it's just not good..."

"...okay?"

Myles paused for a moment, searching for comfortable wording, "When this thing...well, woke up, I guess...*then* I recognized it and eventually, it led me to you."

"To me?" Korbin asked as he wiped a thin layer of sweat from his forehead; he then grabbed his t-shirt and lifted it off the skin of his chest, shaking it back and forth to cool himself.

"Yes. I followed my senses and they led me to you; this thing is festering inside you; I can actually feel it right now. I don't know what it is exactly or what it will do but at some point, you're going to find out. It's energy's been increasing more and...more..." Myles paused and looked down as he reached only a few inches out ahead of him; *...don't touch anything; not the kid, not that entity, nothing.* Even at that three-foot distance, Myles could feel heat radiating from Korbin—actual, physical heat.

"Sorry, what were you saying?" Korbin asked. Myles looked up at Korbin's face and he was dripping sweat; his shirt was soaking rapidly and Korbin kept swinging his head around, rubbing his neck.

"I was saying...the entity's energy...is...increas—ing; are you alright?" Myles asked and Korbin shook his head, attempting to jolt his mind back to a coherent state.

"Yeah man...um...I really don't know...I; ugh, fuck! What the hell? Did we just get a warm-front?"

The hot scratching in Myles' mind turned into a burning drill, digging into his consciousness and he slowly backed away; *Tonight? You serious? This thing decides to do something tonight?!* "No—no warmfront. I think the thing I'm telling you about is actually doing something...right now."

Korbin dropped his backpack to the ground and walked a few paces away from the building, toward the track; he took a few deep breaths and coughed out the last one, panting heavily as he bent over, resting his hands on his knees. Myles cautiously walked toward him, "...you alright?" *No...he's definitely not.*

"Fuck! How'd it get so goddamn hot?!" Korbin shouted as he rose up and pulled his shirt off.

Myles looked back when a couple guys opened the building door, "What's goin' on? Is he okay?" one of them asked. Myles just shook his head and looked back at Korbin, who was bent over again, still panting. The guys then walked out and approached Korbin from behind. When one of them touched his shoulder, Korbin shot upward, yanking his shoulder away.

"Don't touch me!" he shouted, staggering further out.

"Dude, you need some help?" the other student asked with no response from Korbin, "...who is that?" he asked quietly and his friend just shrugged.

Panting nervously himself, Myles closed his eyes and focused on his *E.S.P.*—on the red smoke within the victim it was now torturing. The image immediately appeared but was now a burning red flame; it brightened as it shrunk into Korbin's chest. Holding onto that image, Myles opened his eyes again. The flame continued decreasing in size, matching Korbin's increasing struggle for air. When the flame was the size of a softball, it was now a blinding white with a red halo and resided at the center of Korbin's torso—his core.

The flame exploded, completely engulfing Korbin and Myles' muscles stiffened with a stabbing burn; his fists clenched and his jaw locked open. When the blinding light subsided, the former red smoke and flame was now a transparent red shell; *Let go. Let go, son of a bitch. Let go. Let go!*

Myles snapped out of the grip and stopped himself from falling; then he looked at Korbin, who—when Myles experienced the blast—had fallen to his knees with a big, deep gasp of air, then keeled over and started heaving violently; the other two students were taken back and just watched in panic while two more students came out to investigate.

Korbin heaved until his stomach was empty, eventually throwing up blood as his stomach continued its purge. When it finally stopped, Korbin slowly rose his torso upward, struggling to inhale a deep breath; his eyes rolled back into his head, turning black. The bones in his face cracked in various locations and he let out a loud, painful scream. He fell to his side on the ground and brought his hands up to his face; his scream never stopped and eventually sounded out with short, exhaled breaths as his face continued breaking and contorting.

One of the students approached the boy in agony and Myles grabbed his shoulder, pulling him back, "Get back!" Instead, Myles moved closer to Korbin, taking careful steps; by the time he circled around to Korbin's front, he knelt down and examined his face; it was a broken, distorted mess, full of blood.

"Shit!" Myles jolted back but on another disfiguring crack, he noticed Korbin's skin split open, release another flow of blood, then slowly seal back together.

Korbin's gums throbbed as large fangs stabbed through and pushed their way around his human teeth. He gasped again and let out another scream that masked a whimpering cry of pain. He stomped his feet on the ground and his hands shook as they cradled his mouth. Finally, Myles caught Korbin's eyes and Korbin reached out to him, "Help me! Please!" he cried out as his eyes leaked tears. Frozen in place, Myles just stared at him; when he broke his gaze, the first place he looked was up, discovering the sky was brightly lit by a full moon. He looked back down at Korbin, then up again; *You've got to be kidding. You have* got *to be fucking kidding! He's a goddamn w—*

Myles eyes shifted to the four students staring at him and Korbin and he quickly stood up, "Get back in the building!"

"What are we gonna do?! He's like, dying!" a student asked.

Myles quickly walked toward them; he grabbed two of them by the shirts and shoved them toward the door, "Get back in there now or *you're* going to die!" Three of the students started back toward the door but one ignored Myles and jogged back to Korbin, circling to his front. When he laid his eyes on Korbin's face, they widened and he jumped back, tripping over his feet. He quickly stood and sprinted back toward the door, "Get back inside! Get back inside now!" This time, the other three students obeyed and even picked up speed. Myles' jaw hung open, slowly walking backward as he watched Korbin; the disobedient student turned back, grabbed Myles' shoulder and pulled, "C'mon man!" he shouted. Myles turned and ran inside with the students, locking the closed door behind them. He pushed his way through the crowd, placing himself right next to the glass and as he stared out into the open field, he reached behind him and drew his gun.

Korbin released a fresh, whimpering cry with every lingering mutilation of his body and they were muffled by the jagged fangs that filled his growing mouth; his oversized gums protruded from beneath his lips like a great white shark; his mouth stretched outward, splitting his upper lip and flattening his nose. The tearing cartilage echoed in his ears as they stretched.

Each of his bones jumped out of place and snapped at random moments, reforming their shapes and further deforming his body; when his left shoulder dislocated, his right forearm nearly pierced his flesh in a compound fracture. His fingertips throbbed—ready to explode—as black claws stabbed through his fingernails; his fingers snapped backward at each knuckle and his flat palms erupted with bone shards, pushing against his skin as the flesh and muscles swelled around his fingers. When his left arm broke in half, he rolled onto it, bending it at the break and he screamed to the top of his lungs; his voice cut out mid-scream and he began *hacking* like something caught in his throat. The hacking quickly dissolved into a deep growling.

The weakest points of his skin split with each stretch of muscle and bone then immediately healed itself. Hair grew over his entire swelling body and his pants tore at the seams; his leather belt broke in half and even his feet split his shoes apart, forcing him to kick off the remains. Now lying on his back, his chest suddenly rose up, pulling his back off the ground then slammed back down; the convulsion repeated five more times.

When his body stopped slamming, Korbin's blurred vision was finally going black as he lost consciousness; before the darkness consumed his eyes and mind, the vision of Shanna popped into his mind.

The curse grabbed the part of his mind where Shanna resided and cranked on it; he roared as a throbbing shock slowly traveled through his head and body and Korbin finally submitted to the dark unconsciousness. As select pieces of its body finished their transformation, the new, steaming body of the former student laid on its side and gradually came to rest.

Myles and all the students watched in awe from behind the glass; while he held a firm grip on his gun, pointing it down at a slight angle toward the window, most of the students pointed their cell phones out toward the motionless animal. In his peripheral vision, Myles saw one student's phone pointing at him for a few seconds, then turned back toward the window. He felt a select stream of energy radiating toward him from the same student; without making physical contact, Myles was reading the student's thoughts: *"Who the hell is this guy and why does he have a gun?"*; Myles looked back out the window, then tightened his grip on the gun as he braced himself for what everyone was seeing.

The *animal* outside rose its head for a moment, then dropped it back down and laid motionless for another few seconds. It slowly curled its shoulders upward, bracing itself on its paws and strained to push itself up; its legs trembled underneath its massive body. As it stood on all fours, its legs quickly spread, catching itself from falling. It shook its head with a loud, exhaling snort, then dipped it to the ground and curled its back upward; its spine cracked as it stretched. It stretched its front paws, followed by the rear paws, popping in juicy crackles. When it finally took a step, it wobbled again and shook its head. It turned toward the window and locked in place—right at the student that was filming Myles and who turned to record everyone behind him. The animal curled its lips and its walk toward the window immediately progressed to a jog, then a short, sluggish sprint.

Myles and every other student backed away from the window but the animal's target turned just in time to see it slam its head into the glass; the lack of momentum and force merely vibrated the window and the animal staggered backward, shaking its head again. Regaining composure and maintaining its jagged snarl, it turned and slowly crept along the brick wall, sniffing with each step. It then turned and crept the opposite way, still sniffing the wall. When it was right in front of Myles, it looked up and their eyes locked. As the psychic stared into the consuming black eyeballs, the animal shifted its head slightly and when the light caught its eye, a hidden red color glimmered at him.

Completely numb from adrenaline, Myles lost the grip on each of his abilities but, somehow—with a struggle he failed to notice—he held the grip of his empathy. He didn't even have to close his eyes for additional focus; he tapped into his *E.S.P.* with ease and the vision of the curse's new red shell immediately reappeared in his physical sight.

The animal snarled more, cautiously ducked down in a defensive stance, and started to shake; then it lifted its head and looked behind its massive body, never looking back before running off toward the dorms. The crowd of students pushed up against the window, looking for it.

After a few silent seconds, they all burst into frantic chatter; those that weren't talking to one another were either sending text messages on their phones or typing about the occurrence on their laptops. As Myles still glared out the window, however, one student shouted: "Who was that?! Was it a student?!"

The sudden echoing voices pulled Myles from his trance and the first person his eyes caught was the overeager cameraman. Myles approached him and looked him straight in the eyes, over the phone's camera pointed at him, "I'm Myles. I was invited to do a seminar at the campus; I carry the gun, with a permit, just for protection. I'm not here to hurt anybody."

The student's hands began to shake, "I-I, uh...I didn't actually ask that, did I?"

"No, you didn't." Myles answered, "I heard your thoughts and, quite frankly, I didn't ask for enough money." he walked back to the window and peered out into the darkness—into the trees; *You know who that was; help him. Can he even* be *helped? Stop...you're not gonna know that now. You have to find him. Go help him; keep your distance—your gun ready and go help him. Go grab his things; don't let anyone find out who he is.* Never taking his eyes from the window, Myles backtracked to the door; he reached for the lock, feeling the door until his fingers touched the little metal rectangle. He gripped it tightly and twisted until the door unlocked and he stepped outside. The students all yelled at him for being insane and to come back in the building.

With all the students watching, Myles checked in the distance, toward the trees; there was no sign of the animal. He quickly scanned the ground; he grabbed Korbin's pants and checked the pockets; *...wallet; good.* He then grabbed the other torn rags of clothing and Korbin's backpack. After a final check, he turned and ran back to his car.

# 17

Fifteen minutes before Shanna and Jake began a casual stroll around the dorm building, Amanda spotted them outside from her window and ran down.

Jake's calm demeanor eased Shanna's nervous mind, especially after he promised to talk in a mature manner; there was a sincerity in his voice that she immediately recognized from years before.

While it took him a minute to find words he was confident with, the first ones out of his mouth were the simplest, "...I'm sorry, Shanna."

A soothing warmth flowed through her body, washing away her anxiety—her loathing of his recent attitude—and she smiled a bit; *Make sure he really is. He sounds serious, but double check,* "Really?"

"Yeah. I really am." Jake insisted.

"Thank you." she replied.

"You're welcome. I know I was being a real asshole and, looking back, I was really stupid with our relationship. I should've accepted the issues and addressed them with you. But...hindsight, right?"

"Right." she said with a nod and they walked in silence for a few seconds.

"I can't stand the idea of not having you in my life—especially because of my stupidity. So, if you're willing...I want us to be friends again...the way we always were."

An endearing chill swelled Shanna's heart and her smile grew much larger, "That's all I want, Jake. But...is it gonna be a problem that I'm seeing someone else now?"

Jake smiled and took a deep breath, "Um...it'll be hard at first. To be honest, I don't think I'll ever like anyone that you date; but I think I can get over it. I want you to be happy—it still sucks that it's with someone else—but if you're happy, that's all that matters." Shanna turned and wrapped her arms around Jake's waist and he squeezed his arms around her shoulders.

A jealous rage pulsed through Amanda's body as she watched from around the corner of the building. Maintaining her distance, she cautiously followed as Jake and Shanna continued walking. Careful not to scrape any excess pebbles or dirt, Amanda practically tiptoed behind them but stopped at a rustling in the trees; she looked over and spotted the animal that put the activity center—and now the dorms—in a panic, as it emerged. Amanda's eyes widened; the animal's mouth hung open as it crouched; strings of drool hung from its lips. It coiled

214

back and jumped into a full-sprinted beeline toward Shanna and Jake. Amanda stood frozen.

It already jumped by the time they turned to see what was thumping in the grass next to them; it tackled Jake to the ground and began to devour him. Jake's athletic strength did nothing as he desperately tried to fight off the onslaught of scratches and bites. The animal's claws sliced open pieces of Jake's flesh and its teeth dug deep into his muscles, tearing them off his bones. Jake's screams were easily matched by Shanna's and all the while, Amanda just stared in a temporary paralysis.

Missing vital pieces of skin, Jake was drenched in blood; it clogged his throat, muffling his screams to loud gurgles. As with the pain Korbin felt during his transformation, Jake wailed out in crying screams.

Finally overcoming the shock and panic, Shanna quickly pulled out her cell phone with trembling hands but immediately dropped it; the distracting sound pulled the animal's attention directly toward her. Staring at the scratched device, she bent down to pick it up but stopped short. The sound of thick, heavy footsteps on the sidewalk approached; the blood covering its paws sloshed on the pavement. Shanna slowly lifted her head to see the gigantic animal staring right at her; its upper lip was curled over its snout and when it drooled Jake's blood on the pavement, Shanna focused her hearing toward her ex-boyfriend, listening to his final blood-drenched breaths.

In three quick steps, the animal was immediately in front of Shanna; she fell back to the ground and frantically backed away but its front paw stepped behind her shoulder, blocking her backward movement. Staring into its black and red eyes, Shanna closed her eyes as she began to cry; *Oh God, please help me.*

As the animal's mouth opened, revealing every one of its grotesque, blood-soaked teeth, Amanda quickly ran into the small clearing toward the animal's side, waving her arms, "Hey! Over here!"

Its head turned and it immediately stepped away from Shanna, cautiously prowling toward Amanda. In a few steps it was half way between the two girls; it curled its lips, crouched down—preparing—and took a deep breath. As Amanda lowered her arms, the animal lunged at her with a loud roar; it knocked her to the ground and sunk its teeth into her shoulder. It lifted her off the ground and thrashed her. At the sound of a gunshot and an irritated yelp, it dropped her and backed away. Students inside the dorm appeared from around the corner of the building and froze at the sight.

Thirty feet away, Myles had his gun pointing right at the animal and they stared each other down.

Never breaking its gaze, the animal slowly prowled to the side, back toward Jake's body and stopped on the sidewalk, growling at Myles.

Still numb from adrenaline, Myles' pulse was racing as he panted lightly. The grip on the gun's handle was growing more and more slippery as his palm leaked sweat; his hand's vibration kept shaking it out of place; *You gotta do it; no you don't wanna, but you have to do it. Yeah, he's in there but he just killed someone—it just killed someone;*

216

When the animal made a sudden change in stance, Myles fired off four more shots, hitting it with each bullet.

After another irritated groan, the animal carefully sidestepped to Jake, hovering over his mutilated corpse. When the tiny sound of metal against concrete echoed underneath the animal, Myles realized one of the bullets had purged from the wound—causing no ill-effect. Finally, the animal wrapped its jaws around what was left of Jake's neck, lifted its head, turned and jumped into a sprint, disappearing into the trees. Jake's corpse dragged heavily along the ground.

Myles closed his eyes and carefully lowered his gun. After a few deep breaths, he glanced over at Shanna, who was staring at nothing; after a few moments, she fell back to the ground, unconscious.

"Shit." Myles said. He looked over into the clearing where Amanda was struggling to move; a pool of blood drowned the grass beneath her wounded shoulder. Myles shook his head and glared into the tree line then backtracked, running into the group of students, "911! Someone call 911!" he shouted. One student obeyed and as Myles ran back toward his parked car, the numbness began to wear off.

*Good; his light's on;* Myles' tires squealed as he cranked the wheel, pulling into Billy's driveway. He parked the car and ran out, sprinting up to the porch; he rang the doorbell three times then began pounding on the door and his fist was raw by the time Billy answered.

"What?! What?!" Billy shouted with a scowl as he opened the door, "Myles? What the hell's wrong?"

"Billy, I'm sorry. Can I come in?"

Billy stepped aside and Myles pulled the screen door open; before entering the house, he stopped and looked back. Holding onto his auric sight, the animal's red shell glowed brightly in the distance, remaining in the same spot; *Stay there you shit. It's probably eating...ugh.* Myles gagged as he finally stepped inside the house and Billy shut the door behind him.

"What's going on, Kiddo?" Billy repeated.

Myles paused for a moment, staring at the floor as he held his breath. He looked up at Billy with a sigh, "I can't go into details right now—though I'm sure you'll find out soon enough—but I need a couple things from you."

"What?"

"Okay..." Myles began, "...this'll sound really weird, but I need a pair of sweats, a long sleeve shirt, gloves..." he paused with hesitation on the final request, "...and I need whatever prescription medication you have."

Billy stared at Myles with a confusion, "What *kind* of medication?"

"Pain killers, if you have them. You still take meds for your knees?"

"Yeah but...I kinda need them?"

"I know but...okay, something happened tonight; some shit that...pretty much, only *I* have any hope to handle. But I need something for heavy sedation—heavy, *heavy*, sedation. I don't know if it'll work or not; I don't want to risk over-the-counter meds failing and I don't have access to the good hospital stuff. You're the only one I know that has anything so, please." Billy sighed and shook his head, "I swear I'll buy you a new supply but I need as heavy sedatives as I can get, *now*."

"You can't even tell me what happened?"

Myles closed his eyes, took off his hat and ran his fingers through his hair; his eyes returned to Billy as he put it back on, tucking his hair behind his ears, "I can't even say it, man. It's too bizarre, even for me. Look...you'll probably see it on the news tomorrow—if not tonight. Please Billy. Please. Trust me."

Billy shrugged his shoulders, "Alright, alright. I have pills and I have shots; which do you need?"

"...will it kill someone if they took all of it? I'm not going to hurt anyone, but will it?"

Billy's face cringed and he never blinked, "Uh, yeah unless they're not human."

*Bingo!* "Give me *all* of it."

While police interviewed the witnessing students, they fought rolling their eyes as they skeptically wrote down notes on their paper pads. The only viable piece of information their minds opened to was the description of a long-haired man in his thirties, wearing a black hat that was carrying a gun that saved everyone else. Tempted to disregard the extraordinary testimonies, the police immediately put out an *A.P.B.* for Myles and a big, hostile, wild animal.

219

The ambulances carrying Amanda and Shanna had already left for the hospital and Shanna remained unconscious as she lay secured in the stretcher; the second paramedic sat patiently in back with her, occasionally checking Shanna's vitals and continually finding nothing out of the ordinary; then her unconscious mind went to work…

*Shanna stood in her back yard at night. Just to the right of the back door was a white shed and surrounding the yard was a chain-link fence. Her shadow on the ground was crisp as her back was illuminated by the porch light. She stared straight at the back of, what looked like, a little girl with long brown hair petting a large Rottweiler behind its ear. As the dog dipped its head, the little girl walked to its other side, never turning her head; she pet behind the other ear. The ground sloshed as her feet stepped in a mix of a strange, thick black puddle and a gelatinous substance. As the dog raised its head and locked eyes with Shanna, her eyes widened and her pulse jumped. The dog just licked its lips.*

*"…stay, puppy." Shanna said. The dog then bobbed forward—as if to walk—then stopped and sat back on its hind legs. Her pulse jumped another notch.*

*"I said 'stay', puppy." she repeated.*

In the ambulance, Shanna's heart rate sped up a little and her arm twitched. The paramedic glanced over her body, then checked the monitor; *…must be dreaming…*

*The dog looked at the little girl and her hand gently slid down the side of its neck. Finally, the dog started toward Shanna.*

*She took a step back and it stopped, "I said 'stay', puppy!" she shouted and the dog whimpered. As it continued forward, her pulse continued to rise and she backed away until her back hit the side of the house. She panted as the dog drew closer, stopping every few steps to stare at Shanna. Its tongue hung out of its open mouth—almost smiling at Shanna; she began to calm.*

*"Aww, come here, puppy." she said, coaxing the dog with her hand. She bent down, making kiss-noises and it continued walking.*

Back in the ambulance, her heart rate dropped back to normal and her twitching ceased...

*Eventually, the dog was in reaching distance and Shanna pet its head. The dog leaned into her hand, coaxing her to scratch behind its ear. She smiled as she catered to the dog's simple desire and knelt down. The dog's eyes squinted with delight as she massaged the other side of its face at the same time.*

*Stepping up the affection to a more playful manner, she gently held the dog's face with her hands and pointed it directly in front of hers.*

*"You're such a good puppy." she said, then the dog's entire head morphed into the head of the animal that killed Jake...*

Shanna's upper body exploded off the stretcher, snapping the securing strap and she released an ear-piercing scream. The paramedic fell off his seat and his own heart jumped into his throat. He quickly grabbed a small bottle and poked a fresh syringe through the cap; he cringed from the deafening scream. When the syringe was full, he pulled it from the cap, squirted and flicked out any potential air bubbles; lacking an I.V. tube, he injected it straight into Shanna's arm.

After a couple seconds, her screaming died down and she fell back on the stretcher. The paramedic quickly fastened the remaining straps over her body and when he sat back down, he took a deep breath and held his chest.

The driver looked back, "You got it back there?"

"Yeah..." the paramedic answered, "...scared the hell outta me."

Shanna remained unconscious the rest of the ride to the hospital.

# 18

9:02PM—Keeping close watch on any movement of the curse, hiding in the woods, Myles stopped in a small diner in town with a sign that read: *Open 24 hours!* He sat down and ordered a coffee. Only ten minutes passed before two police officers calmly walked in, right over to his table.

"S'cuse me...Myles?" one officer asked as his partner stood just half a foot behind him; Myles calmly nodded, "How you doing tonight?"

"Doing alright." Myles answered.

"Mind if we step outside?"

"Not at all."

Myles stood up and the officers let him pass before following him out the door.

Standing outside, a sense of relief caressed Myles' shoulders as they exuded no intimidation, "We're following up with…some *unusual* reports at the college campus—one of which involving an armed individual."

"Yes, sir." Myles answered confidently, "That was me."

"*Are* you armed?"

"Yes, sir."

The officer nodded, "Where are you keeping it on your person?"

Myles motioned his head back, "Holstered on my waistband in back."

"Okay, I'm going to ask you to put your arms out to the side; for the duration of the interview, I'm going to remove the weapon for your safety and ours. Do *not* reach for it." Myles nodded and raised his arms up and out sideways, clearing his waist. The officer asked him to turn and Myles obeyed, allowing the officer to remove his pistol; he handed it to his partner, "Alright, Myles, would you be willing to come to the station and give a statement about what occurred at the campus?"

"Yes, sir. That's fine."

The officers guided Myles to their squad car and, ignoring the handcuffs, allowed him in the back seat.

For two and a half hours, Myles was interviewed about his side of the story; all he could think about was his gratitude for being a Concealed Carry holder and its single ounce of granted leniency; with a *thank-you* for his bravery and quick thinking, he only received a $500 citation for carrying his gun on the campus and was driven back to his car outside the diner; *Oh that could've been so much worse.* He sat back down, surprised to have no additional interrogation from any workers, and refocused his mind on the curse.

<><><>

5:55AM—The sun rose and Myles' eyes drooped as he took another drink of his coffee. He covered the sun with his hand and focused on his target in the distance; too far to see the details of its consistency—red shell of the animal or red smoke of the human—he could only conclude that it hadn't moved from that spot the entire night. He chugged the last of his coffee, then paid the bill at the register by the front door and left.

Following the curse—with his eyes and mind, as the sensation calmed to a mere warm chafing—led him to a thick forest of trees off *Stumptown Road*. Noticing a house sitting fifty yards back in an open yard, across the street from the woods, Myles looked back at the side road he drove passed. He pulled a quick *u-turn*, backtracked and turned onto *Cedar Lane*. When he stopped the car, he looked to his left and through the thick brush, he saw another house; *It's got to be too thick for them to see much. Just hope you're early enough before they see your pretty blue box on wheels.*

Myles shut off the car and got out. He opened the back seat and—already sweating—put on his hooded sweatshirt, the gloves and grabbed the sweat suit that Billy donated; *he probably won't get these back intact.* He closed

225

the back door, then reopened the front and locked the whole car. He walked to the side of the road and stopped at the edge of the trees; now, clearly, the curse returned to its red-smoke form. With a deep breath, he crossed over, into the trees.

The dew-soaked ground was soft—some parts actually muddy—but Myles still crept around the trees and through the brush; *...no sounds; or as little sound as possible. Don't need anyone giving you shit.* Despite his efforts, his lack of *covert* training allowed leaves and twigs to crunch beneath his feet and he cringed with each one, scolding himself. Traveling no more than thirty yards, ten minutes passed before he looked back at his car with an irritated scoff; *Screw the silent treatment; you're taking way too long. Pick it up.* Disregarding the sounds now, Myles picked up his pace.

The red smoke was appearing closer and closer; after another fifteen minutes, he finally reached the small clearing within the trees where it slept—where Korbin was passed out; *Ugh...finally.* Returning to silent mode, Myles carefully stepped into the clearing but as his foot touched the ground, it slipped and he braced his hand on the tree; *...fucking mud.* When he pulled his hand from the tree, it actually stuck a little and came off with a quiet peeling sound. He looked at the tree to find it stained in a dark, glistening red; he looked down at his feet where he slipped and instead of mud, he was standing in a pile of fleshy pieces that used to be Jake; *Oh God—skin or intestines...* His body suddenly lunged forward to vomit, but he stopped himself and forced it back down. He took a few deep breaths then continued into the clearing.

Stepping carefully, Myles noticed four subtle shimmers in the light—one right after the other. Every one of his bullets was forced out of the animal's body and the realization that they were useless churned his stomach. Now standing over the naked young man, Myles' eyes widened at the surrounding forest floor; a pile of shed hair surrounded Korbin. Detached black claws lay near his hands and the grotesque, pink-tinted fangs sat near his mouth; a couple were actually still inside, protruding from his lips. Myles looked up and all around; most of the clearing was clean but when he looked back at where he entered, he saw the entire bloody mess of last night's meal and he quickly shut his eyes. He cringed as a rotten scent of waste filled his nose; he turned his head away from the horror scene and looked around for the stench's source. A few feet from Korbin, in a small pit, was a basketball-sized pile of feces, covered with flies. Myles covered his mouth with his hand and looked away, returning his attention to the blood-covered Korbin.

With no sleep, putting the tight grip back on his abilities, fighting the sensations of Korbin's curse and lifting his dead, sleeping weight, Myles inevitably strained through his fatigue. Careful not to touch Korbin's skin with his own—despite his precautionary long sleeves and gloves—Myles only wasted a few minutes dressing him and when he was finished, he rested him back on the ground for a moment; he shook his head in the attempt to stay awake, then looked around the clearing; *Okay; drag the kid through that disgusting opening. Then, in as dry an area you can find, hop him on the shoulders and muscle through. Oh yeah...that simple.*

The dragging went surprisingly smooth and when he reached a firm spot of soil, Myles squatted down, lifted Korbin off the ground and worked him onto his shoulders; *...oh my God.* With Korbin securely balanced, Myles took a deep breath, then improperly held it as he squatted the hundred-some pound body up to a standing position and finally exhaled. He braced his quadriceps and began walking.

When he reached the edge of the woods, a shock of excitement shot through his body as he laid eyes on his car. Before he actually crossed into the opening, he examined the road through the trees; barely able to see through the wooded wall and going on his best guess that no cars were around, he continued onward, toward his vehicle.

Myles dropped Korbin right by the passenger door and even *he* started to fall. Desperate to allow it, he groaned as he, instead, braced himself with whatever strength his rubbery legs still had and unlocked the door. He kept looking around, finding no one in sight; he opened the door, then quickly lifted Korbin and struggled to shove him in the back seat. Careful of his bare feet, Myles pushed them into the car and shut the door. He leaned his body against the car for a moment until the sound of tires and a running engine crept into his ears. He lifted his head with wide eyes and sluggishly ran to the driver side door. Myles opened it, hopped inside and shut the door as he glared into the rear-view mirror. The approaching car passed right by *Cedar Lane* and Myles sat back in the seat, shutting his eyes in relief.

*No! Don't sleep. Get back home. You got shit to do.* Myles reached forward, started the car and turned it around, heading back to go *through* Platteville, and back to Racine.

# 19

Outside Shanna's hospital room, the doctor assured her parents that she was perfectly fine with no injuries and that the outburst in the ambulance wasn't anything to worry about; he added that if it was an indication of a night-terror brought on by the incident, that there would most likely be more to come.

Assuring the validation of his theory—as Shanna slept on the bed—her subconscious conjured another dream...

*Shanna stood, all alone, in her kitchen in the middle of the night and all the lights were off. Staring straight ahead at the back door, a strange urge compelled her to walk toward it. She tiptoed across the cold tile floor, cringing with each sliding sound of her bare feet; Don't wake them up. She continually glanced at the ceiling until she reached the door.*

Looking out through the window, two people stood in front of a little child's playhouse; the two people appeared to be chatting but she could not see their faces. She cupped her hands around her eyes and pressed them against the window; still unclear, the two people looked like Korbin and Amanda and they looked right at the door—right at Shanna. Amanda waved 'hi' and Korbin waved his hand, inviting her outside.

Shanna nodded with a smile then looked back at the ceiling; *They won't know; we'll be quiet.* She looked down at the door knob and slowly wrapped her hand around it. The slight rattling echoed throughout the house's entire first floor and Shanna cringed; she looked at the ceiling to the sounds of her parents shifting in their bed; *...still sleeping.* Even slower and more careful, she turned the knob and the teasing mechanism clicks were as loud as firecrackers and she cringed again. After another shift in the bed upstairs, Shanna looked down at the knob, took a deep breath and in one fast motion, she twisted it completely, pulled the door open, pushed open the screen door and stepped outside. As both doors slammed shut, she looked at them with confusion; between the last turn of the knob and stepping outside, there was no sound.

"Get over here, crazy." Korbin yelled to her.

Shanna looked at him, then up to her parent's bedroom window; somehow, she still heard them shifting in the bed, signaling their uninterrupted sleep. She shook her head and walked over to the playhouse to join the small gathering.

"Hey guys." She greeted; both Korbin and Amanda held out their hands and Shanna kissed the top of each one, then continued to hold them.

Korbin turned his head back toward the door, "Look...there she is again."

"Hmm?" Shanna asked as she turned around; silhouetted by the porch light—hiding her face in shadow—was the same little girl from the last dream, walking back and forth and in circles. Partially blinded by the light, Shanna barely noticed the little girl's hair was now blonde. The ground sloshed as she continually stepped her feet in the same mysterious puddle. Shrugging it off, Shanna returned her attention to Korbin and Amanda.

Amanda smiled and looked down at the ground with hesitation, "So we're thinking of buying a house and...we think we found the right one."

"In this market?" Shanna asked with wide eyes, "We can't afford one with our grades."

"No, it's cool," Korbin chimed in, "We got some extra credit and then they let us paint it for a down-payment."

Shanna looked down at the playhouse, examining it from her vantage point, "...well it looks solid. What kinda plastic is it built with?"

"Military grade kindergarten." Korbin said.

Shanna nodded with approval, "Nice. Nice find, you guys. Does it have a security system?"

Amanda shook her hand, "Oh it comes with a guard puppy!"

"Yeah," Korbin added, "But you have to let it bite you."

Shanna laughed and looked at Korbin to find the lower left half of his face suddenly torn open and that segment of his jaw missing. Though she didn't jump, her adrenaline flow did.

"It's really not that bad," Amanda added; Shanna turned back to Amanda, whose throat was torn out, and she gurgled blood with each breath. When Shanna looked back at the house, it was gone and, in its place, the puppy had turned into the animal that almost killed her at school and it stared at her; it stuck its tongue out and licked its lips with a low grumble.

"Ugh...alright." Shanna said as she let go of their hands and laid down on the ground, "Just a little chunk though; I have a party to go to and I don't want anyone to catch anything."

As she stared at the sky, the animal stepped one paw over her and it slowly lowered its head with an open mouth; Shanna stared at its enormous, crooked fangs until they were out of sight; all she could see was the animal's shiny black eye. When the red tint shimmered at her, she looked away at its shoulder; Don't stare. It's rude. Its teeth sunk into the side of her neck and ripped off a chunk; the sound of her flesh tearing away echoed in her ears and the raw anatomy underneath began to burn.

"Damn; this is really uncomfortable, you guys."

Korbin and Amanda just smiled.

The animal bit down again, harder and pulled off another chunk of skin and muscle—more violently. In a fierce, sudden motion, it sunk its teeth into her cheek and ripped it off.

"Ow! Okay, enough! I don't want the house anymore!"

The animal wrapped its mouth around her whole face now and bit; she screamed as it pulled her face off. It started digging its claws into her chest and stomach and when she

*screamed her voice was silent; all she could hear were her*
*panting breaths.*

*Kicking and punching at the animal did nothing and*
*when it finally clamped down onto her throat and yanked,*
*her body gradually fell colder and colder until her eyes were*
*consumed in total darkness...*

Shanna's body shot up in the bed as it did in the
ambulance; instead of screaming, she was only panting
heavily and this time, she was actually awake.

Her loud gasp pulled at the attention of the doctor
and her parents and they ran into the room.

"Hey, hey. Shanna?" Vikki asked, grabbing Shanna's
hand as Rich caressed her head, "You okay sweetie?"

The doctor approached her on the opposite side of the
bed, "Shanna? How are you feeling?" She nodded and
mouthed the word, '*okay*' as her breathing slowed down,
"I'm Doctor Thames. Do you know where you are right
now?"

"...hospital." Shanna answered, placing her palm on
her forehead.

"Do you know who these two are?"

"...mom and dad."

"What are their names?"

"...Rich and Vikki." Shanna answered, passing the
quick assessment.

Thames put on his stethoscope and placed it against
Shanna's chest; after replacing it in different spots, he
moved it to her back and repeated the process. He
eventually took out the earpieces and returned the cord

around the back of his neck, then placed his hand in front of Shanna's face, extending his index finger.

"Shanna, can you just follow my finger?"

She removed her hand as she lifted her head and locked her heavy eyes on the doctor's finger; as he moved it around, she followed it flawlessly.

"Are you feeling any numbness? Nausea? Aching?" Thames asked.

"...just really tired."

"Yeah that's what's left of the sedative; it'll pass. Well everything seems alright. Shanna, do you remember what happened before you got here?"

Shanna looked back at the doctor as her memory jumped right to Jake's death—her close encounter. As her eyes filled with tears, her jaw began to quiver and shifted her eyes to her mother, "...I...it *killed* him. It tore him apart." she said in a quiet, nasally tone. When she broke down, sobbing heavily, both her parents wrapped their arms around her, "There was so much blood..."

"Shhh..." Rich sounded out, "...try not to think about it."

Shanna let out a loud cry, "God...he just came t—to tell me—just came to tell me 'sorry'."

Watching the family with a sorrowful look, Thames walked behind Rich and leaned close to his ear, whispering, "There's some things we need to go over yet, but I'll give you guys a little time."

Rich nodded and the doctor left the room, closing the door behind him while Rich and Vikki comforted their daughter.

<><><>

Thirty minutes from Racine, Korbin finally started to wake; the only part of him that moved were his eyelids, struggling to open. In the attempt to speak, the slightest, innate flex of his vocal muscles ached with a searing throb. After another painful, failed attempt, his face started to cringe but Korbin's mind released the flex of even those muscles; having each nerve wrenched violently in its own vice was an entirely new sensation; he shuddered at the thought of trial and error-coping—more aching.

Pulling into the garage, Myles reached up to his visor and pushed the button, shutting the garage door. He quickly got out of the car and walked out the garage's side door, looking all around; none of his neighbors were outside; *Good. Just keep your asses inside for a few more minutes, please.* He ran to the back door of the house, unlocked it and pushed the heavy door wide open; he slid the metal holding clip on the screen door opener, leaving the door wide open then headed back to the garage.

He looked at Korbin for a moment—assessing the process—and shuddered at the chafing burn of Korbin's curse; *...not touching it but still feel it—bullshit deal. Well...he's still out; just prop him over the shoulder again.* He reached into his pocket and put the gloves back on. As he grabbed Korbin and started pulling him out of the car without care, the limp body let out a sudden whispering grunt.

236

Myles jumped, almost dropping him, "You're awake! Okay, hang on, hang on." He gently set Myles back down on the seat then stepped to the side—in front of Korbin's face—and held up his head as his shoulders hung over the edge. Korbin's barely-open eyes focused on Myles as he knelt down, "You remember me?"

Korbin gave no response.

"Myles...I did the seminar two weeks ago and I was talking to you last night?"...nothing, "Can you understand me?"

Finally, Korbin's throat flexed just a bit and he coughed an attempted word.

Myles leaned his head down, "What?" Korbin coughed again, then squeezed his eyes shut, squeezing out a tear, "I'm sorry. I can't understand."

"...*hurts*." he coughed out.

Myles' eyes widened and he nodded; ... *'hurts'; of course he hurts—after all that.* "Okay...I'm not going to hurt you or anything. I'm going to try to help but first, I have to get you inside. It's going to hurt though, so you need to bear with me."

Korbin managed a big, deliberate blink.

"That mean yes?" Myles asked and Korbin blinked again, "Good! Good idea," *Why the hell didn't you think of that?* "So twice for no?"

Korbin blinked twice in confirmation.

"Good. Alright...you ready?"...*blink*, "Okay; I'm sorry about this."

Now with extreme caution, he pulled Korbin out of the car, over his shoulder and Korbin let out another whispering grunt. Myles shut the door and paused a moment, "Now get ready, I'm going to move as fast as possible and get you to a couch...here we go."

Myles walked fast steps to the garage's side door, turning sideways to fit Korbin through, then picked up the pace to the house; he maneuvered sideways through each door until he reached the living room. He dropped to his knees by the couch, ducked down and rolled Korbin onto the cushions. Noticing Korbin's face buried against the back of the couch, he quickly rolled him front ways, then propped his legs up the rest of the way.

He quickly ran back outside, looked around and still saw no one; *...better not have been spying through a window—not like you'll do anything about it.* He shut the side door on the garage, backtracked to shut the screen door, then shut the heavy door, and locked the deadbolt. Walking into the kitchen, he took off the gloves and rested his head in folded arms on the counter; *No sleep! Not yet.* He dragged himself off the counter and returned to the living room.

Myles walked over and sat down in front of Korbin's face, taking a deep breath, "Okay...you understand me?"

*...blink,*

"You remember me from last night?"

*...blink,*

"Do you remember what happened after we talked?"

*...blink, blink,*

"'No'..." he chuckled and shook his head, "Alright; Um—well, no bullshit...last night, while we were talking, you started looking real sick and then turned into—"

*Don't say it;* "...well, it was a full moon last night and you changed; do the math. Anyway, from what I saw—depending on your conscience, this may or may not be hard to hear...you—er...*it*...killed one person and severely injured another," *Don't mention the aftermath of that kill,* "I saw you had something—some force—latched onto you and I tried to tell you about it but...I was too late." *...such a coward...goddamn coward—stop!* "Now, tons of people saw this happening; it's going to be on the news, I'm sure, and all over the internet—camera footage, the whole works; but, I don't think anyone knew it was you. I grabbed your things—wallet, backpack, clothes—and brought them with me. I don't know anything about...*any* of this, besides what I've seen in movies so, I'm taking precautions based on those. I'll keep you here, hidden for the next two nights—the last two full moons—and see what happens from there. I'm going to chain you up in the basement—I know that sounds stupid but, like I said, I only have the movie references—but I'm also going to dose you as heavily as I can. I actually shot you last night and since bullets didn't do anything, I'm pretty sure the sedatives won't kill you; I don't know if they'll even work, but I don't think they'll kill you. Afterward, if my theory is even close to being right, I'll do what I can to try and help you."

Korbin carefully flexed his throat and coughed out three words; missing them, Myles apologized and leaned his head closer, "...can't...move...hurt."

Myles pulled away, "Well...I can't stress enough that nothing I say is certain, but my guess is you can't move 'cause you're so damn stiff and sore. What your body went through last night...*psshh*...that probably would've killed a regular person."

*...blink*

Myles nodded and stood up, "Okay, um...you just rest. I have to run get some stuff. I won't be gone long though, alright?"

*...blink*

"Okay, I'll be back in a little while." Myles said as he left the living room and walked out the back door, locking the deadbolt.

When the silence of Myles' house became Korbin's only company, the image of Shanna popped into his mind and his pulse rose; the sudden euphoria numbed his muscles just enough to utter the words: "*...I need you.*"

The back door unlocked and Myles walked back in, heading right toward Korbin, "I don't know if you'll be able to move—or talk—before I get back but, here's your phone, just in case. I programmed my number in your contact list, so just call if you need me—if you're able. Alright...back in a while."

As the door locked a second time, Korbin closed his eyes and immediately fell back to sleep.

# 20

*Okay, mental list: chain...big, thick, long chain; locks; well that covers the kid—God, that better work. Basement door—that's got to be...what—four feet from the counter? Okay, six foot four by fours; just measure and cut when you get back. You still have at least nine hours. Then what? Silver bullets—where the hell are you going to get silver bullets? Who says silver even works? Precaution; okay, just get something silver—anything.*

For the entire drive to the nearest hardware store, Myles sorted through any and all possibilities—solely on what fiction has taught him through the years. With no definitive answers or solutions, he started to sweat as his blood boiled and he forced his back muscles to relax when they began to cramp from tension; *...insane— completely...fucking...insane; this better be a nightmare you're about to wake up from.*

Myles' anxiety eased when he arrived to a parking lot that wasn't even one-quarter full; a good portion of the vehicles belonged to employees, sitting in the blue lines, furthest from the building. Staring at the front entrance, a sudden *what-if* scenario flashed in his head, playing out everyone's reactions as he traveled through the store with such specific items. He saw their eyes, full of confusion, glued to him; many whispered to one another while others just shook their heads.

When he conjured the image of someone recording him with a cell phone, he snapped back to reality; *First...just stop; look at how many cars are in the lot. Exactly...zero! Second, if you don't go in there like a petrified madman, no one will be the wiser—probably. Besides, think of how many people go into this store every day, without a damn clue about home repair. They'll be so worried about which screwdriver is a* "Philips Head" *they won't even see you; the others that know what they're doing won't give a shit. Calm down.* Finally, he left his car in the barely-filled lot, sticking out like a sore thumb and walked inside.

He grabbed the only steel, gray hardware cart in sight; perfect for heavy bulk items, it had a solid, flat panel on the bottom that held four separate, vertically arched bars; each inside bar connected to the outside one with a short crossbar. He walked in front of it and the moment he pulled it along, the left rear wheel screamed, *"Look at me!"* with a loud, back and forth vibration; *...really?*

Myles first headed for his chains and after searching a few aisles with no luck, a hardware associate directed him to them. He debated for a couple minutes before deciding on a comfortable thickness that was stocked at only twelve feet long. His debate of sacrificing thickness over length lasted only a few seconds and he quickly filled the cart's entire bottom with fifteen rolls of chain. The locks weren't located much further away and he grabbed fifteen of the heaviest locks on the shelf; *Okay...four by fours.*

Retreating to the outside yard, two young employees were standing at the treated lumber rack chatting and one held a broom. When Myles appeared in their sight, they immediately parted and the sweeper quickly started brushing on the empty concrete; in a moment of customer critique, Myles looked around and felt a surge of surprise and approval at the well-kept yard; *Store's dead right now and the yard's immaculate; let them chill.*

He pulled his cart up to the rack and left it sitting as he scanned each labeled unit until the sweeping associate approached him.

"Can I help you find somethin'?" he asked.

Myles continued looking for a few seconds then turned to the associate, "I'm looking for six foot, four by fours?"

"Yeah; that's actually further down the rack on this level."

"Okay. Thanks." Myles said. He continued quickly along the rack until he found his four by fours, then jogged back to his cart; sandwiched between rough pavement and steel, the vibrating wheel grew even louder. He pulled the chains and locks off the cart first, then filled the cart with the wood until they reached the bars;

*Why not start with the wood? Give yourself a break—no sleep.* He then started stacking the wood onto the attaching crossbars. When there was nothing else to hold them in place, he finally stopped stacking, then got behind the cart and pushed it toward the door at a slow, weighted pace.

While the chain, locks and wood were easy finds and, to his surprise, no one gave him funny looks, a sense of embarrassment tickled Myles' nerves when he asked about silver. The only available options were a sterling silver light fixture or a little pendant, which he stared at with a look of skepticism; *You really don't even know what you're going to do with this. Are you supposed to get silver into the body or will it work if it just touches his skin? You going to try beating him with a light fixture? Oh, like wrapping a tiny little pendant around his neck is going to do much— maybe that's all you need? Okay, okay—test run; save some money, get the pendant and put it on him. If nothing happens, then you know silver's bullshit. If something happens, you go get the light fixture—unless you find something better.* He carefully removed the pendant from its holding place in the rack then pushed his cart to the checkout lanes.

Back at the house, Korbin's consuming pain slowly subsided; in slow, careful attempts, he was finally able to move his arm and he picked up his phone, telling it to dial: "Dad". The voice-mail immediately picked up and Korbin cleared his throat with a deep breath, preparing to talk; the beep sounded just as his chest pain halted him from inhaling any further.

"*Hey, it's me,*" he began in a weak, hoarse whisper, "*Dunno what you heard yet. I'm not hurt; been sick in the dorm. Talk later.*"

He ended the call and looked at the screen, finding no new messages. Opening his text message application, he went right to his conversation with Shanna and began tapping the screen with his thumb but stopped when the back door opened. Korbin just watched as Myles ran in and out of the house, bringing in the triple layered bags of chain each time.

When the last bag was in, he stayed outside for another ten minutes, stacking his new collection of wood in the garage. He finally returned inside with one single four by four and set it on the floor; he stood up and leaned against the counter, lightly panting. As he absorbed the chafing burn of Korbin's curse in his mind again, he looked into the living room to see Korbin's eyes finally open entirely and glossing over all the items. He walked over and dropped to one knee in front of Korbin.

"Uh...probably still really bad, but...how you feeling?" he asked.

Korbin inhaled another breath, wincing when he reached the shortened pain threshold, "*I can kinda talk now—move my arm.*"

Myles nodded, "Well that's something." He pulled the pendant out of his pocket, "Okay...I'm going to try something. This is silver—supposedly." he pointed out, placing the pendant a few inches from Korbin's eyes; he removed it from its cardboard holder and let the chain drop, straightening out; *What does it matter? He's not going to be wearing it; just put it on him.*

Myles hovered the pendant over Korbin's hand and slowly lowered it onto his skin, draping the chain over the side—nothing. He then lifted Korbin's sleeve, exposing the still blood-stained arm and repositioned the pendant—nothing. Finally, he placed the pendant on the back of his neck—nothing. "Well, that answers the question. Silver does *not* work."

He stood and walked to the kitchen but stopped to look at the pendant; *Wait...does it work only when he's changed? Ohhhh no; don't even think about braving that. You are* not *going to try getting close enough to test silver when he turns into that thing. Unless you find someone that makes silver bullets, silver does* not *work.* Myles leaned against the counter—out of Korbin's sight—and as the adrenaline subsided, exhaustion consumed his body like the pull of a black hole and he braced his arms on the counter just as his knee buckled; he tightly squeezed his eyes open and closed, then immediately yawned.

"*Ugh...Jesus Christ.*" he whispered and he shut his eyes. As he started to dream, the knowledge of his lingering tasks shocked his brain back to consciousness; with a loud grunt, he grabbed a marker from the drawer, picked up the four by four and took it to the basement door; he struggled to keep his eyes straight and clear as he marked his measurement.

After cutting the wood to his specified eyeball measurements five hours earlier, Myles reclined in his living room chair and finally allowed himself some sleep; his eyes popped open when his phone alarm went off at 6:50PM

When he pushed back on the chair, raising it up, he lowered the footrest and sat perfectly still for a moment; while his eyes were once again closed—tempted to travel back to a *R.E.M.* state—he focused all his energy back to the grips on his abilities; *Let nothing inside.* Ten minutes later, consumed by the chafing burn and the tension of keeping his abilities at bay, he allowed his auric sight to seep through into his consciousness. Before he opened his eyes, he could see Korbin's curse had turned from the red, dripping smoke into the hot red flame—preparing for its next emergence. He finally opened his eyes and saw Korbin was wide awake.

Myles leaned forward in the chair, "Korbin...how do you feel?"

Korbin's eyes glanced over to his rescuer, "Still sore—think I can move my legs but...I don't *wanna* move."

Myles nodded as he stood from the chair; he walked over to Korbin and knelt down in front of his face, "Alright...I need to take you downstairs and get you prepped so...I have to move you. We have less than an hour so it's got to be now. You want me to carry you or you want to try with me?"

"I'll try." Korbin said.

Myles nodded then ran back to the small table next to the chair and grabbed his gloves; when he returned, he grabbed Korbin's hand and wrapped his other arm around his waist and carefully helped him up. Korbin's face cringed as he coughed with a whimpering groan that continued as Myles pulled him to his feet. Wrapping Korbin's arm around his shoulder and holding most of his weight, Myles started walking; barely lifting them off the ground, Korbin dragged his bare feet forward, gasping and groaning the entire way.

It was already 7:10PM when Myles rested Korbin on the basement floor in a space he cleared earlier. He quickly removed his glove and pulled out his phone, checking the time, then placed it back in his pocket and put the glove back on. He unraveled the chains and quickly wrapped them around Korbin's entire body. By the time Myles finished, Korbin was cocooned in thick metal, fastened together by randomly placed locks, and he laid on the floor—wincing with pain. Myles then headed upstairs.

In fast and heavy footsteps, he came back down with a glass of cloudy, white liquid and one syringe; he knelt down in front of Korbin and showed him the glass, "Alright, um...this is going to taste really disgusting, but this is over half of a large supply of pain killers;" then he held up the syringe, "so is this. Like I said...I'm pretty sure it won't kill you; I just have to take the precautions." Myles put his hand under Korbin's head and lifted it upright, putting the glass to his lips, "...ready?" Korbin nodded.

Myles slowly poured the liquid into Korbin's mouth and the steel mummy cringed as he forced the drink down his throat. When the glass was empty, Myles set it down, grabbed the syringe and placed it over the small chain opening he left to expose Korbin's arm; because of the chain's constriction, the vein protruded just enough but when Myles poked the needle into the skin, the vein moved. He tried again and missed. After two more failed attempts, Myles wiped away the tiny streams of blood; *...forgot paper towel.* Underneath the red fluid, however, the skin already healed and he gently pinched on the vein; *You better hold.* He stuck the needle in and, finally hitting the vein, he pushed the medicine into Korbin's body; blood immediately oozed out around the needle.

When he pulled the needle out, a squirt of blood shot out at Myles' shirt.

"Shit!" he yelled. He quickly put his gloved thumb over the wound, stopping the flow. After a minute, he hesitantly removed his hand, wiped away the excess blood and Korbin's skin was flawless—no needle marks.

"Alright, Korbin...I'm—" he began, looking over at Korbin's face to find him unconscious—completely sedated. Myles took off his glove and pulled out his phone: 7:32PM; *Get upstairs and block the door.* Myles quickly looked around, grabbed the glass and syringe then ran up the stairs, slamming the door shut.

He dropped the glass and syringe on the counter— cringing at the careless move—then looked back to find them still intact. He then walked back to the door; the fresh-cut four by fours were stacked neatly, ready for their bizarre purpose. Myles picked up the first piece, placed one end flush against the door and proceeded to push the other end against the side of the counter; his momentum suddenly stopped as the temporary brace hung passed the counter's edge too far—half an inch.

Myles leaned over and examined the wood's end and scoffed, "...dammit."

He set the four by four on the hallway floor, then reached back to grab another; again, the tip slammed against the corner of the counter, extending too far. With a low grunt, he tossed the wood next to the other piece in the hallway and grabbed another; then another...then another. His stomach churned as his body swelled with panic and when the next piece failed, he quickly placed it back on top of the pile; he lined it up with the remaining pieces—all equal length—all too long.

"Fuck!" he yelled, chucking the top piece against the couch; *Off by half an inch! Why didn't you take your time and get an accurate measure?! You had tons of time! Stupid son of a—*

The muffled sound of chains rustling on concrete traveled through the kitchen floor and Myles stopped. He put his ear down, flat with the linoleum surface as the chains continued; his eyes widened as his mouth gaped wide open; *...shit! Your gun!*

Myles sprinted to the garage and into his car. He grabbed the gun and struggled to pull it from the holster under the dash, "C'mon!" Finally remembering to push on the spring-lock, the gun dislodged. He grabbed it, the used clip and two spares, then ran out of the garage and stopped; he heard nothing. He looked over at the small basement window at the bottom of the house; *...it can't* *get you from there.* He tiptoed over the cement patio and ducked down to the window's level.

Through the blurred glass, Korbin's head rested right above a small pool of vomit and blood but, other than the momentum of his changing body, he hadn't moved; *...still out.* His facial bones started to break and reform with distortion as they did the night before.

Over the next several minutes that Korbin transformed, Myles loaded the magazine into his gun and cocked a bullet into the chamber. The entire change was happening as it did the other night but the constricting chains were cutting into the growing body and the wounds instantly healed around the metal links.

When the change appeared to have finally finished, the animal slowly rose its head—slower than when it woke last night. Its head kept rising and dropping as the neck muscles failed to hold it. Eventually, the animal started to roll around and when it rolled toward the window, Myles caught its black eyes; they were half open and its jaw opened and closed with low grumbles.

*It's working; son of a bitch...it's holding.* Only a few minutes passed when the top chain—around the animal's suddenly-tense shoulders—snapped.

Myles' eyes widened and the animal's sluggish movement quickened in deliberate and frantic motions. Trying to free itself from the bindings, its head and body jerked in repetitious gestures and its hind legs pushed itself in half circles on the floor; its growling grew with fierce intensity and aggravation.

*...shit; it's* not *holding. What the hell you going to do? What the* fuck *are you going to do? You have nothing barricading the door—oh like* that's *going to do a damn thing! ...the necklace. It didn't work before—you don't know if it'll work now. Are you seriously going to—no choice.*

With another loud *snap* of the chains, two more broken ends rattled on the floor as severed pieces flew across the basement; *Go now!*

Myles sprinted back into the house and grabbed the silver jewelry from the counter top and just as he reached the door, he stopped; *How you going to get close enough?* A louder growl echoed through the floor, catching Myles' attention; then he looked at the back door and sprinted back outside.

Bursting through the garage door, he skimmed around the front corner of his car to the far corner of the garage and grabbed the rake leaning against the wall. He shook as the adrenaline tainted his blood and suffocated his body; his pulse was racing and his stomach practically turned inside out. After a minute of constantly looking back toward the house—maintaining an ambiguous mental countdown—he finally managed to secure the chain around the rake's prongs, his trembling hands failed to fasten the links together.

"C'mon you bitch!" he shouted and on the fifth attempt, the hook finally latched and he sprinted back to the house.

Stopping at the basement door, he gripped the door knob and paused, closing his eyes, "*God...*" he whispered, "*I know I don't pray to you...ever; but please, keep me safe. If*

252

*I'm going to die tonight, make it quick and painless."* At the sound of another louder growl, Myles' eyes popped open and he yanked on the door.

He descended the stairs quickly until the last step where he stopped; he peeked his head around the corner and the animal's eyes were already locked on him; its lips slowly curled as its mouth opened; another chain had already broken. Myles pulled his head back out of sight and took a deep breath then emerged from the stairwell.

Holding his long weapon at the ready, he walked forcefully to the next room but stopped as the animal spun around, facing its head toward its captor and started pushing forward along the floor. Though not seeing it with his auric vision, Myles cringed and held back the urge to vomit as the curse's sickening energy burned its way through every level of his consciousness.

When the animal was only ten feet away, Myles held the rake like a hunter's spear with the silver accessory aimed at the animal's head and it continued pushing forward; *God, help me; please keep me safe; don't let this thing—*

With a foot of distance suddenly between the animal's head and the rake, the animal squinted its eyes and quickly whipped its head to the side with a low, whimpering grumble. It immediately refocused its eyes on Myles and when it straightened its head in front of the weapon again, it immediately pulled away a second time.

*...yes. Yes!* Myles followed the animal's head with the rake and it continued to pull out of the rake's path; *Touch its head.* Myles reached further and rested the rake on the

animal's head; it froze and trembled, sizzling underneath the silver. A small line of steam rose into the air. The animal groaned until Myles removed the rake—peeling off a strip of burned hair and melted flesh—and then it dropped its head for a moment. The animal jerked its head up with a snarl as it regained composure. Myles slammed the rake back down on the animal's head.

He looked up at the ceiling—at Heaven, "*Thank you.*" he said in a shaky whisper; *Okay...just keep the rake on it; you can manage another night without sleep. Just, don't let it melt a hole in its brain—in Korbin's brain.*

For the rest of the night, Myles kept the silver pressed against the animal—frequently changing spots on its head and the exposed spaces of its body.

When the first rays of morning sun gleamed through the window, Myles hesitantly removed the rake, pulling it away. The animal raised its head and let out a few soft moans before dropping it back down and closing its eyes.

Myles watched as the animal transformed back to its human form. Its hair dropped as it shed from the shrinking body. The claws grew out until breaking at the tips of Korbin's fingernails and the teeth pushed themselves out, falling onto the floor. Half an hour passed before Myles could recognize Korbin and as his body completed its transformation, Myles closed his eyes, embracing the euphoric relief and immediately succumbed to his exhaustion.

<><><>

Myles woke that afternoon in a panic. When his eyes regained focus, he found Korbin surrounded by fur and detached claws and fangs; the chains were embedded beneath his healed skin; *Oh God, that's disgusting; now you have to cut them out.*

Still hoping this would all be a repeat of yesterday morning—Korbin remaining unconscious for the next several hours—Myles walked upstairs, grabbed a large, serrated knife from the kitchen, and headed back down for the makeshift surgical procedure, only to find Korbin waking up; *It's not the morning; he was already passed out for those morning hours. He's just going to have to suck it up.* Myles dragged Korbin back into the other room where the cement floor led to a drain; after a sincere apology, he began to cut.

After two hours of synchronized slicing, unlocking and fishing the chains from Korbin's flesh, Myles was covered in the student's blood. Beneath the chains, Billy's clothes were shredded so Myles grabbed some of his own and re-dressed Korbin before taking him upstairs. After showering himself, Myles brought a hose down to the basement and washed whatever blood he could find down the basement drain.

When he returned upstairs, Korbin was once again paralyzed by pain as he laid on the couch. Myles knelt in front of him, holding the silver necklace he removed from the rake, "Okay; again...I'm sorry about the extra pain but I had to get the chains out of your skin."...*blink;*

"Remember this necklace? Well...turns out it works. I was actually able to keep you—*it*—at bay. So I'm going to put it on you; tonight, I have to chain you up again—I'll probably just pin the necklace down by the chains—but...I don't know, I guess we'll see what happens."

Korbin blinked in approval and Myles wrapped the chain around his neck. He then took the wood pile back out to the garage and proceeded to cut the last half-inch off each piece in preparation for the next night.

As the day progressed, Korbin regained a sense of movement; but as the time drew closer to moonrise, he started groaning with a burning sensation underneath his skin and a new throbbing in his head gradually increased every few minutes.

Myles immediately took him downstairs and individually wrapped Korbin's arms, legs and torso with silver wire he'd bought at a different hardware store in the late afternoon. Keeping the silver pendant around his neck, he re-wrapped him in the bloody chains—and a few freshly purchased ones—and again, dosed Korbin with Billy's drugs; *At the very least, he won't feel whatever that extra pain was—had to be the silver.*

When Korbin fell unconscious, Myles went back upstairs and barricaded the door with the, now correctly sized, four by fours. His gun was holstered behind him while gripping the rake—armed with an additional silver necklace from his trip for new chains—and he walked outside, peering into the basement window.

Besides small amounts of steam from his body, Korbin never moved the entire night; there was no rustling around...and no transformation; *Silver fucking works*. When the sun rose again, Myles went into the living room, sat in his recliner and fell asleep.

# 21

Amanda laid unconscious in the hospital bed, attached to numerous tubes and sensors; her heart rate was steady. In the *I.C.U.* at *Southwest Health Center*, Amanda's mother sat next to the bed, reading a magazine and continually glancing up at her daughter with disappointed anticipation.

The emergency surgeons managed to re-attach the severed muscles in Amanda's shoulder but determined the likely result of her injury would render her arm useless; at the doctors' suggestion, her parents highly considered amputation.

However, beneath the heavy bandaging, Amanda's shoulder had already begun repairing itself. Her severed nerves actually regrew with fresh endings. Bypassing the thick, surgical stitching, her muscle fibers fused back together with perfection. The cells of her protective flesh re-bonded to become whole, creating solid damage-less skin. Yet her body failed to repair the scar—the constant reminder of what happened and of what she would become. Invisible to the unworthy eye, the curse that plagued Korbin made its way over and through Amanda's tiny body and her eyes slowly opened.

<><><>

Shanna texted Korbin the moment she and her parents arrived home. As anxious as she was to hear from him, she failed to notice his lack of response, fighting the terrorizing images eating away at her subconscious.

At 6:03PM—sitting on the couch while Rich prepared dinner—Shanna's heart jumped to her throat as her brain released a dose of—much needed—euphoric chemicals throughout her body. Korbin's text was the first thing to finally consume her consciousness with a sense of optimism and she wasted no time in opening the message:

"*Hey u. I finally got ur text. sorry i didn't respond. I got hurt too and i'm at home right now...thats why I can't be there. Dunno what hurts more, my body or that i'm not there for u. I'm so sorry and when I'm cleared to move, ill come see u. K?*"

Shanna's eyes widened as the euphoria faded and her stomach churned; *Oh my God! What happened?* She immediately began tapping her thumbs on the screen: "*Oh my God! Korbin! How bad are you hurt? Did you go to* the hospital? Do you want me to come out there?" She hit send and Korbin's response chimed her phone within seconds:

"No. I want u to rest and get better. Doc says just a few sprains and Im just REALLY sore. the thing, like, tackled me and sent me flying. "

Shanna took a deep breath and continued tapping on her phone: "I'm not actually hurt, though. I just got really scared so it's fine."

...new message: "I'll be fine babe; my concern is u getting better. The faster u feel better, the better I feel :)"

Having already trickled back down to her chest, her heart sunk just a bit. The message's price for a small growth of endearing goose bumps was an underlying despair; she shook her head and typed another message: "...you sure?"

...............new message: "S'all good, really. When we both get better, we'll meet up. I promise."

Shanna smiled, embracing another wave of euphoria as she typed: "Alright :) Just keep me posted ok? Get better soon :*"

...new message: "I will!"

Shanna locked her phone and set it down as she let herself sink into the couch; she closed her eyes and instantly drifted to sleep...

*Further into the yard, behind the shed, the same little girl's hair—now blonde with a few brown streaks—glistened in the moonlight as she whispered in the ear of another little girl with blonde hair. Shanna struggled to recognize her but as her eyes traveled down, the enormous hole in the girl's chest tipped her off; Samantha James. Her blue skin blended perfectly with the tint of the night sky. The mysterious girl ran off toward the opposite side of the house—her feet flinging the black puddle up in the air.*

*Samantha looked at Shanna and smiled as she waved, "Hi."*

*"Hey..." Shanna replied.*

*"...I don't have a heart." Samantha stated and Shanna just stared at her, "Maybe someone can give me theirs?" Then Samantha walked a few steps over where Jake suddenly appeared with his back to Shanna.*

*He looked over his shoulder with a calm look, "I can always be with you." Shanna remained motionless and silent.*

*Samantha walked in front of Jake, blocked from Shanna's view; with a loud* thud *and* crack, *Jake gasped for air and started grunting. Through the opening between his legs, Samantha's legs trembled as she balanced on her tiptoes; she side-stepped, catching herself each time she fell off balance. Jake grunted as if something was tugging at him and at the sound of a loud tearing, his head slumped down, motionless, as he still remained upright.*

*Samantha stepped to the side, in full view, as her hands were stuffed into her chest's large cavity; when she pulled her hands away, Jake's heart started beating and as she looked at Shanna, she grew taller.*

*. As Samantha's limbs grew and her face molded into a new one, Shanna cringed when Amanda was suddenly standing next to Jake.*

*"Now you can't resist us." Amanda said with a smile...*

Only twenty minutes passed before Shanna woke in shock; her eyes weighed three thousand tons as she pushed herself up on the couch.

Her dad peeked from around the kitchen corner, "You alright?"

Shanna nodded, "...dozed off again."

Rich sighed then returned into the kitchen for a moment. He walked into the living room with a glass of chocolate milk and handed it to Shanna.

"Thanks." She said, taking the glass as Rich headed back to the kitchen. She stirred the milk with the spoon he left in the glass, then took a sip; her tingling nerves and racing pulse took their time calming themselves. She gripped the glass firmly with both hands as it displayed the slightest hint of trembling.

The doorbell rang and Shanna jumped; her anxiety shot right back up. She set the glass on the table and let her head fall into her palm; *...oh my God.* Even when Rich opened the door for Molly, Shanna's shivering muscles ached. Nevertheless, she slowly stood from the couch and met her friend halfway for a big hug.

"My God," Molly began, "How you feeling?"

"...been better." Shanna answered as they parted and walked back to the couch.

Shanna plopped back into her original position while Molly sat one cushion over, facing Shanna and pulling her knees close to her chest. "Well it's good to see you finally awake."

Shanna tilted her head back, "...barely. I haven't really slept since I woke up in the hospital."

"No?" Molly insisted.

"Nope;" Shanna answered, shaking her head, "every time I finally fall asleep I keep having nightmares then wake up after only a few minutes; and my body, like, tenses up while I'm dreaming so...double exhaustion."

"Wow. I'm sorry Shanna; but, still, I'm glad you're alright and awake—even a little bit. I went by the hospital twice and you were out both times."

"Thanks." Shanna said as she looked at Molly, "I'm sorry for worrying you."

"I forgive you." Molly added with a smile.

A tiny smirk barely made its way across Shanna's face and she turned her head back; she sipped her chocolate milk, "...what have you heard?"

Molly paused for a moment and a look of hesitation consumed her eyes, "...you really wanna talk about it right now?"

"Not really but I'm asking for something specific."

Molly shifted her knees down onto the cushion and sat on top of her feet, "Well, besides you, just that one

263

student was killed and one injured that went to the hospital."

"...you don't know who they were?"

"No." Molly said shaking her head and her eyebrows slowly turned upside down with concern.

Shanna dipped her head, staring right at her hands resting in her lap, "The injured one was Amanda...the one that was killed was Jake."

Molly's jaw dropped, "...no?"

"...mm-hmm," Shanna assured, "I was standing right next to him as it happened." Tears leaked from her eyes.

Molly's hand rose to cover her mouth; her other hand reached out toward Shanna but quickly recoiled as she looked away, "...oh God; *Jake?*"

As Shanna's chest convulsed with crying hiccups, Molly scooted closer and wrapped one arm around Shanna's shoulders and caressed her head with the other.

Rich peeked from around the corner for a moment, then shook his head with another heavy sigh as he looked away. He returned to the frying pan on the stove's front burner, where mushrooms and onions sizzled as he stirred them around; he then reached over to the pan on the back burner, poked the two steaks and turned them over.

He looked back into the living room and noticed Shanna compose herself; he paused for a pondering moment, staring at them as if they were eight years old again; he calmly approached.

"Hey, um..." he began in a soft tone, catching Molly's attention, "...I need to make a quick phone call; can you just, keep an eye on the food, quick?" Molly nodded as she wiped her eyes, "Okay...I'll be right back."

Rich walked down the hall to a small office, leaving the door open just a crack as he pulled out his phone and dialed his wife.

"Hello?" Vikki said over the phone.

"Hey babe."

"Hey, hun; how's everything? she asked.

"...I dunno; Shanna had another nightmare and Molly just got here but she started cryin' again; so did Molly."

Vikki sighed, "What are we supposed to do? She hasn't slept in days."

"I think I'm gonna get her on some sleeping meds." he answered in a defeated tone.

"You think she's gonna go for that?"

"I think so but, quite frankly, I don't care; she needs sleep."

"Yeah, she does; what are you gonna put her on?"

"I dunno. I'll grab some samples from the office and...just start seeing what works and what doesn't—just so she can get some sleep. Then we can figure out long term help."

"Okay."

Back in the living room, Molly gently pushed on Shanna's shoulders and Shanna pulled away from her friend. Molly caressed her head a few more times, "Have you heard from Korbin?"

Shanna nodded her head as she sniffled, "Yeah, he said he got hurt by the thing too. I offered to go see him but I mentioned my nightmares and he wants me to get better first. He promises we'll meet up when we're both better."

Molly nodded in acceptance, "That's really considerate of him." She looked away and the slightest hint of confusion hung in her eyes; *...does he not wanna see his girlfriend? Oh stop; it's Korbin. He's always been that considerate.* "I'm gonna go check on the food quick; okay?" She pushed herself off the couch and walked toward the kitchen.

Shanna nodded and wiped her face. She leaned on the couch arm and laid her head in her hand; with a deep sigh, she closed her eyes and immediately dozed off...

*Once again in the darkness of her kitchen, Shanna faced the back door; as her parents shuffled in their bed upstairs, she looked up at the ceiling for a moment, then returned her eyes to the door and locked her gaze. She took a step and the floor groaned lightly; No...take normal steps. The door was silent when you opened it normally. Picking up her pace into a calm stroll, she reached the door in total silence; she turned the knob and just as she was about to pull the door open, a voice giggled and said, "...they'll never find me." Her momentum froze and her veins burned with adrenaline.*

*Obeying her sense of direction, Shanna slowly turned toward the kitchen corner then took a few short steps toward the table. The voice released another muffled giggle—fighting the urge to laugh—and Shanna quivered as her neck hairs*

266

stood straight out. When she finally reached the table, she ducked down and sitting on the floor, facing the wall between the two furthest chairs, was the recurring little girl; her hair was now evenly mixed with blonde and brown. Shanna stared at her for a moment, then crawled under the table and as she was about to whisper to her, she stopped; Talk normally.

"Excuse me." she finally said, and the little girl turned with a deep, heavy gasp and Shanna jumped, "No, no, no, no, no; I'm not gonna hurt you."

Pinning herself against the wall, the little girl panted heavily as she stared at Shanna, "I know," she said, "you just scared me."

"I'm sorry." Shanna said with a sympathetic grin.

"It's okay."

Shanna smiled and crawled further under the table, "Who are you?"

The little girl smiled and crawled under the table, meeting Shanna halfway, "I'm us."

Shanna stared at her with confusion, "Who's us?"

"...us." she repeated then crawled closer, with only an inch of space between their faces, "...say thank you."

"For what?" Shanna asked.

"For being alive; it could have killed you."

"...I'm eternally grateful."

The ceiling echoed with quick footsteps and Shanna's anxiety had a reverse-effect; she immediately pulled herself out from under the table and ran over to the stairs. She watched from the first floor, waiting for her parents' the sprinting steps to carry them into sight but the footsteps stopped when the little girl's scream echoed from the kitchen.

Shanna continued watching for a moment—nothing. When she walked back into the kitchen, she noticed a long, dark streak on the floor, stretching from under the table and out the back door. When her feet began to move of their own will, Shanna examined her body and flexed her muscles to stop but her feet continued onward, stepping over the streak until she was right in front of the door. When she opened it, the back light turned on, throwing the smallest amount of light on the streak, revealing a deep, red glisten; ...blood...oh God. That poor girl! To her surprise, unlike the sound of first hearing the girl's mysterious voice, her body didn't experience a physiological reaction—no adrenaline, no anxiety, no nauseating fear.

Still under the command of her body, Shanna walked outside and when she reached the shed, the ground sloshed as she stepped in the same puddle of thick liquid and goo; it was warm with a tacky consistency. When the stench of iron filled her nose, Shanna turned around; her shadow wasn't blocking the light but the substance was still black. It wasn't until she lifted her foot, allowing it to trickle back to the grass, that she saw the same shiny red as the streak inside and she still felt nothing.

That anxiety-switch flipped right back on when an invisible force pulled her feet out from under her—splashing blood everywhere—and dragged her to the middle of the yard. It raised her right to her feet and a deep growling sounded right behind her head, breathing down her neck. The force turned her around and standing outside, just in front of the *door, was Amanda with a pistol aimed right at her. One second passed and, in a consuming light, the bullet exploded from the gun without a sound...*

Rich and Molly watched Shanna from a few feet away; every muscle in her, now, rigid body tightened and locked her spine in an arched position.

"Why can't we wake her up?" Molly asked.

Rich shook his head, "Unless she starts flailing around or harming herself, it's better to let it ride out. If we wake her, she may wake up in a worse shock—maybe swinging at one of us—but if she wakes from it on her own, she's more likely to forget it happened."

Molly glanced at Rich, pondering a moment, "But she hasn't forgotten any of them so far."

"...I know." Rich added in a defeated tone; finally, Shanna's body relaxed—slowly releasing every muscle and allowing herself to drop back into the couch. As she sunk into the cushion, she released a little whimper and the flesh around her eyes turned bright pink as she began to cry. In a few sobbing breaths, she let out a loud yell and her eyes popped open.

Rich cautiously approached her and crouched down, "Shanna?"

Still sobbing, she squeezed her eyes shut for a moment then turned her head toward her father, "...I can't take this anymore, Daddy."

Rich stepped forward, right next to the couch and placed his hand on Shanna's cheek as he kissed her forehead, "I know, sweetheart," Shanna closed her eyes again and rolled over, burrowing her head into Rich's chest and crying even louder; he wrapped his arms around her shoulders and kissed her again, "Shhh...it's okay sweetheart. It'll be okay, I promise."

Molly went into the kitchen and filled a glass with cold water; then she grabbed a fresh dish rag and ran it under the faucet. She walked quickly to the bathroom and grabbed the box of tissues, then returned to the kitchen for the glass and rag and walked back to the living room. She set the glass and tissues on the table next to the couch, handed Rich the cold rag and took a seat in a chair at the far end of the living room. She pulled out her phone and started a new text message to Korbin:

*"I'm sorry for adding extra pressure but as soon as you get better, you need to come see Shanna; she really needs you."*

*...message sent*

# 22

After two days of rest and recuperation, Korbin could finally walk on his own but the pain lingered nonetheless. He was unable to lift his arms above his shoulders and turning his head required a full torso rotation. Limping more on his left leg than his right, he walked as if he'd ridden a horse, nonstop, for the last week. Despite the firing of his tortured nerves—serving as his only reminder of what happened to him—he embraced the pain and forced himself to move as needed.

Myles brought him home to Muskego, taking Korbin's father, Jim, by surprise. When Jim saw his suffering son and the man escorting him inside, his stomach churned with demanding curiosity. Myles introduced himself and asked if he could sit down—urging Jim to sit down as well—and proceeded to inform Jim of the curse that plagued Korbin. It wasn't until after they pulled up an instantly viral internet video and a local news report on Myles' cell phone that Jim's skeptical mind opened.

"Just, uh...just gimme a minute." he began hesitantly. He scrolled back through the footage and watched again as a shaky camera phone recorded Korbin's entire transformation.

"Consider this, Mr. Voss..." Myles interjected, "...police found remains of the one person that was killed; there really was only a few pieces left but coroner confirmed the remains were real. And...look at how much pain your son's in."

Jim looked over at Korbin with concern.

"I blacked out, Dad. I couldn't tell you anything about that night so all I have to go on is all this pain, the blood stains I woke up with the next day and *his* word." Korbin said wearily and Jim looked back at the video, paused on a frame showing the animal looking through the Activity Center window, "Dad...you don't have to believe the video, or the news report...or Myles; just believe me."

Jim rubbed his head and scoffed, "I'm sorry bud; I'm sorry you're hurt and I wish I could believe this is the real reason why, but...c'mon. Even *you* said you blacked out; how do you know someone—or even this guy—didn't...like, drug you?" Jim glared at Myles, "...no offense."

Myles smirked, "Uh...none taken. If you really believed that though, I think you would've kicked me out

272

by now. If I was so deranged, I probably would've done something to harm you already."

Jim shook his head and stood up, walking in a circle, "This is...*insane*." he looked back at Korbin, "What do you believe?"

"I believe Myles." Korbin answered confidently.

Jim paced another small circle, then redirected his gaze at Myles, "...and you're a psychic?"

Myles nodded.

After another small circle, Jim sat back down and looked at Korbin, "Look, bud...the way the details connect is peculiar and...interesting but...I'm sorry; I just can't accept it. However, I trust you. If this is something you gotta go along with—for...*whatever* reason—I trust you won't let it get you seriously hurt; it's bad enough that whatever you did put you in this much agony."

In a sudden impulse, Myles rolled his eyes and dipped his head with a heavy sigh; his eyes widened when he realized the challenging tone of his gesture; *Oh that's great...piss the guy off.*

Jim looked over at Myles with a condescending glare, "Well what do you expect? Here I am goin' about a regular day—at most, worrying about my son being sick in his dorm—then you bring him in, badly limping, and start talking about curses and psychics!"

"I know, I know; I'm sorry, Mr. Voss;" Myles began, nodding as he held his hand up in defense, "It just comes as a shock to me when someone can't see passed skepticism, despite any presented evidence."

"C'mon! You've shown me a video and some digital news reports. How easily could someone forge *either* of those?!"

"Yes, you're right;" Myles added, "It was an impulsive reaction and I didn't mean to offend you. I'm sorry."

Jim stood back up and walked his circle again—faster steps now, "Do you have any proof?"

"That you can see in person? Not that I can think of; the full moon cycle's done until next month."

Jim stared at Korbin for a moment, then back at Myles, "You can't do some psychic stuff?"

*Here we go again; how many more people do you have to show off to? When this is all over—if you survive—just keep your mouth shut.* Myles looked at Korbin—at the curse—with hesitation and inhaled deeply as his eyes returned to Jim, "Can we go out to the back yard?"

Jim nodded and started toward the back door through the kitchen and Myles followed.

Using most of his energy to keep Korbin's curse from penetrating his consciousness during the demonstration, Myles took Jim's hand and struggled to pass the skeptical barriers of Jim's subconscious mind.

Myles' vision was hazy and weak as the chafing burn lingered in his mind—scratching at his brain stem—and it trickled all the way down his spine as it clawed to break in; he focused even harder, keeping it at bay and triggering the small pressure of a future headache...

*...need something big;* Within Jim's perspective, passing through his memories of the last sixteen years—raising Korbin as a single father—Myles finally came to a moment in time that captivated his attention and the tiny sudden ounce of adrenaline increased his strength, allowing him to push the curse's effect away just a bit farther.

It was the morning when Jim woke in his bed to find an empty spot next to him; casually calling out the name, *Sara,* he got up and started looking around the house but soon panicked when he could not find her; *...a little farther—the day before.*

Coasting one day earlier, Myles continued watching through Jim's eyes; a baseball game aired on television when the front door opened and a young woman with long hair—that covered her face—dragged her feet inside; she was crying heavily as her head faced down at the floor.

"*...Andrew.*" was all she said; she continuously repeated the phrase and every time she attempted to elaborate, she cried louder and harder. Eventually, Jim lifted her up and took her to their bedroom; Korbin peeked from his bedroom doorway.

"It's alright bud. Mommy's just tired." Jim said.

He laid Sara in the bed and took her shoes off; when he reached for her hair and brushed it away, the face of a woman in her early twenties was almost perfectly clear; *What the...?* Myles immediately tapped back into his own memory...

The Jane Doe lying comatose in the hospital when Myles visited Oma—the woman that first introduced him

275

to Korbin's haunting curse—had the same face as Sara; *...the same woman. He married Jane Doe?! The curse didn't jump to Korbin; it was passed down from his mother!...*

Returning to the present reality, Myles released Jim's hand and paused a moment. He then slowly looked up into Jim's eyes with a look of concerned curiosity, "...your wife, Sara, went missing and you never found her."

Jim's eyebrows turned upside down and he opened his mouth to speak but paused a moment before finding a desirable response, "Korbin could've told you about that."

"True," Myles replied with a deep breath, "but did you ever tell him about her time in the hospital? With bandaging around her chest and wrist?"

"...no." Jim answered as his eyes widened, "You saw that?"

"Not in your memory—my own. I saw her face in *your* memory, then I remembered. When your wife was lying in a coma, I was visiting my grandmother at the same time; their rooms were just down the hall from each other. Long story short, I heard growling from Jane Doe—Sara's room, went to look, saw flashes of the curse that has Korbin right now—though I didn't know it was a curse then—it got a hold of me and I immediately felt it was bad. My only question is...why was she in the hospital?"

Jim looked away for a moment and took a deep breath, "Well I didn't marry her until a year after she was outta the hospital. We found her behind a pub; she'd been mugged and hurt really bad. We called the ambulance and they took her; that was the last I saw of her until she was out of the hospital. Her family got word, took her home to recover, then she moved back and we started dating."

Back in the house, Korbin laid on the couch, staring at his phone as his thumb swiped across the screen. He stared intently at every photo he had with Shanna, embracing every intoxicating thought about her, conjured by both memory and fantasy. When he finally came to the photo they took just before parting last year—outside the bar—he stopped and gently ran his thumb over her face and inhaled deeply; suddenly...his mind went blank. After a moment, he glanced up, toward the open back door; *What am I doing home? What's dad doin' outside?* He forced himself off the couch—confused by the pain—and headed toward the back door. He stepped outside just as Myles was finishing his explanation to Jim, of why he wouldn't be able to find Sara; *Who the hell's that?*

As Myles regretfully explained that he would need a closer contact to see where she was, he was oblivious to the backdoor's commotion; when he finally stopped talking, Korbin chimed in..."What's goin' on?"

Myles jumped as he turned around, dropping every one of his defenses. The moment he laid eyes on Korbin—without any physical contact—Myles' consciousness fused with the curse and he froze as he slipped into its burning grasp...

The same stabbing sensation he felt in his arm during his first encounter foxed at the base of his skull, trickling throughout his body. An ambient, growling breath sounded as he stared into a consuming red cloud. As his consciousness focused on the void, an image slowly appeared; *...the curse's consciousness?*

278

When the image revealed itself as Korbin—standing straight up, perfectly still—Myles cautiously approached him. Within the curse's grip, he felt Korbin's energy radiating stronger than anyone's he'd ever felt in the past. Despite the stabbing pain, Myles was still, somehow, in complete control over himself and his abilities and after a moment's pause, he allowed himself into *Korbin's* mind…

The first image that consumed Korbin's mind was Shanna's face and Myles immediately recognized her from his reading with Amanda; *So, Korbin,* you're *that strange girl's competition.* Eventually making his way beyond Korbin's fixation, Myles finally fixed his focus within Korbin's perspective and proceeded with his analysis.

The last memory Korbin had before his curse transformed him—even before Myles approached him— he was with Shanna in the college library; watching her gather her books, Myles' *E.S.P.* actually absorbed Shanna's energy at a lesser level than Korbin's and he quickly refocused his mind but as he attempted to transfer himself to her consciousness, nothing happened. He tried again to no avail and after a third time, he finally gave up; *So…you can still feel other energies through the curse, but can't read multiple people. Nope; this wasn't difficult enough.*

Still in Korbin's perspective, Shanna had asked Korbin if he was sure he didn't want to join her at the gathering she was going to and, admitting a priority for homework, he denied with a heavy regret. She walked over to his side and gently pressed her lips against his.

After a short, passionate kiss that triggered the euphoric river of brain chemicals to Korbin's body, Shanna left and he went back to his homework while Shanna's face continually appeared in his mind; *Well he's clearly stuck on her.*

Traveling further back in time, Myles viewed Korbin and Shanna's entire relationship up to that point. He continued traveling back, viewing all of Korbin's life until he reached the same stopping point he saw when he first read Korbin in the lecture hall—the thick wall of fog that refused to dissipate. This time, upon reaching the wall, it finally disappeared and Myles actually pulled himself from Korbin's now five-year old perspective, standing outside his body and everything became still.

The ominous growl returned and was now directly behind Myles, melting the back of his neck. As Korbin and everyone else stood frozen in that time, Myles glared at the slowly lifting fog, then looked back at Korbin; *...guess you can't see through their eyes if they don't remember.* Myles turned back to the fog and walked into its clearing as it pulled back like a vaporous curtain.

*Wait...get your bearings quick; you tapped into the curse's consciousness, then into Korbin's—where, apparently, you can feel the energies of others around him. Before, when his memory ran out, there was just the fog; now the fog lifted but the only way to move forward was to leave Korbin's perspective—viewing everything from your own eye...third person mode—then everyone froze. Obviously, Korbin can't see what he doesn't remember—the curse is remembering. It's showing you everything and everyone its host has—or had—ties to. Okay...this is painful but...definitely fascinating.*

Myles continued through the fog and as he appeared to reach the end of it, more frozen people emerged; he was back in Korbin's house and the little five-year old stood peeking from his door, staring at the next door over. Myles walked into the bedroom where Jim stood over his wife, Sara—Jane Doe—and her energy was just as strong as Korbin's. Hesitantly, he crouched right in front of her and, with a deep breath, shifted his mind into Sara's consciousness. Nestled in her perspective, Myles paused from the moment Sara laid crying in the bed and pushed forward in time; *Let's see where she is...*

# 23

*Follow her. Find out where she wound up;* Myles pushed himself forward through Sara's consciousness only to an abrupt halt. He stood in the same red fog he reached at the edge of Korbin's memory and backtracked to her last memory he could see.

She was a naked mess and crouched low to the ground with another person directly in front of her. Myles stepped out of her mind, into his omniscient role and time froze. He suffocated on the hostile vulnerability again. Searching for a threat he noticed the surrounding trees and familiar stone path; the lack of horizon cued him to be standing at an elevated level and he quickly turned. Behind Sara was the highest edge of a cliff and across the void was a second, mirroring rockface. Between them both, five hundred feet below was a three-acre lake and beach; *...bluffs. She ran to Devil's Lake?* Seeing nothing, he returned focus on Sara and the other person and his eyes widened…

*What is Oma doing here? How the hell did she get up here on her own?!* Myles' eyes filled with rage; *What the hell is Oma doing? And what's that bitch doing to Oma?!* Oma's face was straining in pain. Myles glared impulsively at Sara, ready to defend his family but the pain in *her* face calmed him; …*The curse is hurting them?* Oma was knelt down, eye to eye with the young woman; one of her hands was placed on Sara's head and the other over her chest. Oma was withered and decrepit now; her body seemed to have devoured its own muscles, leaving behind only sagging scraps. Myles was careful not to stare at Sara's body; *There's nothing after this…what the hell happened? Go back.* Myles focused his mind to continue back through the curse then froze…

The growling breaths behind his head now circled slowly around him, inches from his face; *It's watching you…taunting;* he jumped as an appendage grazed his shoulders. Myles' pulse raced and he struggled to swallow the lump in his throat. When the invisible entity faded, Myles forced his mind back in time; *Forget all that for now. If Oma took care of it before, she had to have been able to do something again. But…that's probably how she died. You don't need to see that. Go back to what led to all of that…just get your eyes away from it…*

Traveling back—passed what appeared to be the night that led to Sara's suicide—right to the house where she cried on the bed, Myles stopped; *No...a little further.* He continued back, noticing a bizarre incident at a grocery store before she returned home but he kept going. Traveling over the previous and, apparently happy, five years of raising their son, Myles approached Sara's time in the hospital.

One night, when he and his parents were at home, Oma made her way into Sara's room; *Hold on; just start at the beginning—before this; look at everything going on. What's the beginning? All the way to when she was born?......no; you've got some of your own questions. Go to her mugging—the start of her and Jim's life together; that's beginning enough.* Myles continued further back, passed the hospital to the night Jim found her behind the pub.

Sara's twenty-one-year old hands trembled like an eighty-year-old as she gripped the knife. Huddled behind a dumpster on the side of a corner pub, her heart pounded against her ribs; every nerve in her body was electrified, convulsing her muscles. The tighter she squeezed the knife, the more it slipped in her warm, sweaty grasp.

Quickly switching the weapon to her free hand, she wiped her moist palm on her pant leg but sweat persisted. She switched the knife back to her first hand and finally placed the serrated blade against her wrist; each tooth pushed against her flesh, creating a lasting indentation; just before pushing the blade, she froze as hesitation locked her muscles in place; she stared into the night with

284

a wet blurry gaze. She looked back down at the knife, surged with scalding bravery. She gripped the handle, pushed the blade firmly onto her wrist and thrusted back and forth.

Violent shocks blasted up her arm and into her brain as she sawed through her wrist; as the flesh peeled back, blood quickly poured out and every severed nerve shocked her brain harder and harder. Tears welled in her eyes and she whimpered through her tightly pursed lips. Blood and tissue sloshed with each slice of the blade until she finally cut the artery. As red liquid spewed from her wrist, she sliced faster and harder, finally reaching the bone. Halfway into the marrow, Sara finally screamed.

She yanked the knife from her nearly-severed hand and, now shaking violently, lifted her arm, turning the blade toward her chest; she almost dropped it as the handle slipped in her blood-covered hand. Pointing the blade over her heart, she took three deep breaths, and thrust. As the knife pierced her chest, it suddenly stopped its forward motion. The tip pierced her skin and only part of her chest plate. Sara let out another loud scream and pushed on the knife handle; it slowly dug its way through the bone and the moment it reached the other side, its forward momentum shot the blade into her heart and almost through her back.

She gasped as blood poured violently from her chest—leaking internally, internally, all over her remaining organs and she fell back onto the pavement. As she stared into the sky, her body's temperature began to decrease and fatigue spread throughout her limbs; the burning ache of her wounds dulled to a slight throb. Slowly, her nerves shut down; fewer and fewer signals reached her brain as she lost feeling in her body from her scalp all the way down to her toes.

Sara sat up. All the sounds of the surrounding small Wisconsin town became a quiet echo; she turned around and looked at her dying body lying on the ground. Her eyes widened and her jaw dropped as she stood up; she looked at her hands finding no wounds. There was no blood on her—not even on her shoes. She placed her hand on the dumpster and the normal cold, hard texture didn't even register; nothing did. The cool breeze in the air, the scent of garbage...nothing. She'd done it; she killed herself.

As quickly as the smile of relief grew on her face, it disappeared; nothing happened. There were no welcoming bright lights; there were no fiery pits of hell opening for her...nothing.

Hearing only distant echoes of the living and feeling no sensations brought the smile back to her face; then a small burning sensation crept around her wrist; the tingling of a waking limb trickled into her hand, through her fingers and her smiled vanished again.

Sara's eyes squinted as she stared at her hand...nothing. She looked up and froze. After a moment, she stepped back to her bleeding corpse. She took slow, hesitant steps until she finally stood over her wounded arm; the bleeding stopped. She jumped as the same tingling surged in her chest. Staring wide-eyed at her body, she knelt down looking straight at her wrist and watched as it slowly began to heal itself; all the severed fibers of flesh, tendons, and muscles were growing back and re-attaching themselves. Sara squeezed her eyes shut and shook her head then looked down at the knife protruding from her chest; regenerating skin scabbed around the blade and she gasped. She stood up, turned, and started to run when the pub door opened and a small intoxicated group of people strolled out of the door, searching around the building.

"Now I *know* I heard a scream out here." one man said.

A small force pulled Sara to a stop. As the small-town, blue-collar group continued searching—drawing closer to the grisly scene—the force grew stronger and stronger. Sara was actually moving backward, sliding toward her body; even after digging her feet into the ground, she turned and saw herself drawing closer and closer.

There was no friction for her to grip; her spirit was returning to its vessel as it healed itself and returned to life. She fought—tearing her arms away from nothing—sprinting forward but still moving backward; she leaned forward, trying to crawl on all fours as she began to cry but the invisible force just sucked her back. She finally stopped moving and fell to the ground—giving in as she cried.

As Sara's spirit re-entered her body, a twenty-some-year younger, Jim, approached the dumpster and stopped. Despite how easily his height allowed him to see over the top, he crouched down and cautiously peeked around the corner; when a motionless foot, covered by a slipper-like shoe came into sight, he stopped and his eyes widened.

"...*oh shit.*" he whispered. As his heart sped up, he took a deep breath and continued around the dumpster to find Sara's body lying in a pool of blood—her hand almost severed and a knife sticking straight out of her chest. Jim began trembling and stood up, "Here! I found her!"

Everyone quickly gathered behind him; some gasped, a few others cringed, but they all just stared at Sara. Jim looked back and no one did anything.

"...*you think she's dead?*" a man asked in slurred speech and no one responded.

Careful not to step in her blood, Jim walked over, close to her face and slowly crouched down. Still shaking, he swallowed the knot in his throat.

"...*my god...*" he whispered. After another moment of examining her body, he reached his hand out but quickly pulled it back, grabbing it with his other hand; he squeezed tightly as it trembled. He took a deep breath, exhaling heavily then reached his hand out again, directing his fingertips to the side of Sara's neck; the closer he came, the slower he moved. The air reeked of the iron in Sara's blood and Jim gagged at both the stench and sight; he swallowed again, keeping the vomiting urge at bay. His hands shook even harder and more visibly as his fingertips brushed her cold flesh and, with a shudder, he pressed his index and middle finger into her neck. He held the spot for a few seconds—no pulse.

"She's gone." he said with a subtle nod. As he pulled his hand away, Sara's hand lifted gently; it brushed against Jim's arm and he jumped, falling back; his eyes and mouth gaped wide open as he stared at Sara's arm lifting in the air. His heart beat so fast and hard it began an irregular rhythm—almost skipping beats. His blood crashed through his veins as he pushed himself up against the fence, panting heavily; everyone else backed away, swearing and questioning what had just happened.

Sara's lungs sucked a deep, gasping breath. After a few more, Jim shook his head and approached Sara once more—faster now, less careful. Standing near her face, he looked down at her; her eyes slowly opened.

"Get an ambulance!" Jim shouted and one of the onlookers quickly ran back to the pub.

"Don't move," Jim began speaking to Sara, "you're hurt really bad. We're getting help for you."

Sara did not respond; when her eyes fully opened and re-focused, she looked at Jim; her throat clenched and she released a loud, violent scream.

Jim jumped again but remained upright as Sara's strong hand quickly reached up and grabbed his shirt. Pulling herself up close to his face, she locked on his gaze as tears poured from her eyes; with a broken voice, she said: "...*I'm sorry.*"

Jim's eyes were frozen and even as she fell unconscious, he never looked away...

*Well she definitely wasn't mugged. Go see what Oma was doing in her room.* Myles now moved forward along the time-line of Sara's memory—the curse's memory—passed the day he first met it in the hospital, right to the moment Oma reached her door that night, alone.

Releasing himself from Sara's consciousness, Myles stood outside her hospital room next to Oma and time was actually moving; *...well what the hell? Thought everyone froze when you stepped out of someone's consciousness.* When a nurse asked Oma what she was doing, Oma convincingly explained she just it necessary to give the *poor* Jane Doe a prayer. Hesitantly, the nurse obliged and allowed Oma to pass; *Not that anyone could deny a* "fragile" *little old lady.*

Inside the room, Oma walked right next to the bed and gently grabbed Sara's hand; she squeezed it with both hands and held it close to her chest. She dipped her head as she closed her eyes and stood absolutely still; *Uh...what is she doing?* Oma did nothing but hold Sara's hand and keep her eyes closed.

Myles focused on Sara's consuming curse and his auric sight translated it to that same dripping red cloud; he walked around and looked at Oma's face; it was calm and straight; *Just look and see what's going on in Oma's mind.* Myles focused his energy, preparing to transport into Oma's consciousness but nothing happened. He tried again and he remained right where he was standing; *What the hell?* He tried once more, this time flexing his muscles and his mind, holding it—pushing to get into Oma's mind—but, still, nothing happened; *Seriously?! You can't even get into* Oma's *mind?! What the hell is that—*

Oma inhaled deeply and gripped tighter on Sara's hand. She squeezed tighter and tighter, then began trembling.

290

"...Oma?" Myles' voice echoed. When her jaw dropped, blood dripped from her nose and she let out a soft whimper, "Oma!" Myles ran to the door and walked right through it; he frantically looked around, "Help! I need help over here!" Then, he stopped and paused; he looked over at the nurses sitting at the front desk, then back toward Sara's door; the nurse that allowed Oma to pass waited patiently for her to finish; ...*they can't hear you,* genius. *This already happened.*

Myles shook his head and walked back into the room. Having already released Sara's hand, Oma rested one of her palms on Sara's bed railing, panting heavily. She held the other hand up to her face and Myles walked back around to see a trickle of blood seeping between her fingers. He looked back at Sara and focused on her curse; now, only a small, glowing red hint of the dripping red smoke remained over the middle of her chest it laid flat against her skin. Myles' eyes widened and he looked at Oma; *You subdued it. How the hell did you do that?*

Finally, Oma turned and walked out of the room; through the small door window, he noticed the, now concerned, nurse examining Oma's bleeding nose and they walked back to her room; ...*Okay...now what drove her to the bluff at Devil's Lake? With Oma?* Myles focused his *E.S.P.* back on Sara, returned into her consciousness and continued forward in time...

As Myles viewed from her perspective, Sara stood in the produce department of the local grocery store with a cart full of food and supplies; she examined a large tomato then placed it in her bag.

Right after she grabbed another tomato for inspection, a dark-haired man she barely noticed stopped in front of Sara's cart and slowly turned his own to pass by.

"Excuse me." He said in a polite smile.

"Oh! I'm sorry." Sara responded, quickly moving her cart and catching just a glimpse of his face. They both shared a small laugh and the man continued on. As he passed, a thick cloud of his cologne radiated right to Sara's nose; she looked up and froze.

Absorbing all her thoughts, an instant memory immediately clicked in Myles' *E.S.P.*; the scent instantly pulled the image of another dark-haired man—a lover—whom wore the same cologne as *this* man. A small fire of her curse burst through Oma's bindings; it remained over her heart, trickling inches out along her chest and was now a straight rising smoke—no drips. Though it failed to consume her entire body, Myles burned in a sensation of fire and he immediately jumped out of Sara's mind.

Standing next to Sara, she and everyone around them froze; *Oh, come on; not again. Will you all just* move?! Instantly, time and everyone continued moving; *...you just have to ask? How stupid—why does this have to be a learning experience* right *now?* Myles returned his eyes to Sara who was now trembling lightly. The tomato in her hand had been obliterated by her grip and dripped all over the vegetable shelf. When he looked closer, he saw Sara's eyes welling with tears.

"...*Andrew?*" was all she said in an almost non-existent whisper. Sara dropped the tomato's remains and left her cart as she walked toward the exit, increasing speed with each step.

...*shit.* Myles quickly ran and followed her to a used minivan. He passed right through the closed passenger door as Sara got in the driver's side. She peeled out of the parking lot and onto the road, cutting off one car; the driver honked angrily at her and Sara maintained her reckless course; she cried heavier and heavier the whole ride home...

The tires squealed as she pulled into the driveway, parking on a crooked angle. Sobbing uncontrollably, she was slow to turn off the car and step out.

She left her door open and walked with a hunch. She gasped heavily as she dragged her feet to the front door, then slowly opened it—almost collapsing onto the hardwood floor.

As Myles saw in *Jim's* memory, Jim ran to her and all she said, in a broken, hoarse voice was: "...*Andrew.*" Her cries inhibited her from any other words and Jim took her to their room where she just repeated the same thing. Standing over her, trying to talk her down, Sara just turned away and continued crying. Jim kissed her cheek and left the room.

Throughout the remainder of the day, Jim attempted to console his wife but when she was not crying, she was completely shut down—avoiding conversation or sleeping—and gave no response. Eventually, Jim went to

Korbin's room, explained how mommy was not feeling well so they needed to leave her alone. Both he and Korbin respected Sara's space and when Jim was ready to sleep, he prepared a blanket and pillow on the living room couch...

At 9:02PM, Sara squirmed around on the bed as she remained sleeping; the small visible portion of the curse was turning into a red flame as it still remained over her heart.

"...Andrew." she said in a low voice and Sara's sleeping eyes slowly opened; she rose from the bed, walking in a haze, and left the bedroom; she walked right out the front door.

Myles followed her until she started to run; when she burst into a sprint, more and more distance gradually grew between them. As Sara ran out of sight, he gave extra focus on his *E.S.P.* Despite his current omniscience, he barely caught her as he transported himself back into her consciousness; traveling forward through her memory, he found himself an, impossible, four hours later and one hundred fifteen miles away in Baraboo, WI.

Myles stepped out again as a spectator. Drenched in sweat—dried blood from cuts on her feet—Sara continued sprinting through a heavy brush of trees on the outskirts of town. Myles never blinked as he watched her; *How the hell did she manage that? Yeah, she has that curse but, c'mon...it's bound. That little escaped portion must've given her a physical boost.* When he focused his auric sight over Sara's heart, he noticed the spot was a complete, red flame; *that's what it looked like when Korbin was about to—*

Sara finally slowed to a stop. When she uttered the word, "*Andrew*" once more, the red flame exploded and coursed its way through her entire body. She froze as it turned into an imprisoning red shell around her body. Unlike Korbin, she broke free of the initial paralysis and struggled to move forward; she somehow increased her pace into a ragged jog until she reached the tree line and fell face first into a chain-link fence. Her head cracked against the metal pole and the fence links echoed in a wave around the proximity.

Sara clenched her muscles as she climbed over the fence into the back yard of a two story-ranch house. After a few steps, she collapsed and, just like her son, she began heaving the contents of her stomach until nothing but blood spewed from her mouth. She convulsed as her body began its change into the exact same beast as her son. Only *this* animal woke and stood with no struggle and it slowly prowled around the yard. It stopped at the sound of a door opening and closing, then turned toward the back door of the house; it froze preparation.

A young girl with dark hair, wearing pajamas, cautiously emerged from around the shed. She walked out to the middle of the yard, searching all around until she turned and locked eyes with the large predator. She froze and the animal prowled toward her, snarling. From twenty feet away, it lowered its stance and prepared to attack, when an even younger girl in pajamas ran out to the first one's side; her blonde hair glistened in the porch

295

light. The second her little movements came into the animal's view, it jumped into a full sprint and attacked.

The blonde's tiny body flew another ten feet along the wet grass and the animal jumped over, wrapped its jaws around her and threw her against the shed; it picked her up and began tearing her to pieces. Her screams were muffled by a lack of air as blood drowned her throat.

When the animal finished and lifted its head, the older girl looked at the back door in a panic and started flailed her arms.

"Hey!" she shouted and the animal redirected its attention back to her. It crouched down and took three slow steps; the dark-haired girl matched it by backing up three slow steps; the animal jumped on top of the girl and began its second course.

The back door slammed open and the animal turned toward a man aiming a rifle right at it; he fired a shot into the animal's head and, whimpering with pain, it just cringed, maintaining a defensive stance; the man pulled back on the bolt and fired again with the same result. He fired his last four bullets into the animal's head and body with no fatal consequence. Eventually, it ran off, leaving both fresh kills behind.

Myles continued hesitantly into the yard, toward the carnage. The gunman dropped his rifle and grabbed his head with both hands; his eyes were wide as he glanced back and forth between the two girls then he sprinted back into the house. As Myles prepared to recalibrate his focus, another little girl—the youngest—emerged.

296

She stared obliviously at the other two girls' mutilated bodies then walked out to the grass. As she looked ahead at the older girl, she continued forward and stopped to see her foot drowning in a pool of blood and parts of what used to be the little blonde. She froze in place, staring at the corpse. When a woman burst through the door and grabbed her, the little girl gasped and immediately began to cry.

*Stop!* Time froze in place and Myles walked over to the two remaining females. He stared at the crying little girl as a familiar energy radiated from her; *You know her...that's the girl—the one Korbin likes. That's the one the weird girl is obsessed with! Ho...ly...shit—*

Myles' throat collapsed under the curse's grip, choking him. It lifted him into the air with the same loud roar from the hospital when he was a child. Myles grabbed for it but latched onto nothing. His feet flailed and kicked at the air in front of him; he grew lightheaded as he gagged. When his eyes rolled back, the entity released him and he fell to the ground. He grabbed his throat, coughing as he gasped for air.

Myles then flew through the air from a violent tug and landed in the middle of the yard; he turned over onto his back and could feel the entity straddling him. With a loud roar, an appendage swiped down, crushing Myles' chest; three razor claws dragged across, cutting open his shirt and torso and he screamed in agony. Myles turned over and pushed himself onto his feet that were running before he was upright. He hopped the fence and barely passed the tree line before he was stopped by the red fog.

Hearing the entity stomping toward him, Myles gathered whatever remaining focus he had and struggled to back his way out of the curse's hold. The stomps increased speed, pounding heavier and heavier; the entity exhaled a growling snort. Myles dug deep as it closed in, and finally pushed his way out, returning to the world in the present time.

# 24

A heavy weight lifted when Rich realized he was still able to separate his home life from work. It had been years since he felt any serious concern for Shanna's well-being and he actually considered calling in sick. Overwhelmed with uncertainty—whether or not he could remain focused on his patients at work—he struggled to suppress the worries about his daughter. Nevertheless, arriving at the office, his mind instinctively switched to work-mode, allowing him to carry on as always.

Shifting his attention back to his family later that night, Rich returned home with a sample box of sleeping medication and gave it to Shanna, "Starting tonight, just take half a tablet. You'll, most likely, feel a little loopy but it should allow you to finally get some sleep."

Shanna took the box and immediately opened it; the tablets were only a quarter of an inch long and a centimeter thick; *Half of one? What's* that *gonna do?* Her skepticism didn't last long as it was drowned with a surge of excitement and the last two hours of the evening dragged in her anticipation.

At 7:30PM, Shanna popped a tablet from the container of plastic and foil and snapped it in half; she set aside the smaller of the two for tomorrow night, then filled a glass of water. The miniscule tablet would've been lost forever if dropped onto the carpet and she just stared at it for a moment; *You really need to wash this down with water? You could've just stuck it in some food or something; it'll prolly just dissolve on your tongue. Whatever...play it safe.* She tossed the half-pill in her mouth and guzzled down the water. When she finished, she went into the living room and sat in her corner of the couch, staring at the television.

After a half an hour, the characters on the screen began to move in little circles; Shanna shook her head and they returned to normal. A few minutes later, she looked up to see the pictures on the wall moving in even larger circles and as she looked back down, the television was twisting back and forth—as if on a swiveling mechanism.

"...Dad?" She said, holding her head and staring at the floor.

Rich looked over and grinned, "Bedtime!"

He helped Shanna walk up the stairs to her room and when she was nestled into bed, he kissed her forehead, "G'night sweetheart."

He backed out of the room, shut off the light, and pulled her door shut—leaving it open by an inch.

Shanna's eyes were wide open as the medicine stepped up its reaction with her brain and spinning-inanimate objects were suddenly replaced by random hallucinations.

One took her to an unrecognizable metropolis. She sat in an outdoor cafe, eating a cheeseburger; *...world domination with cheeseburgers! It's genius!* Another hallucination placed her in a park around numerous friends and family at a large cookout. A large cast-iron grate sat over a bonfire and Rich was flipping steaks, hotdogs and burgers; *Oooooo burgers! A big* moo *party in our tummies. Moo...cow...okay, there's cow burgers, turkey burgers, veggie burgers...anyone ever make steak burgers? Shut up...they're both from cows;* bear *burgers! You could make a burger out of anything. Wonder if Korbin likes burgers; of course he does. You've seen him scarf them down plenty of times. Jake liked burgers—God...wonder what Jake tasted like for that animal...Jake Burgers!*

Shanna gasped as she buried her face in her pillow, fighting a quiet giggle; *Shame on you, Shanna. That is so disrespectful. You are sooooooo going to hell. Damn...all this talk about burgers—gots a rumbly in the tumbly.*

Shanna rose from her bed and left the room. She looked down the hall to find the light off in her parents' room as Vikki had already gone to bed. With a small grin on her face, Shanna walked softly on the already-muffling carpet and stepped cautiously down the steps. Halfway down, she actually missed a step but caught herself on the railing before she fell; she fought the urge to laugh, covering her hand over her mouth as she stood back up. She looked around and raised her hands, whispering: "*I'm okay. I'm good."* then continued down the stairs with additional caution.

She looked down the hall to Rich's office and the light was on; *...he's occupied. Coast is* clear. She continued in soft steps to the kitchen and went straight to the fridge. She grabbed the large foil-covered plate and placed it on the counter. She reached back in the fridge and pulled the mayonnaise, ketchup, and mustard bottles, setting them on the counter. Finally, she pulled the open bag of hamburger buns from the bread holder and set it down with the rest of the feast.

Shanna grabbed a paper plate from the cabinet, then lifted the tin-foil, covering three left over hamburgers on the glass plate; *Can't microwave...daddy'll hear.* She placed the cold slab of meat on top of a bun, coated it with the condiments and placed the other half of the bun on top. She squished the burger, flattening the buns, and the meal's colorful taste enhancers oozed from the sides; she grabbed it and took a large bite. Her eyes rolled backward as she chewed and she sighed pleasurably; *oh it's fantastic, even cold! Sucks that Jake'll never have another one of these. Amanda should be the one never having a burger again.*

She finished the burger quickly then grabbed another bun and slapped a glop of mayonnaise on the bottom half followed by a smiley-face with the ketchup and mustard and immediately dug in when the creation was finished; *Amanda...psshh...she could stand to use a couple burgers. Then, maybe she'd actually be kinda cute. Of course, you still wouldn't touch that—and she'd still be a pain—but at least she'd be easier on the eyes. Maybe she'd attract someone that actually was a lesbian. Then again...can't really blame her. She was probably all neglected growing up—sheltered. God...she probably doesn't have anyone to explain the ways of life to her...that's why she's so messed up. Maybe that's one of your purposes in life; but, God...you were so cruel to her. Would she even listen to you anymore? Try...you should try. She's a good girl; and honestly, she's not that much of a pain and...kinda cute. Wonder what it's like to be a lesbian. Who knows? Maybe it could be interesting. You should email her. Yeah...email her. Everything that happened was because of shock; she's not bad. Email her and make amends. If no one else likes it, fuck'em; if it has to be just you and her, fine then. Go email her.*

Shanna scarfed down the rest of the burger, then paused as she grabbed her chest; her face cringed with discomfort as the air-bubble pushed its way down to her stomach. Leaving everything out on the counter, she left the kitchen and crept back up the stairs to her room.

She laid on the bed with her phone and opened her email application. After entering Amanda's name as the recipient, she started tapping her thumbs on the screen, continually deleting misspelled words and her eyes finally grew heavy. Forcing them to stay open, she eventually finished the long, apologetic email and after tapping "send", she shut her eyes and fell right to sleep.

<><><>

Following the call of a dangerously increased heart rate, the doctor and a nurse rushed into Amanda's room

303

to find her convulsing in the bed—the first sign of life after her shoulder healed itself. They attributed the convulsing to her hot body temperature and when they noticed the one hundred thirteen degrees on the monitor screen, the doctor immediately administered a fever reducer and a sedative. Within a few moments, Amanda's eyes rolled back into her head and the slightest tint of blue seeped through her bright pink skin. Declaring Amanda's tongue-choking, the nurse sprinted out of the room and returned in a few seconds with surgical clamps. The nurse and doctor immediately pried open her jaw and pulled her tongue from her throat. Pinning Amanda to the bed, they watched the monitor and her body temperature remained at one hundred thirteen degrees.

Her convulsing soon dramatically decreased but her fever was slow to come down—too slow for the doctor's preference—and she hesitantly called for another, smaller dose of the fever reducer. Still holding Amanda's tongue with the steel clamp, the medical duo eased their hold on her. The doctor looked her over while the nurse examined the monitor; Amanda's heartbeat had slowed only two, unacceptable points. As the doctor turned to the nurse, Amanda's heart rate jumped back up and her body contorted her joints into locked positions; almost mirroring her daughter, Amanda's mother was frozen as she watched with wide, tear-filled eyes.

The doctor called for a second dose of sedative and moments after it entered Amanda's veins, her body gradually released its grip and she slowly lowered back to the bed. Her heart rate finally dropped to a constant, moderate pace and her body was decreasing in temperature.

The following day, Amanda slowly woke with her vision in a blurry haze; when her arms stopped as she tried to lift them, she looked over and her eyes managed to interpret thick straps, binding her wrists. She attempted to move her legs with the same result and saw two additional straps wrapped around her ankles. The weight of her exhausted muscles pulled her head back down to the pillow and she relaxed her body into the bed.

Only a second passed before a sense of panic flowed from her brain, down her spine. The monitor's beeping increased pace and when she lifted her head, the dizzying vertigo dropped it back down. Her body temperature rose as her stomach churned.

"...*help*..." she whispered with her eyes closed; she swallowed, holding back an impulsive heave, "*I need help. I'm gonna throw up.*"

Emily walked back into the room with a cup of coffee and sat back in her chair, only to stand right back up when Amanda moved her head. She set the cup down and rushed to Amanda's side, "Hun? You okay?"

Amanda shook her head, "...*gonna throw up.*"

Emily quickly looked around then ran into the bathroom; she came out with a small wastebasket and the moment she lifted it to the side of her daughter's face, Amanda turned and vomited into the plastic container.

A nurse quickly entered the room, "Everything okay?"

"I don't know," Emily said, "She woke up—said she was going to throw up."

After two more violent heaves, Amanda arched her back, pulling tightly on the straps, and screamed. The nurse urged Emily to back away and immediately examined Amanda. "Amanda, what's wrong? What hurts?"

"Everything!" Amanda screamed.

"What are you feeling?"

Amanda sucked in a deep breath and clenched her jaw, "Burning! Burning ache!" Then she screamed again. With a clueless scoff, the nurse ran to the phone on the wall and called for a doctor over the loudspeaker.

A new doctor arrived within a minute of the call and the nurse informed him of Amanda's symptoms, explaining the previous night's convulsing and choking, followed by her current nausea and pain. As the doctor approached, Amanda turned her head and blood spewed from her mouth all over the floor and her bed—barely missing the doctor's white coat. She then coughed blood up and onto her gown as she let out another scream.

The doctor looked over at the monitor—at her rising temperature and pulse—and, again, administered a sedative. This time, Amanda settled immediately back into the bed; a wave of euphoria relaxed her muscles. With barely open eyes and a jelly-like body, the nurse put on a pair of rubber gloves and started wiping the blood from Amanda's mouth.

The doctor stepped around the puddle on the floor, walked into the bathroom and washed his hands. He came back out, looked at Amanda—who was passed out—and invited Emily out into the hallway.

"Are you alright to talk?" he asked just outside the Amanda's door.

Emily ran her hands through her hair and closed her eyes for a moment, then nodded hesitantly.

The doctor looked back in the room where Amanda laid motionless and the nurse monitored her vitals. He then turned back toward Emily, placing his hands in his pockets.

"Well, it looks like we have her stabilized now. Unfortunately, we're still waiting on the results from her second blood test and until those come...I really don't have any new updates for you."

"You think it's rabies?" Emily asked.

The doctor thought for a moment, "Mrs...?"

"Blythe."

He nodded, "Mrs. Blythe...honestly, that's what it looks like. Unfortunately, I can't explain why her first blood test would've shown up negative."

Emily closed her eyes and shook her head, then stared into the room for a moment, locking her eyes on Amanda, "What happens if it *is* rabies?"

The doctor shook his head, "Again, at this point, we can't know for certain. Usually we administer the necessary immunizations immediately but if blood work came back negative, they wouldn't have done so. If, somehow they come back positive this time...I don't know...maybe it hadn't manifested until now and we may still have time to take preventative measures."

"And if not?"

"...typically if rabies isn't treated in time, the victim rarely ever survives." Emily stepped back and covered her face with her hand and the doctor reached to touch her shoulder, "but...like I said...maybe it didn't manifest until just recently, so, if blood comes back positive, we may have caught it in time." Emily turned toward the room and looked at her daughter again, wiping tears from her eyes.

"...I understand this is hard for you, ma'am; I can't imagine what you're going through and I wish I had better answers." The doctor added.

"...so, my daughter could die?" Emily asked in a soft tone.

"It's possible, yes." The doctor answered, "But until we know for sure, there's a fifty-fifty shot."

Emily closed her eyes and shook her head as she inhaled a deep breath. The doctor guided her back into the room and over to her chair. He put his hand on her shoulder as she sat down and then crouched next to her, "Just bear with us, Mrs. Blythe; we're doing all we can. I'm going to take another assessment of Amanda and start looking into everything further." Emily nodded and he stood up, heading to Amanda's side. Emily pulled her cell phone from her purse, pulled up her husband's contact information and began typing a text message to him.

# 25

The morning after her second outburst—Amanda calmly woke; she lifted her head to find the silhouette of her mother sleeping in the chair and though the hallway was active, her light was still off. Feeling not one tingle of discomfort, she simply laid her head back down and waited for someone to come unbind her; *You're fine—ready to go home now.*

A nurse quietly walked into the room and turned on the light; he checked the monitor, then turned to Amanda, checking her vitals.

Emily woke a couple minutes later and walked over to her daughter, asking her how she felt. Emily's relief was unsettling as the notion of Amanda contracting a fatal disease drowned her mind. She just grabbed Amanda's hand and kissed her forehead.

A half an hour later, the doctor arrived with a different nurse and repeated the vitals check in a shortened procedure; the nurse carried a rolling cart with gauze and bandaging on the top tray. The doctor informed Amanda about the blood tests they took and Emily's grip tightened on Amanda's hand; "...*negative*" was all Emily heard and the crushing weight of uncertainty immediately lifted from her shoulders but, already knowing her status, Amanda had no response.

Next, the nurse released both of Amanda's wrist bindings and helped her sit up; the doctor pulled the shoulder of her gown forward, revealing brown and pink-stained gauze over her shoulder. He put on a pair of latex gloves and proceeded to carefully remove the bandages. As her wounded flesh began to expose, the doctor's eyebrows cringed and he cocked his head to the side. The further he removed the bandaging, the higher his eyebrows raised and when the gauze was pulled completely off, his eyes were wide open; despite a deep, noticeable scar, Amanda's shoulder was completely healed.

He invited Emily over and when her eyes locked on her daughter's non-existent wound, her jaw dropped. The doctor closely examined Amanda's shoulder from the front, up to the top and around the back; the flesh was completely sealed back together with no scabbing. He proceeded with a few tests for nerve response, mobility and strength; she moved her arm perfectly as if nothing happened.

The doctor rolled Amanda's gown back over her shoulder and explained to her that, due to her severe reactions the last two days, they were going to keep her bindings on for one more day; if everything remained stable, they would remove them the next morning. He then told her, somehow, her wound had completely healed and there was no need for additional bandaging. Finally, he mentioned they'd have to run a few more *official* tests to ensure her arm had recovered, as it appeared.

He admitted his own confusion regarding Amanda's rabies-consistent symptoms without any traces of the disease. When he came to the topic of her shoulder, he fell speechless. Unable to give any final answers on either matter, he told Emily they wanted to keep Amanda in the hospital for a few more days for observation and if there were no more noticeable issues, they would release her.

The following day, Amanda's bindings were released and for the next three days, she laid in the bed drawing on the sketchpad her father brought on a visit; she put no effort into the doodles on the paper as only one thought consumed her mind...Shanna.

The moment she was home, Amanda politely denied her mother's offer for food and went straight to her room. She immediately powered up her entertainment system and played *Pearl Harbor* from her digital collection. She then walked over to her easel, where she picked up a pencil and started marking on a large pad of paper.

She had not even drawn a recognizable mark when her mother knocked on the door. Amanda opened it and

Emily handed over her cell phone, "I was throwing your clothes in the wash and it was still in your pocket."

Amanda smiled and took the phone, "Thanks."

"You're welcome." Emily said, pulling the door shut as she left.

Amanda pushed the "Home" button on the phone and nothing happened. She tried again...nothing; ...*battery.* She plugged the phone into the wall charger and set it on the television stand.

Her phone chimed as it came back to life. After another minute—as it progressed beyond the loading screens—she picked up the phone and checked her social media applications. Eventually, she opened her email application and, nestled between various junk-mail notifications, was a message from Shanna; Amanda's heart dropped to her suddenly churning stomach and she immediately trembled as she closed her eyes; *Please be good. Please be a good message. Please, I beg you...be a good message.* She slowly opened her eyes and raised her thumb over the screen—directly over the message—and paused. Finally, she dropped her thumb on the glass, triggering the phone's censors and the one-week old message opened.

Amanda cringed; the entire message was full of misspellings and inappropriate letter casing and punctuation. With a little effort, her eyes translated it to:

*"Hey Amanda. I wanna apologize for what I said to you. It was a really shitty thing to say. I never said anything like that to anyone and I didn't mean it to you. I was just freaked out at the situation but that's no excuse. I feel really really*

*awful. You're not a bad person, Amanda, you're just a little different but that makes you really cool and I'm not just saying that. I really mean it. You have a really interesting outlook on life and you're an AMAZING artist. Maybe you can teach me how to draw someday cause I suck haha. You know what, though, I'm still recovering but I think we should get together and hang out sometime. You can come visit me if you want. My address is 3407 Shirley Lane in Baraboo. I don't know when I'll ever leave my house again so feel free to just come by. Okay, I'm gonna go to bed...I'm SUPER tired. Goodnight!"*

Amanda giggled and bit her lip; she closed her eyes and pressed her hands against her forehead; *She cares. She really cares! Shanna wants to hang out with you; she wants you to teach her how to draw. She wants to be around you...to be with you. She—she wants you...she loves you.* Amanda closed the email and opened the phone's map application and immediately typed in Shanna's address.

Back in Muskego, Korbin tilted the phone from his mouth as he dipped his head with a heavy sigh; the words, *"couldn't find anything"* and *"trial and error"* dug a hole in his chest.

"Well what am I supposed to do?" he asked.

"Right now...just stay close to home." Myles answered over the phone, "We've been lucky so far; we don't really know anything other than the results we've gotten. I mean, you haven't changed since after the third night so the moon theory seems accurate; but I don't know if something else could set it off or not. Know what I mean?"

"Yeah." Korbin answered reluctantly.

"I'm doing all I can, bud; so...all you can do now is just sit tight."

"...alright."

Korbin hung up the phone and sat down on the couch, scowling as his eyes drifted. He searched and searched his mind for some trace of memory when he was transformed but came up with nothing; all he could pull out were the final moments when his fever hit, right before he collapsed and the agonizing soreness the morning after.

When his mind shifted to Shanna's face, endorphins immediately soothed his tense body and he finally relaxed; *Go see her—no...you can't...not until you figure this out. What if you never figure it out? Then you'll just have to— you'll figure it out. She's all you have; she's your world.*

Then, as his body grew warmer, Korbin's memories and his entire consciousness blurred together; at the center—in crystal clarity—was Shanna's face. He lost his sense of time, place and specific memories; all he could see was her face and all he could think was to be with her and an even bigger—more intoxicating—dose of euphoria flowed through his body; *...God, this is amazing.*

The trance cut out and Korbin snapped back to the living room; *Wha—what the hell? The hell was that? That was amazing. Whatever kinda daydream that was...get it back. Get it back now!*

He frantically looked around then grabbed his cellphone off the floor, waking it; *...what were you just doing? Before that amazing dream?...fuck it; just get it back! He* quickly opened the phone's photo album and immediately started scrolling through—passing up numerous photos of him and Shanna; *C'mon, c'mon c'mon come on!!!*

He came to the photo of him and Shanna outside the bar four months earlier. He grinned hesitantly, then closed his eyes with a deep breath, attempting to recreate the trance; *Concentrate...Shanna...Shanna.* He failed as the photo proved to only be a blurry reflection in his mind; *COME ON! You just had that shit! Shanna...Shanna...* As the images severed their connection from Korbin's reality-senses, he groaned in frustration; soon the intoxicating scene was just a memorable haze.

Korbin opened his eyes after another moment and frowned as he stared at the photo on the phone. He clenched every muscle in his body as he stood up. Walking down the hall, he squeezed the phone in one hand while his other hand became a tightly clenched fist. Turning into his room, he slammed the door shut and crashing objects echoed through the thin wood. After the crashes died down—muffled by a pillow—he screamed in one prolonged note, "*Fuuuuck!*"

# 26

Amanda gave a little extra push on the gas pedal late the next morning. When she saw almost no traffic on the road, her excitement heightened; the stimulation overdose triggered her anxiety and she started to panic.

She continually took one hand off the wheel to shake out the tremors—alternating each hand. Her stomach dug a hole in itself as her pulse raced; she even almost crashed in a brief lightheaded moment. Eventually, she recomposed herself and a smile returned to her face.

The smell of freshly ground coffee filled the Madsen's kitchen and the coffee pot chugged as it brewed the beverage.

Vikki pulled a coffee mug from the bottom shelf of an upper cabinet and set it next to the coffee pot while Shanna sat at the bar-counter with a bowl of cereal.

Rich walked in from the hallway and grinned, "Finally awake, *Lazy?*" Shanna scrunched her face and stuck her tongue out as her father walked toward her; he handed her a small sheet of paper with writing and she looked it over.

"Just talked to the psychologist and this is the earliest she can get you in." he said, leaning on the counter.

"Mmkay" Shanna said, shoving a spoonful into her mouth.

Rich walked over and kissed Vikki as she mixed creamer into her coffee, then grabbed the empty mug and filled it almost to the brim, drinking it straight black.

Shanna ate another spoonful, "That's like, your fourth cup this morning, *Junkie.*" Rich looked over, turned the corners of his mouth upside down and bobbled his head back and forth with a loud, mocking groan and they both laughed.

"Really?" Vikki interjected, "That's how you greet family?"

Rich wrapped his arm around Vikki's shoulders, pulled her close and kissed her again, "That's true love, babe."

"Probably as good as it's gonna get." Vikki answered with a joking grin; all three laughed and Vikki sat at the kitchen table.

Shanna looked back at the paper, "She good?"

Rich nodded, "Yup. Any of my patients needs to see someone, I send'em to her. I think you'll like her; she's a real sweetheart."

"She's not gonna put me on any more meds, is she?"

317

Rich smiled and shook his head, "No; you need a psychiatrist for that and I don't think you need one at this point. Lately you've just exhibited symptoms of Post-Traumatic Stress; you just need to get things out and learn how to cope." Shanna nodded and took another bite of her gradually softening cereal, and Rich smiled, "Don't like that hazy effect, huh?"

Shanna dropped her spoon in the bowl, sat back in the chair and crossed her arms as her gaze burned a hole through Rich's eyeballs; he just chuckled.

"Babe, really? Was that necessary?" Vikki asked.

"*Whaaaat*? Oh c'mon, I'm just teasing you."

Shanna's only movement was her jaw chewing the last bits of cereal, "...it's not funny."

Rich scoffed, "C'mon, it's a *little* funny."

"*Seriously*?! That crap had me hallucinating and drunk dialing people!" Shanna snapped.

"...don't forget the munchies."

Vikki snorted in her mug and fought a laughing urge; she put the cup down and quickly grabbed a napkin— more to hide her smiling face than clean the dribbles of coffee.

Shanna quickly turned with wide eyes, "*Mom*?!"

Vikki's body shook uncontrollably and she pulled her hand away from her mouth, "I'm sorry sweetie."

Shanna turned back around and pressed her forehead into her hands; she closed her eyes and shook her head, "...oh God."

"It's okay, Shanna," Vikki added, "It's one chore off my list; you cleaned out the fridge for me." She and Rich lost control and burst into laughter.

"She just can't clean up the dishes afterward...*or* the candy wrappers." Rich added and Vikki snorted, pulling them both into a deeper laughing fit.

Shanna covered her face with her hands and they failed to cover her swelling cheeks; her body shook as she giggled and her parents laughed even harder. The contagious laughter finally grabbed hold and Shanna released her grip.

After a few minutes, they all finally calmed and the kitchen was quiet again. Shanna took her bowl to the sink and dumped the remaining mush; after chopping it up in the disposal, she rinsed the bowl, turned and set it in the dishwasher, "Okay, dad, really—are you gonna switch me back to meds like that?"

Rich shook his head, "No. Are these new ones working for you, though?"

"I been getting sleep..." she answered with a shoulder shrug, "...but it gives me a nasty taste in my mouth. It's like something's *inside* my tongue and everything tastes awful."

"Yeah, that's a common side effect."

Shanna nodded, "Well it's better than getting drunk off a tiny little tablet and waking up with no memory of the crap I did the night before."

Rich fought a small chuckle, "Okay, okay; I'm sorry, Shanna. You really needed sleep so I picked the strongest medicine we had samples for. I mean, I knew you'd be feelin' off kilter, but I figured you'd go right to sleep. So...I'm sorry."

Shanna smiled and nodded, "Whatever."

The doorbell rang and Shanna took the first few steps to leave the kitchen.

"I got it," she said—her voice trailing off as she distanced herself from the kitchen, "You guys just keep enjoying my misfortunes!" Rich and Vikki both smiled.

Shanna froze in shock when she opened the door. Mirroring her greeter, Amanda stood perfectly still as she gazed in Shanna's widening eyes; Amanda licked her lips and slightly moved her jaw in multiple attempts to start a sentence. Finally, she tightened her stomach and pushed a gust of air out of her lungs and up her windpipe; in a shaky, whispering voice, all that came out was, "...*hi*."

Shanna failed to muster any strength to hide her shock; her jaw dropped and her eyebrows flipped; *What the hell? What's she doing here?! How did she find out where I live?! Who the hell did she talk to?! She's stalking you...she's stalking you! She's fucking stalking you!* Shanna's eyes grew more and more tense and her panicking aggravation crushed her shock, allowing her to finally move and speak, "...what are you doing here?"

"I, uh—I came to see how you were?" Amanda replied, shrugging her shoulders.

"I'm fine." Shanna answered in a flat, stern tone.

Amanda stared at her for a moment, then hesitantly grinned and nodded. Shanna looked back into the house, toward the kitchen then sneaked out, shutting the door

320

behind her; Amanda immediately stepped back, giving Shanna more room.

Without even thinking, Shanna crossed her arms and slightly curled her torso in a defensive stance; turned away, her shoulder was on point, directly at the uninvited visitor's face. She stared at Amanda as her brain struggled to process words.

Amanda took a deep breath, "I'm glad you're alright. I'm feeling better too." She pulled back her shirt collar and Shanna barely glanced at it; *So what? She's got a scar— holy shit, you can't even pretend to be nice—even with an obviously fake facade?......nope. Now you can see that she's a little creep—stalking you at your house. Jesus...it really is the quiet ones;*

"How did you get my address?"

Amanda released her shirt and cautiously folded her hands together, "...you gave it to me."

Shanna's eyes widened and she shook her head, "Excuse me?"

"In your email at the beginning of the week. You said you'd be home and I should come by; you typed your address for me."

"Umm...no, I didn't." Shanna replied in a condescending tone.

"...would you like to see?"

"Yes, I would, actually." Shanna added.

Amanda pulled out her phone and opened its email application; she tapped on the *Inbox* and slid her finger up the screen, navigating down to the message and turned the phone toward Shanna; there it was, just as Amanda

321

said. Shanna's eyes widened and her neck tightened as she fought the urge to scream. Amanda handed her the phone and Shanna reluctantly grabbed it; even more hesitant, she paused for a second, then started to read—closing her eyes and shaking her head throughout.

Shanna returned Amanda's phone and retreated back to the wall in her defensive pose, staring off into the yard, "When did you get that?"

"I didn't read it until yesterday but it was sent early in the week."

*...the meds. You emailed her when you were high on those goddamn meds. So...maybe she's not a stalker; maybe she didn't follow you home or hack the internet for your info; but maybe she did.*

Amanda took a deep breath and smiled obliviously, "If I can be honest for a minute...I was really happy when I got that. I was scared, but somehow, I knew deep down that you didn't hate me; but that email just assures me that...I really do have a chance; *we* have a chance to be together. Maybe it's not meant to be now, but someday, I believe it's meant to."

Shanna squeezed her eyes shut and clenched every muscle in her body; *Is she really that blind? She doesn't even see how surprised you were at the email she got! Just...calm...down—no, not for her sake; you don't wanna get sued or go to jail for beating some sense into her.* "Look," she finally began, "I'm sorry for talking down to you just now. I'm also sorry about that email message; it should've never even been typed. I was...really drunk, when I typed that and I have no memory of it. I'm sorry that it gave

322

you any sort of impression or hope; but as I told you before...I'm not interested. I will *never* be interested—not with you or *anyone*."

Amanda's face was blank, "But...when you're drunk, you lose your inhibitions and things you say are typically your true thoughts and feelings."

"Well, not this time; I can assure you."

"...but, I—"

Shanna held up her hand, "No, Amanda; don't bother. I understand you're here because of the message; that was my fault and, again, I'm sorry. But, in general, you being here, at my house is really awkward for me—like, really uncomfortable. So, now, I'm gonna politely ask you to leave and not come back; you need some gas money for the trouble?"

Amanda stared at Shanna for a couple seconds, then shook her head and turned back toward her car; Shanna turned and walked back in the house, locking the door knob, the deadbolt and latching the chain. She watched from a small window as Amanda carefully backed out of the driveway, turned and drove off.

Rich stepped in from the kitchen, "Who was that?"

"...no one." Shanna said, shaking her head; in a heavy, dragging pace, she turned and walked upstairs.


<><><>


With a third addition of anxiety on her plate, the week's duration was a random mix of flying and dragging. Every uncomfortable sensation and thought took the day

323

and stretched it by seven hours; but the thought of Jake's approaching memorial—her unwillingness to face his parents—compressed the days by *twelve* hours. Now that the day was actually here, her stomach churned, just as it did when she broke up with him that summer.

When they pulled into the parking lot, Shanna requested her parents ask Jake's parents to leave her alone until the ceremony was done—fearing a large, conspicuous breakdown. When Rich and Vikki gave Shanna the "*okay*" she finally entered the funeral parlor; she kept her eyes on the floor, only glancing to the right as they walked along a designated path. On the outside of the people-circle, were various collections of Jake's belongings and the second Shanna's eyes told her brain what each item was, she looked back at the ground, pushing down her creeping sentiment. Unfortunately, when she came to his letter jacket, a slew of high school memories took over and she began to cry.

Too distraught to notice the time, Jake's service was suddenly over and as everyone left to reconvene at the reception's separate location, Shanna and her parents stayed behind.

As the last guest walked out the door, Jake's parents glanced over at the Madsen's; Shanna slowly lifted her head and her eyes were closed. With a deep breath, she opened them and Jake's mother was staring right at her with a tiny smile, fighting to hide her tears. As Shanna's eyes welled up, she started walking. Meeting her halfway, Jake's mother gently placed her hands-on Shanna's shoulders, who broke down to a heavy sob before she even looked up. Jake's mother hugged Shanna firmly as did his father.

"It's okay, hun." Jake's mother said softly.

Keeping their allotted reception time in consideration, Shanna rode with Jake's parents, in the effort for a one-on-one chat. She denied his mother's offer to sit in the back seat with her.

"I'd like to talk to you both on the same level." Shanna insisted, climbing into the back seat—still staring at the floor. Jake's parents stopped for a moment, reminding Shanna's parents of a few directions and then climbed in the car. Between the time their doors shut to the moment the car pulled out onto the road, Shanna was completely silent.

"You okay, hun?" Jake's mother asked.

Shanna nodded, "...yeah." She inhaled deeply and finally looked up, "Okay, um—there's just some things I wanna tell you and...it's feeling pretty difficult. So, please...just—uh...just bear with me." Jake's parents agreed and Shanna sat forward, "I just want you to know, the reason I broke up with Jake was because we just grew too far apart and our lives were going separate ways. Neither one of us disrespected or dishonored the other but we'd both become different people. I never *once*, stopped loving your son but...I wasn't *in* love with him anymore and...I had to move on." She paused, fighting back the urge to cry some more; she took another deep breath and a few more tears trickled down her cheek, "I can't help but feel re——...responsible for what happened; if I—"

As Shanna broke down again, Jake's mother unbuckled her seat belt, turned around and hugged Shanna once more. She gently caressed Shanna's back, then wiped another tear from her own eye, "*Shhhh...*" she sounded, "Shanna? Hun? I need you to listen to me..." she grabbed Shanna's arms and gently nudged her backward, creating a distance between them, then looked Shanna straight in the eyes, "...don't start thinking any of this is your fault; you're parents told us how you've been since it happened and if you lay this unnecessary guilt on yourself, you're never going to get better." Shanna nodded as Jake's mother caressed her head, "Jake told us everything—how he screwed up. He even said—and we all agreed—that you were completely right to move on. He said he got mad and that you probably thought it was at you; he didn't say what happened to his nose the day of your big fight, but he was only mad at himself and he was so sorry he took it out on you. He said he still loved you but you were right in that you both had grown apart." Shanna looked down and wiped her eyes; with a quiet sniffle, even Jake's father wiped his eyes clean. Jake's mother tapped her finger on Shanna's chin and gently pulled up, locking eyes with her, "Hun...this was a freak incident with no one to blame. No matter what, Jake will always love you; and so will we."

Shanna grinned and leaned forward, hugging Jake's mother again; Jake's father reached back with one hand and gently squeezed Shanna's arm, "Love ya." After another moment, Shanna sat back in the seat and the hole in her chest slowly began to heal itself as they made their way to the reception.

After finishing the food on her plate, Shanna drank the last of the soda in her glass, then grabbed her purse and excused herself to the restroom.

Sitting in the stall, she was consumed by fatigue; were it not for the cold seat, she may have been found sleeping on the toilet—another cause for anxiety.

The silence of the empty bathroom cracked as the door opened with two women, speaking in older, middle-aged voices. Shanna sat right up and froze; *...what the hell are you nervous about? It's a public bathroom. Oh shut up, just don't say anything.* Inevitably, her ears perked and focused on the conversation right in front of her stall's door.

"It's so sad. He had so much potential."

"Oh, I know. I mean...damn. All the sudden...gone."

"I can't even imagine what his girlfriend must be going through."

Shanna's eyes popped open—full alert now—and her hand covered her mouth.

"Who's that?"

"Umm...I can't remember her first name, but she's Doctor Rich Madsen's daughter; but yeah, she's already dealt with awful deaths of loved ones."

"What, recently?"

"*Nooooo.* This was, like...I dunno, fifteen, sixteen—maybe seventeen years ago. She had two sisters that were killed by a drunk driver; and I mean, like...they were unrecognizable—mangled in pieces."

"Really?"

"Yup."

"Wow...that poor girl; that poor *family*."

"Exactly."

The chatty duo finally left the restroom and Shanna removed her hand from her mouth, breathing normally again; her dried eyes were once again soaked with tears. Finishing in the stall, she went to the mirror and wiped her eyes; she grabbed the makeup kit from her purse and added an extra layer of flesh tone; her pink cheeks barely showed through. When she finished, she put away the makeup, grabbed her purse and examined her face once more before heading back to her table; ...*as good as you're gonna get.*

# 27

Five minutes after Rich started driving home, Shanna fell right to sleep in the back seat and her subconscious immediately started pulling images from her memory. From the dreams she was having, to Jake's death and all the way to the vague recollection of her, supposed, sisters' accident, her mind was consumed by a rapid sequence of images. They quickly sped up faster and faster until her mind could no longer discern one image from another; everything went black...

Shanna gasped and immediately woke as Rich pulled into the driveway, right into the open garage. Vikki quickly looked back at Shanna.

"You okay?" she asked. Shanna sighed and fell back into the seat, nodding as she rubbed her eyes; following her parents, she got out of the car and headed inside.

Rich pushed the button for the garage door, then unlocked the door to the house. As Shanna followed, she found herself in a pondering haze as the images she just dreamed about continued cycling through her head; her attention focused, specifically, on the faded, forgotten memory of her sisters' car accident, and the image of her backyard from all her previous dreams; *Why do those feel so related?*

Having dragged herself upstairs to her room and sluggishly changed to her sleeping attire, Shanna fell onto her mattress and pulled the covers up over her; she closed her eyes and was sleeping within seconds.

"Shanna?" Vikki called out from the bottom of the stairs, "Did you take your medicine?" Receiving no response, Vikki walked up the stairs and paused when she noticed Shanna's darkened room. She carefully peeked her head inside and watched her daughter for a moment; Shanna's breaths were deep, calm and steady. With a small grin, Vikki backed out of the room and left the door open a few inches. What she failed to see was Shanna's rapid eye movement as she dreamed…

Shanna's eyes opened and she rolled over, finding herself in a twin-sized bed, dressed in a t-shirt and pajama pants; her body was tiny with short limbs and no womanly figure—five-years old again.

She looked over to an empty twin bed in the room's opposite corner; the covers had been pulled back; *Where's K'istin?* Shanna shoved her covers off and got up toward the door. She peeked her head out and pulled it right back in at the sound of quick footsteps.

A taller, ten-year old girl with dark hair—Denise—wearing pink pajama bottoms and a white, long-sleeve t-shirt stepped out from her room and immediately stopped; she stepped slowly and softly all the way down the hall and down the steps, cringing at every little groan in the floor or loud swish of her feet on the carpet. Eventually she reached the stairs and descended.

After the ten-year old finally reached the bottom floor, an eight-year old girl with blonde hair—Kristin—wearing an oversized t-shirt down to her shins, emerged from the room, "*Denise!*" she whispered loudly.

As Kristin followed Denise's path, Shanna stepped into the hall.

"*K'istin!*" she called in a whisper.

Kristin jumped and turned, grabbing her chest, "*You scared me, Shanna! Go back to bed!*"

"*What are you doing?*" Shanna continued.

"*Nothing. Go back to bed.*"

Shanna pouted for a moment, then Kristin pointed her finger back toward Shanna's bed; after a short moment, Shanna obeyed her older sister and Kristin continued downstairs.

Laying back on her pillows, muffled whispers and footsteps seeped through the floor and eventually, Shanna got up again and followed her sisters...

She sat in the middle of the stairs, watching through the railings and listening to her sisters whispering until the back door opened. It started to creak then stopped and was followed by more whispering; when the whispering was finished, the door continued opening with a light groan and Shanna cautiously continued down the steps.

When she approached the threshold between the kitchen and the living room, she saw Kristin standing at the screen door, watching intently; Denise could barely be seen through the door's glass. Shanna gently pressed her little toes against the kitchen linoleum and tiptoed across to the back door until she was three feet behind Kristin.

"*I wanna play too.*" Shanna said and Kristin jumped again; she balled up her fist and swung at Shanna.

"*Stop that!*" Kristin whispered fiercely.

"*I'm sorry. Can I play?*"

Kristin shook her head, "*We're not playing; Denise is checking something.*"

Shanna pouted again, "*...I wanna play too.*"

"*We're not* playing *anything.*"

"I wanna play toooooo!" Shanna shouted—her quiet pitch quickly increasing.

Kristin jumped over and put her hand over Shanna's mouth, "*Okay! Okay! You gotta be quiet first.*" Shanna nodded with a smile and Kristin removed her hand, "*You go hide under the table, then I'll tell Denise she has to find you. Okay?*"

The corners of Shanna's mouth stretched back to her ears in an enormous smile and she quickly ran under the table to the far corner. Kristin looked back out the door into the yard and paused; she hesitantly grabbed the handle and pushed the door open, letting it slam shut and

Shanna jumped; her belly fluttered with excitement and she giggled.

A loud growl erupted from outside, followed by a loud thud; an even louder crash sounded right after and sent a shock down Shanna's little spine... then came the choking screams. Obeying her youthful curiosity, Shanna carefully walked out from under the table and the screaming stopped when she reached the door.

In front of the shed was a large, hairy animal with its head dipped down to the ground; it tugged on something; after three attempts, it finally removed what it was chewing on and when its head lifted, a small pink and red chunk of flesh hung from its mouth; ...*what is that?* Shanna shifted her eyes further into the yard and spotted Denise, who—in turn—spotted Shanna and immediately started waving her hands and shouting.

The animal immediately turned to Denise and Shanna looked up at the ceiling as heavy footsteps moved quickly across the floor. She ran back under the table and the animal let out another roar—the sound followed, then, by Denise's scream.

The heavy steps descended the stairs and Shanna's father appeared, sprinting across the kitchen floor, holding a rifle. He slammed on the door handle and the second he was outside, his gun echoed throughout the house. Shanna's mother appeared immediately after and she sprinted through the kitchen. She looked out the door and gasped—shouting in frantic, whimpering cries for her daughters as she leaned over on the table.

Five more gunshots fired and then there was only Vikki's cries. After a few seconds, Rich came back inside and grabbed his wife. She shook her head and slowly turned toward Rich, "Oh God, no; please no; not both of them."

Rich shook his head and squeezed his eyes shut, "Both of'em." he said and as Vikki stepped back, screaming, Rich wrapped his arms around her and held her from collapsing to the floor. He picked her up and guided her back into the living room.

With wide, terrified eyes, Shanna hesitantly climbed out from under the table and walked to the door, stepping outside. Further out in the yard, Denise lay motionless on the ground; matching the portion on her neck and chest, a big black substance in the grass surrounded her body. Much closer, however—in front of the shed—was more of the same substance that actually glistened in the porch and moon light; covering her face and throat, Kristin's blonde hair was pink and red now and her shirt was drenched with the liquid beneath her body; *Ooooohh I wanna play in the puddle!*

Shanna carefully stepped off the porch and when her feet hit the grass, she stopped; scattered near the big puddle was half of Kristin's arm and small chunks of her flesh; *What are those? Whose hand is that?* She walked further out and her feet immediately submerged in the thick, warm puddle; she lifted her foot and as the dripping liquid thinned on her foot, its black color faded to a deep red. Shanna reached down and touched it; she spread it around in her fingers, cringing at its tacky consistency.

She looked down at Kristin, then over at Denise and finally back at the severed arm; again, she examined the red substance on her hand then returned her eyes to Kristin's consuming puddle and her lip trembled, "K'istin I don't like this game; it's scary." Shanna received no response from her lifeless sister, "K'istin? K'istin, help me out of the puddle!"

She froze for a second, right next to Kristin's body, then reached down, "K'istin!" Shanna brushed Kristin's hair aside; Kristin's eyes and jaw were wide open, stained with the same substance surrounding her in the grass; her throat was torn out and her torso was sliced open in multiple places. All that remained of her right arm was a bloody, dislocated stump. Shanna's eyes were locked and she started to shake. The door slammed opened again.

"Shanna!" Vikki yelled.

Instantly broken from her trance, Shanna's sudden screaming popped her mother's ear drums while a river of tears cascaded down her cheeks; Vikki squeezed her tightly and sprinted back into the house...


As she did in the ambulance after her attack in Platteville, Shanna's upper body shot up in her bed and she screamed—switching from ear-piercing cries to deep, grumbling moans.

Rich and Vikki ran to her room and turned on the light; watching Shanna thrash her lungs and throat, Rich turned and leaned his forehead against the wall while Vikki nervously ran her hand through her hair.

"What do we do?" she asked in a raised voice.

Rich took a deep breath, then pulled his head off the wall and walked over to Shanna's bed, "Here; I'm gonna pin her arms down and try to hold her. You just try to wake her up." Vikki nodded and as Rich wrapped his arms around their screaming daughter, Vikki sat down in front of her and gently grabbed her face.

Cringing at the sound, Vikki kept repeating Shanna's name, coaxing her from the sleeping state and Shanna kept screaming. Rich scoffed and Vikki pressed her fingertips against her temples. She then placed her hands on Shanna's face and tapped her cheeks with no change. With a deep sigh, Vikki dipped her head in defeat; when she looked back up, she took a deep, holding breath, then lightly slapped Shanna's face, breaking her scream.

Vikki's eyes widened and she continued calling Shanna's name, gently tapping her cheeks again. Shanna slowly returned to consciousness in frantic, confused moaning; when she finally opened her eyes, Rich pinned her flailing arms tightly to her body; all that moved was her head twisting back and forth as she absorbed her surroundings and her parents both relaxed with a big, relieving sigh.

<><><>

Despite the tense awakening in the middle of the night, Rich and Vikki woke up at 7:30AM without any debilitating fatigue and their morning routine brought them to the kitchen table with their full coffee mugs.

When Shanna came down and walked into the kitchen, she stopped for a moment.

"How you feelin' sweetie?" Vikki asked.

Straight-faced, Shanna calmly walked over to the table, pulling up a chair and she glanced at each one of them for a few seconds before asking: "...how did my sisters die?"

At the end of Rich's revelation, the lighthearted kitchen became a cold, dead tomb of uncertainty. Shanna revealed her dream from last night and her parents reluctantly confirmed every detail as true. Though Shanna could understand—even sympathize with her parents for hiding this past from her—she now lingered on a strand of deceit and they said nothing as they all sat at the table.

"...do you ever forget them?" Shanna asked, finally breaking the silence.

Vikki shook her head, "No sweetie—not ever."

"Shanna," Rich chimed in, "it's like we said...we thought the best thing for you would be to forget. You were so young and...to see something like that at such an age. We didn't even wanna tell you the car accident story. We both agreed it best that you just forgot."

Shanna buried her face in her hands and took a deep breath, "So...instead I had to find out like this—being attacked by the same thing, years later?"

"You know there's no way we could've known this would happen again." Rich added.

"Maybe...but what if it had been some other way that I found out?" Shanna continued in as sympathetic tone she could muster—her mind now trying to balance every emotion at once, "Didn't you think I would've rather found out from my own parents?"

Vikki shook her head, "Of course we did, Shanna. But, again, it was such a freak thing at the time—it seemed so far removed that you would never find out."

"I found out about the car accident story at Jake's reception."

"...how?" Vikki asked.

"It doesn't matter how," Rich interrupted; he pulled his chair around close to Shanna's, "look...Shanna...you're smart enough to know that your mom and I were only looking out for your interests." He grabbed Shanna's hand and sandwiched it between both his palms, "We love you and we loved your sisters; but, please, don't blame us for what's happened—then or now."

Shanna's lip quivered and she shook her head, "...*I don't blame you.*" She said in a quiet whisper. She then leaned forward and wrapped her arms around her father's neck, "...*I'm sorry, Daddy.*"

Rich shook his head as he embraced his daughter, "It's okay, sweetheart; it's okay." As he gently rocked her back and forth, Vikki walked over and wrapped her arms around them both; Shanna shifted her nearest arm, wrapping it around her mother's waist and they all squeezed tightly in an affirming hug.

"I love you guys." Shanna said with a sniffle.

# 28

Following Myles' three-day old message saying he'd come out to the house, Korbin laid on the couch, staring off as he waited for the psychic's arrival; stretching the length of the furniture, the only sign of life he showed was the expanding and collapsing of his breathing lungs. He glanced at the clock: 9:43 AM.

His phone vibrated with a new text message. When Shanna's name displayed on the screen, he recoiled to a seated position; before he even opened the message, her face—her entire existence—consumed Korbins mind and he finally fell back into the same, euphoric and blinding trance. Quickly, he skimmed through the short message:

*"Can I please see you? You won't have to drive, I'll come out there but I just really need to see you."*

Once again, losing regard for everything *but* her—forgetting why he was confined to his house and that the man helping him would arrive later that afternoon—he immediately replied, "*Yeah, come out here :)*" Then after pressing "send", he went to his room and put on a fresh t-shirt and jeans.

Korbin continually looked out the window as the morning dragged; he checked the clock: 11:50 AM. He pulled out his phone a few times, checking for any mistakes when he sent his address to Shanna; every number and letter was correct. Still staring at an empty driveway, he returned his attention to the television; while the thumb on one hand flipped channels on the remote, the other hand flipped the phone in circles on top of his knee and his nerves were starting to rage with discomfort.

The faint rumbling of an engine finally sounded through the walls and Korbin sat up—his eyes nearly melting the glass of the living room window. Making eye contact with Shanna, he jumped up, running toward the door. He yanked it open and, for the first time in weeks, Shanna smiled as she laid eyes on him; they hugged each other tightly followed by a long and deep kiss. Shanna caressed Korbin's head and smiled as they pulled apart.

"God; I missed you; don't you know it's all about *me*, ya dick?" she said smiling.

Korbin tilted his head back and *blinked* at her. She giggled and kissed him again.

Sitting on the couch, Korbin held Shanna tightly as she cried and he kissed her head. He rocked her gently until she eventually pulled away and wiped her eyes.

"...*I'm sorry.*" she whispered.

"Don't apologize."

Shanna turned her head away as her face cringed again, releasing another flow of tears. She took a deep breath and maintained the ounce of composure she had left, "God...I just—dunno how much more I can take."

"I know." Korbin replied softly.

Shanna looked at him, then scooted a few inches away, allowing herself to lay down in his lap, "You wanna just go to Australia or something? Somewhere far away and tropical? Maybe a little closer—Jamaica?" Korbin smiled and she nodded, "Yeah...yeah; think you can take care of that? Trip to Jamaica please. Thanks."

"*Pssshh*; *I'll* go to Jamaica. You can come along if you scrounge up some cash."

Shanna's eyes widened, "You're not gonna buy your girlfriend a ticket?! What the hell's wrong with you?"

"*Lots*'a shit, my dear." Korbin answered with a grin.

Shanna giggled, "I guess we got somethin' else in common."

"Hell no; I got some problems but *you*...yeah, you're fucked up."

Shanna's body shot up; her eyes and mouth were wide open, "Really?! You really just went there?!"

"Uh-huh." Korbin answered just before breaking into laughter. Shanna fought a smile and punched him in the stomach; he fell backward onto the bed then Shanna punched him a few more times in random spots; Korbin curled up in defense, still laughing and Shanna started tickling him.

"Yeah. What now, dick? What now?" Shanna said; she clenched her jaw but a smile slowly crept through, onto her face. Korbin caught Shanna's wrists and sat back up.

"Okay, okay..." he began, regaining composure, "...I'm sorry. I was just kidding."

"Whatever." Shanna answered in a condescending tone. Korbin pulled her close and kissed her with no resistance; when they pulled away, Shanna scrunched her face and stuck out her tongue. Finally, Korbin *blinked* at her and she paused; a second after his eyelids reopened, Shanna dipped her head a little and smiled. She leaned forward, kissed him and Korbin grunted as she squeezed her arms around his stomach.

"...*yeah; love ya too*." he uttered in a hoarse whisper.

Now on an unexpected visit, Myles drove up the suburban road toward Korbin's house. As he rounded the bend, he slowed and pulled over to a stop. A young woman walked out the front door and into the parked car in the driveway; she pulled away in the opposite direction. With a questioning glare, Myles continued on and replaced Shanna's car in the driveway...

Korbin answered the door a few seconds after the bell erupted through the house; his head cocked with confusion when he locked eyes with Myles; *who the hell—;* "…Can I help you?"

A blast of the curse's energy shot at Myles with a nauseous acidity and he fought to keep himself upright. Recollecting himself, he mirrored Korbin's confusion, "Uh…can I come in?"

"Is there a problem?" Korbin asked, now condescending.

"There might be." Myles said, overcoming the new frustration as he tried to rationalize, "Did you forget I was coming by today? I sent you a message."

The memory flooded back to Korbin's mind in a heavy pulse and hobbled him backward, knocking him to the floor. Myles ripped the screen door open, rushing to Korbin's aid.

He helped Korbin back to his feet and guided him to the couch. Crouched forward, Korbin held his head while Myles brought him a glass of water, urging him to sip. Finally composed, Korbin looked around, "What happened?"

"I don't know—dizzy spell, I guess?" Myles suggested and Korbin scoffed; he swallowed a few large chugs of water. Myles sat next to him, "Who was that? The girl that just left?"

Korbin inhaled, "Shanna. Sorry, I know you said I shouldn't be around anyone or—"

"Wait…" Myles held up his hand, "So you remember now? That I was coming over?" Korbin nodded and Myles stood, pacing around the living room; *He didn't just forget you were coming today. He was completely clueless to who you were;* "Are you normally this forgetful? Like, do you have an actual, *mortal*, mental condition?"

Korbin's face cringed as he looked up, "What? No. Why?"

"Because you completely forgot who I even was at the door. That wasn't just a brain fart."

Korbin's eyes scanned frantically back and forth, trying to conjure a defense, "No I didn't."

Myles shook his head, "You're a terrible liar." Korbin scoffed and sipped the water; Myles' eyes practically burned his flesh, "I'm guessing this probably never happened until the last few weeks. Is this the first time?"

Korbin froze; *He clearly sees you suck at lying...but if you tell him it happened once already—no...twice! Remember forgetting after he brought you home? He went out to talk to Dad and you didn't even know who he was. Then you hung up with him on the phone and everything went blank. Shit...he'll tell her; lie—no...you selfish asshole. What if you end up hurting Shanna? Tell him...* "No..." Korbin finally uttered with hesitation, "...this happened twice already. Once after you brought me home then after you told me to stay put." He paused and thought for a moment, "...actually, today would make it three."

Myles stared at Korbin for a moment, then continued pacing; *He wouldn't have been able to tell you until now if he kept forgetting;* "Were you doing...or feeling anything unusual? Anything out of the ordinary?" *Unlike everything that's been happening?* "I need specifics."

Korbin shrugged, "I dunno what exactly happened. I, like, hypnotized myself or something. It's like I lost track of *everything* and forgot every time…until I see or talk to you, then it comes back."

"So, essentially, I knock the memory back into you; that's some consistency. Try to think…what are you usually doing right before you forget?"

"I dunno."

Myles sat in the recliner angled to Korbin, "I know it's even harder because you keep forgetting, but you have to dig deep."

Korbin shook his head with a clenched jaw, "I don't know."

"Come on, Korbin. You have to work with me."

"I…don't…know."

Myles scoffed and slumped back in the chair; he rubbed his temples with his thumb and middle finger in a few circles; *Okay…where do we go from here? Where do we go*— The image of Shanna leaving snapped in his mind, "Were you doing anything that had to do with Shanna just before you would forget?"

In another mental flash flood, it all came back to Korbin: Shanna's photos…*forget*; Shanna's messages…*forget*; thoughts of Shanna, "…yes." He finally said under his breath, "It's like I'm drunk and high and it feels amazing."

Myles stood again, pacing around the living room; *So, she's a key;* "You going to tell her?"

Korbin froze, thinking; he shook his head, "…no."

Myles stopped and slowly knelt down to the floor, never breaking his gaze, "…You're *really* going to keep something like this from her? How crazy you are about her...you're actually attempting to hide this?" Korbin lowered his head and stared at the floor; Myles ran his hand through his hair, "Is it worth risking her life?"

Korbin wrapped his hands around the back of his head with no response. He sighed and a moment later, flung himself back against the couch; he slammed his fist into the cushion; Myles sat back next to him, "There's something else you should know,"

"...what?"

"Through the curse, I followed your mom when she disappeared. She ended up leaving on the night of a full moon—why she didn't change immediately, I have no idea; she was in a heavy dream-state and something was, like, holding the curse—but she wound up at a house a couple hours away. There she transformed and ended up killing two little girls."

Korbin tilted his head back and closed his eyes, "...Jesus Christ."

"...that's not the crazy part."

Korbin opened his eyes and slowly looked back at Myles with anticipation.

"Those two little girls, were Shanna's older sisters."

Korbin sat forward with slow deliberation and his jaw dropped slightly, "You're serious?"

Myles nodded, "Mm-hmm; I felt Shanna's energy once before and it was the same when I tracked your mom to her family as a child." Korbin's eyes were locked and his body froze as every muscle clenched; despite the growing cramps, he couldn't bring himself to move, "Now, one thing I'm absolutely certain of...is I think

Shanna woke the curse—not intentionally, but she has something to do with it. *Obviously*, nothing bad happened today, but, based on what you told me about her...I think you need to keep your distance."

The notion of cutting ties with Shanna instantly crossed Korbin's mind but was ripped away even faster as he gradually fell into the consuming haze revolving around his girlfriend.

# 29

Even after hearing Myles' theories, Korbin never came close to any negative feelings toward Shanna; regardless, he agreed—with total compliance, besides text messages—to stay clear of her. When Korbin's father returned home from work, Myles reminded them both they needed to come to his house at the week's end, in preparation for the full moon. For the better part of the next seven days, Korbin hid in his room, battling confusion and despair as he processed the information about Shanna and his mother—conjuring various "*what if*" scenarios and ideas of his own. All the while, his needful desire to be with Shanna grew—manifesting into an aching burn.

At 2:43PM on the day of that month's first full moon, Shanna's text message instantly kicked Korbin into his trance and he didn't even read her message before typing: "*Can I come see you?*"

"*Uh, duh? ;)*" she replied and without hesitation or consideration—even memory of his obligations that day—he slipped on a pair of jeans and his shoes, then grabbed his keys and headed toward his car.

An hour later, after a follow up doctor's appointment Amanda would obey her own urges in the same trance as she drove to the same location.

4:37PM in Racine, Myles hid in his bedroom. On the bed was a small, brown, opened package. Sitting on the floor next to the bed, Myles examined the last silver bullet, rotating it between his thumb and index finger; he placed it at the top of the magazine and pressed down. The bottom projectiles clicked as the last one squeezed into place then Myles picked up the gun and slid the magazine into the grip. When his phone rang, he slipped the gun in its holster, stood up and grabbed the phone from his pocket.

"Hello?"

"Is this Myles?" Jim asked through the phone.

"This is." Myles answered.

"Hey, it's Jim—Korbin's dad."

"Hi, uh...you guys on your way?"

"Korbin's gone."

Myles paused a moment and his eyes started to wander around the room, "What do you mean? Where is he?"

"I dunno," Jim answered, "I got home and his car was gone."

"His car? Did you pick it up from the school?"

"Yeah—about two weeks ago."

Myles bit the inside of his mouth as he wandered around the room in a fast pace, "He didn't leave a note or anything?"

"Nope."

Myles stopped—almost toppling over with momentum—and his jaw dropped, "I know where he went."

Pulling into the Madsen's driveway, Shanna emerged from the front door just as Korbin put his car in park; almost forgetting to shut off the engine, he rushed out to greet her with a big, tight hug and a deep kiss. As before, Korbin regained coherency when he was finally with Shanna and all notions of that day's importance—Myles' theory about Shanna—completely vanished from his mind.

"You feeling better?" Shanna asked with a smile.

"Yep. Much better."

"That's good." Shanna replied; then she grabbed Korbin's hand and pulled, "You feel up to meeting my parents?"

"Sure." Korbin said.

Shanna scoffed and shook her head, "'Kay, something's seriously wrong with you if it was *that* easy."

"Right? Look at who I'm dating."

Shanna swung back and slapped Korbin in the chest and he cringed with a big smile.

As they bantered back and forth, they were oblivious to the next car driving down the Madsen's street. When Amanda came upon the house, she noticed two people standing on the porch; she slowed down just enough to see Shanna talking with Korbin then sped up and passed them. Following the navigation on her phone, she turned and followed a slew of side roads until she was back on *Shirley Lane*. She parked her car roadside a quarter mile away, then got out and trudged through the woods to a nearby tree line. Realizing Shanna and Korbin had already gone inside, she stayed hidden and watched for them to come back out.

Shanna guided Korbin into the living room where Rich and Vikki sat holding glasses of wine as they watched T.V. They turned as soon as the young couple's footsteps brushed against the carpet.

"Mom, Dad...I'd like you to meet, Korbin. Korbin...this is my mom, Vikki, and my dad, Rich."

Rich set his glass down and immediately stood up and Vikki remained seated as she turned. Towering half a foot over Korbin's head, Rich extended his hand, "Good to meet ya."

"You too, sir." Korbin said with a firm handshake. He shifted his hand to Vikki's with a much softer grip, "Nice to meet you, ma'am."

Vikki smiled and looked at Shanna, "Awww, he's polite!"

"Yeah," Shanna began with hesitation, "I dunno where that came from."

Korbin smiled and glared at her, "Shush, you. The adults are talking." Shanna jabbed her fingers into his side and Vikki laughed when he cringed.

"You want somethin' to drink?" Rich asked.

Korbin thought for a moment, "Dark soda's good." Rich nodded and walked into the kitchen, then Shanna and Korbin sat on the couch.

Vikki took a quick sip of her wine then Rich came back with a glass full of soda and handed it to Korbin; he scowled at Shanna, "That's *my* spot."

Shanna pointed to the empty recliner, "There's a chair right there!"

"You're lucky you brought company." he added with a smile. Korbin laughed and took a drink, then Vikki sipped her wine.

"Shanna's been holding out on us." she began, "We've only heard vague details, so let's hear from the source; tell us about you." Korbin just smiled and shrugged his shoulders.

At 6:33PM, the sun was on its last rays of the day by the time Shanna and Korbin finished their conversation; leaving her parents back to their night of wine and television, they walked down the driveway, heading toward the road.

Their voices and the closing door immediately alerted Amanda's attention; when they gained a fifty-yard lead down the road, Amanda started to follow.

Korbin gripped Shanna's hand firmly and she rested her head on his shoulder for a few steps.

"How're you feeling?" Korbin asked.

Shanna lifted her head and shrugged her shoulders, "I guess I'm alright. I mean, I feel better around you but, in general, things seem like they're calming down."

"Still having the nightmares?" ...*shit. What nightmares was she having again?*

"Only when I forget to take meds." Shanna said, shaking her head.

Korbin nodded, then lifted her hand and kissed it, "Well that's something, isn't it?"

"I guess."

Korbin thought about the words for a moment, analyzing the tone with each step, then gently nudged his girlfriend, "Sounds like you got somethin' else."

Shanna grinned, "I got a shitty poker face."

"Yeah, you do." Korbin confirmed.

"Dick."

Korbin wrapped his arm around her shoulder and squeezed; she looked at him and they kissed. Stumbling over their feet, they started laughing.

"Oh, *that* was graceful." Korbin said and Shanna kept laughing. Regaining their footing, they continued walking and when the laughter died down, Korbin tugged at Shanna's hand, "So, c'mon. What's up?"

Shanna sighed, "Well...right now, I guess I'm just kinda disappointed with my parents."

"How come?"

"...hiding the truth from me." she added.

Korbin paused for a moment, "Can I ask, what truth?"

"Uh..." Shanna began then paused for a moment and Korbin stopped; he turned to Shanna and grabbed both her hands.

"...you don't have to tell me." he said.

Shanna shook her head, "It's just so bizarre."

Korbin pulled her close and locked his eyes with hers, then *blinked* and she smiled, wrapping her arms around his waist and squeezing. As Korbin returned the hug, the final rays of light faded into darkness and the full moon completed its rise into place.

"*Phew!* Think I just had a hot flash." Korbin said, shaking his head. Shanna smiled then lifted her head with a confused look.

"You turning into a woman?" Shanna asked. Korbin forced a smile as he shook his head again, dismissing the sudden vertigo. He turned into the moonlight and Shanna cringed at the beads of sweat dripping down his forehead, "Holy sweat-ball."

Failing another forced smile, Korbin shook his head again and exhaled a heavy breath. When he turned back to face Shanna, he stumbled and quickly caught himself, "*Gah*...what the hell?"

With a sincere look of concern, now, Shanna held out her hands to catch him, "You okay?"

Korbin nodded then fell into Shanna; she quickly caught him, bracing her legs firmly to hold his weight.

Another voice yelled out from down the road, "H—He—Help!".

"What the hell?" Shanna said. She gently pushed Korbin up for balance and when she let go, he collapsed to the ground and immediately curled into a fetal position.

"Korbin!" She yelled and he grunted with pain; he breathed heavily and his muscles clenched.

Shanna looked down the road again, then back to Korbin, "Shit!" She burst into a sprint, leaving Korbin by himself. When she came upon the mysterious person calling for help, her jaw dropped when the scrawny girl turned over.

"Amanda?!" She shouted, "Wha—what the hell?!" Frantically, she glanced back and forth, then checked her pocket; there was nothing but empty fabric rubbing against her fingers, "Shit!" She started sprinting again, toward her house.

Lying helpless on the isolated road, both Korbin and Amanda simultaneously progressed into their damned transformations as Korbin first experienced one month earlier. Their torn stomachs spewed blood; their bodies broke, shifted, and grew as their likenesses faded into the consuming curse.

Lights beamed onto the road as a car peeled out from the Madsen's driveway and, within seconds, squealed to a stop on the side of the road next to Amanda. Shanna and Rich jumped out of the car and as he examined Amanda with a small duffel bag at his side, Shanna ran back to Korbin.

Unable to see clearly, Rich carefully picked up Amanda and pulled her in front of the car lights; he jumped back when he saw her distorted face, "Uh, miss? Miss, can you understand me? I'm a doctor." he said and Amanda began convulsing. Rich immediately opened the bag, quickly searched through it then stopped at the sound of a loud crack; he looked over at Amanda to see her face extending outward, followed by her growing limbs and he froze. The moment the light glistened off her jagged set of fangs, he stood up and ran over to his daughter.

Before Shanna even reached Korbin, she stopped in her tracks when she noticed the same contortions Rich just witnessed; her jaw dropped and she slowly stepped backward. She screamed when her father tapped her shoulder.

"Shanna? What the hell's going on?!" He asked in a shaky voice. Shanna shook her head and immediately looked back at Korbin whose snout was glaring under the moonlight. A flash crossed her mind of the night Jake was killed; the animal's snout glared in the moonlight, just as Korbin's was at that moment.

"Oh my God; Shanna, run! C'mon!" Rich ordered as he pulled Shanna's arm and she obeyed; they sprinted back to the car and just as they passed Amanda's head, Shanna's scent filled Amanda's animal-like nose. They slammed the doors shut and Rich popped the gears to *reverse*, quickly spun around, switching them to *drive* then peeled away.

"What was that?!" Rich demanded, "Shanna! What was that?! Do you know?!"

Shanna sat in the seat with her eyes and mouth gaped wide open. As they pulled back into the driveway, Rich jumped out of the car and stopped as Shanna remained sitting; he ran to her door and opened it, ordering her get out. With tear-filled eyes, she finally obeyed and they ran inside the house.

They both stood at the door, speechless; Shanna trembled as her heart pounded against her ribs while Rich leaned against the stair railing, panting short, shaky breaths. Finally, Shanna gently grabbed Rich's arm, "Daddy? The thing that killed Denise and Kristin...did you shoot it?" Rich looked at her for a second, then nodded, "Did it die?"

He looked back at her with realization ran up the stairs.

"Did it die?!" Shanna repeated.

Never looking back, he reached the top of the stairs and circled around the top railing, "Not that I saw." He called out. Shanna cringed as a frustrating ache strangled her nerves and she wrapped both her hands around her head.

From the hallway, the toilet flushed and the bathroom faucet turned on; when it turned off, Vikki calmly walked into the kitchen. When she saw Shanna standing at the front door, visibly tense, she called to her.

"Is Korbin alright?"

357

The kitchen window exploded into microscopic shards as one of the animals burst through. Vikki screamed and both she and Shanna quickly turned to see the animal look around quick, then lock its eyes on Vikki; its crooked fangs displayed clearly beneath its curled lips. Vikki and Shanna stood frozen and as Rich took his first step back down the stairs, Vikki's head instinctively turned and the animal lunged forward, knocking her to the floor. She screamed helplessly as it started biting and clawing; Vikki braced her arms and hands against its large head, losing the fight as it bit through her hand.

Shanna ran into the kitchen; the animal swiped at her before she even crossed the threshold—missing by an inch with its long reach. Shanna jumped back and fell to the floor then the animal continued tearing Vikki to shreds.

"Get outta the way!" Rich yelled. Shanna glanced quickly to see her father pointing a rifle and she immediately crawled to the side. The gunshot blasted and Shanna's ears rang through the perforation. The slug pierced the animal's flesh but it just kept feeding as blood oozed from its body; in a sudden lunge, its jaws were wrapped around Vikki's neck, digging through the tender meat and she gagged as blood filled her throat.

"Oh God! Mom!" Shanna screamed and Rich fired the gun again; the slug hit the animal right in the head and as blood ran down onto its snout, its body pushed the first slug out onto the floor and the wound closed flawlessly.

Rich's eyes widened, "...Jesus Christ." Still trapped in its teeth, Vikki's torso lifted off the ground as the animal raised its head toward Rich; never taking its red-shimmered eyes off him, it cautiously dragged Vikki further back into the kitchen. When Shanna finally broke her screaming, she stood and started after her mother; Rich immediately dropped the gun and lunged forward, grabbing Shanna's hand just before she ran to the kitchen. Fighting her forward momentum, Rich tugged hard on her arm, pulling her close and he wrapped his arms around her waist.

"Shanna!" He gripped tighter and climbed his arms up around her shoulders, holding her right against his chest; he placed his mouth right next to her ear.

"*Listen to me!*" he ordered in a fierce whisper, "*I can't kill it; we have to get out of here now!*"

"...mom." Shanna said in a crying voice.

"*Now Shanna!*"

She surrendered and Rich turned her toward the front door before releasing his grip, "*...quick and quiet.*" They both skimmed across the hardwood floor and rushed out of the house.

Leaving the door open, they sprinted to the car and jumped inside. Rich started the car and the doors locked; the tires squealed as he backed out onto the road. He then put the car in *drive* and the tires squealed again as he peeled away.

The car already jumped to fifty-three miles per hour when Shanna buried her head in her hands and allowed herself to sob. "...God, mom."

Rich clenched his jaw and as tears filled his eyes, he gave his head a violent shake, "There's nothing we could do."

Shanna dropped her hands and looked up at the road, "...then where are we going?"

"Into town." Rich answered.

"But what is—" Shanna began; following her peripheral vision, she looked out her side window. Matching the car's current speed of eighty miles per hour, the animal came right toward her and its eyes reflected a yellow tint.

"Dad!" she screamed and the second Rich turned his head, the animal lunged at the car, latching its claws into the hood.

Naturally avoiding the danger, Rich's driving instincts forced his hands to crank on the steering wheel, turning the car at a sharp angle and it skipped into a demolishing roll.

Stopping upside down in the open grass next to the road, Shanna panted heavily and her eyes were locked in a haze; blood from her head poured down her face and filled the cuts on her cheeks and after a few moments, her eyes finally started to move. She carefully turned her head to look at her father whom wasn't even in the seat; she looked in the back, finding it completely empty.

Noticing the missing section of glass, she peered through the driver side window and found Rich laying in the grass; his broken spine protruded against the side of his neck. "...daddy?"

Crushed by the car, the animal's severed upper body propped itself up and—leaving its legs behind—crawled toward the scent of fresh blood. Even at just a quarter of its full running speed, it reached the car in only three seconds. Focused on the still-beating heart of its prey, it crawled faster and faster. When it reached the car, it lunged its head into the passenger window.

Shanna screamed at the stabbing pressure crushing her shoulder and collarbone. The animal tugged on her three times but failed to pull her from the car as she was hung up on the door; with a final tug—triple the force of the first three attempts, it pulled her from the wreckage and her free shoulder dislocated as it hooked on the door frame.

Shanna's legs kicked frantically at the ground. The moment the animal released her shoulder, she pushed the ground with her feet and spun around—face to face with her attacker. The animal bent its arms in a crouch as it snarled. Shanna sprung her legs out hard, kicking its face twice then she started pushing herself back toward the car. The animal instantly latched its claws onto her foot and pulled itself forward on top of her. Pinned to the ground by crushing weight, Shanna groaned painfully from the searing ache in both shoulders and she strained to breathe. As the animal rose its head and opened its mouth, the moon flashed the same yellow shimmer as before and Shanna barely exhaled three whimpering breaths.

The animal lunged its head down and clamped onto Shanna's dislocated shoulder; instead of a scream, she released a hoarse, whispering cry. The animal tugged upward, tearing skin and muscle off the bone and chewed. Shanna lifted her leg, repeatedly kicking it. The animal pulled back, growled, and clawed her face, neck, and chest; it bit on her shoulder and tore off a large chunk of flesh. Shanna's eyes widened and she stared into the sky as her body grew cold, losing nerve sensation. The animal lunged for her throat but stopped and looked up, over the car; its lips curled in another snarl and it pushed itself off Shanna, crawling away.

Down the road, with Jim as his passenger, Myles spotted an indiscernible commotion but the sudden increase in his mind's scratching burn alerted him to slow his speeding vehicle; creeping closer, he saw the totaled car in the grass and he came to stop; the animal was snapping and swinging its paws at something on the ground. Myles stopped the car fifty yards from the crash site and after instructing Jim to stay put, he got out. He quickly looked around, finding no one else in sight and he removed his gun from the holster as he continued forward.

Relieved of the weight, Shanna's breathing returned in short, fast gusts of air; her profuse bleeding rapidly dropped her temperature. After one, throat-tickling breath, she started coughing and blood shot up all over her mouth; when the coughs stopped, her attention focused up over the car, at the sound of both animals fighting.

The strength of Shanna's lungs and beating heart grew weaker; she breathed faster and harder until the oxygen flow finally ceased; all the sounds in her ears faded to a muffled echo and her vision slowly dissolved into a black void.

The still-in-tact animal slammed its paws down and clamped its jaws on the crippled animal's throat; it shook violently until the hairy flesh separated from the rest of the body and the outmatched torso fell lifeless.

Dropping the chunk to the ground, the victorious animal looked over at Myles and its eyes blinked rapidly; its legs trembled and it caught itself once before falling over. It looked at Myles again with a lazier gaze then finally collapsed to the ground.

His gun aimed, Myles cocked his head with confusion after spotting the upper half of a second animal; he looked away for a moment. Beyond the inevitable adrenaline, the scratching burn faded and when he looked back at the animal with his auric sight, the vapor-like shells consuming both animals began to break off and disappear into the sky. When it all finally disappeared, Myles realized the scratching burn was gone and the animals convulsed as they changed; *...curse is gone?*

He looked over and saw Shanna standing next to the car, staring at the fallen animals. When she turned and stared into Myles' eyes with a blank expression, guilt and horror rotted his stomach; *...oh no.* He scanned the entire scene, only seeing a man with a broken neck other than the two animals. Redirecting his eyes toward the car, he squeezed them shut and shook his head; hesitantly, he approached the scrap-metal and cautiously walked around to the opposite side where Shanna's lifeless body lay covered in blood. Myles lowered his gun with a deep sigh and ran his hand through his hair; he grabbed a handful and squeezed it as he clenched his jaw.

He snapped out of his guilt-ridden trance and looked around again; *Shit...you have to get Korbin out of here; but who's that other one?* Myles ran over to the two animals—in mid-change back to human form. Still unrecognizable, he knelt down and watched as their hair and fangs fell out, claws detached, and bodies reshaped. After another few minutes, Myles identified Korbin once again but his jaw dropped when he saw Amanda lying on the ground. He quickly walked over and—avoiding her bloody neck—grabbed her wrist finding no pulse; *Oh God.* He pressed his fingers against Korbin's neck and felt a weak pulse beneath them. With a compulsive nod, he sprinted back to his car and drove it to the scene.

Before stepping back out to retrieve Jim's son, Myles glared down the road then back at Korbin, "Okay, Jim…we're going to get Korbin and stick him in my car. Then we need to drive further down and, hopefully, find his car and belongings. You have to drive it back home, understand?" With a dazed look, Jim hesitantly nodded.

After one more quick check and—an emphasis on holding his empathy at bay—Myles and Jim lifted Korbin off the ground and dragged him toward the road. Myles opened the door, then they set Korbin onto the seat, shoving him in. They quickly sat back inside and continued driving down the road, toward the Madsen's house.

364

Fighting the urge to investigate the house's open-front door, Myles stopped at the edge of the driveway, where Korbin's car was parked. Jim quickly opened the door but Myles stopped him; *Keys...probably in Korbin's pocket. Where did his change start?* He looked back at Korbin as he lay unconscious; he turned around and reached his arm back, placing his hand on Korbin's shoulder as he searched his memory. Jim stared at Myles for a few moments, stuck his head outside to keep watch then pulled himself back in the car. After another minute, Myles opened his eyes and turned around; he flashed his brights down the road where barely-visible scraps of clothing lay scattered on the ground.

"Look ahead," Myles said and Jim obeyed, "...that leather shit isn't his so skip that. His pants should be up there with his keys and wallet." Jim wasted no time and sprinted down the road, losing his breath after only ten feet. Myles glanced at Korbin again; *...using your abilities* that *time wasn't so bad. Maybe you* are *getting stronger.* He stuck his head out the window, glancing around the car, finding nothing. To his surprise, the moment he pulled his head back in, Jim was standing on the side of the car, jingling Korbin's car keys. With an affirming nod, Jim got in his son's car. As Myles put the car in *drive*, he glanced over at the house; walking backward, toward the backyard were the spirits of Shanna, Vikki and Rich; their eyes never left Myles' gaze. Giving no second thought, he moved the car forward and Jim backed out of the driveway, following Myles as they started back to Muskego.

# 30

It finally all came crashing through Korbin's consciousness. The transformation—Jake, Amanda, Vikki...Shanna—the onslaught of memories forgotten in the acidic haze of his curse—suddenly scorched Korbin's mind and he woke up in his bed, screaming.

Jim burst through the bedroom door in a panic and ran to his son's bedside while Myles looked in from the hallway.

"Korbin? You alright, bud?" he asked.

Never looking up, Korbin shook his head, "...I remember—everything."

Jim stared at him for a moment, then looked out at Myles watching with heavy, sympathetic eyes; he lowered his head in defeat. Jim invited Korbin out to the living room—when he was ready—then gently rubbed his son's head and left the room.

Korbin sat in his bed, cycling through all the horrific images left by the curse; at the memory of killing Jake and Vikki, his guilt hollowed out his chest and squeezed his heart like a python…but that was a pin-prick compared to the memory of Shanna. Though he hadn't actually killed her, the curse connected him to Amanda's memory and he saw every grizzly detail from the car accident, right to his girlfriend's devouring; the nausea in his gut was drowned in his sorrow and his insides began to tear themselves apart. Just as he was about to lay back down, he remembered Myles' face and, wearing nothing but a pair of gym shorts, he ran out to the living room.

Preparing to ask his father about getting in touch with Myles, Korbin was taken back to find the psychic already sitting in the living room. His jaw hung open as he stared at Myles with wide eyes and his voice cracked as he attempted to speak, "I—I…I remember it all."

The look of sorrow increased its weight in Myles' eyes, "…I'm sorry. I'm sorry that…all this happened to you."

In subtle glances, Korbin examined the living room and finally decided on a place to sit; he lowered himself into a chair cushion with his eyes pointed at the floor in a blank stare, "…Shanna's dead. *Her whole family…because of* me!" he said as the muscles around his eyes squeezed tightly.

"It wasn't you." Myles corrected, "It wasn't you. You couldn't—"

"I even remember forgetting about you—every time. You kept warning me, then I kept forgetting everything. I went to see her cause I forgot I was going to change—forgot that thing was inside me."

Myles shook his head, "It wasn't your fault. Whatever that curse was about—who or whatever…*conjured* it, made sure it would destroy lives. It wasn't your fault." Korbin rested his elbows on his knees and buried his forehead into his palms; after a few moments, he let out a gasping breath as he started to cry. Myles leaned forward, "…Korbin?…Korbin." After a few short breaths, Korbin looked up, forced his lungs to inhale deeply; he exhaled a slow breath then looked at Myles, "…I can't even imagine how hard this is but…the curse is gone. I don't know how or why, but it's not in you anymore. It's not subdued or hidden; I see absolutely no traces of it; it's gone."

"…*so is she.*"

Sitting in his small home office the following week, Myles cringed while sorting through his accounts and finances. A fellow colleague covered Myles' lawns while he was off assisting Korbin; while not much, sacrificing a little extra from his contract payout in Platteville scratched his ego; *at least someone covered your ass.*

A notification woke Myles' phone; welcoming the distraction, he opened it in a heartbeat. It was a news bulletin describing new recent deaths—a small family in Baraboo, WI. Myles closed his eyes and exhaled as he dropped his head; he flipped the phone on its screen and slumped back in his chair.

"...*how could you let this happen?*" He whispered to himself as guilt trickled through his veins.

The guilt was immediately washed away with a comforting warmth he had not felt in years—a loving energy stored in the back of his mind and it gently squeezed his shoulder, then grasped his hand; ...*Oma?* With no fear—no hesitation—Myles opened his eyes and smiled, "Hi, Oma."

His grandmother knelt beside him, holding his hand; she looked up at him with a small grin, but sorrowful eyes. His smile faded, "What's wrong?" She only stared into his eyes in, what one would perceive as, a look of pride; it still could not hide her sadness, "Why won't you talk to me, Oma?" Myles pleaded. As her lip quivered, his grandmother caressed his cheek; all he could do was reciprocate a gaze of despair. She reached her hand higher and palmed the side of his head. Myles closed his eyes, savoring the moment, not knowing if it would ever happen again. When a soft pressure consumed his mind, he inhaled to his lungs' full capacity and held it; a slew of new memories graced his consciousness.

<><><>

...*what the hell?* Myles was in a cafe. After a moment he finally remembered it was his grandmother's, The Sweet Kraut; it maintained a polished design scheme with earthy colors. Tables and chairs were dark brown and walls were off-white; various works of German painters hung on the wall, as well as prints of pre-twentieth

369

century musicians. Despite the old-time elegance, the food and friendly service drew in people of various ages and ethnicities.

The cafe had already quieted down after the Sunday breakfast rush. Despite being one hundred percent German, Ava utilized some polish dishes in her meals; everyone flooded the place for her Paczkis. Still, Myles was in a haze—the relief of a hangover's end. Rather than being tied to his own body—or another's by seeing their own thoughts—his consciousness took him from one spot to another; ...*you're, what...a camera?* Eventually he found himself watching the interaction between his grandmother and mother...and himself; ...*why don't you remember this?*

"I'll call you tomorrow." Ava's daughter, Tricia, said to her mother as she pulled her long, frizzed hair into a pony tail. Next to her, seven-year old Myles wolfed down his own Paczki; he finished it in thirty seconds. Tricia smirked as she shook her head, "You must've hated that." After a moment of staring into his treat, his mother's voice finally registered in his mind and he looked up at her.

"Huh?"

Tricia shook her head with a smile, "Say 'bye' to Oma." Ava smiled and knelt down with her arms outstretched, "Tschuss, Myles. Oma loves you."

Myles stepped forward and wrapped his arms around Ava's neck, "Tchuss, Oma. Love you too!" He said with his mouth full. They parted and Ava wiped the jam off his mouth then stood. Tricia hugged Ava and then turned with Myles toward the door. Passing a young woman

370

dressed in her Sunday best on the way out, Tricia nudged Myles out of their path, "Careful Myles!"; he glanced up, "Sorry!"

"That's ok!" The woman said with a grin. The door shut behind Tricia and Myles as they turned on the sidewalk. As the woman approached, Ava smiled and retreated behind the glass counter full of desserts and pastries, "Guten Morgen! I'm Ava. What can I get you?" She said.

"Hi Ava. I'm Claire." She glossed over the contents of the glass case, "It all looks delicious."

*Claire? Who the hell--no she looks, like...Korbin's mom?! Sara's not her real name? She probably had no memory after the hospital. Government gave her a new identity?* The door opened again and when Ava looked up, her eyes locked and for a split second, her heart stopped. Her lungs pulled the deepest breath they could manage. Her neck clenched as she choked, forcing herself to swallow. The young man that just entered wore an off-white sweater with black dress pants and shoes. As he approached with a casual swagger, hands in pocket, Ava's body cramped as every muscle clenched; she was paralyzed. Drawing closer to the counter, the young man locked eyes with Ava, grinned with a nod and the slightest wink; he looked at Claire, "See anything you like hun?"

"All of it!" Claire said. She looked at the young man then indicated toward Ava, "Danny, this is Ava. Ava, this is my boyfriend, Danny."

An invisible dagger stabbed Ava's heart and it sunk down to her gut, churning her stomach; now she clenched

371

voluntarily just to keep everything down. In an automated blur, Ava trudged her way through the interaction; her eyes absorbed every detail of Danny's face once more before they walked through the door. When the couple was finally out of sight, Ava's eyes welled and she rushed through the kitchen doors. The push handle clanked through the heavy back door as Ava emerged; she dropped the two-by-four doorstop down behind her as she had for the last fifteen years. She stepped to the side of the doorway and leaned against the wall, burrowing her face in her hands; she inhaled deep and rubbed away the tears. She reached into her pocket and pulled out her pack of cigarettes and lighter; she trembled as she placed one in her mouth and lit it. The drag she inhaled was long, deep, and it burned her throat. She inhaled again, and again, and again only to reach a small measure of comfort from her forty-eight-year habit. The moment she shut her eyes in a savoring moment, Danny's face flashed across her mind; Myles saw it; ...*Oma who is this guy?!* Ava squeezed her eyes and pressed her hand against her head. Recalling that wink he gave her in acknowledgment, she felt herself break again and she froze; Myles' vision blurred.

The light surrounding Ava changed from the morning sun to a mix of deep, night-blue and incandescent yellow. Myles was pulled away and placed in different spots of Ava's living room until he was stopped in front of a shelf. He recalled that shelf and all Oma's knick-knacks but all he could focus on was the old black and white photo of his grandparents—Oma and his Opa, David. Taken when they were in their twenties, it was perfectly preserved and well suited in its rustic wood frame. Myles was pulled closer and his focus directed at his grandfather; *shit, he looks a lot like...*

Transported near Ava again, she regained her movement and as her eyes relaxed, tears rolled down her cheeks. Cigarette smoke rose from the ash tray and trickled up her face. She slammed the last bit of whiskey from the bottom of her glass and sluggishly set it down next to the near-empty bottle. She poured the remaining alcohol and the glass slipped a little in her grip; *Aw Oma, what's wrong? Who was that guy?*

Danny's face flashed again but this time Myles recalled the photo of his grandfather; *Stop!* He focused on the memory of Danny's face next to his Grandfather's photo...David's face. They were different men, but the similarities were remarkable. From their bone structure to the hair flow, they could have been brothers but when Myles saw the memories of both men winking at Ava, in different times, a chill shot down his spine and churned his stomach. With complete independence from any other muscle, each man's right eyelid quickly slid down the eye, but stopped just short of completely shutting; the matching subtle nod sealed Myles' anxiety.

"It can't be David." Ava said in calm, slurred speech. Myles waited for another memory to come forward, but there was nothing. She sat silent—her mind blank, "But what if it is him? My husband? Is this my debt?"

*...debt? What debt, Oma?*; Ava's memory shifted to the young woman that day, Claire. She absorbed every detail she could about her innocent face for reasons known only

to the whiskey. Recalling how Claire looked at Danny, Ava's jaw clenched and the back of her neck radiated; *...what do you have against Korbin's mother?*

Ava knew the consequences of her choice from years ago—her cruel intervention in fate's natural order. She knew she would pay in suffering, just as those whom suffered by her hand. While she fought and hid her agonies, she endured her punishments for the remainder of her life.

Yet, in that day's shock, she could not tell if Danny's resemblance to David was a coincidence or another punishing blow—seeing her husband with another woman. Were it not for her drunken despair, she may have been able to find that answer but she definitely would have convinced herself only *she* was at fault.

Driven by rage and navigated by the liquor, her mind fixated on Claire's face, "...I only saved him; I saved my husband." Ava said through her teeth, "I saved him. That's not selfish. Not selfish!" Claire's face flashed across Ava's mind and her glass flew across the room just as fast, shattering against the wall. She buried her face in her hands and sobbed, "Why do you torment me? ...he's not yours. He is not for you. He is mine! Meins, du Schlampe!"

A blast of energy blurred Myles' vision and shook his core. Quickly sitting up straight, Ava was frozen; her eyes stared straight ahead, filled with influenced rage and her mind was locked on Claire's face. "You will never have him, Claire;" she said in a gritty whisper, "you will never have anyone, Claire; your love will destroy everything to which you give it. You are an awful animal...a beast."

*...Oma? What are you doing?* Ava inhaled deeply and closed her eyes, "I curse your love Claire, to match the beast you are; you will forget all that you are; all people you love will forget your existence; you will forever mourn a lost love and never remember him; your agony will summon the beast inside and destroy all around you; I curse your love Claire, to match the beast you are; I curse your love Claire, to match the beast you are..." Her voice slowly dissolved to silence as she chanted and if Myles could see himself, he would be as transparent as the ghosts he fears; *...Oma! You didn't!*

Time froze and, in another haze, Myles found himself back at Korbin's house. In the same perspective, he watched Korbin hopelessly drag himself through the house to the kitchen; It was the present time. Korbin sat at the counter, grabbed a nearby pen and notepad and wrote:

'To whoever finds this, please do not try notifying anyone of the choice I made. Do not try to find my family. I love them so I've driven far and left my identity behind to save them from grief and shame. I've already said my 'goodbye' to them. Please just notify the proper authorities to dispose of my body. I apologize it was you who came upon me. Thank you.

In an instant, Myles was ripped away.

When his own mind returned to that present moment, he coughed out the air in his burning lungs and opened his eyes.

His grandmother was gone; he searched the room, finding nothing—not even a trace of her energy. Recalling the proud look on her face and her loving energy, he smiled for a moment then froze at the notion that Korbin's mother, Sara, had an entirely different identity—a different life. Then his eyes widened and his muscles locked recalling the very last vision, "…Korbin."

Unable to overcome the awful memories burned into his mind, Korbin slowly folded a piece of paper filled with his handwriting and slid it into his back pocket. He walked to the kitchen and his stride held no life; his muscles activate as necessary to reach his destination but his spirit was gone—nothing but an empty shell. He walked right to the counter and stared at the butcher block. Every metal handle shimmered silver and he pulled out the large butcher knife; he ran his thumb across the blade. With almost no pressure, he slid his thumb up, drawing a sliver of blood. He licked it off his thumb, wrapped the knife in a towel, and walked to the front door.

Outside, he locked the door but when he turned toward his car, he froze. The furthest corner, out of sight, sunk down as the last tire deflated, matching the visible three; his lifeless face never flinched, even as Myles stood from behind the rear corner.

"Hey, Kiddo..." Myles said in a pleasant tone, "I noticed your tires were a little full of themselves so I brought them down a bit." Korbin just stared, never blinking. Myles shrugged and gestured the subtlest nod, "Sorry. Bad joke." Myles took a step then paused when Korbin matched him in the opposite direction, "Where you headed?" Korbin said nothing and Myles nodded, "Okay...no bullshit. I know where you're going—*were* going. I know what you were planning. You've got a very effective and, uh...*sharp* tool for the job. You've got your note for your dad's closure. It's very considerate of you to carry it out away from home. However, please consider something..." Myles swayed to one side and Korbin stepped back, "...Don't worry; I won't come any closer. I understand the agony you're feeling; the madness in your mind right now feels unbearable. There's no right or wrong way to deal with such a thing, especially what you've been through...but if you let me, I will do my damnedest to help you." Korbin's eyes and lip twitched; *He's breaking down. Approach...carefully*; "Korbin, think of everyone you would leave behind. Your problems would be over, yes, but your dad and everyone else that loves you would live with this the rest of their lives..." Myles took a step and Korbin was still as he swallowed the lump in his throat, "It'll be difficult but I promise, you will never be alone in this. Not ever." Korbin clenched his empty hand into a fist; *Hold it. Okay, take the gamble...say it*; "Korbin, everyone that knows anything about this,

377

knows it was not your fault. They know you had no control and that you were dealt...probably the most impossible, shittiest hand anyone could ever get; if you let this false guilt consume you...Shanna would be devastated."

Korbin released his grip, dropping the knife, and whimpered as he fell back into the garage door. He keeled over and Myles rushed to his side, kicking away the knife; *She's his trigger;* He braced Korbin as he fell to his knees, exhaling a strained and silent cry, then embraced him. After a few moments, Korbin's cries calmed enough for Myles to continue, "It's alright, Kiddo. I know." Myles grasped Korbin's shoulders and forced his focus, "Look at me..." Korbin obeyed, almost completely blind from tears, "I get the pain you're feeling, but you cannot do this because she's gone. I swear to you, she does not blame you." Korbin shook his head and Myles loosened his grip, "...what?"

Korbin wiped his eyes as his chest convulsed; he gathered himself with a few deep breaths, "...not just Shanna." His voice was hoarse, "...I killed people. I murdered them."

"No. No you did not." Myles assured.

"...can't get them out of my head. I—I can feel them dying. You c—can't imagine..."

Never relating to anyone his entire life as a gifted individual—not even his grandmother before she passed—Myles recalled the night his mind was raped by every Dahmer victim; he finally felt what it was to share a relative bond in a manner he fully understood,

378

"Actually…I can imagine vividly." Korbin paused and stared with questioning eyes. Myles shook his head, "It's not important. Here, do you have your phone?"

"No."

Myles nodded, "Okay, I'm going to message your dad and let him know you and I took a trip. I'll let him know about your tires too."

"Wha—? Trip where?" Korbin asked.

"I have an idea."

<><><>

The first forty-five minutes of the drive was filled with a heavy silence as Korbin stared out the window; slumped in the seat, he appeared to be sleeping—or even dead—except for his eyes. His despair was obvious in those cringed eyes and that was the only life he showed; consumed by his soul-feeding despair, the rest of his body was practically numb.

Myles continually looked over, noticing no change. He sighed quietly at the lingering relief in his mind; other than Korbin's last transformation—the curse's departure—this was the first time Myles was in close proximity to Korbin without any overbearing sensations. It was because of this relief that his own guilt lingered just below it; *You suffer when this kid's mind has some sort of peace. Now you get peace while his mind is haunted by the shit he's been through. God…what did he do to deserve this?* He thought about Korbin's family; Korbin's dad flashed through Myles' mind, then his mother—*wait…Oma's curse made this kid's mom forget she was cursed; her own family forgot about her. Why hasn't his dad forgotten her or Korbin? Why didn't Shanna forget…or anyone else for that matter? Do curses evolve…or…break down from generation to generation? What the fuck?*

Korbin nervously swallowed a lump of air then turned his head forward and looked down at the floor, "How—" he stopped to clear his throat, "—how long has it been?"

Myles' eyebrows raised a brief moment as his eyes stayed on the road, "…about a week."

"…how…" Korbin said, then stopped.

Myles glanced at him for a moment, "How what?"

Korbin continued staring at the floor then shook his head, "…I don't even know what to say. I dunno what to think."

"I bet."

Korbin hesitantly glanced at his chauffeur, "Does anyone know yet?"

Myles shook his head, "No; and we're going to do our damnedest to keep it that way."

"…what if it comes back?"

"I don't think it will." Myles began, "I suppose that's one good thing we can pull out of this mess."

"How do you know?" Korbin asked.

"Because I saw it leave your body and disappear. There's absolutely no trace of it in you anymore. The only reason any of this happened in the first place was because it was inside of you—like…hibernating. *That*, I could feel; I didn't know what it was, but I felt it. Then…it woke up." Myles answered with an assuring confidence; Korbin

380

shook his head and returned his eyes to the floor, "...I'm sorry, Kiddo. Like I said before, I can't imagine what you're going through right now but...the hard part's over, you know?" *Really—Stop; at least it's an answer. Of course the psychological damage is going to be bad but maybe he can use that answer as a motivator.*

Korbin clenched his jaw and squeezed his eyes shut, "I killed her...I *killed* her."

Myles sighed, "Korbin...*you* didn't do anything; *it* did it." Korbin shook his head, "...just, trust me. I think I have a way that'll get you some closure."

Korbin shook his head and looked up at the road ahead; he glanced at Myles for a moment, then turned back to his window and continued staring at the road for the rest of the trip.

An hour and a half later, they passed a bright orange sign that said "*Detour Ahead*"; when they came to the turn, the road was blocked off and, with a loud scoff, Myles passed it. He immediately activated his *GPS* and examined for other alternative routes. When he found one, he turned at the very next intersection.

Following the blocks in a zig-zag pattern, Myles finally turned onto *Shirley Lane*. He passed a few houses until he came to another "*Road Blocked*" warning but continued forward until he reached the barricades; not even a quarter mile away was the Madsen's house. Myles parked his car on the side of the road where both he and Korbin got out.

They looked around and nothing could be seen around the long road bend; they slipped through the gap between the barricades and headed toward the Madsen residence.

When they reached the house, Korbin's eyes widened as he stared at the police tape blocking the edge of the lawn and driveway; he stood frozen as Myles waited for him on the other side. After a few moments, Korbin's pulse raced and he breathed heavily but, with hesitation, he finally ducked under the tape.

Myles wiped the sweat from his forehead as they continued forward; he occasionally stopped to hone his abilities but it wasn't until they reached the side of the house that he fixated on an invisible energy. A subtle, cold chill dribbled through his nerves and he squeezed his eyes shut, flexing all his muscles; *don't freak out. You* have *to do this.* Fighting the sudden anxiety, he instructed Korbin to keep following as he headed toward the back yard.

When they cleared the back corner, Myles stopped and stared straight ahead. Korbin cautiously peered over his shoulder and saw nothing but a fair-sized back yard with a shed, "...what?"

"...hang on a sec." Myles answered quietly as he stared at Shanna with her entire family; they all stared right back at him, "Wait here, alright?" Korbin nodded and Myles stepped forward into the yard. Now isolated between the living and the dead, he closed his eyes, inhaling a deep breath; he reached far into the depths of his consciousness...attempting to awaken his empathic ability.

Korbin watched for several minutes as Myles just stood there, seemingly doing nothing; eventually, Myles exhaled a deep, *heavy* sigh and dropped his hands to his knees. After a few deep breaths, he stood back up and looked at Korbin, "Okay...just a couple more minutes." Korbin nodded and Myles continued toward the family of spirits—cautious in his steps.

He held his arms tight to his body, focusing his empathy to a mental containment; *Don't let it spill out.* His steps slowed as he drew closer to the group and the chill grew colder. He stopped at arm's length from Shanna and stared in her eyes for a moment then looked at the remaining family.

"Hello," he began in a soft, trembling voice, "My name is Myles; I'm not going to hurt any of you. Um...I'm—uh...I'm very sorry for what happened to all of you. With your permission, I'd like to see how Shanna is feeling but...*none* of you are allowed to touch me in anyway. I *forbid* you from entering my body or my mind."

With a deep breath, Myles nodded and stepped closer to Shanna. Standing only one foot away now, he slowly lifted his hand, opened his palm and placed it an inch away from the side of her head. He closed his eyes and opened the gates of his mind, allowing Shanna's consciousness to join his; her memories filled his mind with every perceived sensation.

His face cringed and he exhaled a muffled grunt—stopping himself from crying out in the Shanna's emitted despair, "Korbin didn't know, Shanna. He didn't know what would happen; he didn't know. The curse took away all control." He clenched his jaw maintaining control of his empathy, "Please, Shanna. Please believe me. He didn't know. Korbin loves you and he's *so* sorry for everything. Please...please..."

Myles' reaction slowly calmed. Recomposing himself, his face relaxed, "One second Shanna..." He reached his free hand back toward Korbin and carefully motioned him forward. Confused, Korbin stepped forward, hesitating; Myles circled his hand forward again and Korbin continued toward the medium. He stared into the empty yard for a moment then looked at Myles, "What're you doing?"

Myles held his hand up, "...give me your wrist." He whispered. Korbin extended his wrist and Myles' fingers wrapped around in a firm grip, "...I don't know if this will work but...just...close your eyes and think about Shanna—the best parts...every little detail." Korbin obeyed and shut his eyes. The first and most cherished was the little quirks in her mouth; the mocking faces she made, the subtle differences in her smile for each occasion. He recalled the fire in her spirit; that spark opened the floodgate of his adrenaline while her innate compassion and kindness soothed his soul. Her eyes...whenever she looked at him...he felt all the loving words she could never think to say.

Korbin's breath was snatched from his lungs; his mind blanked as gravity pulled him in every possible direction and he fell to one knee. When it released its pull, his breath returned and he opened his eyes. All color had disappeared. He examined his hands and body, then looked around the yard; there was no green in the leaves or grass; the blue in the sky was gone. Everything was silent and completely still.

He stood up, "…Myles? What—" Korbin's eyes locked on Myles, frozen in place then scanned over to himself. He examined his own body, still standing with his wrist in the psychic's grasp. His trembling, disembodied hand reached toward his physical shoulder.

"…dick." Shanna's said with a sniffle and Korbin jumped. There she was, standing in front of them, staring right at Korbin; she smiled through her tears. For the first time, he could not tell whether she cried from joy or sadness; he failed to notice the answer as her color slowly returned. Never breaking his gaze, he approached her and they embraced tighter than they ever could in the physical world. They separated just enough to kiss, interrupted by the broken rhythm of Shanna's crying breath. She smiled and pressed her forehead against Korbin's.

He sighed, "…I'm…oh God…I—I'm…so…" Shanna laid her hand on his cheek and shook her head. She pulled back to find his eyes closed; she wiped away his tears with her thumbs.

"Look at me." She said. Korbin shook his head but obeyed. He looked up, locking eyes with his smiling lady and she slowly *blinked—his* blink. Korbin forced a smile as he fought desperately not to break down and his color slowly returned. Shanna pressed her forehead to his once more and held it, "Only meant for you…always." Korbin coughed out a whimper and she grasped his neck with one hand, then grabbed one of his hands with the other and kissed his fingers. She pressed his hand to her cheek then tilted his head up; they kissed one more time parting slowly—savoring every sensation.

When they pulled apart for the last time, Korbin opened his eyes, and Shanna was gone. He looked around and saw no trace of her. When the notion that she had moved on settled into his mind, he saw all surrounding colors completely restored. A big, long gust of wind picked up; he closed his eyes again and inhaled a slow, deep breath.

Korbin opened his eyes; he stood next to Myles with his wrist still wrapped in the psychic's hand. Myles' grip relaxed as he recollected himself. He took a few breaths then turned to Korbin with a calm, content look in his eyes, "Let's go…"

The drive back was silent; Myles occasionally glanced over at Korbin as he stared out the window. He was torn whether or not to reveal the visions Oma bestowed upon him—that his mother was dead…having flung herself off the cliff after Oma destroyed *her* curse—that Myles' grandmother sacrificed her remaining lifeforce for Korbin's mother. Despite the closure he sensed from Korbin, it was incomplete. Myles felt a piece missing from him and had no idea how long his cursed memories would last; *He's got enough to deal with. Let it be.*

Korbin's muffled voice bounced off the window and Myles glanced over, "What?"

"How're we gonna keep this secret?" Korbin repeated after turning his head.

Myles nodded, "I've actually been thinking about that. What do you know about body modification?"

Korbin stared with questioning eyes and Myles just turned on the radio.

# 31

Meeting again at *Steve's Pizza Palace,* Myles sat with Billy and Jessica, whose faces were plastered with bewilderment and ears were deaf to the surrounding commotion.

"You really think people will buy it?" Billy asked, leaning forward.

Myles grinned, "Honestly, I'm betting no one besides his friends notice he's been gone. They're so wrapped up in the insanity of what happened, they probably won't even notice when—or if—he returns; but that's why we're going this route…in the chance they *do* notice.

"What about all the video footage?" Jessica chimed, "That's all over the web. All those students saw it first-hand."

"They saw *someone*—not necessarily Korbin." Myles said. The uncertainty was plastered all over Billy and

388

Jessica from their faces to their posture, "Trust me. This will work, one way or another. You two will be fine. *Everything* will be fine." *...Wow. That's a notion you've never said—or even thought*; "I'll be damned if I let him exist in exile." Immediately connecting the reference, and just hearing the sincerity in Myles' voice, Billy nodded in complete acceptance.

"Excuse me…" came a voice behind Myles. He turned to see Molly standing with the slightest hunch—a shelled posture. Having never met her, Myles would not know that even this small change was a far cry from her typical, uninhibited persona, "Um…I'm sorry to bother you but…are you the one that came to the school, like, a month ago?" With a blank stare, Myles nodded; Molly extended her hand, "Hi. I'm Molly. My friend Shanna told me you were talking a lot with our friend Korbin…"

Myles' skin tingled with a warm chill; *She needs closure*; Being accustomed to his solitude for so long, the compassion he felt for these kids kicked him with slight surprise. Even more so, his apprehension to shake her hand, skin to skin, faded quickly. He reached out, wrapped his hand around hers with a firm grip and shook it, "Myles. Nice to meet you, Molly." He said with a nod.

"You too." Molly replied; she paused a moment, glancing at Billy and Jessica, "Um…if you get a moment, I was wondering if we could have a word."

Myles nodded, "Sure..." he looked back at his company, "…excuse me a moment." He stood and accompanied Molly through the crowd to a back corner, "What can I do for you?"

389

Molly sighed with hesitation; she closed her eyes for a moment, "I'm not sure if you know or not, but…my friend, Shanna was—" her voice broke; she clenched her jaw to restrain her cries, but tears immediately flowed, "she—she and her parents were killed over all this—this…whatever this shit was."

"Yeah. Korbin told me." Myles said. Molly hid her mouth behind her hand; her face cringed, fighting to hold her sobs, "I understand you all were very close." Molly nodded as her shoulders and chest convulsed; she waved her hand in apology, "Take your time."

Molly wiped her glistening eyes after a few moments, "You're a psychic?"

"…Mm-hmm."

"Do you know—" she sighed, "…is she okay?"

Myles took her hand between both of his and gently squeezed, "I'm sure it feels awkward to ask that question, which doesn't help; to this day it still feels weird to me. However, I actually had the same talk with Korbin. I, personally, made contact with Shanna." Molly's convulsing stopped; in her desperate hope, she stared in Myles' eyes with wonder, "You and Korbin both have my word, she and her parents are just fine. Everything is resolved and all she wants is for you and Korbin to live your lives—and to always keep her close, as she will for you both. If not, she'll be upset; I believe her words were something like, 'I'll come back and haunt your asses;' or…something." Molly laughed and Myles grinned, "Okay?"

Molly nodded then leaned forward and hugged Myles, "Thank you." Her face cringed, squeezing out more tears; she wiped them away as they parted and she returned to her own group. Myles inhaled deeply and returned to his table.

"Everything alright?" Jessica asked. Myles nodded.

"So now what, Kiddo?" Billy continued.

Myles paused for a moment then shrugged. In the split second before the rest of the dinner meeting continued, the seedling-idea of his future sprouted; *Maybe it's time to finally be* you.

# 32

Near-silent cries sounded from some of the audience. Even the attending skeptics were hooked on Myles' story and their eyes reflected the slightest touch of remorse. Switching demeanor with Myles on the stage, David Caine was slumped back in his chair, defensively crossing his arms and legs; he even clenched his abs to maintain a straight, objective face while Myles sat back, completely loose and relaxed.

"When Chris' dad told me he was missing, I exhausted my efforts to hone on that curse; it drained the hell out of me and I came up with nothing."

Never breaking eye contact, Caine scoffed in amazement, "And...what? That's it?"

"Until I heard about the Madsens' deaths...yeah. I haven't felt that rancid energy or seen *him* since—two and a half years, now. I figure he's either...no longer with us, or just hiding with no intention to be found. Either way, my gut tells me the curse is gone."

"That's what you meant earlier, when you said '*what he was*'?" Caine asked and Myles nodded.

Mirroring the audience as he had the majority of the night, Caine was frozen, "...and you have no idea what happened to him?"

Myles shook his head, "Nope."

"...wow." Caine added, shaking his head, "Okay, I gotta ask this...with everything that happened—people getting killed, you covering for this person, revealing the story to us now—on *national* television...did anyone ever come after you? Police? F.B.I.? I mean, are you even worried about getting in trouble now?"

"Well I'm not too worried now but, yeah, I got questioned. There was actually a good six or seven months where there was talks about me being charged—"

"Charged?! With *what*?!" Caine shouted, "I mean, I know I just asked you with the chance of this answer but I still can't believe they'd try to nail you with something."

Myles chuckled, "I hear you; and I'm not telling anything different than what I said to them that entire time. Um...oh man...I think one charge was aiding and abetting; another was harboring a fugitive and even a conspiracy to cover. There was even a small thing about lying to the police in Platteville."

Caine's eyes widened and he flashed a look at the audience, then looked back at Myles, "And none of them stuck?"

Myles shrugged, "Well, no. I mean they really didn't have anything on me to actually charge; I didn't hurt anyone or do anything illegal; D.N.A. testing proved the attacks to be from a wild animal; they couldn't even find a judge—or attorneys—that would take the case until the end of this pursuit. The only judge that would even touch the case just held some little private trial and said, even if it were a legit case, above all, I was trying to help someone get rid of a severe problem; I wasn't helping to commit a crime or hiding any evidence admissible in court. All the evidence remained at the scenes and were made clear to the police and public. What could they even do? Arrest someone for completely turning into some animal that kills? It's ridiculous! But it happened; people can believe what they want but the fact is, this kid turned into a creature and it was that *creature* that killed those people. It had nothing to do with his mind not being right; it had nothing to do with violent urges. He had an uncontrollable force consuming him and it took over for the sole purpose of carnage." The entire studio fell dead silent and *everyone's* jaws dropped; realizing his passion caused him to lean forward, Myles stopped and slowly sat back in the chair, "...anyway—um...with no substantial evidence, the judge ruled it as a mistrial and I was acquitted of all charges."

Caine took a deep breath and shook his head; he glanced at the audience with a chuckle then looked back at Myles, "That's a really amazing story, Myles—really. Now, um...I understand that you actually brought one of the survivors with you—the *only* survivor from the university. Right?"

Myles nodded, "That's right."

"Let's bring him out," Caine turned to the audience, "Ladies and gentleman, please welcome Korbin Voss."

The audience erupted in the softest applause as Korbin appeared from behind a stage wall wearing khakis and a long sleeve t-shirt. The left side of his face was scarred; the top of his left ear was missing; large claw marks sprawled across his jaw and neck, creeping further down under his shirt. He gave the audience a small wave; he patted Myles' shoulder and shook Caine's hand as he sat down.

"Welcome to the show, Korbin."

"Thanks for having me." Korbin replied.

Caine began his brief interview with the *lone* survivor and Myles looked on with a chest-swelling pride; *Cannot believe the body mods and bullshit story worked this well. Not one single person has caught on, and even Korbin's energy is much more balanced. Guess those scars worked as additional closure—even if they're manmade; a new form of therapy?*

"So, you were wounded by this thing, right?" Caine continued, "You didn't notice any...*effects*?"

Korbin's mouth quirked into a bashful grin, "Well, no but, thankfully, it didn't bite me either—just clawed the hell outta my face and chest. I dunno if that actually does the same thing as it does in movies, and I really don't wanna find out."

"Yeah neither would I. Any chance you'd be willing to show the extent of the damage?"

Korbin breathed deep and nodded; he stood up and lifted his shirt. Behind the microphone wire, scars stretched from his neck and shoulder, down his chest, onto his ribs. His pec was slightly deformed, "Took a lot of therapy and surgery but I'm fully functional again. My pec took the worst of it though—ripped right through a big chunk."

"Geeeez," Caine exclaimed and Korbin lowered his shirt as he sat down, "Well thanks for showing us. So, um…you knew Shanna?"

"…Yep." Korbin answered with a heavy tone; the sorrow and regret appearing on his face, "We were really close—me, her, and our friend Molly."

Caine nodded, "What about Amanda?"

"Uh, no. I wasn't close with her."

"I gotcha. What about…this *Chris* guy—the one that…started all this. *That* guy." Caine continued, pointing to a paused frame of the cell-phone video.

Managing to hide it, Korbin shuddered inside then shrugged his shoulders, "No. Actually, word around campus was that he wasn't even a student; he was just visiting some friends that attended UWP."

"And no sign of him?"

Myles shook his head, "Not to our knowledge, no."

Caine chuckled and shook his head; he glanced over at the stage director whom held up two fingers, signaling the "*two-minute*" mark. Caine returned his attention to his guests, "Well fellas, we're actually just about outta time, but I'd like to ask you, Korbin—as I asked Myles—would you ever be willing to come back and elaborate on your story?"

Korbin shrugged, "Maybe. I'll, uh…have my people call your people; right? That's how it goes?"

Everyone in attendance finally laughed, savoring the lighthearted moment after listening to such despair. Caine clapped a few times, "Well Myles, Korbin, I wanna thank you *very* much for coming on and sharing your story."

They both shook Caine's hand and Myles nodded, "Thanks for having us."

"Our pleasure, guys. Alright everyone, have a great evening and we'll see ya next time."

The main camera pulled back, capturing both Caine and Myles as the credits rolled and after the cutting to the sponsor logos, the broadcast faded to black.

*…clear.*

# ABOUT THE AUTHOR

Evan Miller is a creator in various disciplines with a Bachelor's Degree in Digital Filmmaking. His roots, however lie in drawing and painting. He has since added digital art to his creative arsenal and is always working to hone his skills and vision.

As a Wisconsin native, it was only fitting to incorporate his home state into this story. After years of development and evolution, *Within* is his first completed novel.

# DESIGN SOFTWARE ACKNOWLEDGEMENTS:

*COVER FONT:*

*Copyright (c) 2010, Caroline Hadilaksono & Micah Rich <caroline@hadilaksono, micah@micahrich.com>, with Reserved Font Name: "League Gothic".*

---------------------------------------------------------

*SIL OPEN FONT LICENSE Version 1.1 - 26 February 2007*

---------------------------------------------------------

*PREAMBLE*

*The goals of the Open Font License (OFL) are to stimulate worldwide development of collaborative font projects, to support the font creation efforts of academic and linguistic communities, and to provide a free and open framework in which fonts may be shared and improved in partnership with others.*

*The OFL allows the licensed fonts to be used, studied, modified and redistributed freely as long as they are not sold by themselves. The fonts, including any derivative works, can be bundled, embedded, redistributed and/or sold with any software provided that any reserved names are not used by derivative works. The fonts and derivatives, however, cannot be released under any other type of license. The requirement*

399

*for fonts to remain under this license does not apply to any document created using the fonts or their derivatives.*

*DEFINITIONS*
*"Font Software" refers to the set of files released by the Copyright Holder(s) under this license and clearly marked as such. This may include source files, build scripts and documentation.*

*"Reserved Font Name" refers to any names specified as such after the copyright statement(s).*

*"Original Version" refers to the collection of Font Software components as distributed by the Copyright Holder(s).*

*"Modified Version" refers to any derivative made by adding to, deleting, or substituting -- in part or in whole -- any of the components of the Original Version, by changing formats or by porting the Font Software to a new environment.*

*"Author" refers to any designer, engineer, programmer, technical writer or other person who contributed to the Font Software.*

*PERMISSION & CONDITIONS*
*Permission is hereby granted, free of charge, to any person obtaining a copy of the Font Software, to use, study, copy,*

400

merge, embed, modify, redistribute, and sell modified and unmodified copies of the Font Software, subject to the following conditions:

1) Neither the Font Software nor any of its individual components, in Original or Modified Versions, may be sold by itself.

2) Original or Modified Versions of the Font Software may be bundled, redistributed and/or sold with any software, provided that each copy contains the above copyright notice and this license. These can be included either as stand-alone text files, human-readable headers or in the appropriate machine-readable metadata fields within text or binary files as long as those fields can be easily viewed by the user.

3) No Modified Version of the Font Software may use the Reserved Font Name(s) unless explicit written permission is granted by the corresponding Copyright Holder. This restriction only applies to the primary font name as presented to the users.

4) The name(s) of the Copyright Holder(s) or the Author(s) of the Font Software shall not be used to promote, endorse or advertise any Modified Version, except to acknowledge the contribution(s) of the Copyright Holder(s) and the Author(s) or with their explicit written permission.

*5) The Font Software, modified or unmodified, in part or in whole, must be distributed entirely under this license, and must not be distributed under any other license. The requirement for fonts to remain under this license does not apply to any document created using the Font Software.*

*TERMINATION*
*This license becomes null and void if any of the above conditions are not met.*

*DISCLAIMER*
*THE FONT SOFTWARE IS PROVIDED "AS IS", WITHOUT WARRANTY OF ANY KIND, EXPRESS OR IMPLIED, INCLUDING BUT NOT LIMITED TO ANY WARRANTIES OF MERCHANTABILITY, FITNESS FOR A PARTICULAR PURPOSE AND NONINFRINGEMENT OF COPYRIGHT, PATENT, TRADEMARK, OR OTHER RIGHT. IN NO EVENT SHALL THE COPYRIGHT HOLDER BE LIABLE FOR ANY CLAIM, DAMAGES OR OTHER LIABILITY, INCLUDING ANY GENERAL, SPECIAL, INDIRECT, INCIDENTAL, OR CONSEQUENTIAL DAMAGES, WHETHER IN AN ACTION OF CONTRACT, TORT OR OTHERWISE, ARISING FROM, OUT OF THE USE OR INABILITY TO USE THE FONT SOFTWARE OR FROM OTHER DEALINGS IN THE FONT SOFTWARE.*

Made in the USA
Monee, IL
03 June 2023

34834006R00239